THE TOWN

THE

TOWN

BY

CONRAD RICHTER

---

1 9 7 8

ALFRED A KNOPF

NEW YORK

Published April 24, 1950
Reprinted Twelve Times
Fourteenth Printing, October 1978

ACKNOWLEDGMENTS

The author acknowledges his debt to the rich historical collections of HENRY HOWE *and* SHERMAN DAY; *to the excellent manuscripts of* JOHN BUTZ BOWMAN; *to obscure early volumes, manuscripts, newspaper files and personal records made available by* H. C. SHETRONE, *director, Miss* HELEN M. WILLS, *reference librarian, and Miss* BERTHA E. JOSEPHSON, *head of the Department of Documents, of the Ohio State Historical Society; by* SYLVESTER L. VIGILANTE, *head, and* IVOR AVELLINO, *assistant, of the American History Room of the New York Public Library; by Col.* HENRY W. SHOEMAKER, *Pennsylvania state archivist, and Mrs.* ETHEL S. DAVENPORT, *assistant; by Librarians Miss* EDITH PATTERSON, *Miss* ISABEL CRAWFORD SCHOCH, *Miss* NELL B. STEVENS, *Miss* CATHERINE T. SHULENBERGER, *and others; and to the help, firsthand material or counsel of* W. T. BOYD, *Mrs.* SAMANTHA RIGGS, *Miss* EDNA STINE, *Miss* AUGUSTA R. FILBERT, *Misses* ANNA *and* MARY BOYER, MARION S. SCHOCH, *Miss* AGNES SELIN SCHOCH, MILTON T. JARRETT, FREDERICK RICHTER, *Mrs.* ANNIE NEIDLINGER *and many others.*

Finally the author wants again to set down his obligation to those men and women of pioneer stock among whom he lived both in the East and West, whose lives and whose

ACKNOWLEDGMENTS

tales of older days gave him a passionate love for the early American way of thought and speech, and a great respect for many whose names never figured in the history books but whose influence on their own times and country was incalculable. If this novel has had any other purpose than to tell some of their story, it has been to try to impart to the reader the feeling of having lived for a little while in those earlier days and of having come in contact, not with the sound and fury of dramatic historical events that is the fortune of the relative, and often uninteresting, few, but with the broader stuff of reality that was the lot of the great majority of men and women who, if they did not experience the certain incidents related in these pages, lived through comparable events and emotions, for life is endlessly resourceful and inexhaustible. It's only the author who is limited and mortal.

CONTENTS

CONTENTS

THE TOWN

CHAPTER ONE

TOWARDS EVENING

Hit all comes with bein' a woman.

LAMB IN HIS BOSOM

SAYWARD awoke this day with the feeling that something had happened to her. What it was, she didn't know as yet, or if it was for better or for worse, but inside of her a change had taken place. She wasn't the same as last month or last year. That much she could tell.

She lay beside Portius studying this thing out. Twice, she recollected, she had such a feeling before, the first time when she was no more than a stout chit of a girl. She lived in old Pennsylvany then with her mammy, pappy, brother and sisters. She had woke up in the middle of the night with the singular notion that her life was over and done. Now wasn't that a funny way for a young girl to think? Well, if her time on earth was done, then it was done, she said to herself, and she was much obliged for being told so she could get ready for heaven. It sobered her but she couldn't say that it frightened her any. She reckoned she could get along in the next life, if she tried, as well as in this one.

That day or the next her pappy came home and told how the squirrels were leaving the country. Before the week was up, her life by the Juniata was over and she was following the trace westward along with Worth and Jary, Genny and Achsa, Wyitt and Sulie, lighting out with all they had on their backs, traipsing for another land, saying goodby to old Pennsylvany, the only state she ever knew up to then and would never lay eyes on again.

The second time she felt such a change inside her was the time she and Portius got married. Not when she stood up and heard Squire Chew say the lawful words nor during the frolic afterwards. No, it came deep in the night long after all the folks had gone home, all save her and Portius. They were in the cabin alone. She lay in bed with her new man a sleeping beside her like he did now. But she had no notion to waste this hour in foolish deadness to the world. No, she wanted to study out what had happened to her tonight. Never before had she known a man or what it was like. Oh, she had heard enough about it. They was some who played it up to the sky, but as far as she was concerned, it wasn't all it was cracked up to be.

Just the same, as she lay there still as a mouse, she could feel the change in her, something she had never known before, a running along her blood and stirring in all her veins. And if she didn't know it then, she did a couple months afterwards that it was life.

Now this third time she wouldn't be sure. Not always could you put off Death and she wasn't as young and spry as she used to be. No, she had lived a mighty long time. She was in her late forties and she thought her mam an old woman when she gave up and died at thirty-seven. Now she lay quiet till daylight came a sifting in the window. Then she got up, making no noise. Outside she stopped a

[4]

minute on the way to the backhouse to look around. This
was the top hour of the day and foolish were them who
reckoned it the bottom, for the world like a human rested
up at night, and that's why it was never so fresh after the
first hour of the morning. The fields looked as if they just
came out of the dye kettle. The town lay like it always lay
there, with two streets already on the river bank and cross-
way streets at either end reaching out and closing her place
in. Just to see it made her feel old for fair. Why, when she
came here as a girl, all this was solid woods. Not a white
folks cabin for miles east or west, south to the Forks or
north towards the English Lakes. Anywhere you turned,
the trees stood so close and thick that Jary had to suck for
breath. The first year you hardly saw another white person. These days folks were always stopping off from their
old states to settle down at Moonshine Church.

When she came back in, the fire looked like it was out,
but she knew there would be coals a glowing and winking
down under the ash and that the water in the big kettle
would still be good and warm. The others could lay abed
a while till she washed herself all over, for so busy was she
Saturday and Saturday night with ten others to get washed
that she had to wait for Sunday morning when it was gen-
erally too chilly for these younger ones. She pulled off
her old robe and bedgown. Let the girls look down the
loft hole at their mam naked if they liked. They would
only see how they'd look themselves thirty or forty years
hence.

Now why, she wondered, did a woman's hams have to
get heavy just when she needed them supple and light the
most? Could those hams spell out that no more child would
rise up between them? And why did her breasts, that used
to be stout as wood ducks, hang down now like old shook-

out meal bags? Ten babes, counting the one that lay over yonder in the burying ground, had drunk from those bags months on end. Were those tits a telling her now that they didn't have to stand up and feed greedy mouths any more? Was that it? Was that the change that had come on her, that never could she give flesh, blood and breath to a squalling young one again?

Seven years back she would have thanked her lucky stars to know she had no more on the way and never could have another even if she wanted. But now that she was a scutched tree, that it had come true like winter or taxes, she didn't know as she liked it so much. Not that she could do anything about it. Never could you go back once the door closed behind you. You could dig in your heels and grab holt, if you wanted, but you had to go on. Even them that had to pass to another world went without making too much fuss about it.

As soon as she had her clothes on, she called the boys from the loft over her and Portius's room, for they had chores to do — Resolve, the first, a man already and a lawyer like his pappy; then Guerdon with his Yankee gimber jaw, always a scheming to get out of work like his Grandpappy Luckett; next, freckled Kinzie who was going on an appointment to the government academy at Annapolis in the fall. Then it was the girls' turn — Huldah, sly as a young fisher fox with her black eyes and eye winkers; next Libby with her fine hazel eyes, fat bottom and teasing ways; Sooth who would be a beauty some day with her white skin, red hair and sweet mouth; and Dezia, ten or eleven, the little oldest Bay State lady you ever saw. After that she called Portius, a winking and blinking in the morning like an untamed, uncombed lion with weak eyes. Last of all she sent one of the girls up for her two littlest, no more than babes in the manger, both of them unexpected and coming a long ways after the rest, Massey who couldn't keep still and Chancey who hadn't dare to run, a rubbing their eyes and holding fast to each other, for they were two against the rest.

Once they were all in the kitchen, Sayward felt better. Her chances to have more young ones might be gone, but she had made hay while the sun shone. Why, seeing them all come down in the morning made her think of that light-handed professor at the Ferry House last winter who took more things out of Portius's old high hat than you could shake a stick at. What's more, Resolve was itching to marry and fetch his bride home. Before she'd know it, there'd be more young ones a landing at this cabin. She couldn't figure out where they'd put them all. Maybe Portius was right and they did need that big house he wanted to put up.

Come to think of it, she had no time to think of getting old or of Death or of how she felt when she was young and spunky. She better forget mooning now and get to work. She could be glad her changes had stopped so she could have all her snap to tend what she had. The wars were over now. The Indians and Old England for the second time were peaceful. But her young ones weren't. They hadn't signed any peace treaties. What was coming, neither they nor her nor anybody else knew, or whether it would be good or bad, but however it came, she had a notion it would be plenty.

CHAPTER TWO

THE DARK AND
ANCIENT EARTH

The babe is wise that weepeth, being born.
ZOROASTER

WHAT sin had she done, Sayward asked herself, for that sin to be visited on the youngest of her children? She had asked it ever since he was born. Not that she said it to anybody, just in her own heart. Those she gave birth to before him had been stout and hearty enough. One or two might have been on the slim side like her sister, Genny, used to be. A mite more flesh on their little ribs and haunches wouldn't have hurt. But they had nothing wrong with them. They could fight like wild kits, go it tooth and nail, daylight and dark.

Now this last one had come puny and ailing. Mrs. Coven-hoven said she never saw such a delicate babe. She told Sayward right off not to expect to raise him. He was like a flower budded out in the fall before the frosts. He had come too late. Sayward should remember that her oldest boy was a grown man before his youngest brother ever lay in her womb. Likely all the best sap had been used up by them that came before.

Genny said, did you ever see a boy's flesh so pure? Why, you could look right through at his blue veins going about their business, which you weren't supposed to. That's what was the matter with him, she claimed. His thin hide couldn't keep out the chills and fever. Genny wiped her eyes. He was Heaven's child, that's what he was, and Sayward might as well make up her mind that the Lord wouldn't give him up long.

In her heart Sayward rose up to deny it. That wasn't the Lord talking. It was Genny Beagle, and nobody had to listen to a woman's say-so. It was true that Chancey took all the young ones' sickness that came around. Usually he was the first to go down and the last to be free. He had spells, too, that nobody knew the name of. She told Portius never to speak the name of any new plague or pox in the house or Chancey would surely catch it. But that didn't mean he had no chance, that the Lord's black ox had tramped him. No, she had health and stoutness to spare, if he hadn't, and more than one feverish night she felt it was her will and the Lord's that held him up till morning. Then from daylight on, his five sisters could watch and tend him, for their young brother was the apple of their eye, especially when Death prowled near.

Today Sayward had put him by the window in Portius's room, and there he would sit for hours looking out and never opening his mouth. What he saw only he and God knew. Sometimes from his face and the faraway look in his eyes she thought it must be another world than this that he mostly lived in. Just what world it could be, whether the one he came from or the one he was going to,

Sayward did not claim to know. But ever had he such shy ways, even to her, that he made her think of some creature of the deep woods she had known as a girl, one of those wild things that came into the world and went out of it without the benefit of human minds or hands, and while here followed paths no human feet had trod.

Portius wasn't partial to the young ones coming in his office, but Chancey was his clerk, he said. No matter how private a client's law business, the boy could stay and listen if he wanted. He was four years old now, and the rheumatism had left his heart too poorly to race around. To see him sitting stock-still on his stool while the others tore and ran always bothered Sayward. Even when Portius hoisted him to his back and took him along to town yonder, his puny white body stayed behind like a pack on her heart.

The little boy sat by the window. Summer had come out of Kentucky into Ohio, and the window stood open. It was raining. Out through the window he could see his sister, Massey, and the Patterson girl trying to run between the drops like his mother said. But never could they. Wet as fish they would come in every time. Now he could run between the drops, Chancey believed, if only he could run. He could feel himself small as a tomtit and thin as paper slipping right through, swimming all the muddy rivers that ran between the potato hills in his mother's garden and crossing the great lakes in the side yard on a chip for a keel boat and with a straw for a pole.

After while he heard a whispering at the door to the windsweep that led to the kitchen. As he looked, the string was stealthily pulled, the door opened and Massey's white head pushed through. He could see Ellin Patterson's black head close behind her.

"Chancey!" Massey whispered, though he was looking right at her.

Oh, he knew pretty close what she wanted. Only yesterday when he was sick, Libby had put him on the old cedar bucket in the kitchen to do his business. It set in a dark corner and she claimed she couldn't see it was filled with boiling water to scald it. He had risen up with a howl, and all day he had known anguish. Even now his mother had something soft and comforting under him on the stool.

"Chancey!" Massey whispered again, for she feared her father sitting at his law table with the strange man and little girl before it. "Don't it hurt sitting on it all the time?"

"No," he lied and gave her a dark look to go about her business, but never a ripple marred the innocence of that wide speculative gaze.

"Chancey," she went on. "Will you let Ellin see how bad you hurt it?"

With great dignity the little boy made as though he didn't hear. Massey only bent forward and raised her whisper.

"Why won't you? She won't hurt it or nothing. You showed it to A'nt Ginny."

The little boy shut his eyes to thrust the pain from his mind. It was still raining. He could feel the dampness like a great mittened hand reaching through the window, touching walls and bed, nudging the desk and cold dark fireplace. Under its dank fingering, he could smell the chinked logs, the bitter ink and the slept-in odor of his mother's and father's bed. Once he opened his eyes and peeped. They had gone. Near him at his father's law table were just the strange man and the strange little girl. She sat white and stiff as a china chick in a glass dish, while the men's deep voices like bumblebees droned and rested.

Sometimes when the voices ceased, when all he could hear was the running of the tiny feet of rain on the roof, when the mist rolling over the world outside the window seemed to roll over him, too, then the close sheets-and-blankets smell of his mother's and father's bed took him off somewhere. It was like a path, more like a beam of motes, for he could follow it without feet.

Only a moment or two it took, and he was there. This was the Effortless Place, the Unencumbered World. Never did he feel heavy or tired here, for he could leap and run without moving his legs, and speak without his lips. Scarcely did he even think about having a heart, for here he seemed all in one piece. He could do anything he liked. He need only wish for a thing, and there it was, more wonderful than he had any notion and sometimes in colors he never saw before. And the people mostly were like nobody he had ever noticed around Moonshine Church. They knew what he wanted to say before he said it. Why, then, he wondered, could he never recollect just what they said that pleased him or what they showed him that gave him wonder? So long as he stayed in the Effortless Place, all was crystal clear. But once he got back, a mist lay on his mind, and he couldn't remember till something brought it up. Perhaps it was a strange face in town or the sunset sky with painted clouds banked like continents with stretches of bottomless green sea between. Then some memory returned like a flash and was gone, leaving that indescribably blissful feel of the Dream World like a soft phosphorescent glow behind.

It was always a dark moment when something tore him away from that world. Today he sat very still on his rude stool, struggling with the black feelings he ever found waiting to spring out at him from the shadows of the cabin

when he got back. Often had he wrestled with these old
enemies before, the heavy rain feeling, the melancholy
gray-sky feeling, the sad, old, sooty fireplace feeling, and
the sick and bloody earth feeling, while all the time something like a severed muscle in his chest palpitated and quivered.

Then he heard the sound again and knew what fetched
him back. It was the strange little girl's father crying out
loud. Oh, that was a terrible sound for a small boy to hear,
a grown-up man giving way to his feelings. His hair was
rough and brown but it could not disguise his narrow, gentle head. He held it to one side tenderly. His eyes were sad
and brooding. He looked like a man who had never laid
a hand to a tool in his life. He was afraid, he cried to Chancey's father. Never had he known anything like the forest
out here choked with monster trees and vines. He was
afraid his strength would not hold out till his place was
cleared and the ground planted to keep his loved ones alive.
Chancey saw the little girl look up at her father with sudden terror, holding fast to his white hand lest she lose him,
and how then would she ever find her way back to her
mother, sisters and brothers again? Chancey could see it all
as the man sobbed, the bright house they had left in the
eastern city, and now the dim hut in these Western woods
with the wild solitude shutting them in.

Did his mother hear the man cry out, the little boy
wondered. She had mighty sharp ears and heard a great
deal more than she let on. Mostly when she wanted anything in this room she sent one of the girls in. But today the
door from the windsweep opened, and there she stood herself in a clean apron. Her face was grave but her eyes
looked mild at the man who had cried out and at his little
girl.

"Supper's ready, I'd like you folks to stay," she said.

The man and his little girl got up quickly. They were like two rabbits in the woods ready to break and run at the sound of a foot in the brush.

"I have plenty and won't make company of you," Chancey's mother promised.

But the man and his little girl couldn't stay, he said. They were away from their place in the woods too long now. They had just come to see about title and deed to his land. It would be dark before they got home as it was. The rest of the family was back there in the woods alone and would be worried if they didn't come. No, they couldn't stay even for the special dishes. Chancey saw water come to the little girl's mouth at the sound of sweet milk, but her eyes stayed fast on her father's face, and her feet were ready with his to go. They couldn't leave quick enough, and off they went. Chancey stood at the office door, something in him hurting as he watched them go, the man who had cried out he was afraid and his little girl holding fast to his hairy white hand. When the mists swallowed them up, the boy felt an inconsolable loss. Sooner would he have gone with them if he could, for he knew just how they felt in this gloomy and alien world.

His mother had to call him twice for supper, and then Massey was obliged to fetch him. Still he went slowly. He was loathe to leave those two out there where he could not see them. He didn't want to break the cord that stretched from his heart to theirs departing in the mist and rain. He felt closer to them than his own family. Oh, never would he breathe a word of this even to Massey, but in his heart he knew that those he lived with here in this house were not his real people. No, they were only his foster people with whom he had been given by his real parents to live.

Who his real father and mother were, he did not know, only that they must be like he was. His three brothers were old enough to be his uncles and four of his sisters acted like cousins. You could tell they had different blood than he the way they quarreled and fought, laughed and shouted, ran and jumped, while all he could do was sit out his small, puny life on his stool.

Now he looked up unwillingly as Massey dragged him in. There they were as he knew they would be, in a long square around the table, his father in his white collar and black stock standing up to carve, and at the other end his mother in her apron and cap. In between were all the rest from Resolve down to Dezia and then a gap of years till you came to Massey and himself.

As he climbed his bench, the little boy heard the worst. They were talking about Nilum. A pang went through him at the name. Why couldn't they wait till tomorrow? Then it would be bad enough, but at least the tragedy would be over and this terrible anguish done. Now he would have to sit and hear them tell again why the Shawanees were killing Nilum. It would be at sunset tonight, just a little time from now. They claimed him the fault of another Indian's death. But the real reason, Chancey's father said, was that Nilum was too friendly to the whites.

Now who would have dreamed that with all the mean and ugly and drunken Indians, it was good, kind Nilum who had to die? More than once Chancey had seen him out at the barn using their grindstone or sitting in their kitchen eating his mother's bread. His Indian name was long and hard to say, so the whites called him Nilum. It meant nephew, Chancey's mother said. Once when a family in the woods had nothing to eat, Nilum had carried off the white boy. The family was much afraid but Nilum sent him back

with his pants over his shoulder. Nilum had tied the bot-
toms of the legs with whang and filled them with corn.

"I was out and talked to Nilum," Chancey heard his father tell Resolve. "It's an interesting case. Shows you the
basic difference between Indian law and ours."

The little boy sat hunched and rigid on his bench. Now
he would have to hear his father tell the whole terrible
story again, how he had gone out to Shawaneetown, and
Nilum himself said it was no use. Oh, life was sweet to him
as any other man who lived, he said, but he was judged
guilty by his people and must die. The white people
shouldn't try to stop it. If they tried, he and the other Indians would go only deeper in the forest and carry it out
just the same, for it was Indian law and custom. He said,
"You tell white people forget about Nilum. Now I take a
rag and wipe away all remembering from white people.
Now nobody feel bad about poor Nilum any more." Chancey wished he had never heard those pitiful words of
Nilum. Ever since, he could see nothing but Nilum kneel-
ing by his open grave and the father and three brothers of
the dead Indian firing their rifles into Nilum's breast just
as the sun went down.

Oh, this, Chancey knew, was why he hated to come
back from the Dream World to the dark and bloody earth.
Once when his mother told him the story how a family she
knew had only six grains of corn to eat, he had to cry out
for her to stop. His mother had looked at him as if he had
done wrong. And now at supper all of them looked at him
as if he did wrong that he couldn't touch his food. How
could they eat tonight and talk about Nilum?

"If you don't like this, you don't know what's good!"
Huldah told him crossly, taking his plate and cutting the
meat finer as if that might be why he had no stomach to-

night. As she passed it back, she smacked her red lips over
a tidbit from the tenderest portion that her father had
served his littlest.

"You should be thankful, Chancey. The starving heathen
would be very glad for it," Dezia preached at him.

"A man must do his duty at the table," Guerdon told
him. "Your insides are plumb empty. I kin hear your big
guts a growlin' at your little ones."

Of all who claimed to be his brothers and sisters, only
little Massey guessed what ailed him, for she was just a
year older than he, and for two months every year they
were the same age. The stretch of years between them and
the others made them closer.

"Maybe the Indians will wait tonight, Chancey," she
whispered. "Because they can't tell when the sun goes
down in the rain."

Something inside the little boy rose instantly, and with
it a flood of feeling. It shot from his eyes like a warm flame
gratefully enveloping Massey. Good old Massey. And now
that warm flame that had licked around Massey was enveloping the whole room. For a long moment the brown
face of his mother looked beautiful and serene, and the
steam curling over her teapot hung like in a picture. A
secret inner rosy light glowed from the cherry cupboard
and even the hard earth that had pushed up between the
puncheons purred like Aunt Genny's cat. He could eat a
little now, he believed. Strength and well being rose in him
with every bite, for all was well now with Nilum.

Not till supper was almost over did he notice the cries
of children at play. His spoon halted suddenly in his rigid
hand. He listened. The sound of rain on the roof had
ceased. From somewhere came a sudden revival of saw and
hammer. The ferry bell rang, showing that someone was

out and wanting to cross the river, while from some open
town door or window a cornet started to play, Christ My
All, making sad drawn-out tantarara on the late afternoon
air.

"It's getting lighter," Hulda said with satisfaction, for she
was going out tonight.

Their father looked out of the window.

"The mist's dissolving into air — into thin air," he declared, and then, as if that reminded him of something, he
lifted his head and began reciting half to himself and half
to the room in his low, deep, courtroom voice.

> Our revels now are ended. These our actors,
> As I foretold you, were all spirits and
> Are melted into air, into thin air.

He didn't stop there, but went on, his deep voice linger-
ing lovingly over the cloud-capped towers, the gorgeous
palaces and great globe itself.

> Yea, all which it inherit shall dissolve,
> And like this insubstantial pageant faded,
> Leave not a rack behind. We are of such things
> As dreams are made on, and our little life
> Is rounded with a sleep.

There was something about it that made Chancey shake
with terror. Oh, well he knew what his father meant. It
was Nilum's elegy he was giving. The little boy climbed
over the bench and stumbled from the table. From the
open kitchen door he could begin to see the town through
the mist. Once it was all their land, his mother had said,
but now there were houses and half a public square. The
mist was rising over it in twists and swirls. Already he
could make out the different buildings, the brick front of

the old store, the two-story house of the new, the brown
shape of the mill. Farther this way loomed the long low
ferry house, the church with the new steeple, the tan yard
and the stillhouse with smoke floating about like mist. The
latter was almost gone now. Rows of houses stood with
their wet roofs shiny under the sky. People were out on the
street with the cows and pigs that had been there all the
time, not minding the rain. Up the lane by the academy
marched old lady Winters' flock of geese like a row of
scholars reciting with their necks stretched out.

A faint something caught his eye. At first he didn't know
what it was, a patch of color high over the boat yard. He
could see clouds through it. Then it grew and blossomed
like the tree of life. Another tree of life shot up near the
mill. An arch joined them, and there it stood, fragile and
dazzling, the mysterious bow of the sky, reminding him of
nothing so much as something from that other world he
knew. It shone with color, yet nobody painted it. Nothing
held it up and nothing could tear it down except God.

"Ta-ra-ra!" played the horn.

He could hear town children squealing with delight
but Chancey's heart went cold. Never had he thought he
would sometimes dread to see a bow in the sky. But now he
thought he couldn't bear it. Not today. Already the sun
must be shining up there through the raindrops, his father
said, and that's what made the bow. Soon, the boy knew,
the sun must be out everywhere, for the rain was over. Perhaps it was already shining in Shawaneetown with every
Indian watching it sink farther and farther toward earth
until it touched the horizon and struck like a hammer.

Every moment, the little boy thought, the bow must
fade, but the delicate colors lingered like everlasting. The
first of the night flocks of woods pigeons making for their

roosts flew under it. The dark ferry crossing the river passed slowly through. Now why did that send a shiver down his spine? He strained his eyes far as he could see. Did the man who had cried and his little girl see it? Where were they in the dark forest now? Why did he keep thinking of and feeling for these two he never saw before? Was it that they knew nothing of Nilum and with them he would have oblivion and peace? Or could it be perhaps that the little girl like a china chick might be his sister, his true sister, and the man, who held his narrow head tenderly to one side, was his father kept from him ever since he could remember? He recollected now how the man had smiled to him when first he came and had laid a hand on his head as he passed. The little boy could still feel that hand. The impact of a great secret went over him. It must be he was his real father, he told himself, and that was the reason he had cried.

CHAPTER THREE

THE BRIDE'S BED

Beyond that under their shirts they're all alike.
In the dark you couldn't know one from the next.

THE TIME OF MAN

Dᴵᴰ a young one, Sayward wondered, ever know how its mother felt for it? Likely not. Perhaps some dark night long after its mammy was dead and gone, such a one now grown up might recollect the glimmer of light around it when it was little. But hardly could it guess how tender its mother had held it in her mind, how loving, how anxious for blessings on it, how constant and everlasting, year in and year out, even when it was a grown man going about his business.

She didn't believe in being partial. She did her best to love one like the other. Yet you couldn't help but carry the baby of the family around in your heart the most. And when that littlest was puny and ailing, you prayed more times than you could cipher that he might live and have his chance to go through life like the others, for all things were possible to God.

Just the same, after she had managed to drag Chancey

alive through ill omen and pestilence, she fretted once or twice that for his sake she might regret it some day. She hated to reckon she had ever gone against the will of God. She felt relieved when it turned out one day that his small lips could talk and hardly could she hold the gratitude in her heart when she found his little mind flowed clear as spring water. But she didn't like him wanting to be alone so much. Her eight others throve on sociability and their fellows. Now this last one would sooner drag himself to a window inside or some corner outside with his own self for company.

That didn't go down so well with Sayward. Even the Bible said it wasn't good for man to be alone. Didn't she know? Hadn't Chancey's own pappy been a solitary in the woods when first he came to this Western country, holing up in his cabin of buckeye logs and hearing no voice for weeks on end but his own or some frogs' wild croaking? Some went so far as to say he'd still be there if it hadn't been for her. That was nonsense. Also she didn't like what Genny hinted, that there might be a queer streak in Portius's family, and that's why he never breathed a word of his folks or why he left the Bay State. She told Genny mighty quick there was nothing to it. But to herself she promised that she would do for Chancey all she had for his pappy, keep him from shutting his mind up in himself, throw what life and living with folks she could his way, for in all mortal creatures, she reckoned, was a great hankering to live or never would they have come into this living world.

That's how she came to put overnight company in to sleep with Chancey. He might avoid them by day and hardly speak a word to them even when he ought to. But

he could rub shins and elbows with them by night. It would
be sociability for him and it wouldn't hurt him. It might
even toughen up his thin skin a little, get it used toward all
these folks he was put on earth to live with and make the
best of.

To little Chancey, night was the dark ages. Of all the
torments he found waiting for him in life, night time was
the worst, to have to lay yourself down in the dark and try
to make your thoughts leave your mind and your body
give up life for a kind of death. Night came so often and
lasted so long. Weekdays had a change on Sunday and
every once in a while on public day. But night had no
holiday. Every afternoon at the melancholy hour when the
shadows started to fall, he could see it waiting there ahead
of him, the dungeon he would have to lie in chained hand
and foot till morning.

Could he only run around all day like the others, he believed he might be more satisfied to lie still at night. But to
sleep the dark hours through was a trick that baffled him.
Never could he get the hang of this strange coma that
gripped his brothers and sisters, father and mother, so that
until early morning they lay as if struck by lightning or by
some mysterious nocturnal drunkenness, their heavy breathing filling the cabin. Oh, it was hard for a little boy to lie
there wakeful and think up things to pass the whole live-
long night. He didn't know what he'd do without the
Yankee clock down on the log wall. It never stopped talking to him, gave him something to look forward to, that
golden moment at which it struck. Each time he lifted his
head from the bolster and counted. At the end he prayed
it would strike just once more and that much nearer morn-

ing. Then when the pitiless silence ensued, his heart always sank knowing that until he heard it again, the whole eternity of an hour would have to be lived through.

Just the same he felt grateful to that clock for staying awake with him and keeping his mind company. A whippoorwill's voice was only part of the darkness, but when the giggers came, they seemed like a piece of day in the night time. He could lie on his floor bed and look out the low window and see their torch light moving like a small sun far over there on the river and hear the giggers' voices when the wind brought them right. The best was when the blacksmith worked at night to let a keel boat get off in the morning. He thought no sound so cheerful and alive in the dark as that ringing anvil. It put iron in his soul and sweetness in the long black hours to know that some human was awake like himself, that it wasn't wholly a season of gloom and the dead.

But the worst was when company came and he had to give up his bedfellow, Guerdon. Hardly a week that some strange man or woman didn't stay overnight in the cabin, and most always Chancey had to sleep with them. His mother would say something like this.

"You're welcome to spend the night if you don't mind sleeping with Chancey. He's such a little feller, you'll hardly know he's there."

And seldom did they. He might as well have been a lump in the bed tick for all the notice they took of him, but every minute of the long night their presence and parts from head to toe tormented him. Some were worse than others. One night he had to sleep with a hairy man whose spines pierced his tender young flesh like a porcupine whenever he turned or rolled against him. Another time his bedmate was a little dried-up old woman who lay in her

place like it was her coffin, never moving or breathing all
night that Chancey could tell except that every once in a
while she made a fine sound like a cat spitting.

Now why did the family make such a joke of the awful
time he had to sleep with the bride and bridesman! They
came from Spring Valley. Chancey's father had done some
law work for the bridesman, and the pair had their heart
set on him to do the marrying. When he said he was no
squire and couldn't, they were so taken down that Chancey's mother took pity on them and sent for the new Squire
Matthews and had the bridal pair to supper afterwards.
When Chancey went to bed, they were still in the kitchen.
Later he heard them come into the room below where his
mother and father had their bed. At last he heard his
mother say the fateful words.

"We'll make you welcome to spend the night. But you'll
have to sleep in the loft with Chancey. He has a bad heart
and we can't move him. But I'm sure you won't mind. He's
such a little feller and don't take up much room."

That was the time Chancey's heart even sank the deep-
est. Soon Kinzie and Guerdon came up. Resolve was out
somewhere and would come in later. The little boy looked
sadly at his bedfellow, Guerdon, whom he knew would
sleep three in a bed tonight with his other brothers. He always had to give up his bed with Chancey when company
came. But Guerdon acted like it didn't matter to him.

"Oh, man, are you goin' to sleep with a mighty pretty
woman tonight!" he told the little boy.

"I'd sooner sleep with you," Chancey said to him.

"Shh! Don't talk like that. You'll make her feel bad if
she hears you. She likes you. I could tell the way she looked
at you at the table."

Yes, he could talk that way. He didn't have to sleep with

her. He could lay down and sleep with his brothers. Every now and then while they undressed, he heard Guerdon whisper something to Kinzie or Kinzie to him. He couldn't catch what they said, but they'd snort and gurgle and hold it in till they shook, and that's the way it went till they had their night shirts on. Then they came over to Chancey's bed and stood there in their skinny legs looking down at him.

"You better not sleep on your side of the bed tonight, Chancey," Kinzie told him. "You're supposed to sleep in the middle."

"What for?"

"So the bed stays in balance. You're such a little feller. If you was on one side and those two on the other, it would throw the whole business out of kilter."

"Yes, and so they don't fight, too," Guerdon put in. "A bride and a bridesman is liable to scrap with each other the first night, and this way you keep each one on his side where he belongs."

With grave faces they lifted their small brother up and set him down squarely in the middle of the bed. Then they left him there, but long after they got in their own bed, Chancey could hear them whisper and choke together till in time they grew silent and after that started to snore.

Only he on this loft was awake when the bride and bridesman came tiptoeing up. Chancey peeked. The bride held the candlestick in her hands. It was true what Guerdon said that she was a pretty thing with snowy skin, brown hair and a yellow flowered dress with tucks and ruffles. Except that she was strange and would constrain him, he didn't mind too much sleeping with her. She looked soft and quiet and like she wouldn't snore. But why did this old bridesman have to come up too? Why couldn't he sleep outside on the bench or in the barn on the hay? He looked rough and scaly on the outside as a persimmon butt. The soil of his calling stuck to his hands. So deep was it embedded in the cracks of his skin, it looked as if he never could wash it out. Just to lay eye on him gave the little boy the feeling that if this horny and brushy old ploughman ever crawled between the sheets, he'd corrode and puncture them and next morning leave a dark scaly print of himself on the linen.

"You ain't a goin' to leave him 'ar?" he asked hoarsely.

"I think we better," she whispered. She seemed uncertain.

"Hold on. How kin we get in our bed with that damned tyke in the middle?"

"We'll have to," she whispered. "You're supposed to sleep on that side and me on this."

"Not me! The squire said we were man and wife, and nobody could part us."

"We can't move him on account of his heart!"

"He's asleep and he won't find out." Chancey felt the heavy, soil-caked hands under him.

"Let me be!" the little boy yelled.

The snoring of the two grown boys in the other bed stopped abruptly like halted clocks, then went on. Almost nothing would wake Guerdon and Kinzie once they got to sleep. Their mother said they were bad as Lymie Hollins who slept through the time the flood carried his house down the river.

The bride pushed the bridesman away.

"Now you better be good!" she hissed.

Chancey meditated. She might be little but she could take care of herself. That was the way with women. They might look slight, and mild as butter outside, but inside

[27]

they were spit and fire. The bride blew out the candle. The little boy could hear them undressing in the dimness. He felt the bride creep lightly in under the covers on one side of him. After while a heavy grunting crocodile crawled in on the other.

Oh this, the little boy knew, would be the darkest night of his life. He felt like a small fence stretched between a raging lion on one side and a soft white lamb on the other. The nights of the hairy man and the old woman who spat like a cat seemed mild and peaceful now in comparison. Never had the loft felt so sultry and filled with dark lightning. For a while he tried to make himself thin as a sassafras leaf lying spaceless and harmless between them. But the soft feel of the bride on one side and the hard scales of the bridesman on the other kept bringing him back to human shape and misery.

If only the bridesman had lain still as the bride, but he kept reaching his claws over as if wanting to eat her.

"Remember the little feller's heart!" she whispered.

"It kin stop deader'n a doornail for all I care," he growled.

"Listen!" she halted him. "I don't hear him breathing any more."

That held the bridesman and Chancey held his breath. On and on he held it till the bride sat up in alarm. He wished he could hold it all night but in the end he had to let it go with a loud whoosh, and the bride lay down with relief and a sharp warning. But the bridesman wasn't satisfied. If he couldn't torment with his hands, he would with his feet. He would reach one leg over below the little feller and kick at her. It startled Chancey. He didn't know what to make of it. The picture in the dark of this old man scaled like a snapping turtle, cavorting himself playfully with his feet filled the little boy with horror. Once when a horny leg struck him he gave a loud bleat.

Downstairs he heard the creaking ropes of his mother's bed.

"Is Chancey all right, Mrs. Jones?" she called.

Instantly the bride sat up, and her soft hands ran quickly over the little boy's form till they found his heart.

"Why, I think so, ma'am," she called back, guardedly. "He must have had a nightmare."

"I'm glad it's no worse," the voice said, relieved, and the ropes creaked once more.

Now why did his mother call out like that, the little boy wondered. It must have been a warning, for almost never had she done that before.

The bride must have reckoned it the same.

"Now you lay quiet, Mr. Jones!" she whispered so sharp that Chancy reckoned it would take all the wildness out of him. But no sooner did he reckon all was still than the bridesman started talking again.

"I can't sleep here and you can't neither," he told her.

"I was asleep a half dozen times already, but you woke me up," she came back tartly. "Now why don't you settle down and try to go to sleep your own self, Mr. Jones?"

He snorted at that, kept thrashing and turning like he couldn't lay still. Once he heard her asleep and breathing peacefully, he jumped up like it made him mad. Chancey could hear him pulling on his pants and boots. Down the steps he went, a feeling his way as if he had to go out bad. The little boy counted the minutes like pearls till he'd come back. How peaceful it seemed. Chancey had room now to let his body out to its natural size. He could feel the bride lying there softly beside him. Her presence was like the time the strange little girl sat white and fragile as a china

chick in his father's office. She and the bride both gave out
the same kind of soundless purrings. He could feel them
rise up around him like soft streams of quivering tiny marks
in the dark air. It acted on him like the hum of bees and
flies, made him sink down in the bed. It put over him a
kind of spell as when Massey or Sooth combed his hair.

When he woke up he couldn't believe it. Why, he
couldn't remember a night that passed so soon. He never
slept and yet it was daylight, while the last he remembered
was the dark. He couldn't even recollect the clock striking
twelve. Yes, it must be so, for Resolve was still out when
he minded last and there Resolve snored with his brothers.
But where was the bridesman? The bride lay where she
had all the time. She was awake now and likely her stirrings
had woke him. In the far away kitchen he could hear his
mother, and now the bride slipped quietly out of bed, holding her yellow dress around her. She picked up her shoes
and stockings and ran without a sound down the steps.

For a long time after she had gone, the boy lay there
tasting the warm pleasure of his bed. It was like basking at
the fire. He had actually slept. When he came downstairs,
the boys were gone to their chores, and both bride and
bridesman had vanished. They were over at the store, his
mother said, on their way back to Spring Valley. Chancey
went to the kitchen door but he couldn't see them.

"What time did Mr. Jones get up?" Chancey's father
asked as he sat down for his breakfast.

"All I know is he was sitting on the bench outside the
kitchen when I came out, and that was just daylight," Sayward told him.

"He couldn't have slept very well," Portius said.

"I think Chancey kicked him out!" Sooth cried.

"Is it true, Chancey, that you slept with the bride all night alone?" Libby teased him.

Huldah's black eyes glittered.

"I hear that when a baby comes, Mrs. Jones is going to name him after Chancey."

"Now that's plenty!" their mother said sharply, turning on them. "We had enough carrying on for one night."

CHAPTER FOUR

THE HAY SCALES

Two gills a day — the thing is clear,
Twenty-three gallons make the year.

OLD ALMANACK

IT seemed strange but now that Portius was away, Chancey wanted desperately to believe him his real father, for Portius was at the state capitol trying to get his bill passed. In his mind the little boy could see him moving among the legislators in their fine black coats and starched white collars. In his mind's ear he could hear his father's voice echoing from the capitol walls, telling that the citizens of Washington township wanted a county of their own, for now they had to travel days and nights through forests and waters to reach their county seat.

Oh, Chancey had heard the story a thousand times, how this county was vaster than some states, how the folks down at the far end didn't give a hait about them up here in Washington township which they reckoned belonged to Canada or old England perhaps. Four times, he knew, his father had taken his bill to the capitol, and three times it had been thrown out. But this year, the girls said, it was sure to go through, and when it did, his father would be one of the new county's four judges and perhaps his honor, the president judge himself.

All day yesterday and so far today the little boy had been sitting at the window, waiting to see his father come riding triumphantly home on his black horse, Brig. Now what would a president judge wear, he wondered. Would he come in a scarlet robe, with a three-cornered hat on his head, and when he kissed him, would he still have that peculiar sweetish tobacco-whiskey taste that was his father's?

He listened too hard, his sisters said, and that's what gave him his ear ache, though often had he had it before. Now he let his mother swathe his head in a red flannel rag sweetened with oil. Still his father didn't come, not until they put him on the bucket in the corner. He could hear Massey racing for the house. What she cried out, he couldn't tell and there was nobody to tell him, for his sisters hurried to the door and paid no attention when he called. There wasn't even anybody to wipe him. He had to get to the window on his own shaky legs while his fallen britches tried to hobble him and his heart leaped like a crippled rabbit.

Now who was that poor sick man a coming on foot for the house, the little boy wondered. His face was unshaven, his clothes dirtied, and when he walked, he reeled a little from side to side like a run down top. Not even the girls must have known him, for they drew back when he came up the step and in the house. Only Chancey's mother kept standing at her place like she wasn't scared and let him greet her. And that's how the little boy knew who it was.

He turned bitter eyes on his daughters.

[33]

"Have you no welcome for your father?" he scourged them.

None of them came forward although Huldah stared at him boldly.

"You've been dramming and you're drunk!" she sneered at him.

"Yes, but I'm not stupid, Huldah," her father retorted. "You may remember what I tell you. Tomorrow the stupid person will still be stupid, but the drunken man will be sober." His eyes glowed like coals at the boy by the window. "So my little Chancey is the only one who will kiss me!" he said, and the little boy felt a shiver run along his back. He held up his britches higher and his face, too, blindly, till his father came, and he tasted the sour mixture of tavern doors, of the bucket, of sleeping rooms and other unknown dregs of the flesh.

Oh, how, Chancey asked himself, could he have wished this man staggering to a bench to be his real father? Now his soiled hands fumbled through his pockets and fetched out pipe and pouch. Presently Libby at her mother's word, brought a hot coal on the fire shovel, and as he drew, his eyes vanished in his stubble till his face became a clay chimney with the smoke pouring out.

"Climb up and I'll mitigate that torment," he said and the restless hands pulled the boy to his knee and worked back the rag of flannel. Then his bluish, white-coated lips began plying a soft soothing stream into the painful ear.

All the time Chancey's sisters stood there, more composed now, but watching and waiting, exchanging looks with each other. You could see them consumed by unspoken questions. Only their mother went about her business as if nothing had happened.

"Where is Brig, Papa?" Libby dared at length to ask.

"In safe hands," her father answered between puffs, but he didn't look at her. "The hands of one still more unfortunate than your father and farther to go."

"You sold him!" the girls cried together. Consternation reigned. Even his mother's fingers, busily cleaning his father's hat, were utterly still for a minute.

"Then we'll never see Brig again!" Sooth cried.

"Your saddle, too, Papa?" Chancey whimpered.

"Would you have me carry it home on my back?" he demanded sternly.

"Where did you meet this man — in a tavern?" Huldah scorned.

"And you had to walk all the way home, Papa?" Massey cried.

"Then your bill was thrown out again?" Libby asked him.

Their father gazed at one after the other with sovereign disdain.

"No. The legislature passed the bill. By a good majority I may say."

Little squeals rose from the girls.

"Then we're in a new county!" Chancey tried to look out of the window but could see nothing. Light was breaking everywhere into the darkish kitchen. It wasn't as bad as they had figured.

"And you're the president!" Massey shouted.

"The president judge, you mean!" Dezia corrected her.

Their father didn't answer right away. His stream of smoke was missing Chancey's ear and going down his neck.

"No," he said thickly.

"Are you just a judge, Papa?" Sooth asked him.

"I am nothing," he said.

"Hasn't the governor told you yet?"

[35]

At the word, "governor," Chancey felt a trembling in his father's knee.

"The governor has made his appointments. But I am not named."

"Not you, Papa?" Sooth told him. "Why, you are the one who wrote the bill and got it passed and made the new county."

The little boy felt his father breathing heavily.

"Your father is an agnostic. He doesn't claim to be personally acquainted with the Almighty. He never gets happy or the jerks at camp meeting. His morals are in doubt. He's not that monument of virtue and rectitude to hold the scales of justice for the people."

The little boy looked quickly to his mother. How could she sit there at the table so calm, her strong brown hands keeping on peeling potatoes which Huldah or Libby could do as well, and never a word of sympathy for his father, only that cruel expression that sometimes steeled her face. If she were his own flesh and blood, never could she be like this, for now his own heart was twisted with pity for his father.

"Who are the judges then?" Huldah braved to ask him.

The names came thickly from his mouth. There were a squire and storekeeper from Tateville and Talcott Simms from Moonshine Church.

"And the president judge?" Huldah persisted.

Chancey felt himself slide to the floor as his father got to his feet. Looking up, he saw his father's face twitching in a horrible grimace and he knew that at last they had got to the place of torment.

"Mr. Zephon Brown," he told them.

"Him a judge!" Libby cried. "Why he's just a skinflint farmer and tax collector!"

Nobody else said anything. When Chancey glanced around the girls were looking at their father as if this was the lowest degradation of all. In self defense he took down the brown jug that hung on the rafter and poured a cupful. The sweetish fumes filled the room and the fiery liquid spilled down his chin and waistcoat. Afterward he stood there inclining a little this way and that, the spasm still distorting one side of his face.

"He's also an elder in your mother's church," he told them. Then with careful dignity, the jug in one hand and pewter cup in the other, he made his way to his office in the front room.

That was a painful afternoon. Chancey's ear ache was gone, but a greater ache filled his small breast. Aunt Genny and Mrs. Weaver along with others came to the kitchen. Was it true that Portius had lost out to Zephon Brown, they wanted to know. But how did he lose his horse and have to come home afoot? It was Genny spoke most of the time. And what was Sayward going to do about the load of hay Portius ordered before he went away, for Zephon himself was down the road this minute fetching it, and Sayward would hardly need it now, having fodder for her cows till pasture came in again!

The little boy sat tightly on his stool. His mother claimed that God was good and kind, but it looked like God was cruel, playing with his father like a cat with a mouse. First He had given a fine new horse to his father as a judge to ride on. Then he took the judgeship away, and now when the hay for this fine horse was coming, He had taken the horse away. Chancey peered out of the window. How he hated the sight of the triumphant Zephon sitting high as he could on his load of hay driving his best pair of horses. God had not taken Zephon Brown's horses away.

Where the road came nearest the house, he halted his team and called Massey outside to tell her father he was to meet him at the hay scales.

"Even his hay's come up in the world," Mollie Weaver said. "He don't want to sell it by the load any more."

"You better go over your own self, Saird," Genny warned her sister. "He'll skin the eyes off Portius today."

Chancey's mother made no reply but the little boy could tell by her face that she had no intention of going, for that would admit to all that his father was drunk and couldn't take care of his own business. She sat bitter-faced and still. Then the other door opened and Portius stood there. His eyes were bloodshot but no blood flowed in his face. His eyes darkened a bit at the sight of his sister-in-law. Then majestically he made his difficult way across the room.

"Most potent, grave and reverend signiors, my approved good masters," he said with irony, looking out of the window. With both hands he fitted on his gray beaver hat which Sayward had meantime cleaned.

Then he came toward Chancey. The little boy had no notion of his intent until he saw Mollie Weaver put her hand to her mouth and heard Aunt Genny draw her breath.

"I don't believe I'd take a little feller like him along today, Portius," Genny told him.

He straightened and stood there, regarding her with those fiery gray-green eyes.

"It happens to be my custom to do as I please, Genny," he informed her. "You can ambulate where you please. You can gossip in every kitchen in town, and probably do. But this lad has been deprived and hindered by the powers that be. I want to show him some of the spiders and scorpions created by their Maker to crawl upon civilization."

Over his shoulder as they went, Chancey had a glimpse of his mother's cruel face, but never a word of protest from the lines that were her mouth. She was letting him go. Now he would have to see and bear his father's shame and drunkenness in front of the whole town.

Once outside, his father set him on his shoulder and his course for the road. The wagon with its wide swaying load had gone on, and his father followed about as unsteadily. Sometimes the little boy found himself almost at the fence on one side, and sometimes almost in the ditch at the other. It was nicer to lay back his head and look at the sky. When he pitched this way, the clouds went flying that. And when he pitched that way, the clouds all came sailing back. It gave him the most extraordinary sensation. Where before had he felt the heavens whirling around him like this, the sense of rising and falling in space, while soft blue and white worlds like vast seas floated around him, soothing his ears and dragging his memory with long forgotten impressions?

The hay scales were new and belonged to George Roebuck. They stood by his store, the handsomest spot in town, Chancey thought, for across the road was the Ferry House and a little beyond, the ferry on the slow tide of the river. When Chancey and his father got there, Zephon Brown had already driven under the very high shed with its little roof house far above. Anselm, the clerk, waited as if he expected the driver to get down from the load while they weighed the wagon, but Zephon's half closed eye looked back at Portius reeling after. He gave a little cough, blew himself up a bit and kept sitting there while Anselm lowered the chains and put one around each hub. The great clicking windlass turned, the pulleys screeched, the four wheels lifted one by one clear of the ground, and presently you could see Anselm up at the window of the little roof house, moving the weights on the pair of great black steel-yards.

Now what were the men down here nudging each other for? Chancey wondered. They had done it ever since Zephon had kept sitting like a king on the hay. The little boy looked at his father. He seemed to see or understand nothing that was going on. He talked to no one, steadying himself at the hogshead on which he had seated Chancey. Never had the little boy seen his features so dissolved and run together. Anselm came down with the figures on a scrap of paper. This was the gross weight, this was the weight of the wagon. Portius paid no attention. Zephon's black man, Caesar, came up on foot to drive the load off to the Wheeler stable, and Zephon slid down from the wagon.

"Now shall we settle?" he asked, turning his head so that only his half-closed eye was on Chancey's father.

"I'm at your service," he agreed thickly.

Zephon gave his little cough.

"I'd like the cash, Portius."

For the first time Chancey's father seemed to come out of his lethargy.

"Cash!" he fetched out, trying to keep his balance. "Why, there isn't that much cash in the new county. Fortunately I brought some with me from the old. Shall we retire to the Ferry House? We'll seal the bargain with a clincher."

More than once Chancey had been carried by the Ferry House, by the tantalizing smells and the sound of the fiddle that came out of it. These had made him itch to see what it was like inside, but now that he was in at last, he felt cheated. Why, it looked bare as a barn, with sand on the floor, a few worn brown benches and tables and a high counter they called the bar. Even the man behind it, Sam Sloper, the proprietor and ferryman whom everyone called King Sam, looked disappointing, and today there was no fiddle. Chancey's father set him on the bar with his heels hanging down. Zephon Brown looked disapproving at the little boy sitting among the mugs and bottles, as if this was a sure way to make a drunkard out of a child. Zephon and Chancey's father drank. The men drank from mugs drawn from a mysterious looking barrel. Chancey's father reached in pocket after pocket, fetching out silver shillings, paper shinplasters and banknotes each of which latter Zephon looked up in his Banknote Detector.

When the money in full lay on the bar, Zephon Brown stroked his hand over his mouth as if in apology for the condition of the man with whom he must do business.

"You're entirely satisfied, Portius?"

"Oh, I'm perfectly satisfied. I feel I have a bargain. I hope you have no regrets."

"Regrets? No indeed," Zephon concealed a smile. He carefully drained the last drops from his mug. "Well, I'll have to be going."

Chancey's father seemed almost asleep. Suddenly he woke up.

"But you can't do that," he said thickly.

"How's that?" Zephon asked in good humor as to a child, pocketing the money.

"Why, you belong to me! I bought you," Portius told him.

In the eyes of the men standing back of his father, Chancey glimpsed a sudden wild light of astonishment and exhilaration. Elbows poked into neighbors' ribs.

[41]

"What do you mean?" Zephon looked startled.

Portius gave him his sodden and majestic attention.

"You acted in this transaction entirely of your own free will, didn't you?"

"I don't know what you're talking about," Zephon protested, but his face had paled.

Bracing himself at the bar, Portius turned further and further until he could gaze direct at the other. Here he stood swaying and making horrible grimaces.

"You're an adult sober and in sound mind, aren't you? You had no reservations in adding your own body and weight to that of the hay, did you? You demanded cash payment in full and received and acknowledged it. Your purpose surely wasn't to cheat me, was it? Not in front of so many of your fellow citizens?"

Zephon looked frightened for the first time.

"If there was anything amiss, Portius — "

"Ignorance is no excuse in the eyes of the law." Chancey had never seen his father's face so terrifying.

Zephon cast his good eye at the door.

"Let me give you some sound and gratuitous advice," Portius leered at him. "Do not try to escape. It will only be used against you in court."

"You can't hold me!" Zephon cried, but he made no move to go. Instead he figured hastily on a piece of paper, then from his pocket counted out a small amount of silver and banknotes on the bar. "If you noticed my forgetfulness, you should have called my attention to the mistake in the first place," he declared angrily.

"Not so fast!" Portius said. "You must know that a thief may discharge his debt to his victim after he is caught. But he cannot so easily discharge his debt to the law once it's broken."

"What'll you take to let him buy himself loose, Portius?" King Sam behind the bar propounded.

"Not a shilling." Chancey's father waved it aside with an unstable hand. "The defendant may be willing to traffic in his human soul. I'll have none of it. The only possible condition that might absolve him of duplicity and debt would be for him to solemnly and truthfully swear that he had no intention to charge in the first place, that the hay was a gift bathed with the milk of human kindness and warmed by the sun of human brotherhood – "

"I'll never do it!" Zephon shouted.

Portius turned, his face working in grim and righteous retribution.

"I only stated a hypothetical case, in which I should be helpless to bring against you charges of sharp practice and connivance, of scheming and intent to defraud, of willful extortion, of acceptance of moneys secured by fraud and, in the event of your running away, of the perfidious breaking of your bond!"

Never had Chancey seen such a look on anyone's face as on Zephon Brown's while hurriedly he counted out a further sum, threw it on the bar and rushed from the Ferry House. The barroom broke into such wild yells of delight as to startle and frighten the little boy. Even on King Sam's wintry face the thin sun of a grin had appeared. Boatmen and loafers surrounded Chancey's father and shook his hand, while the latter stood like a tipsy king surrounded by his backwoods court.

"It's my intention to treat those present, Sam," he stated. "You may also mix up a little rum and warm milk for the boy."

Chancey wished his father hadn't said that. Now no matter how much he disliked the taste, he would have to drink it. More than once had he tried the watered whiskey handed out at the house to children on festive occasions. Never could he keep it down long and this, he knew, would be the same. He would have to throw it up in front of everybody here or over his father on the way home.

CHAPTER FIVE

A NAME TO CALL
IT BY

Spit on your hands and take a fresh holt.

EARLY SAYING

SAYWARD was put out. Whoever heard of such a thing as being ashamed of the name of your own home town? But that's how some folks felt about Moonshine Church.

The first time she heard it was when Portius told her a fight was on between their town and Tateville for the county seat. Then Zephon Brown stopped her on Water Street sober as an owl. He told her the court house would likely go to Tateville, and Moonshine Church to the dogs. She better sell off her land for what she could get while she had buyers for it.

"I wouldn't a thought he'd speak to me after what he tried to do to you," she told Portius. "Anyway I didn't thank him none for it."

To herself she guessed that Moonshine Church could

get along by itself. It wasn't doing bad for an upstart town along the river. All day long you could hear the broken tune of the sash sawmills like giant horseflies buzzing and lighting, stopping and starting, whining and skipping, for the saws cut only on the down stroke. Griswold's Race from Crazy Creek had to be dug wider. Five mills took water from that race now, three of them sawmills. Even that wasn't enough to fill the bill for the town. A thousand feet of boards was a good day's sawing, and that had to be cut out of soft poplar logs. Oak and hickory took longer. Truth to tell, the hardwoods were mostly broad-axed. If you went up in the hills, you could hear the chip of hewing all day. House and barn timbers were in great demand, and it didn't pay to use walnut or cherry any more, for they fetched a better price boated down the river.

Oh, Sayward knew what Zephon Brown was after. He wanted her to sell him some of her land cheap, but he could go suck his thumbs. She had no trouble finding buyers. Her trouble was holding on. Every month town men came and plagued her to sell. They offered good inducement. She had sold all Water Street in parcels and lots, why wouldn't she sell this? But that piece of three acres down town she let Oliver Meek have, taught her a lesson. Oliver gave her four hundred dollars. She thought that a pile of money. But after while he sold it to Seth Collins for seven hundred and fifty. Seth didn't hold it long till Colonel Suydam gave him a thousand, and now the colonel had cut it up into six parcels and was asking three hundred dollars a lot. Why, he was making more clear profit out of that one piece of her land in six months than she had got for it after holding on to it for nigh onto thirty years, clearing it in the bargain, chopping down the butts and vines, burning out the stumps, grubbing the wild sprouts that for years tried to come up, and working the ground till it was fit and fine.

"If anybody makes money out of our land after this, it's going to be the Wheelers," she told Portius.

And who had a better right, she'd like to know? Who came here when all this ground was nothing save a howling wilderness? But it wasn't them that came first like her father who made anything out of it, she noticed. There was Billy Harbison, one of the earliest. He was beat out of his first place by Zephon Brown and induced to sell pieces off his second till now when movers in red-wheeled wagons were coming in ready to pay good money for bottom land, Billy had none left. Their old neighbor, Mrs. Covenhoven, had sold out long ago when Big John died, and now strangers were selling high-priced town lots off that farm. Till it was done, it would fetch a small fortune, but Martha Covenhoven wouldn't get it. No, it wasn't the old settlers that reaped the harvest, save for those stubborn few who held on to their land till the cows came home.

Now Portius was all for Sayward selling out. It would make more land available for the town to build on, he claimed, and the more folks Moonshine Church had, the more argument to be the county seat.

"Lawsy me!" Sayward said. "If Tateville's entitled to the court house, let them have it."

It didn't bother her any. Everybody knew Tateville was bigger than Moonshine Church. It was richer, too, they said, with ditches dug on both sides of its main street, and sidewalks laid in brick or stone and no team had dared to drive over them. Besides, Tateville had a wool mill with she-didn't-know-how-many-looms, and when men and boys came out from work their faces and hands were red as blood from the new dyed wool. They looked like Indians, Mollie Weaver told her.

So let them have their county seat, she said, but do you think folks like the Meeks and Suydams would hear to it? No, they fought Tateville tooth and nail. To hear them talk, you'd half believe the world would go flat as a pancake if the court house went to Tateville. Even General Morrison worked like a horse trying to get the county seat in Moonshine Church. The shorter time men lived here, it looked like, the harder they fought against losing something they never had. The way they were riled up and talked, you'd reckon a county seat was like heaven with golden streets, with pumps that fetched up whiskey instead of water, and where folks were always washed so all-fired clean and white of their sins that a person from another settlement couldn't stand looking at them till he smoked up a piece of glass like Jake Tench had the time he claimed the sun spotted like a rattlesnake.

The new Moonshine Church Weekly Centinel blackguarded Tateville and the Western Repository Gazette of Tateville ran down Moonshine Church. That was all right. But it went too far when it poked fun at the other town's name.

"Whoever heard of a seat of justice with a name like Moonshine Church?" the Tateville paper printed. "Our very prisoners at the bar would snicker. Shawanee County would be a laughing stock to the nation, the name of its seat an offense to all of Christendom."

That's when folks in Moonshine Church started getting up a petition to change the name. Sayward told them they had a right to their opinion, but so had she, and she wouldn't sign it. For one thing, it had been Portius who named it Moonshine Church, and for another, it always seemed like a decent commonplace name to her. Why, it sounded right and natural as her own name. She didn't see in her mind a church made out of moonshine when she said it any more than she saw a boy hopping out of the grass when she said johnny-jump-up. She always reckoned johnny-jump-up a pert flower name and Moonshine Church a pert name for a town. But now these later comers wanted to give it some stale old second-hand name. Make it Syracuse, they said. Make it Portland. Make it Concord, Albany, London or Berlin. One woman even said, make it Jerusalem.

That woman was in the kitchen tonight. So were some other women and men. They were waiting for the Corporation meeting to be over. Portius called it the Corporation because not every crossroads settlement had a bill of incorporation by the state legislature. But to most folks it was just the select council of trustees elected by the freeholders, with the president, the mayor. As a rule they met at the academy or the back room of one of the taverns, for they had no town hall as yet. Tonight this was supposed to be a secret meeting to decide about the name and they came over here to the house of their lawyer. But secrets traveled fast in Moonshine Church, and now seven others sat in the kitchen waiting to hear or to have their say when the meeting broke up.

It lasted a long time. You could hear the sounds of wrangling back and forward over there like the wind in the old days coming through the deep woods. After while a door sounded and Sayward heard a rap on the door to the sweep. Those waiting in the kitchen braced up, expecting to see somebody come out with news, but that was only Portius telling her what they had made out beforehand.

Now she put the coffee on to boil and ham to fry and set
the table with her new white crockery plates and heavy
white cups and fine wooden handled knives and forks and
pewter spoons. In time a rumble sounded like putting
through a motion, then a racket of chairs being pushed
back over a plank floor and a stumping of boots as they
came out.

Those men of the Corporation looked surprised to see so
many crowded in the kitchen. Most had to go back for
chairs and benches from the other room.

"Any of you ladies object to tobacco?" Major Hocking
asked with a cigar in his hand. He lived in the two-story
house at High and Race streets, and never had he been
in war except to sell goods to the army commissary, but
everybody called him Major.

"I do," the Fly Trap said. She was the one who wanted
Moonshine Church called Jerusalem, a thorny maiden lady
who kept two boards hanging up in her house smeared
with molasses. Whenever they got full of flies, she would
smack them together.

"In that case, I'll put it out," the Major said courteously.
He threw his cigar in the fire, but back in the chimney
corner old lady Winters sat and puffed all the harder on
her corncob pipe, her eyes black with disdain.

"It smells mighty good in here, Mrs. Wheeler," one said.

"It ought to. It smells like my coffee," this from Oliver
Meek, the storekeeper.

"I bought the coffee at George Roebuck's," Sayward
said mildly, and the men laughed, set up by the sight of their
plates filled with ham and their cups with the steaming
black coffee.

"I have a petition to read to you, gentlemen," the Fly
Trap announced, standing up and unrolling a long paper.

A NAME TO CALL

"I call it 'Resolved to Change the Name of Moonshine Church to Jerusalem.' "

The councilmen drew long faces. Oh, they didn't say they wouldn't listen. They just didn't save any racket. Their chairs scraped and bumped as they sat down. Now and then for a minute they'd put on pious faces as if to hear, then they'd take fresh bites or smack their lips over coffee. Cups, knives and forks clattered by mistake and on purpose. Trustees turned to their neighbors to ask them to pass this or that or could they have another cup of coffee? Hardly one looked at the Fly Trap. It took a long time for her to read all her "resolves." The minute she was done, talk broke out in the open like the academy after school, but not about the paper. Oliver Meek plagued John Quitman how a teamster hauled sixteen barrels of whiskey from Cincinnati in ten hours, what did he think of that? Quitman, who owned keel boats and barges, answered it didn't scare him. He said the teamster was lucky he didn't break his horses' legs, for the state corduroy road was worse than no road at all, being mostly mudholes that let horses down to their bellies and full of floating logs besides. So it went. They talked of the census and each had his own reckoning for the town and the county. They told what banks had gone bad lately, and how much such and such buildings cost.

Sayward couldn't help thinking. Helped by her girls, she waited on the table and other company, seeing that each had enough to eat. But she couldn't help remembering how it used to be in the old days. Most of the men then had to come a mighty long ways through the woods, on foot and with night dogs snapping after. It wasn't often they didn't fetch their families along. Their women and young ones wouldn't have missed it for the world. Oh, at first those

[51]

oldtime settlers would talk what was afoot in the woods, about some house raising or taxing. But the main part of the evening was sociable, for fun and frolic. They told stories that made you wipe your eyes one minute and scream and holler the next. Your insides warmed and your hearts stretched. Till it was over you felt like a brother and sister to all, if you didn't beforehand. You hated to see the night go so fast. And when the hour for parting came, you never knew if you would see each other again. You stood at the door and watched them off through the snow or leaves, a whirling their flambeaus to keep them lit, a calling back something they forgot or maybe their third and fourth farewells. "Goodby!" they'd call. "Goodby!" you'd call back. "Goodby!" "Goodby!" Fainter and fainter they sounded till all you could make out was their light like pale spook fire in the dark woods, and when you turned back in the house, it looked lonesome and desperate without them. She could feel that choked feeling for your friends and folks come over her now. Even when you lay abed with your head on your bolster, your heart still tramped along with them through the dark woods till they got home.

Now these men tonight at Moonshine Church were different, town bodies, reckoning town things. Figures of money and time and such entered in their talk. Hardly one spoke that he didn't mention so many dollars or hours and days it took to do something or so many boats tied up last week at one time and how many tons they carried. They were good enough folks and friendly to her and Portius, if not to the Fly Trap, but they weren't the settler folks she and Portius used to know in the woods in the old days. She recollected now how Granny MacWhirter used to complain of how folks changed since the Revolution. Be-

fore the War, Granny used to say, it had no classes. A poor
man was good as a rich man and welcome at his house or
table. Sayward never hardly could make Granny out. She
reckoned Granny was just getting old. The old always
complained of the young. No, she hadn't seen what
Granny meant then, but she was beginning to now.

When rations were over, the council went home, saying
nothing of what it had done. Most of the company went,
too. Only Genny stayed, not to help Sayward and the girls
with the dishes but believing Portius would tell something
of what had gone on. And so he did, but not to Genny. He
would give one of his young ones the honor first.

"Well, Massey," he said. "I understand you're not living
in Moonshine Church any more. Did you know that?"

Quickly the young ones crowded round. So they
changed the name after all, Sayward thought. But they
wouldn't give the Fly Trap the satisfaction of knowing
that they did in part what she "resolved." No, they would
sooner have the Fly Trap on the other side, to go against
her.

"What's the name now?" Genny, sharp as scissors,
wanted to know.

Portius bent over the fire, lighting a taper for his pipe
so a coal wouldn't blacken his fingers. Then he puffed
cheerfully, his eyes green and bright.

"Americus, Ohio! How does that strike you?"

Genny's face hardened.

"Well, I intend to go on calling it Moonshine Church.
So I expect will a lot of other folks." She nodded her head,
took her wrap from the peg and went home.

As soon as she had left, Sayward's children gave their
opinion. Huldah was still out some place. Kinzie was back
East, and Resolve at the Morrisons', but the rest told what

they thought. All through it, Portius sat dragging on his pipe, his eyes dancing, the puffs coming from his lips, but not a word till they were done. That was the way, Sayward reckoned, he must sit in court down at Maytown letting the other lawyers bandy their words, in no hurry to deliver his say-so till his turn came.

Now when the children had their say, he pulled from his pocket a long paper written on both sides.

"I was given an original poem to read to the council tonight. Unfortunately the effort was in vain. But I understand it's to be printed this week in the Centinel. You may want to hear it and guess who wrote it." He cleared his throat.

> There is a prayer of wide renown
> Which I dislike to hear,
> To change the name of this fair town
> We citizens hold dear.
>
> They pray for some conventional name.
> The muses answer, No!
> Such names belong to alien fame
> And not to O-hi-o.
>
> Our cherished name is strong and plain
> 'Tis clear and easy spoken,
> Descending to us by a chain
> That never should be broken.
>
> No poet that the world has heard,
> No scholar in research,
> Can offer a more moral word
> Than that of Moonshine Church.
>
> Oh, let us hand it down the stream
> Of time, to coming ages,

So Moonshine Church may be the theme
Of future bards and sages.

Our kinsfolk slumber here, are blest,
Their wish we shan't besmirch.
Let them still rest upon the breast
Of peaceful Moonshine Church.

So my defense remains the same.
No further need to search.
Dismiss the plaintiffs, not the name
Of guiltless Moonshine Church!

All the time he was reading it, Sayward watched little Chancey. Most times he was in bed at this hour, but tonight was a special occasion, and she had let him come down with Massey in their bedgowns to have a chance at the news and leftovers. As a rule the little feller sat wrapped in his own thinking, but tonight he hung on every word, as he mostly did for rhyming pieces.

Now when Portius finished, everyone but Chancey guessed who was the poet. Most of them reckoned it a woman. Some said the Fly Trap. But none, Portius said, was right. Then he asked Chancey.

"I couldn't tell that it was a woman," he said.

"Why not?" his father asked.

"Because when you read it I could see a man all the time."

"What made you see a man?" his father persisted.

"It was a word in it. I don't know what it was any more, but I knew he wouldn't say it if he was a woman."

"Who was the man you saw?" Libby asked him.

"I didn't see him with my eyes. I just saw him in my mind. It might have been a big man or a little man. I don't know. But I think maybe it was Papa."

They all hollered at that and demanded of Portius if it was true, and when he laughed and admitted it, they said Chancey had been over in the law office so much he saw him write it.

"No, I didn't see him, just in my mind," Chancey insisted.

"I didn't think you wrote the poem, Papa," Dezia said, "because Americus sounds like Latin and I thought maybe you were the one who wanted Americus."

"Well, as a matter of fact, I did propose the name, Americus, too," Portius conceded.

Sayward had sat silent, listening. Now she smiled to herself. Wasn't that just like Portius, being on both sides? First he wrote a poem against changing the name. Then he told the council what new name to change it to. He wasn't satisfied to be the one who named Moonshine Church. He had to name Americus, too. Oh, she could see he had his tongue in his cheek when he wrote that poem. That way he would be on both sides and none could be against him. He would be a judge of Shawanee County yet.

"Now you all go to bed right away!" she told them.

Late that night she awoke and lay sleepless for a while. She turned the new name over in her mind. Americus, was it? Now why did it mind her of the old days? She was like Chancey. It minded her of something and she didn't know what. Oh, yes, she did, too. It minded her when she was a girl and a young married woman. Hardly anybody then save Portius said America. No, they said Ameriky. They said Pennsylvany, too, and Virginny. Americus was something like that. That old name, Ameriky, had a power of strength and feeling in it, and Americus was much like it, having only a trammel tacked on the end.

CHAPTER SIX

COUNTY SEAT

Let justice be done though the heavens fall.

INSCRIPTION ON THE
SHAWANEE COUNTY COURT HOUSE

SOON after daylight Chancey crawled to the window. This was Americus now, his father said, and yet it still could have been Moonshine Church, the same brick red and stone brown and the same weathered gray that logs took on when once they couldn't sprout forth leaves any more.

A good many must have thought like Chancey, for they went on calling it Moonshine Church. Most all at home did. Chancey's father heard them a few days in disapproving silence. Then one noontime he laid down his knife and fork and looked around the table. It was a look like the Lion of Barbery gave. They had seen the lion on exhibition at the Central House, admission a levy for grownups and a fip for children. The man said that a hair cut from that lion and rubbed under the arm pit would make weakly children strong. But Portius wouldn't let Aunt Genny try it on Chancey.

"Our town council has voted to rename this town,"

Portius said sternly. "Of course, it must be ratified by the courts. But meantime, regardless of what you hear outside, I don't want to hear Moonshine Church in this house again."

Oh, the younger ones in the Wheeler house had to watch their step after that, for none of them said Americus when their pappy wasn't around. It sounded too stiff and stuck up. Now Moonshine Church slipped out easy as an old tooth.

The next day their father fetched home a handbill and hung it up where all could see. It had a drawing on it of three men at a fork in the road. They were pushing a wheelbarrow with a little court house in it. The three men, Chancey's father said, were the county commissioners. One road fork led to a cruel monster with a whip. That was marked Major Tate. The other led to a spread eagle over an American flag. That was marked Americus.

"Notice that it doesn't say Moonshine Church," their father pointed out.

Now how did that handbill stir up so much trouble, Chancey wondered. A gang of men came down from Tateville a tearing down every one they saw pasted up on roadside fences and stables. That night Chancey could hear them over in town yelling, "Hurroar for Tateville!" Then some Moonshine Church men came out of the taverns and yelled, "Hurroar for Americus!" The two sides had a fight and the Moonshine Church men threw the Tateville men in the race. Most everybody in Moonshine Church found it easier to say Americus after that. Even Aunt Genny, who never would put the name in her mouth, took to it now. "Right here in Americus," she would say. Why, some folks, Chancey's mother told, were so strong for it now, they felt cheated when Americus got only the county

[58]

seat. They thought they'd get the capitol at Washington and the White House besides.

The night Americus celebrated the county seat, Chancey lay in his bed a listening. When he looked out of the window he could see torches flickering in the dark. They were sure making high jack over getting the county court. Little did the small boy think how he would hate to see that new county court in session, that on it would hang his life and well being. But that's what he found out a few days more. He was in the front room when his father was called downtown.

"If Mr. Abernathy and a client come, tell him I'll be back soon," he told Chancey.

The little feller felt mighty proud. He sat up straight on his stool listening. When a knock sounded, he called "Come in. Papa will be back soon." In walked Mr. Abernathy and an Indian, but Mr. Abernathy couldn't stay.

"Tell your father I'll see him later," he said. "You can entertain Little Turtle till he gets back."

Chancey had no time to think about that. Before he could get up a word, Mr. Abernathy had gone and all the little boy could see of him was his back through the window as he left. When Chancey turned around on his stool, there was the Indian standing by the fire. He was big and gaunt and his face the ugliest Chancey ever saw. He wore a dirty shirt and britches like a white man, but his foot gear was moccasins.

"Maybe my father won't be back today," Chancey stammered. "Do you want to come back some other time?"

The Indian's face stayed brown and hard and unwashed as a big copper penny. His arrogant eyes and fierce hooked nose showed not the slightest notice that he had heard. It gave the little feller a desperate feeling. Now how would you entertain a man that wouldn't listen, especially an Indian man? It would be easier to talk to a stump or stone. More than once Chancey had talked to the big rock down by the run. It was a friendly rock, warm in the sun, and had no eyes to bore through you when you asked such a kindly thing as if Little Turtle was deaf and dumb. Every time he turned to see if his father was coming, those fierce eyes were like pitchy awls a pinning him to the stool.

Seldom had his father looked so good as when that familiar figure turned in from the road. Just the way he walked, you could see he feared neither man nor devil. Powerful and noble as always, he came in the law room, went up and shook hands with his ragged caller, smiling at him like he was his brother.

"How are you, Little Turtle?" his voice boomed, making everything all right. "Glad to see you. Mr. Abernathy told me he didn't know if he could get you to come or not. Where is Mr. Abernathy?"

The Indian didn't say anything. He just looked haughtily at Portius.

"Sit down," Chancey's father said and got a chair for him. He took his own easy chair, but the savage would not sit down. "Mr. Abernathy has told me very little about your case. Now I want you to tell me all you can."

The Indian stood there silent. Only his eyes had life. They looked out black and rude as if to say that he didn't talk such a low tongue as the white man's language.

"Speak up, man! We can't do anything without speaking," Chancey's father cried.

"Me Injun," Little Turtle scorned. "Me talk Injun."

Now what could his father do, Chancey wondered, for he couldn't say much in Wyndotte or Shawanee or whatever Little Turtle might be. He felt sorry for his father, but he hadn't need to, for his father didn't look sorry for himself. He kept sitting there and the two men gazed measuring each other. Then the white man got up and poured out two cups of rum from the jug. Little Turtle showed his first interest. He reached out a claw and the rum went down like water.

Seldom had Chancey heard anybody smack his lips as Little Turtle did over that rum. His tongue ran around the inside of the cup like a dog's.

"Damn Injun! Me half white," he said, opening one eye wide for Portius to look at. "See blue eye!" He held out the cup. "More lum."

"We'll have one more, Little Turtle. That's all," Portius said. He made the cups barely half full.

The Indian took his and held it out. He looked at Portius gravely.

"White preacher say Injun no drink, good man, go up, much happy. Say Injun drink, bad man, go down, much burn." He lifted the cup to his chin. "Maybe white preacher tell damn lie." He drank it down and set it on the desk-table with alacrity. "You want me make mark on talking paper?"

"No," Portius said, sitting down and back in the calm, relaxed way he had when he was master of a situation. "Mr. Abernathy said that you used to be happy and prosperous. Now, you look poor and wronged. I want you to tell me who wronged you. Perhaps I can help you."

"Nobody help poor Injun," Little Turtle said. "Mis' Coe up Tateville say him help poor Injun. Say him my broder. Give me lum. Give me whisk. Give cow. Give horse. Say make mark on talking paper. Me make mark. Him constable. Him take away horse. Him take away house. Take away land. Belong Mis' Coe now, him say. Talking paper say so. Take away pistol white chief give. Now got nothing."

"Does Mr. Coe still call you brother?" Portius inquired.

"Still call broder. I say Mis' Coe, how broder? He say, we all broder. In Bible. Go back to Adam. I say glad him no closer."

Chancey's father laughed, but the boy thought he saw anger kindling in his eyes.

"I take it you signed a note, a judgment note," he said. "We'll have to see about that."

"Me go see long ago. See down Maytown. See white constable. Him say Injun no good. Mis' Coe good. Mis' Coe keep horse. Mis' Coe keep house. Mis' Coe keep land. Mis' Coe keep pistol. All belong Mis' Coe now."

"Maytown isn't the county seat for us any more," Portius explained kindly. "We have a new county up here and the first court's being held here in Americus. I think I can help you."

The Indian shook his head.

"White man court no good. One time Injun get drunk. Act bad like devil. What white man court do dan, hah? Tie um all Injun up. Whip um Injun plaintiff. Whip um Injun defendant. Whip um Injun witnesses."

Portius smiled.

"They won't do it here. Not if I can help it."

"White man all same together." Little Turtle held up a hand with four fingers tight against each other. "Great Spirit make mistake. Take white man out fire too soon. That's how come him white. Great Spirit leave Injun in. Make him better. Bake him red. Mis' Coe say Injun come from across water. Come from Tartar. That why him red. I say how you know Tartar across water don't come from us? Hah!"

Portius laughed heartily. Little Turtle, gratified, went on.

"Long time ago Injun have beaver. Take um to White man town. White man say price. Say can't buy now. Must wait. This Great Spirit day. Must go church. Be good. Keep still. Shut eye. Listen what Great Spirit say. Injun sit outside Great Spirit house. Wait. Hear sing. Hear talk. After while white man come out. Can't pay like him said. Price go down. Go to other white man. Him say same. All trader say one like other. Can't pay. Price go down. Then Injun know. White man don't go church so hear what Great Spirit say. Go so can put heads together. Think how cheat poor Injun."

"Well, I won't argue that with you. It's a good story," Portius said and Chancey thought from his father's quiet smile that he had heard it before. "But if you have any principle and courage left, you won't let Mr. Coe defraud you and your wife and children out of what rightfully belongs to you." He said it with such force and fire that the Indian stood fascinated.

"You get talking paper back? Get land back? Get house back?"

"I'm not certain," Portius declared. "But I can give your shyster friend, Mr. Coe, the dressing down I've always wanted to in public."

"Whip um lash?"

"No, not with the lash," Portius regretted. "However, I can promise to give the gentleman and his thieving practices a whipping with the tongue that will let him stand naked and bleeding a long time in the sight and memory of his fellow citizens."

His words seemed to feed a hunger deep in the gaunt frame of the Indian. His eyes fastened on the white man as

[63]

if to search for any possible fraud to this promise. He stood motionless a long time. When he spoke it was with a kind of rude secret gratitude.

"What matter your boy? No run. No fish. No throw stone. Sit all time."

Chancey felt his father's troubled gaze run over him.

"He's delicate, Little Turtle. Doesn't eat enough. He's not strong, was born sickly."

"Keep um on stool all time, him stay sick all time. Him need run. Give um Little Turtle. Little Turtle make um run. Take um long march. Make leg hard. No give anything eat one day, two day, three day. Make belly hard. Make um sleep on ground summer time, winter time. Make um sleep on snow. Him get hard then, hah. Like iron."

Chancey gazed quickly at his father who offered his pouch of tobacco to the Indian, then filled his own pipe and lighted it.

"I'm sure that's fine for an Indian boy," he said equably. "But I don't know how it would work out with a white boy."

"No hurt um," Little Turtle said quickly. "But might die. Better die than sick all time. Better in ground than sit stool."

"Well, I'm grateful for your kind offer, Little Turtle," Portius said, taking long quiet draughts on his pipe. "We'll think about it."

"No need think," Little Turtle promised. "You go court. Whip um Mis' Coe. Get um back house. Get um back land. You my friend. Me take boy. Raise him Injun. Make him strong like iron. Make him heart hard like stone. Won't die. But if die, go to Great Spirit. Great Spirit make him over better next time."

The Indian turned his head majestically and gave the boy

a long look. It was a keen appraising and not unfriendly look, but Chancey felt the blood in his heart thin and chill like snow water. He looked up and saw his mother standing at the door. A great passion rose in him to run to her but the look on her face stopped him, a strong, bitter look. Could it be that she would give him to Little Turtle? He wouldn't put it past her. She had too many to feed and sew for and wash for as it was, Aunt Genny always said. And more than once Huldah and Dezia had told him that he was the odd one and made his mam more trouble than all the rest put together.

The worst was that old half-blind Jonathan Penny had to stump in their kitchen that night.

"I ever tell ye how I was brung up by the Injuns?" he asked in his high voice that gave Chancey the feeling it had been split by an arrow. "They took me when I was just a little tyke, not much bigger'n Chancey 'ar, and my brother Abel about the size of Massey. We was prisoners and had to live with them and do what they said. Abel was good on his legs and tried to run home. One of the yaller blackguards caught him and run his spear through him. I was 'ar and asked him if he was hurt bad. He said he was. He couldn't walk where they wanted him to, so they finished him off. I was 'ar and had to see it. Then they started whetting their knives and I knowed I was next. I told them, I didn't like it home. I said my mam was mean to me and I was glad to get away from her. Oh, I hoped my mam would forgive me lyin' like that, for I reckoned the sun riz and set on her. But that stopped them a while. They asked me which way was home, and I told them the wrong way every time, so they put up their knives. I knew I was safe then for a while from losin' my hair, but hardly could I stand it for longin' and pinin' for home. I was no bigger hardly than Chancey 'ar, and nights when they couldn't see me, I cried like a baby.

"Oh, that's somethin' you got to go through to know about, kept by the Injuns and sick for home. One time they took me along to the old Sciota salt works and 'ar I seen a white woman I knowed back home. Her name was Mrs. McNally and she was a prisoner like me. She looked at me and I looked at her, but we hadn't dare to let on we knowed each other. The next day I come on her in the woods and she asked was it really me and how did the Injuns treat me and didn't I want to get back to my mother and sisters? I told her I should be glad to but never expected to see them again. Then she set me on a log and combed the lice out of my hair. Just doin' that made her cry and she pulled out some pieces of dried scalp she kept in her clothes and showed 'em to me. She said they was her little girl's hair, just the trimmings the Injuns cut off the night after they killed her. She said she picked them up and intended to keep them as long as she lived. She sat there a smoothin' out them pitiful pieces of her little girl's scalp on the log, a strokin' 'em and cryin' and tellin' me this was all she had left of her family now. By that time we was both cryin' and holdin' on to each other. More'n once after that we had a good cry together at the salt works. When the Injuns I was with left, I give her goodby, and never did I see or hear of her again."

Chancey couldn't hear any more. He looked at his mother. Her face was twisted up as cruel as he ever saw it. He felt he couldn't expect any pity there. Desperately he made his way to the front room and then to the loft where he could be alone. Gloom so steeped him that he never noticed how his heart kept shaking his small frame like a hammer. All the tales of Indian capture and torture he ever heard came out now from the dark recesses of his mind. Most of all he couldn't forget the story and fate of Nilum. Without hope he threw himself face downward on his bed.

Shawanee County's first court of Common Pleas was held on a Tuesday morning in early fall, and Portius couldn't help observing the look that Chancey gave him when he left. He told Resolve it was a look a dog might give you when you took it out to shoot it. What could have got over the boy, Portius asked. Especially on such a momentous occasion. You couldn't ask for a more auspicious day for bringing the refining boon of the courts to this fast growing backwoods town. The sun was out, the air bracing. The county in its entirety seemed to have come abroad for the great event. Long before father and son crossed the footbridge over the race, they could see Water Street filled with horses and men. A sense of gratification as the original author of this improvement to the people came over Portius, and he greeted expansively all he met, stopping here and there with dignity to exchange a few words, to introduce his son, to harken a grave ear to troubles and pass them off with some humorous story. He and Resolve hadn't proceeded half way down Water Street when the bell rang and they could hear the voice of new Sheriff Collier.

"Oh ye! Oh, ye! Court's about to set!"

Back on the bench outside the cabin, Chancey heard the bell, too, and it went through him like a clock's stroke to a doomed man. He knew it came from the Central House where court was to set. The Central House was the largest in Americus and more than once had he seen its sign swinging on Water Street and showing the British frigate Guirrere, being whipped by the Constitution. The inn had a wing on Buttonwood Street with a bell and small belfrey on the roof, and every day from the cabin you could hear it ring. Guests rang it when they wanted the hostler to come and take their horses. The cook rang it at meal time, usually twice. The first time, his father said, was a warning to wash up and be ready, and the second time told that hot dishes were being set on the table. On all such occasions it would ring short and furiously. But now for the holding of court, it rang in slow majesty as if tolling for somebody's death. At the sound of it, Chancey shuddered and pulled the sides of the quilt over his ears.

At noon peering from the loft window, the little feller watched his father with Resolve and Little Turtle come up the lane for dinner, Chancey would rather have died than gone down. He told Massey he was sick, he couldn't touch anything on the table. His mother came up to take a look at him, but he must have looked bad as he felt because she told him he better stay in bed. Not till he saw his father and Little Turtle and Resolve going back to town did he feel relief and that was far too short. As the afternoon waned, so did his well being. Any minute now, he knew, the case might be over and Little Turtle come for him. When on toward supper he saw Resolve returning alone, he was too frightened to go down and too anxious to stay up. When he came to the kitchen door, Resolve was telling his mother and the girls about it.

"Oh, it came up," Resolve said. "First were some applications for store and tavern licenses. Then they granted letters of administration to Mrs. Luckenbach, that widow from Tateville. Then Little Turtle's case was called. They drew lots out of Judge Maidenford's hat to impanel the jury, and Papa got up to present his case. Just as he got started, Judge Brown got up and went out. I don't know if he's a friend of Mr. Coe or if he just wanted to mortify Papa after what Papa did to him at the hay scales. Anyhow he stayed out and stayed out. They couldn't have a quorum without him, and Papa had to wait till he got back. You know, Judge Brown likes to ride into town on that white horse of his, and he came today with his saddle bags bulging with law books. He brought those saddle bags into court to show everybody he knew the law and laid them on the floor under the poplar table we call the bar. Now when he stayed out so long, Papa got mad. He dragged out those saddle bags and set them up on the bench in Judge Brown's seat. He said that if Judge Brown didn't come in, they'd have to go on without him. He said the saddle bags knew more about law than Judge Brown did anyhow. Then Papa started his talk, but mostly he'd address the saddle bags. 'Your Honor this,' he'd say to those old leather bags, and 'Your Honor that.' The people began to laugh. The jury had to laugh. Even the other judges couldn't keep their faces straight. When Judge Brown did come in at last, he was so mad he threw out the case."

Chancey was trembling with excitement so he could hardly talk.

"What does throwing out the case mean?"

"It means like when you throw something out of the window. Papa has to take it to a higher court now and that will take months."

All the girls had laughed at the picture Resolve made of Papa arguing his case to Judge Brown's saddle bags. Now after the girls had quieted down, Chancey suddenly began to shriek and laugh.

"Wasn't that funny, Papa talking to the saddle bags!" he cried.

Resolve looked pleased and a little surprised, for it was something of a feat to make sad little Chancey laugh.

"Something else happened that struck us funny," he said. "That back room of the Central House was so packed that the lawyers and judges could hardly get in. When Papa and I got there, men were standing on the window sills and hanging on the wall and rafters like Madagascar bats. First thing Judge Brown did was get up and order the sheriff to remove them, and the sheriff went around pulling down by the leg anybody who wouldn't get down himself. Well, a big farmer named Junkins from Spring Valley wouldn't come down. He kicked at the sheriff. He said, 'I pay my taxes and I got as good right here as any man.' 'Come on down,' Judge Brown ordered him. 'You're creating a disturbance.' 'Oh, hesh up, jedge,' Junkins said. 'You're making a sight more disturbance than I am.' 'You come down,' the judge told him, 'Or I'll send you to jail.' 'There ain't no jail and you know it,' Junkins said. 'There is at Maytown,' the judge said. 'Sheriff, arrest that man.' 'Let him come,' Junkins said. 'I'll stand a hitch with him like I did the damn thief that stole my hogs. I broke his arm and his ribs and half-broke his neck.' 'Stop!' the judge said. 'You're incriminating yourself. You have no right to take the law in your own hands.' 'Why, jedge,' Junkins said, 'I'd a licked you too, if you'd a come and stole my hogs.' "

At every fresh sally from Junkins, the girls laughed and Chancey with them, louder and more uproarious than they. Resolve looked still more pleased. Never had he had a more appreciative audience. Now what had come over the little feller, he wondered. This morning when he and his father left, Chancey had looked like it was his last day on earth.

This noon he felt so bad he couldn't even come downstairs and touch dinner. And now he looked good and healthy as anybody, laughing and jumping and shouting his merriment louder than the rest. He sure was a singular young one, and it took a smarter mind than his to make him out.

CHAPTER SEVEN

YON THORN HEDGE

*Christmas comes but once a year, but
when it comes, I'll have my share.*

HULDAH WHEELER

THE WORLD had changed, Sayward agreed, getting up
this morning. Only yesterday she was thinking how
time in the old days used to stand still. Late afternoons she
could specially feel it, when the sunlight lay in the cleared
ground and banked against the wall of woods. Nothing
moved, save flies droning. It seemed then that a dead calm
hung over cabin and clearing, like a spell had been laid.
Early mornings when it was still dark, you could feel the
hush, too, as if some time during the night the world had
broken its spring and run down. All had stopped and as far
as you knew, you were the only person left alive. That
wasn't such a far while ago, either.

But today long before daylight, anybody who wasn't
deaf could tell that the world still moved and that plenty
were alive to push it. Lying in bed you could hear town
folks getting up to go to market and country folks fetching
their stuff to town. Many of them came a long ways. They

had to leave home about two or three o'clock in the morning, and them that lived far off had to get up around midnight. They liked to be the first to spread their turnips and horse-radish out in the market shed on the square. Or if they sold their flour and bacon down the river, they liked to be the first in line to unload. Americus was getting a name for herself. This was the place to ship from. Sometimes it had as many as eighteen keel boats and barges tied up here in one day.

Oh, times had changed since her pappy had cut down the first big butts around here. Things moved mighty fast. Only a short while back, it seemed like, she had a cabin full of babies. She could wake up any time of night and know where they were all at. If one barked with the croup, she could lay her hands right on it. Now they were mostly grown or nigh onto it. Kinzie was going to government school back in Maryland. And today Resolve was getting married. This morning he would go out of her and Portius's house and most likely never sleep under their roof again. He and Fay had their own house about half up. Till it was done he could stay with his bride in her father's house on the square, a house different from his folks' cabin as daylight from dark.

When General Morrison first came to Moonshine Church, he lived in the Fitch place on Water Street. Last year he put up his own mansion house. It had blue shutters and a white doorway with side window lights, wood carving and stone steps smooth and even as sawn timbers. You went first in a long room that had no use save to walk through. It ran the whole length of the house and they called it the hall. Upstairs was the same. Those two halls would have made four good rooms, Sayward thought, although she didn't know what use the Morrisons would

have for more since already they had four rooms downstairs and nine upstairs counting the little sew room on the
second floor and them on the third floor that the hired girls
slept in. Not even Major Tate or Col. Sutphen owned so
fine a place. Country folk always stared at it as they went
by, and boatmen who used to brag up the French brick
houses in New Orleans now bragged General Morrison's
mansion house from Tateville to Memphis.

Sayward had been inside a good many times, but never
had she seen it so lively and a flutter as today. Folks had
come by stage, boat and their own carriages. Most were
diked out in the new styles. It did her heart good to see
how at home Portius felt in a big house and how easy he
was with fine company. Not once had he ever breathed to
her what kind of home he had been raised in back there in
the Bay State, but you could tell it must have been of the
gentry, the natural way he bowed and carried himself in
here, and Dezia just like him. Now her own sister, Genny,
held back as if struck all of a heap to think she would soon
be kin to the Morrisons.

Sayward sat herself down quiet and steady-headed, taking things as they came. Just the same, when the wedding
started, it set her heart to swelling. She felt grateful Resolve had picked out such a sensible town body. Fay could
have a ring on every finger save one and three on that, if
she wanted. She would come into plenty some day. And
yet more than once she had asked Sayward how would she
do this or that if she was her. Sayward took care not to let
her tongue run. Even her own girls when they married
would have to get along as best they could without trotting
to their mam. A bride did better standing on her own feet.

Till it was over, she thought this wedding of Resolve's
the nicest she ever saw, and mighty different from the time

she and Portius were made one. This was no squire's dry and hasty tying of a knot just to be lawful, but marriage in the name and spirit of the Lord, and done by His bishop who traveled over two hundred miles just to say the words, although Americus had two or three preachers and circuit riders of its own now. A lady from Maytown sat at the black piano to play a march, and Leah sang beautiful. Everything was solemn as it should be, but you never heard such a lively carrying on afterwards. Plenty food and drink were passed. Sociability and good feelings flowed. Everybody talked so nice to Sayward. Her new daughter came up right off for a hug and a kiss, and after that kept fetching up her friends and relations to meet her mother-in-law. Folks from as far as the Western Reserve told her what a fine boy she had. By the time she and Portius went home, she felt like she had used up all her credit with the Lord. When things stayed bad with her or her family too long, she always felt she had saved up some blessing that the Lord owed her. But when Providence had given her a long stretch of favors, she told herself she better not think this was the way it was going to be from now on. No, she owed the Lord something and she better fetch her feet down to solid ground before He did it for her.

Not till the second night after Resolve's wedding did she recollect about her account with the Lord. That was when Huldah never showed up at supper or bed time. First thing in the morning she sent Sooth down to Amy MacMahon's to see if Huldah had stayed all night, but Amy claimed she hadn't seen her since she saw her on her way to Resolve's wedding. Genny, when she heard it, came running over. If Huldah hadn't come over night, it must be she was in the river, or if not, in the race, Genny said. She set all the boatmen looking for Huldah's long black hair a floating on the water in some deep eddy where the cheesy brown foam went round and round, or for her head a laying on some rocky pillow soft with the flotsam of sticks and leaves that tried to ride the river to Orleans without paying freight. Or maybe, Genny said, some river Frenchman had stole her in the cabin of his boat and poled off with her up stream. But most likely he had gone down, running with the current by the Forks and Maytown, never tying up on shore where decent folk could hear a young girl's call for help, but on and on he'd go with his ill-gotten gains till safe among his own countrymen on the muddy bayous that flowed slow and brown as molasses into the Massasip and thence to the salt sea.

Sayward heard her through. Oh, hardly a word Sayward said to tempt Providence, but deep inside she felt Huldah had never fallen in the river. She was too sure-footed. She could tread a foot log over the race like a cat. And hardly likely had a Frenchman penned her in his cabin, for Huldah would be a match for any eat-frog feller. Oh, nothing did Sayward say out loud that the Almighty could make her rue, but over and over to herself she stuck to it that Huldah was not in or down the river. No, Huldah hated water too much, even the little in the wash basin. For all her handsome looks and ways, seldom would she wash her neck till her mam made her. Then how much more would she shy away from a whole river?

Sayward just felt glad she didn't have Portius home on her hands that day. He had to tend to business that wouldn't wait. His voice when he came back sounded deep as usual, but you could see his hands couldn't find the lawbook he wanted. If only Resolve, her staff and mainstay, wasn't East with Fay to some Morrison kin, but she mustn't begrudge them their wedding trip. Guerdon wanted to go down the river on one of John Quitman's boats a looking for Huldah alive or drowned, but his mother told him to stay at the sawmill so she would know where he was at if she needed him.

All that day and the next, the girls and others kept running in with wild tales of some dead body found in the English Lakes or over some hill and holler. It didn't matter if it was last week, maybe it was Huldah. Now little Chancey was small good save to sit on his stool and watch her with those sad eyes of his. Dezia was her rock, staying close to the kitchen, going about her work like every day, talking matter-of-fact cabin talk of cooking and sewing, of this or that. Oh, if folks who wanted to help only knew what comfort it was to hear small talk at a time like this, to go on and forget your trouble as much as you could, to act like all was common as usual. It held off the burden for a while and left you a little more grit to stand bad things when they came.

It hadn't gone long in the afternoon when Leah and her mam called. Was there news of Huldah or anything they could do? Hardly were they settled in the front room when Sayward saw a stranger making for the door. She didn't know as she ever saw him before, must be some Salt Creeker or Sassafrasser, as Portius called them, from back in the hills. He wanted to know did "the squire" live here and was he home? No, he was down in town, Sayward told him, then something made her say more.

"Is it about our girl that's missing?"

"I don't know right yet, ma'am," he backed off. "Not till I talk to your man."

Quickly Sayward stepped out and faced him before he could get away.

"You can tell me. Is she all right?"

"Oh, she's all right if it's her," he said, but so uneasy that the lightness in her lasted only for a lick.

"Then where is she? Why isn't she here?"

"She's out in the Orebank Valley."

"The Orebank Valley? What's she a doing way out there?"

The man looked mighty sober.

"I kain't tell you, ma'am. I only burn charcoal out 'ar. Accordin' to what I heard, she come to the Holcomb furnace house night before last. She give another name than Wheeler. I had no idee who it was till I come to town this mornin' and heard you and the squire had a young miss that never come home. Now this might not be her at all. She claimed she come from the Bay State."

"What did she look like?"

"Well, she's handsome, they said, fair complected with black hair and eye winkers."

"That's her!" Sayward heard Sooth and Libby say behind her.

"What was she dressed in?" Dezia wanted to know.

Now why did the charcoal burner have to scrouge around and not say anything?

"What did she have on?" Sayward put to him sharply.

"From what I heard, she hadn't much on, ma'am," he said, sober. "She had to holler from the bushes. Now I don't know if it's true. I didn't see her, but that's what they tell me. She claimed gypsies took her clothes and left her that way."

Behind her Sayward heard Sooth and Libby draw in their breaths. She looked around. Yes, either she or the girls had left the door stand open. The Morrisons sitting in their chairs in there could hear every word. Well, it was done now and no use crying over.

"Whose place was this you said she came to?" she asked sternly.

"The Holcomb furnace house, ma'am," the charcoal burner said.

She recollected now how a George Holcomb had set up a furnace on Orebank Creek far back in the hills. This was on the other side of the river near where they found iron. He was hardly thirty, if she minded him right, a single man whose folks, they said, had forges back in Pennsylvania. He had come to see Portius on law business and cut a figure with his rough red hair and fine red sorrel mare. He had ridden up to their door and tied the mare to Portius' hitching post. Huldah could have seen him then if she wanted and most likely did, for there was blessed little those handsome black eyes of hers missed.

Libby and Sooth were whispering to their mother. Did she reckon this true? Oh, Sayward couldn't have told them one way or the other, for she didn't know herself yet. All she knew was how like their Aunt Achsa it sounded, her own sister, Achsa, who had run off to the English Lakes with a man that belonged to Genny. That was a long time ago, and where Achsa was now or if she still lived and cut up her didos, only God knew. Not a word had they had from her since she went and few tales about her. You would think that would be an end to it, but, no, the Lord had said, "unto the third and fourth generation," and here was Huldah. Always had Sayward noticed how Huldah minded her of Achsa, not so coarse or rough spoken, but the same black Monsey hair and wild Indian ways. But hardly had she reckoned Huldah so bold as to do a fool trick like this, stuff her dress in a log some place and go naked to the man she had her eye on, figuring that was the way to win him for a husband.

This story would be all over town till nightfall, Sayward told herself, if not already there. It wasn't likely the charcoal burner had held his tongue in town. Yes, she could see Genny now cutting the square. But she hated it most on account of Resolve's new mother-in-law and his bride's sister. That's the usual way it worked out, the ones you'd like to keep it from the longest had to hear it the first. As for herself, she didn't know what would come out of this, but she had overed it the time Achsa ran off with Genny's man. She reckoned she would over it now. The Lord had put her feet back on the ground like she expected, and she oughtn't to complain if the ground was hard and none too clean.

Mrs. Morrison had stood up to go when Sayward came back in the house.

"Don't you want me to send the General?" she asked. "He could drive out and get Huldah before Mr. Wheeler came home."

"Thankee," Sayward said humbly, "But this is something I got to do my own self."

It was good, she thought, that Portius wasn't off in Tateville, or she'd have no horse. She had Libby and Sooth hitch up Hector in the covered two-wheeler. No, she couldn't take either one along, not even Genny. She would need room to pick up some farmer's boy or woodsy to show her the way. She fetched out a dress and shoes and stockings for Huldah, just in case. Then with a small flask of brandy under the seat, she sat very straight in the two-wheeler and started for the river.

The ferry was just in with a team driving off when she got there. Hector and she were the first on the wide splintery old scow. Before old Mike, the ferryman, could cast off, he was called up to the Ferry House and she thought he would never get back. Now what would they keep her waiting so long for? Could it be true what she heard, that King Sam blamed Portius, among others, for holding court at the Central instead of the Ferry House, and would he now try to take it out on any Wheeler he could?

"Couldn't help it, Miz Wheeler," old Mike apologized as he pushed past the two-wheeler, the pole fitted to his shoulder.

Sayward didn't say anything. She had trouble enough of her own this day without letting King Sam set her teeth on edge. She would make up the time once she reached the other side, for Hector was a good traveler, better in the gig than Brig. He could trot smart where the road lay smooth, was a faster walker up hill and down. It was something to see him step briskly along, his head nodding. It took a good man on foot to keep up with him. Never on the steepest hills did he like to rest. Once started, he was out to get where he was going and back home again. You had to watch out only when some high-lifed rider tried to pass him on the road, for Hector wouldn't let any other horse around him. George Holcomb was such a rider, Sayward heard, even when no drink was in him, running his horse like crazy and spattering himself with mud. Now wasn't it strange that both Huldah and Achsa had took to a man like that? She only hoped for Huldah's sake that George Holcomb would turn out better than Louie Scurrah.

Well, she would soon find out. It surprised her how many folks it had living over here to tell her which way to the furnace. Why, farms were plenty as blackberries on this side of the river. The woods for a ways had melted away like last year's snow. Black stumps sprinkled the fields of clover and grain. Twice she passed country mills with their muley saws a riding up and down. She could tell now her own self which way to go. All she had to do was follow the creek, they said, for this was the water that ran the cold blast in the Holcomb furnace.

She was getting in the woods now. The only clearings she saw were charcoal pits. So Huldah reckoned she'd be safe to do as she pleased way back here and nobody in town would know the difference! She found the furnace in a wild glen, laid of brown native stone with a stone bridge running to the side hill, and down below, a big stone cabin. That was the furnace house, no doubt, and behind it the brush where Huldah must have stood naked and brazen calling that gypsies had taken her clothes. Sight of that brush and cabin fetched Sayward up straight and watchful. Oh, this was no sociable visit she was making, but she would not let her mouth get bitter like it wanted to. Putting on a good face, she knocked on the door.

Whoever was in there must have heard her and Hector coming. Hardly a man or woman in the country that didn't run to the door or window, if they had any, to see a traveler go by, let alone stop. But nobody answered here. She had to rap louder and try the latch. Then somebody came to the door in a bright red check dress Sayward had never seen before, with a bowl of batter in her hand like she was a lawfully married housewife making her man's supper. She gave no start to see her mother, and that showed she had peeked out of the window when she heard wheels. Only her eyes had a strange look that said, now how did you know where I was, but never did Huldah speak it.

"Kin I come in?" Oh, Sayward knew she was welcome as a pig in a turnip patch, so she didn't wait for a bid. She just stepped across the doorlog.

So this, she told herself, was where Huldah came with

nary a stitch on to cover her nakedness! That was two evenings back. Now where in here could a young woman like
her have laid herself down in the night time? It had no loft,
only rafters with a few loose plank for extra stuff and fixens. If George Holcomb had more than one bed, she
couldn't see it, just this good walnut bed standing in the
corner with a blanket, scarlet as sin, laying on top. A man's
things were bunched around. His clothes hung from wall
pins. His boots stood on the floor and his account book
and pipe lay on the high desk in the corner like he just set
them there. But the man himself was no place around that
she could see.

Rather would she have stayed clear of thrashing this
thing out with Huldah, but sometimes you couldn't go on
your "rathers."

"You been living here all this time, Huldah?"

"I've been here since the gypsies brought me."

Sayward let that fiddle faddle about the gypsies pass. She
had no heart for this business. Even on the way in here she
wouldn't admit to herself that this thing could be true.
Why, Huldah looked no more than a child now with her
short skirt and red plaid hair ribbon.

"Anybody else in this house with you?"

"Just him and me."

"You been living with him, Huldah?"

"Where'd you expect me to go?" Huldah jeered so it
sounded like Achsa. "It was night time when I got here."

"Well, I've come to take you home," Sayward said
shortly.

"I'm not in your house now!" Huldah flared at her.
"You can't tell me what to do."

"Oh, yes, I can, Miss Huldah," her mother said grimly.
"What's more, I can pick you up and carry you out to the

rig if I have to. You're coming home with me and he's a goin' to ride his horse along."

The first concern showed in her face.

"Who's going to? What do you want him for?"

"What do you suppose? The least he can do for you now is stand up with you in wedlock."

"Not him. I wouldn't marry him if he was the last man!"

Sayward considered. Well, she could let that go and see what came out of this. There was no use making more trouble than you had to. She also better let Huldah's other dress go till she got her home and got it out of her where she had hid it. Then Guerdon could come over sometime and try to find it. Now Sayward unfolded the plum-colored dress she had brought along.

"You can put this on to come home in. That red check, I take it, don't belong to you."

"Don't you say anything against my dress!" Huldah threatened. "I cut it out and sewed it myself from some goods he rode out and fetched me."

"I think you did a real nice job, Huldah," Sayward told her kindly.

But toward her mam, Huldah stayed sullen as a young spider. She was bound to keep that red-check dress whether George Holcomb bought the goods for it or no. She had made it herself, hadn't she? Besides, he said it was hers. She would come along home with her mother if she had to, but she wouldn't take this dress off, nor would she say much once they got in the rig. After a try or two, Sayward didn't push her. She hadn't looked for Huldah to thank her for coming and fetching her home. As they went, she saw two men watching them from the furnace bridge, but if one was George Holcomb, he never came down to his house to see what this woman with a horse and two-wheeler wanted with the girl. He must have half mistrusted all the time that Huldah wasn't all she made out to be.

When they came to the river, the ferry lay on yonder side. It was supper time and still as could be. You could hear the bell ring plain when Huldah got down and yanked on the wire. Somebody came out of the back of the Ferry House to see who was this in a hurry to get across, but the ferry stayed lying there like a dead thing on the town bank till teams and folks afoot piled up on both sides waiting to cross. When the ferry did come at last, Sayward saw that King Sam himself was on it. Now what did this spell out, she wondered, for the place he liked to be was behind the bar of his Ferry House. Only to usher some celebrated body across on his old scow would he come down to help, for he claimed to be a celebrated body himself and that's how he got his name, for kicking a king out of his tavern once when Louie Philippe of France was over here in Ohio and complained his accommodations not good enough for one of sovereign blood.

No sooner had the ferry landed, till King Sam was out on shore like a marshal, holding up his arm and ordering passengers to come or halt. When all were off, Sayward would have driven on, for she had been first to the water, but he held her back and waved others on till the scow was full.

"I got no room now," he called, and then what sounded like, "You and that young slut'll have to wait."

Sayward sat there swallowing back her dander. Why, lucky he hadn't come any closer to say that or she might forget herself and answer with her horse whip. Nobody could say a thing like that to her face about her own, even if it was true. Oh, she could see that his small brain had schemed this all out and it had worked like clockwork.

Now she and Huldah could sit over here in their disgrace, he thought, and wait till he felt like coming back for them.

Well, maybe they could and maybe they couldn't. More than one person she had seen fording the river to save ferry toll, especially in the late summer and early fall when the water was low. It was good and high now but she recollected one time she and Genny had gone to visit Tod Wylder's woman. This was long ago. The river was high then, too, and Tod had come over with his spotted ox and ferried them across on its back one at a time. Surely, she reckoned, Hector ought to be good in the water as Tod Wylder's spotted ox.

When King Sam saw her drive in the river, he must have wondered had he done right after all, for he called back from his end of the scow.

"Go on back, Miz Wheeler. I'm coming back for you directly."

But seldom had Sayward turned back in her life, and hardly would she now. She pulled Huldah's hand from where she was thumbing her nose at the ferry. All the time Hector was settling in farther and farther in the river. It got no deeper for a long ways, than his belly, then all at once the river started squirting through the cracks and joints of the gig box.

"You kin put your feet up under you on the seat," Sayward told Huldah. As for her own, she'd keep them down on the floor where she'd need them to hold Hector's head up once he went down in some deep hole and had to swim for it. The two-wheeler heaved up over unseen rocks and sunken logs. Deep water lifted first one wheel, then the other, and for a while the rig floated like a snug little black and red boat on the river. Hector was in now well over his shoulders and once or twice the brown water floated over the sway of his browner back. But it turned out that his feet found bottom all the way, not that he couldn't have swam for it if he had to, Sayward reckoned.

When they rared dripping out of the water on the far side and Sayward had a chance to look up, it seemed like half of Water Street was up on the bank a watching, General Morrison among them. He came out in the road holding up his cane respectfully.

"Are you and Huldah all right, ma'am?" he inquired.

"We're fine, thankee, General," Sayward said, matching his dignity with her own, but in her breast it felt warm and good to have kin that stood by you in front of everybody at a time like this, even if they were only kin by marriage.

Once she had time to think on dry land, she reckoned she had been a little hasty fording the river. She might have drowned Huldah and some folks would say she could have done it on purpose. What's more, had she waited till King Sam got good and ready to fetch her, it might have been too dark for half the town to see her fetch Huldah home. Now every tongue would wag in Americus tonight. For a long time to come they would joke about Huldah's gypsies. But Huldah didn't let on she minded. She sat up beside her mam as big as you please. And when she got home, she acted the same way among her sisters. Oh, she was somebody more than they were now, somebody older and wiser. And when they spoke to her, it was almost like should they call her Miss Huldah or Mrs. Holcomb, they didn't know rightly which.

Sayward said nothing to Portius till she and he were in their bed that night and all the girls in the other loft out of hearing. Then they had a grave talk. Oh, she knew and he knew that fetching Huldah home didn't mean all was now in apple pie order. You couldn't send a woman to a man's cabin without a stitch of clothes on and then take her off two nights later like nothing had happened. But Portius, who always knew just what to do for his client, was confounded when it came to his daughter. In the end Sayward had to fall back on herself. Always in the past she told herself if worst came to worst, she would just have to live it down. But something like this could take a mighty long while to live down, and she wasn't young as she used to be. She could only pray the Lord to give her a long life till she could square herself and her family with the world.

The one small satisfaction she had as she went to sleep was the way Huldah had looked up to her and listened when they got home. It was fording the river, Sayward thought, and not knuckling down to King Sam that did it. Huldah didn't know that her old mammy had it in her.

CHAPTER EIGHT

THE BRIDGE

A bridge's business is to stand
And join two severed spheres of land.

RIPHEUS (CHANCEY WHEELER) IN THE

AMERICUS CENTINEL SOME THIRTEEN YEARS LATER

IT was King Sam who started the bridge, and Guerdon
that gave it a good push, though neither one might ever
know it.

This rainy evening the Wheelers were sitting around
drinking green tea in the kitchen. Hardly did Sayward ever
remember feeling better or laughing so much. Was it that
Resolve and Fay had a young one on the way and Huldah
hadn't, which was as it should be but not always was. But
she knew that last night and night before. Was it the tea
then, or why did she make so much high jack tonight? she
wondered. After while Guerdon said he heard they were
spanning the river with a bridge at Maytown. He reckoned
he would go down. He could catch a ride on Sam Hend-
ler's boat and get a job bridging.

Not till then did Sayward remember the old saying how
close laughing was to crying.

"You think you'd like it down there?" she asked, sober.

"Nothin' I'd like better than bridgin', Mam," he told her.

"You'd come back, Guerdie?" Massey wondered.

"Oh, I'd come back some day. With my pockets full."

"Will you bring me a present?" Massey asked.

"I won't stop at you," he said. "I'll bring you somethin' gold, and Chancey somethin' silver and Mam somethin' fixed with ruby stones."

Sayward gave him a steady look to show she appreciated it whether or not it ever came true. Before she went to bed that night she went to the shellbark box Will Beagle made for her long ago. Not often had she looked in this since she was married. Mostly the box held keepsakes, the tattered letter her father had somebody write, a broken breast pin of her mother's, her father's and mother's marriage paper now torn and faded from use as a window light. You could hardly make out a word any more, only the red pictures of birds and flowers. But the most precious keepsakes were the locks of hair tied with thread by her mother long ago. Jary said she wanted something to remember her young ones by once they were grown and nothing was like a curl of their hair to bring them back. You could lift it in your hand and see the tyke that used to be. Wasn't it strange, Sayward thought, how hair never died like the rest of the body! A person could be rotted away in the ground but his hair stayed like it was when he was alive. You could still see and feel with your fingers how he was. The whole lot weighed nothing at all in your palm. Hardly could she believe that her own head had ever been so yellow or Genny's hair like the finest tow. Her sister Sulie's curl was soft as beaver and Achsa's coarse and black as a horse's mane. Not even in the wettest, foggiest weather would the hair on Achsa's head curl, but it did in the old shellbark keepsake box. She only wished she had cut a lock from her own little Sulie in time. Afterward it was too late, when the fire had singed it to the flesh.

The last curl she held up was the shaggiest of the lot. Many a time had she seen that shock of sandy hair on her brother Wyitt's head. Law, how many years had it been since she saw him! And where was Wyitt now? He had gone and never a word from him. The Country of the Western Waters had swallowed him up. She didn't even know if he was dead or still among the living. And now Guerdon was talking of going. Of all her children, he was the closest to Wyitt. Not in looks but in ways. Hadn't she seen the signs ever since he was little? Never would he go in for schooling or be satisfied long in a job. No, he always wanted a new one. Last time it was working in a sawmill. Once he had the smell of fresh sawn boards in his nose, he claimed, he'd be satisfied. That was about a year ago. Now he couldn't wait till he gave it up and went to bridging.

Oh, Sayward knew what was the matter with him. It was his Monsey blood that wouldn't let him be, the same as Wyitt and Worth before him. He thought all he wanted was to go to Maytown. He felt sure once he got there, he'd be satisfied to hang up his hat and afterwards come back to Americus and settle down. But never would he. No, let him have one job for a while and he couldn't wait till he had another.

The next time Portius told of trouble somebody had with the ferry, Sayward kept her counsel till they were getting ready for bed that night.

"Now I think Americus has put up with King Sam long enough," she said.

Portius stood in his stocking feet, his coat and waistcoat off, his white shirt bulging around him starched and full, a mass of wrinkles and sweat stains.

"You want to franchise some other ferry?" he puzzled.

"I'm talking for a bridge," Sayward told him. "One like I hear they're getting down at Maytown."

Portius bent over to draw his shirt over his head as if he didn't hear or want to hear any more, but when his face came bottom first out of the white tunnel, his eyes observed her.

"I never knew you so devoted to progress before."

Sayward had let the upper part of her dress down to her waist. Now she pulled on her bedgown and let it drop so she could draw her dress out from under it. That's the way she had done it ever since she was big enough to know she was a woman.

"So long as the old works, I don't believe in throwing it out for the new. But Americus is getting too big for a huffy old man who reckons he's king and can run his ferry just when it suits."

Portius had taken off his pants. He hung them over a chair where the legs still stood out with the doughty round-ness of their master's hams. You could see those hams now, white and hairy, as Portius stood there considering.

"I've been thinking of it myself but the river's too wide here. It would be cheaper to bridge at the Narrows."

"And make everybody go two miles out of their way?" Sayward retorted. "No, Americus is the place it should be."

That's all she would say. She didn't hold with Zillah Harris that women should stand up in men's meeting and tell what ought to be done. Oh, she believed women had as much sense as the men and as much right to have their way, and as long as she knew anything, women had always done it. Why, forty years back when there was nothing here but a howling wilderness, her pappy had to listen to what his woman wanted, and so did Portius all his life. The men could have the satisfaction of talking it over and carrying it through. But many times it was the women who put it in their heads in the first place. And the place to put it in their heads was not in public but at home.

Long before it came, that bridge was a wonder of the world to Chancey. He felt toward it like it belonged to his family like the barn or pasture, although other folks could use the bridge if they paid. Hadn't his father been the first to talk it! Wasn't Guerdon going to build it, or help anyways, which meant he needn't go to Maytown to be a bridger now. Only last night hadn't their father settled the fight over where the bridge ought to be! For a while it looked like the bridge would get nowhere, for every man in the county wanted it handy to his own house and place of business. They had a monster meeting by torchlight and nobody would give in.

At last Portius got up in front of the crowd.

"Gentlemen," he said, "I move we bridge the whole damn river from Tateville to the Forks."

Chancey knew those words by heart, how some men looked sheepish and others laughed, how the meeting broke up in good feeling with the commissioners setting up three men to view and survey for a bridge.

Sunday afternoon Guerdon carried him over to Water Street, and Massey ran along. Right here, Guerdon said, the commissioners wanted to put the bridge.

"Will it go across the whole river?" Massey wanted to know.

"Clean from this side to that over there," Guerdon told them.

Chancey's gray eyes trembled and strained. A man on the far bank looked littler than the trained monkey a dark man brought through Americus last week on a chain. Between here and yonder yawned a wide gulf with nothing save space and air to hold anything up.

"I can't see a bridge right here," a man standing by told Guerdon.

"I can't see it myself yet," Guerdon told him.

Now never had Chancey seen a bridge save for small rumbly ones over the race. And yet he could look right out there and see it in his mind hanging over the river, though what it hung on, he didn't know. One night he dreamed he saw keel boats floating over him in the sky. What made them stay up, he didn't know, but he could still see them in his mind, and that's the way he could see the bridge, with horses and wagons going across it. Not only that, but teams of oxen and herds of cattle, sheep and hogs trotting over it, whichever way they wanted to go. The bridge wasn't even started yet. King Sam had a case in court against it; claiming it a foolish and malicious scheme to persecute him and ruin his ferry business. And yet Chancey could see it hanging so high over the water that birds could fly under.

He could see it still plainer in his mind when they started to put it up. Now it was like a long house with sides and a roof to keep off the rain. He couldn't tramp that long ways to the river himself, but he could hear Guerdon tell about it when he got home. The little fellow would close his eyes and there all would be in front of him. He could see the river a shining and keel boats and barges moving up and down. He could hear boatmen cursing the bridge men, for they didn't like bridges or fish dams, Guerdon said.

Sometimes he could hear a friendly boatman play his fiddle or blow his horn as he floated by, or see King Sam come out of the back door of his Ferry House and shake his fist at the bridge, while all the time oxen pulled timbers into place or came toiling back from the woods splashed with mud and dragging wagons loaded with butts so heavy they bent down behind to plough furrows in the ground, or so Massey told.

Chancey could see that bridge better sitting at home in a dark corner than if he was there. A couple times when Guerdon went back after dinner, he took him over. All the noise of hatchets, saws, axes and mallets confused him, the voices of drivers bawling at their log teams and of bridgemen pounding where they hung like squirrels far out over the water on the dangerous scaffold. Their cries came so deep and urgent, it sounded like they were falling in the water. Every now and then Chancey froze, for he heard a splash. He felt sure it was Guerdon and wouldn't sit down again till his eye found him safe on the great golden caterpillars of fresh cut timbers, for one day Mr. Jackson's axe had fallen in the river and for two shillings Guerdon had dove into ten feet of water to get it. Back at home Chancey could climb all over the bridge and scaffold. But here it made him giddy just to look at Guerdon standing on a single log high over the dark water.

When he was here at the bridge, Chancey liked mostly to close his eyes. He would breathe the smell of the fresh cut timbers and hear the old men a talking. They sat around him boring the dirt with their canes and speaking a mysterious language of words like gin poles, trustles, cribbing, false work and block and tackle. The word they and Guerdon used that took him the most was "the chord." The way they talked, the chord was the heart and master sinew of the bridge. They argued which was better, trusses or arches, was the footwalk better on the north or south sides, and if the bridge was heavy enough for loaded ox teams. On one thing they agreed, that it had more timber in it already than a frigate, that it would cost a pile of money and take a long time to pay it off. Even the minister would have to pay to cross, they said. Some had the toll all figured out: foot passenger, one pence; ox or horse, 4 pence; horse and rider, 6 pence; cart, sleigh, sled, wagon or chaise and one horse or ox, 9 pence; same with two horses or oxen, 13 pence; same with four horses, 20 pence; horned cattle, 3 pence; sheep and hogs 2 pence. And that was the way it ought to be, they said, for a sheep or hog was worth more ready money than a man.

Oh, those old men knew everything, Chancey told himself. It was a shame they couldn't build the bridge. All they said they backed up with stories of some bridge they built or crossed back in the old states. Two span were nothing grand in a bridge, they said. Old Mr. Tenafly told of one back in New York State of four spans of yellow pine with two roadways, one for going and one for coming. And lame Mr. Troxell said he walked many a time on a bridge across the Delaware with five spans. But the longest span any of them knew was in the state of Vermont over the Connecticut River, two hundred and thirty-nine feet with not even a pier below. Now that was something Chancey would have given much to feast his eyes on, a house of wood stretched and straddled across a river and the middle never sagging or falling in.

Chancey liked to hear the names of those rivers back in the old states, the Kennebec, the Youghiogheny and the Monongahela, the Susquehanna and the Brandywine, the Merrimac and the Rappahannock. But the prettiest sounding was the Juniata, the blue Juniata, Mr. Troxell called it. The sound of any one of those names brought the river it stood for right up in front of him, a wide reach of water like he dreamed about last year. He could still see that river clear in his mind. It was blue as indigo, so blue that even the air over it shone with a bluish light. The wild buffalo standing in it had blue legs from the water. Never had he seen such a beautiful color, and it was a wide river, too. You could hardly see to the other side. He reckoned it must be the Blue Juniata, but when he told his mother, she said you could throw a stone across the Juniata any place and never was it blue, for she had lived on its banks and washed in it. When it wasn't a dirty brown, she said, it was green.

Till it was over, Sayward told herself, she would be glad to see the end of that bridge after all. Oh, it had kept Guerdon around his home town a while longer, and they had all learned plenty about bridges. Even little Chancey kept harping on them. But it was Guerdon who acted the master hand, telling them how he'd a done it different if he had it his way. More than once he said he told Mr. Jackson how the bridge ought to be. "That's impossible," Mr. Jackson would say. "Tain't impossible," Guerdon claimed he said back. But old Jackson would never listen. He couldn't take a point from anybody. He always gave the excuse that if he done that, the bridge would settle when he pulled out the last trustle. Now if he, Guerdon, had been putting it up, he wouldn't have hired any men who got fits or giddy. What's more, he would have hung that bridge high. It might have made a steep pull for teams up the bridge hill, but it would have let boats run under it easy even in flood time.

Many an evening she sat mending his bridge clothes and listening to his bridge talk. The rub was that about the time she and the others got ready for bed, Guerdon was just getting ready to go out.

"Where do you have to go at this time of night, Guerdon?" she'd ask him.

"Oh, I just said I'd be out with the boys a while," he'd say.

His while lasted as a rule till two or three o'clock in the morning and when he came through her and his father's room to go to the loft, he left a reek of rank cigars and barrooms behind him. Now Portius always had a smell of pipe and jugs around his person. Even in the night in his bed he gave out a scent of tobacco and spirits. He wouldn't have been Portius without it, and she was so used to it she reckoned she'd find it slow to go to sleep without it. Why, when she fetched their bolster in from airing, she could always tell which was his end just by laying her nose to it. The scent of spirits would be mostly gone by that time but not the sourness nor the bite of the sharp weed. And yet when Guerdon came home after putting in a night with the bridge gang, he left a trail of stale tobacco and foul liquor behind him that put his father to shame.

Well, she was only getting paid back for pushing that bridge before its time, she reckoned. In her heart she knew she had done it mostly for spite and cowardice, spite against King Sam and cowardice to let her second boy go off from home a bridging. Now she could see what you got for putting in your nose where it wasn't wanted.

But never had she expected she'd get punished as hard as she was, and Guerdon in the bargain, when he wasn't to blame. Before the bridge was done or even the scaffolding knocked away, Huldah told her the bad news.

"Well, Resolve's not the only family man now. Did Guerdon tell you he's married?"

"Married!" Sayward stopped mighty short. "Who to?"

"Something that's no good," Libby put in.

Sayward looked around at the other girls. The worst was written on their faces.

"What's her name?"

"Effie Clouser and she lives up in Fishtown," Sooth said.

Sayward's heart sank. She tried to remember somebody of that name in the scrubby little shanty settlement up the river. She knew now where Guerdon had spent his long evenings.

"She's a slut," Huldah spat out.

Sayward turned on her sternly.

"Who are you to say such a thing! Or any of you for that matter? I can't believe yet that Guerdon's got a wife, but if he has, remember she's your sister."

Through supper that evening Sayward let her eyes rest on her second oldest. Could this be true what they said about him? Of all her children, save her littlest, Guerdon was the one least fitted to stand up for himself in life and get what he wanted. He was good enough company. His black head would throw back and he could sing most every catch Genny could and some that she couldn't. But never could he take care of himself like Genny. He let others impose on him, would stand it till they pushed him too far and then, look out! Something in him would snap. He lacked the staying part and balance the others had, like he lacked all their ten fingers and thumbs, one of his having been chopped off when he was little.

"Is it true you have a wife, Guerdon?" she asked quietly, when, save for Chancey, she had him alone in the kitchen.

Oh, he flushed up at that and bumbled around.

"Yes, it's true, Mam," he said.

"Aren't your father and me good enough to be told beforehand and asked to your wedding?"

"It's not that, Mam," he begged her. "It just happened so quick. I hardly knew it myself beforehand."

She stood there pitying him.

"Well, you and her have my good wishes," she said. "I hope you'll both be happy. When are you going to bring her down?"

"One a these days," he promised. "I'm a moving up tomorrow when the boarder gets out. I'll bring her down soon as she'll come."

"Say her new mam wants to meet her," Sayward said kindly. "Tell her she needn't fret."

Guerdon took his things up to Fishtown next day to stay. Plenty times he stopped in back home after that and usually around meal time, but never was his bride with him. When Sayward asked, he claimed Effie was bashful and couldn't make up her mind. But Genny said likely he felt ashamed to bring her. Though Sayward waited patient enough, never did she come. At last Sayward told him that if Effie wouldn't come to see her mother-in-law, she was going out to see her and take along her wedding present. But she didn't want to come unbeknownst, so she set Saturday afternoon. That would give Guerdon's bride time to have her house cleaned up and herself washed and dressed for the coming Sabbath.

Meanwhile she could spike her own girls' mouths but she couldn't Genny's. Most of what she heard she didn't like, nor how ravenous Guerdon ate when he came home. Carefully she wrapped up in some of Portius's paper the same present she had given Fay, a pair of linen sheets of her own raising, spinning and weaving, and an embroidered bolster case. Oh, nobody would say she was not as nice to a poor daughter-in-law as a rich one, but she complained to herself that the Lord took it out pretty hard on her and Guerdon for the small pride she had in Resolve's fine marriage.

CHAPTER NINE

THE DREAM

*I was just a thinkin', and if I hadn't been
a thinkin', I wouldn't a thunk that way.*

LITTLE MATHIAS COTTLE IN THE FIELDS

T HE LITTLE fellow lay in the entry. Every time they
threw hay down the ladder hole, a little of it stayed on
the entry floor. The fork could not pick it all up for the
manger. It was too short or stubby or it was seed or chaff
or the fine powdery hay dust that sifted down like gray
snow from between the mow planks and hung on the
ghostly cobwebs. In time it covered the floor with a
springy carpet so you wouldn't know there was plain hard
earth beneath.

On this springy carpet face downward, Chancey lay,
and when they called his name from the back door, he gave
no heed that he heard. His sisters were always bothering
after him. Chancey! Where are you, Chancey? Are you all
right? So that's where you've been keeping yourself!
Didn't I tell you to put on your wamus before you went
out! You're as pale as a corpse. Come in now and lay down
a while. Come in and wash your hands; dinner's soon

ready. Come in and see your A'nt Genny. Come in this minute, it's going to rain and if you get wet the distemper will carry you off like the eagle and the little red hen. Not that his mother ever said this, but it must have been she who sent them out to look for him.

In the house he seldom had anything to do. He had to sit all day tongue-tied as a trout and listen to his sisters' chatter. From morn till night it went on, and never a let-up. They sat up to their talk like hungry men to their dinner, but never did they get full. It went all the better when their hands flew. They would throw words over their shoulder or cast them up from their needle or loom. Their tongues were loose on both ends and tied in the middle, Chancey believed. They kept it up at such a rate, gossiping and complaining, jeering and laughing, fighting and singing, all at the same time, till it made his head go round They wore him plumb out, but never did they get tired. Oh, what wouldn't he give to have his brothers back in the house. Kinzie had left him first and all he saw of him now was his scrawl in a letter. Then Resolve went to live with Fay, and now Guerdon, the last brother he owned, had deserted him bag and baggage for Fishtown and left him alone in the cabin with all the women. Of course, his father still lived here, but mostly he was not at home.

"Chancey! Where are you?"

It was Sooth a calling, and she sounded mighty close. He struggled up and stood on the feed measure to climb over the edge of Hector's manger. Then he tumbled in and lay mighty still with his heart pounding while somebody came in the entry door and called him again. Yes, it was Sooth. She went around every place in the barn a looking for him but she didn't think to look in the manger.

When she went out, peace flowed slowly back in the

barn again. His heart let up and the world stopped going around in circles like it did when he stood up in too much of a hurry. He hadn't meant to fall in the manger, but now that he was in, he wouldn't trade it for his bed in the loft. He had hay under him and a cradle around him and could look out the wide cracks and see daylight coming through chinks in the logs. He could look up and see the gray tents of the spiders caught with dust and chaff. They minded him of bird wings about to take off, a lifting him with them. Now why was it he couldn't sleep at night but could in the daytime, especially if it was a place and time he shouldn't with the rain on the roof singing to him and his cradle a rocking when he closed his eyes.

The cow was red with milk white udders. It stood behind the stable and waited for him to climb up. Then he rode it over to town, through the square and up and down Water Street. People looked and smiled at him to see him riding a cow. A driver couldn't get his oxen up the bridge hill, so the red cow gave milk in a big brass kettle and the driver drank it, holding the kettle up with both hands and after that the oxen could pull their load of heavy green logs up the bridge hill easy enough, the leaders with their heads down picking their way carefully step by step into the strange dark tunnel till eight beasts, wagon, logs, driver, Chancey and the red cow all hung over the middle of the river. On the bridge walk and shore the people held their breaths. But the bridge timbers only creaked and groaned. If it stood for that, it would stand for anything, Mr. Jackson said, and now the boy could go back to the house with his red cow, for it looked like rain.

When Chancey heard the rain on the roof, the cow had gone. At the entry door of the barn he saw the water coming down in sheets. He could hardly see the house. Likely that's why he went the wrong way and fell in a pool of water, but he told himself he would have been wet to the skin anyway from the rain till he opened the kitchen door and heard his sisters cry at him.

"Chancey, where have you been? We've been looking everywhere for you! Take off your things. You're wetter than a scalded chicken. What were you doing all this time?"

Chancey suffered them to push him to the fire and pull him this way and that. His shirt came off and then his britches, drawers, shoes and stockings, till he stood there, a grotesque little old man, gaunt as a plucked banty rooster, gaunt with cold, bending down as far as he could to hide his nakedness. He said not a word, only made faint sounds of grief and protest as they rubbed his wobbly body one way or another and jerked at limber limbs that wouldn't stay stiff enough to have stockings pulled over them.

"Now you better tell us where you were!" Libby threatened, buttoning his dry blouse and pinching as punishment some of his cold skin into the buttonholes.

"I was out in the stable," he said meekly.

"Oh no, you weren't. I was out there just a half hour ago."

He considered. He hadn't heard Huldah, only Sooth.

"That must have been when I was over in town."

"How did you get over there?"

"I rode over on a cow," he said gravely.

Now why did his sisters have to set up such a honking like lady Winters' geese when somebody came in her yard?

"Who put you up on a cow?"

Chancey thought.

"Nobody. I got up myself."

"It must have been a mighty little cow. Whose cow was it? Ours?" Libby jeered.

"No. I never saw it before."

"Well, was it an old or young cow and had it any horns and what was its name?"

"It didn't have a name, I think."

"Did anybody see you with this cow over in town?"

"I wasn't with it. I was on it," Chancey corrected her. "And lots of people saw me. They were strange people. But they smiled at me. If you'd ask them, they'd tell you."

"How can we ask them if we don't know who they were? Where's this green cow now?"

"It was a red cow," said Chancey. "I rode it back to the stable. But it's not there now."

They all made those cackling sounds again.

"No, I guess not and never was."

"It was, too," Chancey said mildly.

Then he turned and saw his mother listening. Her face looked uncommonly sober.

"Chancey, I've heard a good many wild tales from you. Now I have nothing much against them. You can make the girls believe them all you like. But you're getting to be too big a chunk of a boy to believe them your own self. You're old enough to know now what's real and true and what's make believe. Now I want you to tell me real and true where you were this afternoon."

She looked so formidable, he let his eyes go a bit out of focus, and that made her look less so, just a brown blurr in the haze of whitish light from the window.

"I rode over to town on a cow," he told her.

"You can't expect me to believe that, Chancey," her voice came back at him just as quiet and mild as before.

"In the first place, folks don't ride cows, and if they did, it wouldn't do them any good because cows are contrary. If you ever tried to take one any place on a rope, you'd find out they won't go where you want."

"This one did," Chancey declared stubbornly. "I rode it up and down Water Street and through the bridge. Mr. Jackson saw me. He said I better go home now, it was going to rain."

A kind of slow bleakness and pain spread over his mother's face until her eyes were blue stones set deep in her sockets and drawn far away.

"Mr. Jackson isn't here in Americus, Chancey. He's down in Hamilton County somewhere putting up a bridge. Guerdon had a letter from him just yesterday wanting him to come down and work. Now I don't know why you say you saw him and rode a cow. Maybe you made this up, maybe you were dreaming. But whatever you did, you give me no other way than send you to bed. You can lay up there a while and study this thing out. When you reckon you know enough to tell when you're make believing or dreaming, you can come down."

If there was one thing Chancey hated more than another, it was to have the ignominy of putting on his bedgown when it was still daylight and going up to the loft before supper. Dezia took him, and all the time she stood over him, his lip quivered. Then she went down and the door to the windsweep closed behind her. All he could hear was the faint flow of voices from the faraway kitchen. They could have a good time together getting supper, and he had to be up here alone. When the sound of laughter reached him he felt himself shrink. They were laughing at him and his red cow, but they wouldn't laugh at him long. He would run away. He would search the world over for his true

mother and sisters, and when he found his mother she
would be a lady with pale golden hair. She would take him
up in her white arms and kiss him and thank God for his
safe return. She would tell how she had missed him all
these years he spent among alien folk who refused to believe his truest words.

All night like a lighted candle in his mind was the memory of the little girl whose father laid his hand on Chancey's head and cried, and they were his really true father
and his sister, and that's why his father had cried, because
he had to go back to Chancey's real mother without him.
They lived somewhere across the river. Their name Chancey didn't remember but it would be a fine name, he knew,
like Davenport or Pemberton or Ormsbee, most likely
Ormsbee, for that was the name that always rang silver
bells in his mind.

By morning the rain had stopped, but the girls said that
the river was very high and still rising, and they all wanted
to go to Aunt Genny's to see it, all save himself who said
he didn't feel good enough to do anything except lay on
the couch. But once they had all left, he put on his cap and
made his way best he could out to Wheeler Street beyond
the barn, where a countryman in a cart took him along to
Water Street. Here a little crowd stood watching the
strong press of high water where it almost came up to the
bridge. The brown flood moved so wide and silent and
queer, like something in a dream, and suddenly it struck
him, could this be a dream like his mother told him to
watch for? He remembered Massey tell of a dream once
where she couldn't stop or go back but had to walk a board
over high water with one white shoe and one black one.
And now all at once he knew it wasn't real, for coming behind him to cross the bridge was a wagon with a white

horse on one side of the tongue and a black mule on the other, driven by a strange looking man with one good eye and a red patch on the other.

The wagon had a step in back and when it moved slowly up the bridge hill, Chancey waded in the water that flowed across the road and climbed up and in.

"Hold on there," said the driver, looking around. "Where do you think you're a goin'?"

"I'm going home to my father and mother and my little sister and all my other brothers and sisters who pray for me every day to come home," Chancey told him.

"And where do they live?" the man asked, surprised.

"Far over there on the other side of the river where the woods is thick and dark and lonely to live without me."

"What's their name?"

"It's Ormsbee, sir."

"Ormsbee," he muttered and shook his head. "Well, I'll take you as far as Kettering's store and he can tell you how to go from there."

Chancey lay back in the wagon box. They were in the tunnel of the bridge now, and the dream was a very clever, deceitful and hard-to-tell dream, because it was just like it had been in real life yesterday when he rode the red cow through the bridge. The hole of light behind him grew smaller and smaller till it was only the white eye of the town looking through a dark telescope after him. Then at last it started to grow light and they were getting out of the tunnel where a tollhouse sat right on the bridge cribbing with no front yard save the roadway and no back yard save the river over which some wash hung.

The pole was down and the tollkeeper's woman came out with her mending in one hand and took toll with the other.

"I have to collect for him, too," she said pointing to Chancey.

"I pay nothing for my folks," the driver protested.

"No, but he's not your folks. He's a foot passenger. He could have crawled on your wagon just to get out of paying toll."

"He's only a little tyke."

"He's a foot passenger just the same, and the law says foot passengers have to pay."

"My father will pay you," Chancey called. "He'll pay you a dollar, he'll be so glad to see me when he sees me."

The sharp face of the woman moved around to the side of the wagon, and at her look, Chancey remembered how she had once thrown the pole down on a driver who forgot to stop and pay and had knocked him off the seat of his wagon.

"Who's this?" she wanted to know.

"Ormsbee, he says his name is."

"So it's Ormsbee now? It used to be Wheeler, unless I miss my guess. Lawyer Wheeler's boy."

Chancey saw the driver's astonished face.

"He's not my real father," the boy said.

"No? Who is then?"

"My father, Mr. Ormsbee."

The woman clicked her tongue, looked at the driver and back to the boy.

"Who told you?"

"It's true," Chancey said solemnly.

"What does your mother say?"

"She isn't my real mother, either. She's just been keeping me for her!"

The tollkeeper's wife looked suddenly angry.

"Now that's enough from you. You go back and tell that

cock and bull story to your mother. Come on. Get out and go back before they close the bridge on you."

The yellow road looked so near and free, Chancey climbed down and tried to make a dash for it, but the toll-keeper's wife caught him and sent him reeling back on the bridge. He ran till his heart stopped him. When he looked around, the wagon had vanished into thin air and all he could see was a white cat in the road where the tollkeeper's wife had been, and that showed still more that it was un-real, for he knew how in a nightmare, people turned into animals and animals into people and one kind of thing into another. His heart still choked off his wind. He had thought for sure he was going to die, but now that he saw the cat and remembered nothing could hurt you in a nightmare, his heart let go of his throat. He could breathe again and everything grew light and airy as it should in a dream.

Twice the little fellow halted and looked around. The wagon of his friend with the patch over his eye was still invisible, but the white cat lay on the pole that stretched across the middle of the road, and that was the tollkeeper's wife watching him. The third time he turned, the cat was gone. Quick as he could, he stumbled into the shelter of the wall of timbers that rose beside the roadway. Here were endless nooks and crannies to hide in, cubbies and cubby holes already brown with dust although suspended over the dustless water. Here were thick timbers and sup-ports, and the thickest was a great arch of half a dozen timbers fastened into one, all bent and curving like a bow in the sky. This was what held the bridge up. As he climbed the easy sloping arch, a stage rumbled through, and he could feel the gentle quivers in the great flexed wooden muscles under his hands.

This was a master place to be, he told himself, lying flat on the top of the arch and looking out on the swollen river. Sometimes it looked like the river stood still and the bridge moved. It made him drowsy just to see the bridge go up stream over the halted water.

Now what was that rapping and knocking? he wondered, after he napped. He looked down inside and saw water flowing over the planking of the bridge. It scared him a little even though he knew it wasn't really true, the fantastic pounding and groaning, the weird hissing and wailing of the river as it boiled up white through the cracks in the planking. He imagined in the sounds of water that he heard voices, a great many voices swelling and receding as the great arch under him rose and fell. They sounded so real, like in waking life when he heard a camp meeting or torchlight procession. But now he told himself he could tell his mother that at last he knew when he was dreaming, for never could that which was happening at this moment be true. He could feel the bridge lifting, lifting. His ears were deafened by a terrible crashing. The bridge seemed to be turning over and over. Then the whole world, and he with it, went down deep in the water, breaking into pieces as it went. What happened to the world he didn't know, but he felt something rise up under him like a great terrapin coming to the surface, and when the water ran from his eyes and was coughed from his nose and pipes, he found himself stretched out on the terrapin's back that was a shell of the bridge floating like an old leaky scow bottom on the flood. He could see the houses of Americus over there and the shore line black with people. Back where the bridge had been, only the unfamiliar wide flatness of the river met his eye.

Oh, Chancey lay there on his raft and watched the town

as long as he was able. Once he thought he could make out the cabin he lived in with the barn behind it. Just for an instant it stood there. Then the revolving wheel of the town shut it from view. Another time he thought he saw boats push out from shore, but they soon turned back. The flood ran too fast and they had to leave him to the river. Already he had gone so far that Americus didn't look like itself any more. It was just a smudge vanishing back yonder behind the hills.

All morning he lay gently rocking, riding his raft of bridgework, breathing the soft smell of the river and watching the country move by. He looked amazed on all the woods and fields and hills he passed, creeks opening their mouths to the river, horses and cows, barns, houses and mills, some of them standing knee deep in the flood. And to think that all these were nameless, vaporous, with no more reality than thoughts and pictures in his mind! Wasn't it fearful how a dream could turn out such an endless lot of things and never repeat itself, all being different? How long would the spectacle last, he asked himself, and how long would he have to lie here, half in water and half out, holding on to boards and timbers, afraid every moment that a worse part of the dream was still to come.

The middle of the afternoon he looked up and saw a town ahead. A bridge like Guerdon helped to build at home spanned the river. Now, he told himself, his dream was nearly done. It was fetching him back to Americus and there was the bridge unhurt all the time. First thing he knew, he'd find himself waking up in his bed in the loft over his pappy's bedroom and office. He could see the walk on the north side of the bridge lined with people, and he stood up to see if he knew any. They all shouted at him but he couldn't make out what they said. Oh, this was most

like a dream, their grotesque yells and the faces they made
and gesticulations. But not a vestige of their meaning could
he get. Just in time he lost his balance and flattened himself
on his raft. For a fleeting moment he saw a row of faces
bent down toward him, then he shot beneath with only a
foot to spare. But not a face had he seen that he knew, and
when he came out on the other side, he sat up and looked
around. Here the flood spread out like a great brown sea
across which a boat with two rowers came swiftly out to
meet him.

The front man, who smelled of chewing tobacco, lifted
him in the boat and passed him dripping like a fish to the
other man who set him on the back seat. Then both men
bent their backs and oars upstream for shore.

"Where'd you come from, boy, and what's your name?"
the front man said.

"You mean my old name or my new name that's really
my oldest name?" he asked them, for he thought that since
he was back home, they better take him to the house for
dry clothes.

"What's that?" the man said surprised.

The back rower held an unlighted pipe between his
teeth. Far ahead was the bridge, and now the town began
to look strange, for Chancey couldn't see his Uncle Will's
boatyard and besides, the town was on the wrong side of
the river.

"How did Americus get over there?" he asked.

"This is Forkville," the man with the pipe told him.

"Is that its real name or just in the dream?"

The men eyed him.

"What dream?"

"Aren't you in a dream then?" Chancey stammered. "Or
are you real?"

"We be," said the man, biting his pipe stem gently.

"Would you mind if you'd do me a favor?" Chancey begged him. "I'd like if you'd give me a pinch."

The man watched him carefully, keeping on rowing for a while. Then he reached forward and gave the skin of the boy's leg a blistering squeeze between thumb and fore-finger.

"Ouch! Thank you," Chancey told him. "Now I think I know that you are real people."

"And who are you?" the rower in the front seat wanted to know again.

"Ormsbee, Henry Ormsbee," Chancey said. "That's my really true name."

The men eyed him strangely, though they said nothing, and presently the little fellow wondered if you couldn't ex-pect people in a dream to admit they weren't real, for never did he see such an unreal town like this one they took him to, built in the water instead of on dry land, and in-stead of walking or driving, they rowed him up the street to a fine brick house where they talked from the boat to a lady and left him.

She was a small lady with very black hair except over her ears where it was white, and she had a gold chain with a cross around her neck. First she gave him a cup of hot brandy milk that made him gasp from the fire. Then she carried him upstairs to a room with sloping ceilings so low at the side that she couldn't walk except at the windows which were carved out of roof and plaster. All the time she took off his clothes and dried him and rubbed warmth in his legs and arms, she asked about where he lived and his people. Finally she laid him in a bed with four yellow posts and white and yellow curtains hanging like great butter-flies on the side. Here she brought him china dishes to eat out of and a tall china pot to sit on and make his water in. The door had an iron latch. When he heard it lift, he would open his eyes and see strange faces there in the hall staring at him.

He lay the rest of the afternoon and whenever he looked, he found the yellow and white curtains still above him and the white china pot still under the bed. When evening came, the room was soft in the candle light. The bed posts looked rich and golden, and the flame of the candle shone in the polish like stars of pointed fire. He had come to this room only a few hours ago, and already it seemed like he knew it a long time. He might even have been born in this room, he whispered to himself, and the lady with the gold cross who was so good and tender to him, might be his secret mother.

Now why did his brother have to come down from Americus and spoil it?

"There's a man down at the door, Henry," the lady told him the next morning. "He's looking for a boy called Chancey Wheeler. They think he came down on the flood."

Chancey closed his eyes quickly, but he could feel the lady waiting. After while he got out of bed and went to the window. Had he not known the dream was over, he would know it now. The water in the town was gone leaving mud over everything. In the street by the front door was Hector and his father's chaise and on the muddy step stood Guerdon. Oh, he would know that familiar, homely figure anywhere in his muddy red shirt and his pantaloons stained with water and mud.

Suddenly the man below looked up and saw him at the window.

"Chancey, that you? Are you all right?" The next minute he came bursting in the house and ran up the stairs a calling.

Guerdon's honest joy at finding him alive sent the pity into the little boy's heart. Never would he tell him that he wasn't his real brother. All the way out of Forkville and north toward Americus, he let Guerdon pour out his talk to him.

"What were you on that bridge for when it went down? You ought to knowed better. I told you all the time that bridge wouldn't stand high water. I kept telling old Jackson, but he wouldn't listen. What were you doing on it anyways?"

"I was lying on the arch," Chancey said carefully.

"I knowed it. The toll woman said you were off. She claimed you got back through in plenty of time, but other folks said they seen you go down the river. All yesterday I wished I was with you. I tried to get to Forkville ahead of you, but it took too long the way the roads were. Then I had to stop every place along the river and ask if they seen any drowned corpse come down. I sure would a hated to go in and find you laying out in the shed with a gunny sack over you."

"What would they have a gunny sack over me for?" Chancey wondered.

"So they wouldn't have to look at your bloated up face and belly. That's why I couldn't get to Forkville in time. If I had, I'd a got out on the bridge. Then I'd a waited for you to come along. I'd a watched my chance and dropped on your raft when you came out from under. Just to keep you company. Me and you'd stayed right on and gone down the river. If we got thirsty we could drink river water. We could a seen the country. You could a got off, if you wanted, but not me. I'd a stayed on till I seen the Gulf of Mexico, and I'd never come home again."

"Why wouldn't you come home?" Chancey asked him, but from then on until after dinner time, Guerdon was silent. Like a bittern that called only in the morning and again toward night, he said little or nothing through the middle of the day. All he talked when they passed teams or folks was to brag Chancey to the skies.

Late that afternoon he started talking to the boy again.

"You're only a little feller, Chancey, but let me tell you something. Never get mixed up lawful with a woman."

"Not even when I'm grown up?" Chancey wondered.

"That's the worst. Have nothing to do with them. Oh, you'll reckon other women might be no good, but you got the master woman. You'll be soft to her. You'll give her all you have. Some times she'll act real nice to you and say nice things. You'll reckon you're the luckiest man alive and her the finest woman. Then some time you'll come home unexpected and find something you wished you hadn't."

"Mush again for supper?" Chancey guessed.

"Worse than that. You know what song I used to sing, 'One night I come a ridin' home as drunk as drunk could be. I seen a head on the bolster where my head ought to be.' That's what you'd find, somebody sleepin' in bed with your woman."

The little boy thought it over.

"I have to sleep in bed with a woman sometimes."

Guerdon clasped him affectionately on one small knee.

"You could a slept in bed with my Effie any time you wanted. Any time you wanted, Chancey, and I wouldn't a minded, either. You're no dark diddler."

"What's a dark diddler?" Chancey asked.

"Don't you know yet? Well, your pap was a dark diddler once on a time. This was a good while ago. Kinzie and me was up in the brush and seen him."

"What did he do?"

"Well, he did something to a woman he had no right to and hadn't ought to."

"Isn't he a dark diddler now?"

"Not that I know of. But that don't excuse him any. He ain't left off that easy. He has a young one by that woman running around right here in Americus. And she ain't much older than you."

"Is it Massey?"

"No, it's not Massey. She's got another mam than we do. Now I don't want to tell you who she is or you might say something and maybe she don't know it yet. But I used to pass her when I went downtown. And when your pap goes down, he sees her too, and don't you forget it. You can guess what he thinks when he sees her a running around and called by another name than Wheeler. And all the time he knows she's a full daughter to him and that other people know it, too."

Hector was about played out when they came through the Narrows and could see the first roofs of Americus ahead against the sky. Some boys saw them. They came and looked in the chaise and then ran ahead. Guerdon said it was to tell the news that little Chancey Wheeler was still alive. By the time they reached town, women stood out in front of their houses to see them go by. Young ones ran a piece alongside to hear Guerdon tell the story. Just before they reached the boat yard, the cannon up at the Ferry House boomed out.

"That's for you!" Guerdon told the little fellow.

Will Beagle was out in the street now. Aunt Genny

came running to kiss Chancey. Tears spoiled her face like
she was kissing the dead. By the time they got to the
square, a whole company of children ran beside the chaise.
Massey among them for a minute and then streaked out for
home. All his sisters stood near the barn on Wheeler Street
waving handkerchiefs to greet them when they turned in
the lane. Chancey looked up the stretch of wheel tracks.
There at the end of it, at the door to the kitchen, stood
his mother. Even at this distance the boy could tell that her
face was cruel with secret feeling. Panic seized him.

"Don't tell her I went down the river on the bridge!" he
begged Guerdon. "She'll claim I'm lying and put me to bed
and I won't get any supper."

But Guerdon wouldn't listen. Chancey couldn't understand how they believed now all the unbelievable things
that happened to him and yet they wouldn't the time he
had just ridden over to town on a red cow. His mother
cooked him and Guerdon a special supper and his sisters
stood around piling more on their plates than they could
eat. All evening company came to hear the story told again
and to make a fuss over him. The minister thanked God
Almighty for "guiding our young Noah on his humble ark
and preserving him from a watery grave."

Never had he seen his mother like she was tonight, meeting everybody at the door, greeting them like they hadn't
seen each other for a long time, swapping words and
talk, listening to the girls tell over and over again what had
happened to Chancey, pouring refreshment to all. It
seemed like she couldn't do enough for everybody who
came. Now what made her like this, Chancey wondered.
It couldn't be jubilee over having him home again, for
only once had she hugged him and that was when he first
came. Had she been his real mother, she would have caught

him up many times and told him how she loved him, covered his face with kisses.

It was toward morning and all were in their beds, when a rapping came on the law room door. Whoever it was had to rap twice, but Chancey heard it the first time.

"Who's there?" his father asked.

"It's me, Collier," a voice at the window said, and Chancey knew it was the sheriff. "Is Guerdon here, Mr. Wheeler?"

"Guerdon? He wouldn't be here," Portius said. Then he must have turned his face toward the bed. "Or is he, Sayward?"

Chancey could hear his mother sitting up in bed.

"Guerdon's not here, Mr. Collier. What did you want him for?"

"Could you tell me where he is, Mrs. Wheeler?"

"Why, out at Fishtown. He lives with his wife's folks and went home around midnight. Is he all right?"

"As far as I know, ma'am. But he had some trouble out there on account of his wife. It happened about one o'clock this morning. I'm sorry to say he hit the man with a stool and the man's dead."

For a minute there was heavy silence downstairs.

"But that don't sound like Guerdon," his mother said.

"I guess his wife wasn't much good, Mrs. Wheeler," the sheriff apologized. "He's had a good deal of trouble with her on account of this old boarder of hers. I understand he came home early this morning and found him there again. The two had a fight and then Guerdon lit out. Well, if he's not here, I reckon I'll light out, too."

"Wait, Collier," Chancey's father said incisively. "I want you to come in and make a search as you would any other place. I'll help you."

"Oh, no, I'll take your word, Mr. Wheeler," the sheriff told him.

Chancey heard his father pull on his clothes and leave the house with the sheriff. Where he went to, the little boy didn't know, only that it must have been nearly morning because he could hear their rooster out at the barn crowing loud and clear while far off in town the other roosters answered him. When the crowing stopped and daylight came in slowly by the window, slow terrible sounds, half aloud and half in whisper, rose from downstairs. The little boy crawled to the loft hole and saw his mother on her knees by the bed, her head down, her hands locked and straining. She still had on her bedgown, coarse and rumpled around her. The bare feet and legs that stuck out of it looked heavy, knotted and indecent.

He drew back quickly. It was as if he had been looking on something he shouldn't. Ever before had he seen his mother strong and unvanquished. Now she seemed humbled, debased, beaten down like the runaway black woman he heard tell of that a Kentucky sheriff took back to slavery. Did Guerdon mean so much to her then, he wondered. Yes, for he was her own flesh and blood. She could cry out and pray from the depths of her heart for him. If Guerdon came back now, she would take him in her arms and tell him how much she loved him. But she couldn't do that for her youngest though he had come back from a watery grave, for she wasn't his real mother.

CHAPTER TEN

A POSY FOR PORTIUS

*All at once she lifted her body and flung her head to the
great sky that reached over the hills and shouted:
"Here I am!"*

THE TIME OF MAN

T HIS was the summer that sickness came to Americus.
Some called it the plague and some cholera, saying
that it came across the sea from the hot countries, and that
seemed likely to Sayward, for the hottest month here was
the worst. For three weeks you didn't see a house fly or
hear a bird. Where they went to nobody ever found out.
Anselm Lengel at Robeauch's died in four hours, and a
Harris boy, whose married sister wouldn't let him in the
house when he came there sick, was found dead on the
river bank in the morning.

Most of those who caught it were poor folk, but Dr.
Pearsall's wife lived in a fine house and she took sick hand-
ing medicine to a patient. While they helped her to her
bed, her face turned black, and before they could get the
doctor home from the country, she had stopped breathing.
Dr. Pearsall said her death was so fast and the contortion

of the muscular system so powerful that the extensor muscles of her arm lifted it from where it was folded on her
cold breast and laid it full length in his lap as he sat by the
bed a full hour after life was extinct.

It was a very bad time for Americus. Forty were carried
off in one week, five out of one cabin, and nobody would
go in to get them out. The council had to appoint a committee of citizens to oversee burying of the dead, and set
the death beds out in the street, to lime the sidewalks and
attend to those in distress.

Sayward had to steel herself when she heard Portius's
name was head of that list. Genny said they might have
picked somebody who didn't have nine children. But who
else could they get that took the part of the underdog like
Portius, Sayward asked herself. She hated to see him go
into the Hill cabin with John Quitman and two of his half-
drunk keel boatmen to fetch out the five bodies, but nobody else would go in for love or money, and somebody
had to do it.

When Portius fell sick, the first thing Sayward thought
of was little Chancey. He took everything that ever came
along, and now God's black ox must surely tramp him, for
even the stout and hearty seldom overed the plague. Portius himself was given only twenty-four hours to live by
Dr. Pearsall, but when the Old England doctor came
around next morning Portius was still among the living.
And so was he the third day. The doctor never told Sayward but he did General Morrison that he was out of cholera medicine that day and all he could give Portius were
pills rolled out of red pepper and asafoetida, so it must
have been the liquor Portius drank all his life that saved
him. He was too pickled and preserved by alcohol to die.
It went all over town, and the taverns did a mint of busi-

ness during the plague. Genny said it shamed her to hear it, but Sayward got down on her knees and thanked the Almighty for whatever it was that saved Portius and the rest of her family, too, for not another of hers that were around here took it. She didn't know about Guerdon, for only God knew where he was at.

It left Portius mighty weak, but at least it left him in his bed and not in the grave. And now the hot drought was broken by thunder showers. Folks began to say that they heard birds in the fields and saw house flies around again, so the worst was over. But Portius looked terrible, the color of ashes. Today Sayward was with him by the bed attending to his wants when through the open doors to the windsweep a faint knock sounded on the kitchen door. The girls had Chancey out while they worked in the truck patch, so she had to leave Portius and go.

That was a picture not easy to forget, leaving Portius feeble and leaden-faced in his sick bed and coming out on this delicate tender young girl standing by the door with a bunch of garden flowers in her hand. Her slender legs looked like they never belonged in that coarse gray calico dress she had on, and her white face had the singular shape of one of her blossoms. Washed and rightly dressed and combed, she would be oddly beautiful, Sayward thought. Now the little girl just stood there, not saying a word.

"You're welcome to come in," Sayward told her gravely, and when the child had as gravely entered. "You live around here?"

"Over along the river," she said and her mouth as she said it looked sensitive as a wild thing. Now who did she look like, Sayward racked her brain, or where did she see her before?

"I feel sure I know you, but I can't call your name," Sayward told her.

"My name's Rosa."

"Rosa what?"

"Rosa Tench."

The sound of the name gave Sayward a turn. For a minute she just stood looking. So this was the child conceived in sin by the pretty school mistress who, they said, looked like a hag now, who would not set foot out of her house since the babe was born, nor would she wash or comb! Why, the girl was no bigger than Chancey, though she must be a year or two older. And now Sayward knew, with the feel of knife in her side, who the girl looked like.

Did the girl know it, too? Her face quivered.

"I brought some flowers for Mr. Wheeler," she said, very low, holding out her handful.

"I'm sure he'll be much obliged to you," Sayward told her, stolid as could be, taking them from her, steeling herself, hardening her hand toward the soft clinging feel of those fingers. Now how much did the child know, she wondered. "Did you bring these your own self or did somebody tell you to?" she asked.

"My father told me." The girl's eyes were like the most delicate of wide slate gray liquid curtains that threatened to be torn down.

"And was he feeling all right when he told you?" Sayward kept on, her face bitter, for hardly could she see Jake Tench in his right mind doing this thing.

"No, he was very drunk," she whispered, shrinking.

So that was it, Sayward thought. She could see it better now. Oh, this was just the trick Jake would play on some highly respectable bigwig like Zephon Brown, send a bastard child to him with flowers when he was sick, but Jake would have to be mighty tipsy to play it on his own foster child and Portius. Why, he had threatened death on any who told Rosa that she was not his own, or so she heard. He would blow a tattletale to hell, he said, for even a broad hint.

Right then she thought she heard Portius calling and remembered how she had left him.

"You want to take a chair till I get back?" she asked. She set the flowers in a crock and went to the front room.

It took longer to get Portius straightened out than she reckoned, and till she got back to the kitchen, Huldah and Libby were there, but no sign of the younger girl.

"Where is she?" she asked them.

"Do you know who that was?" Huldah leered at her.

"Of course I know. What did you do to her?"

"We didn't do anything," Libby said. "We just looked at her, that's all." But her face said, "That sent her home a flying."

"I can guess how you looked at her," Sayward said sternly. She went to the door but Rosa had vanished.

It vexed her that she had to stay so long. Why, it had so bamfoozled her to see the girl here, she had hardly said a word on her own account about the flowers. Now she picked them up and set them in a smaller crock, first dipping the crock in water. Then she wiped off the crock and took it to Portius's room, setting it on his desk where he couldn't help but see the flowers from his bed. Tomorrow when he was better, she would say to him, "Little Rosa Tench brought these over for you."

CHAPTER ELEVEN

THE TWO DIGGINGS

*The sons of revolutionary sires, some of them sharers of
the great baptism of the republic, make the anniversary of
their country's freedom a day of ceremony and rejoicing.*

FROM AN ORATION BY PORTIUS WHEELER

You could tell when Portius was himself again. Then he
would call Chancey Noah like he did for a while after
the bridge went out.

"Noah, how's the old boatman today?" he would say.

Sayward wished Chancey would not look so unhappy
and helpless. That only made his father say it again next
time. What he ought to do was give no notice he had heard.
That's the way she did when he called her playful names,
mostly Juno.

"Now what's Juno?" she asked Resolve one time he was
home.

"She was the consort of Jupiter, the god," Resolve told
her.

"What did she look like?" Sayward asked suspiciously.

"I never had the pleasure of seeing her," Resolve said

smiling. "But I think she was supposed to be on the plump side."

"I thought so," his mother nodded.

So that was it, Portius taking a dig at her and at the same time giving himself a puff. She could be Juno, the fleshy consort, but he was Jupiter, the god. Well, if he liked it that way, it was all right to her.

Never had she seen him so high as lately. Oh, he carried himself grave and dignified as usual, but inside he was pleased as a dog with two tails and a silver collar. Times were good for Americus. The tide of improvement rode high and Portius sat on top, for now he was made lawyer for the new canal company. They were running a ditch to join up the English Lakes and the Ohio. Folks like Will Beagle and John Quitman were wild for a canal. Then boats need never halt for flood or low water but go about their business till ice shut them in. Portius talked canal to all who would listen. He could recite the bill they passed in the legislature far better than the Lord's Prayer. "The act to provide for the internal improvement of the state by navigable canals," he called it.

Now if the town trustees wanted it, you'd think they'd know where to put it. But they fought over it like they had where to set the bridge. Some said the canal ought to run straight down the middle of Water Street with a roadway on either side and the sidewalks cut to five feet. But how would the mills get their power from the race then or their tail water into the river? The canal would be in the way. If they didn't decide soon, Portius said they'd wake up some morning and find the canal had passed Americus by. He kept pestering Sayward. Would she sell the canal company a rightaway through the farm?

Sayward set her mouth. Oh, she knew what he was after, trying to get her to give up the cabin and live in town. She had more than one lot left on the square just in case and on purpose. But it took money to put up a new house, and she wasn't ready yet. On the other hand, neither did she hanker to stay living here at the cabin with canalers hollering and drinking and carrying on a short ways from her door. Some of her young ones were still of mighty tender years to listen to broad talk. And worst of all, she didn't like to see such good rich ground like hers dug up and ruined for ever raising anything on it.

But she told herself she might as well have given in at the start as at the finish. She woke up one winter day and found state men and engineers surveying and appraising her good bottom land. They didn't want just a narrow strip now but a whole canal basin. Oh, Portius went out and made like he never heard of such high-handed doings. He argued up and down with the engineers. But Sayward wasn't fooled. She hadn't been born yesterday. If the canal company lawyer wouldn't have known about this, she asked herself, who would? She even reckoned that Portius had put them up to it, only she couldn't prove it. In the end she made up her mind not to fight the whole state and town to boot. So long as they paid a fair price and didn't try to cheat her. But Portius better walk straight from now on. She wouldn't forgive him easy after this.

They had already dug a good part of the canal farther up north. Now the fourth of July they were starting work down here. A monster jubilee would set it off, half to celebrate Independence but mostly to break the first canal ground in Shawanee county. Sayward didn't have to go up town to see the parade because it would wind up right here in back of the house. Right this minute she could hear the

Tateville Cornet Band marching up Water Street and the Americus Drum Corps coming down Union Street and turning at Wheeler Street with their fifes squealing and their drums rolling through the square. And now she could see Major Hocking, the marshal, on his iron gray, and behind him the veterans of the Revolution, each one, it looked like, in different regimentals. It ought to be the other way round, Sayward thought, those poor old men on horseback and Major Hocking on foot.

And now it sounded like the fifes were marching right into her kitchen, as they turned down the lane. She could stand here at the door and see them all go by, Dr. Haneman, the chief engineer for the canal, and his helpers with their surveying instruments all bright and polished. Behind them came General Morrison, flanked by two Honorable Ploughers, guiding a plough laid on its side and drawn by Petticord's two white oxen. After him marched Judge Devanter and Senator Voorhees trundling empty wheelbarrows, and behind them the Hon. Harold Birchard and George MacKinnon, president of the select council, each with a spade on his shoulder. Now what was the matter with her, Sayward abused herself, curling a lip at these men in high hats playing at sweat and labor? They couldn't help it if their soft white hands hardly knew which end of a plough or wheelbarrow were the handles. General Morrison was a good friend of hers and relation besides. She had no business picking on him. She reckoned it was this tearing up of her land that galled her.

The truth was she had no taste to look at them when they reached her meadow where the canal basin was to be. Some folks already stood waiting, and many more, especially young folks, ran along side the paraders. But they were nothing to the crowd that swept after, like a river of

folks from town. Lucky the hay in her own field had been
made early and the wheat in the other harvested and hauled
off even if the heads hadn't filled out right yet. For now
she wondered if those two fields would hold the crowd.
Never had she seen such a company of people. Why, they
must have come from all over Shawanee County. They
were still pouring like through a sluice gate from the
square, coming from Water and Union Streets where they
had watched along the line of march. She could see them
in her mind's eye a swarming over her corn field and potato
patch. That corn field and potato patch didn't belong to
the canal company and never would, if she could help it,
and yet they had to be tramped down in the cause.

Over the heads of the crowd she could see Dr. Haneman
sighting through his transit, and waving this way and that
to his rodman and chainman. He was making like he was
running a line, locating a few rods of the basin, but everybody knew the canal and basin had been laid out and staked
long ago. After that, General Morrison and the other Honorable Ploughers each turned up a furrow with the white
oxen. The two canal commissioners received the spades
from the bearers and threw some ground in the wheelbarrows. Then Judge Devanter and Senator Voorhees ran the
barrows up on a platform built for the occasion. That's
the way they made a canal bank, Portius had said. The
crowd smiled to see those bigwigs in high hats running
their wheelbarrows up the boards. Now they gave three
"hurroars" and some held their ears for the salute of the
military.

But Sayward didn't hold hers. She felt too glum. This
was her ground they were tearing up. Her pap had settled
it, and she and Portius had cleared it. For thirty years or so
her own hand had helped plough and seed it. Well, she

reckoned, all good things come to an end sometime. She just felt glad her father wasn't here. He'd be liable to take a shot at them. Of his whole family, she and Genny were the only ones left, and now they could know how the Indians felt when the white men ran them off of their land.

Oh, she buttoned up her face and went with Portius to the Independence Day dinner out there under the bower. They had poles set up and laid across on top with green brush. Under the green, boards were laid for a long table and benches. Only the special guests could sit down and eat. The worst was that she had to sit there and listen to toasts praising the tearing up and ruination of her land. The chief canal commissioner gave the first.

"The Fourth of July. The worthies of the Revolution on this day commenced the system of Internal Improvement by breaking ground on the line of our Political Independence."

So that was it, Sayward told herself. Before they got through, they would have God Almighty making the first canal with His flood and Noah a building the first canal boat. Down the line the toasts went — the State of Ohio, the Governor of Ohio, the Canal Commissioners, Our Soldiers and Sailors of the Late War, the memory of Washington. Sayward heard them all stonily. Even Washington, she told herself, was not the father of his country any more. No, he had to be the Father of Public Works and Internal Improvement.

Portius gave one of the best of the day, she had to admit.

"Our Ladies. The only product of Ohio we do not want to see exported."

She hadn't realized before that toast what a hard face she must have been making. Not till he turned and bowed right at her in front of all the company and gave her such a nice

[133]

smile. It was like he might mean all the women folk of
Ohio in general but in particular she was the one he had in
mind. She felt the nerve strings and tendons of her face
give in. It minded her of the night they were married and
she was so provoked at him for going to bed first. Now,
she told herself, she could never go in after him. Then she
saw that he was holding back the blanket for her, and his
eyes had a look in them as toward a lady. She had heard
how sometimes one of the gentry did polite things such as
this or helping a woman over a log. Now today at the canal
jubilee she guessed what he was being nice to her for, but
better that than not give a hait. He knew how she felt and
was trying to make amends.

All that summer Portius acted mighty thoughtful toward
her. Inside, she knew, he was pleased as a basket of chips
over the canal, but for her sake he tried not to show it.
Especially he watched out not to puff the canal too high
when she was around. Instead he would give it a dig. It
got so that when company in the house praised the canal
too much, he would nod sagely.

"Yes, it's a summer that will go down in Americus' history. The summer of the two diggings."

"Two!" the company would say. "Where's the other
one?"

"You mean you haven't heard about Jethro Cox?" Portius would ask. "He's one of the most solid citizens we have
and very well known. He wanted to help in the expansion
of our young city. Knowing the shortage of houses for
emigrants, he built one next door to his own very nice
home and put it up for sale. There was, I believe, no privy,
but he promised to supply one. An emigrant from Maine
by name of Tom Henderson bought the house and paid for
it. 'Now I'd like if you'd build my privy,' he said. But

Cox claimed he didn't know anything about such an article. 'There's nothing in the deed about a privy,' he said. 'If you want one, you'll have to build it yourself.' Well, of course, this emigrant, Tom Henderson, did want and desire the article in question. He brought the deed for me to read and I told him regretfully that Cox was legally sound in his contention. 'Well, then,' Henderson said, 'I guess I'll have to do the building myself.'

"Now the line runs fairly close between the two houses. Henderson looked the ground over carefully and, doubtless after discussion and due agreement with his good wife, he started to dig a hole at the front fence corner beneath Jethro Cox's parlor windows. It wasn't long until Cox came out. 'What are you doing there?' he asked. 'Why, I'm digging for my privy,' Henderson said. 'But you can't do that in your front yard and under my parlor window!' Cox said. 'There's nothing in the deed about that,' Henderson told him.

"Yes," Portius used to end his story, "if we had more self reliant freeholders like Tom Henderson, Shawanee County would be better off. Quite a few of our citizens when they heard about it turned out to see him dig. Indeed some of the select council came and watched. They agreed with me that there was no ordinance that could stop him. Cox shut himself up in his house for a time. Now in view of the fact that the building he was erecting would be practically on the street front, Henderson wanted to do the right thing. He had Lowdermilk, the carpenter, make him a very serviceable and appropriate door with slats below and various figures cut out above so one within could look out and see the sky and know that all was well with the world. In fact he based it on my suggestion. In any event, when Cox saw that door, it smoked him out. He claimed that according to their verbal contract, it was his sacred right to supply the privy and choose its site. He wanted to put it back at the alley, but Henderson said that was too far on cold or rainy nights. I believe they compromised half way back in the garden. You can see it there now yourself if you walk down that way. But they never could agree about filling in the hole at the front fence. Henderson claimed it was Cox's responsibility and Cox said it was Henderson's. So far as I know, the hole is still there. Sometimes I think it is more pointed out and talked about than the canal."

CHAPTER TWELVE

ROSA

They're a strange bird. Nobody sees them come, and nobody sees them go.

BILLY HARBISON

Now he's laid around home long enough," his mother said. "He's crowding eight years old and this fall he's going to school."

Chancey looked at her in dismay. He knew that ropy look around her mouth. Even without seeing it, he could tell she meant business by her voice. She'd put up with a thing a long time. She mightn't like it much, but hardly a word would she say against it. She'd go along with it so far. Then she'd stop, and crowbars couldn't move her.

This was at the dinner table. His father looked up dryly.

"I'm not exactly averse to education. I've been teaching him at home what I could. But school is an apple off another tree. How do you propose to get him back and forward?"

"He can walk like the other young ones."

Chancey looked anxiously around the table. How could he do that when hardly could he go out to the barn without his heart acting like it did? It wouldn't be so bad if school still kept in the small log house that used to stand yonder across the run. His father had been master then they said. But now the academy stood uptown, a big one-story brick building heated by its floor. A low kiln stood at one end. It burned logs, and the fire and smoke went through flues in the floor. That brick floor, they said, kept your feet warm as a toddy. If they were wet, it dried them, but only boys' feet. Girls had to go to Miss Porter's or Miss Bly's school.

"Unfortunately, our boy is not like other children," Portius mentioned gravely.

"That's all he's heard since he's old enough to tell one word from another," his mother said. "He has legs like the rest of us. Old lady Winters told me many a time she'd a give up and died long ago if she couldn't get out every day for a tramp, and she's eighty-four."

"Even at eighty, she probably has a good heart."

"Chancey might have a good heart at eight years old, too," Sayward said grimly. "You always claim a body's innocent till he's proved guilty. Anyway I'm taking him to the new doctor this afternoon."

Chancey looked in alarm at his father.

"He's a quack, Sayward," Portius declared. "He boasted to me himself that he was a stable boy in Kentucky. A horse kicked him and they took him to a doctor. He told me he thought that if doctors could be so stupid, egotistical and well paid, he would be one, too. All the preparation he ever had was hanging up his shingle."

"That's what I like about him," Sayward said. "He tells you what he isn't and what he doesn't know."

"Well, I'm only sorry for the boy," Portius rose from the table and retreated to his law room. The last glimpse

Chancey had of him, his face looked dark and grave, and the boy felt that darkness and gravity spread over him. His father had deserted him. He was left now to the ministrations of his mother and the quack.

A verse he had heard in church kept going through his head as his sisters got him ready for the doctor. It was about a sheep that was dumb, yea, it opened not its mouth. That was plainly himself as his sisters scrubbed, dressed and combed him for the doctor. He was like the ram lamb his mother had sold last week to the butcher. That lamb didn't know what was ahead as they pulled it away, but he did. He couldn't bear to see it going to a place of knives and blood. He couldn't understand how his mother could be so cruel. But she said there were some cruel things in life you had to go through.

She and Dezia drove him away in the chaise. As they came to the doctor's house they saw two-wheelers, four-wheelers and saddled horses from the country, tied outside. It was a big green house but the windows were pale as sightless eyes, and as they walked from the chaise to the front porch, something came out of that house at them. Chancey couldn't see what it was, but as they stepped through the front door, he could smell strange and fearful compounds. He tried to turn back. Almost, he believed now that he could run. But it was too late. Dezia was closing the door behind him, and his mother dragged him into a room where women in pained faces and men with solemnly bandaged heads and arms sat around in silent and dismal conclave.

For hours, it seemed, they had to sit there while the sores and sicknesses of those present and past, the crippled, the cankered and the dying, hid in the dim corners and hovered under the ceiling, a lifeless congregation of invisible vapors and soundless whispers slowly turning and wheeling and pressing in upon his chest. Many of those who had once frequented this room, Chancey felt, must now lie buried in the church yard, but the intangible vestiges of their wretched sufferings still hung here behind the curtains, as their blood and ointments still stained the carpet and walls.

None of the patients he saw go in the doctor's office came out again. Dezia said they went out another way, but fear paralyzed the boy. In time there were so few left in the waiting room that Dezia felt free enough to make him spell out the letters of the framed notice on the wall, and by this he knew that whatever happened to him, his fate was lawfully sealed, for this was the doctor's license hung up for everyone to see, stating that he had the right to practise physic and surgery. There it was for all men to know by these presents that Zephon Brown, president of the Court of Common Pleas of Shawanee County, by the authority vested in him had made it true and according to law, and so had set his hand and official seal. Furthermore, the secretary of the third medical district had sworn that this was a true copy of the license and had so signed it with his unintelligible hand.

Whenever the doctor's door opened now, Chancey's heart shook him. His hour approached. When it came, his mother had to drag him like she had the ram lamb from the barn.

"Now who's this young gentleman?" a brusque cheery voice demanded. "And what's he so pale and contrary about?"

Chancey looked up and saw a tall ponderous man in a long black coat with velvet lapels and collar.

"It's his heart, doctor," Chancey's mother said.

"You're too young to be worried about your heart, young man," the doctor reproved him. He bent down and laid his head against the wildly agitated breast. It was a great head with a shag of iron gray hair that pressed up against the little boy's face.

"Quiet, boy, quiet!" the doctor said as if talking to a horse. "There's nothing to frighten anybody in here." While he spoke, Chancey had to breathe the choking medical scent of that hair, and through it he could see shelves lined with jars of poisonous looking pastes and liquids. A mortar and pestle stood on top of the cabinet, and on the table below were strewn evil-looking knives, scissors and forceps, while in the midst stood a white basin half filled with blood, and now he could make out drops of blood scattered over the brown table and floor, while over in the corner crouched and grinned what once upon a time had walked the earth as a man or woman but of which now nothing remained but its bones like a bundle of dried roots of a blown down willow tree.

The doctor seemed unusually sober when he raised his head, as if it were tragic to have found what he had in one so young. He went on methodically to examine tongue, ribs and other more private parts. When he finished he took down a jar from the cabinet and poured out a few many-colored pills in the boy's trembling hand.

"They're only sugar balls, my boy. Try one. They won't hurt you. Also they won't cure you."

"How is he, doctor?" Sayward asked.

The doctor seated himself as though figuring out what to say. He looked extremely sad and resigned.

"Did you see Mrs. Crane and old Mr. Oliver in the waiting room? They come to me, the aged and the palsied, the weary and the worn out. If we knew what was waiting for us farther on in life, Mrs. Wheeler, the woe and death of all our hopes, the wormwood of the approaching grave, I wonder would we waste our lives in vain regret for one who must die so young."

Chancey felt his heart turn over like a startled squirrel in a cage, while behind him something dark and silent and very terrible made ready to spring at him. He thought Dezia saw it, too, for her face was faintly paler. Only their mother stood there as if she hadn't heard.

"What can you do for him, doctor?" she asked.

"I'm sorry, Mrs. Wheeler," he said, "but I can't cure your boy."

Chancey saw that familiar bitter look come on his mother's face, but not a word of complaint did she make.

"No, I can't cure him," the doctor went on, "but Nature can. Nature made us what we are in the first place. But we must give Nature a chance. Don't tie up this colt in the stable. Put him out to pasture and let him run."

"He isn't tied up, doctor," she said. "But it seems he can't run."

The doctor nodded, leaned back and put his thumbs under his vest. Now who did he remind him of, Chancey wondered. Then he remembered what his father had said. The stable boy! The doctor's hands, he remembered, had run over him gentle as over a colt's legs.

"I want to tell you something, Mrs. Wheeler," he said. "You and I and all creatures in captivity are lazy. Where we get it, I don't know, certainly not from the devil. But I know why we get it. Because we shut ourselves up from Nature. Let me tell you a case I had of a storekeeper who came to me sick and ailing. I told him to walk. He got mad as a wet hen. That's what was the matter with him, he said. He was worn out walking up and down behind the counters of his store. But that's not the same thing, I told him. Go to Nature. Walk the streets and the country. That's my prescription. He followed it and it cured him. Now let me tell you another. When I was a stable man, I had a mare that was balky. She got lame as soon as you started out with harness on her. But I noticed she didn't limp in pasture. And she didn't limp when I put her oats and hay where she had to walk across the stable yard to get them. After while I had her walking down the alley to another stable where I'd feed her. In the end I used to drive her out in the country to feed her and she'd run without limping all the way home. I had her hardened up and cured in no time. You do the same. That'll be fifty cents."

Chancey looked at his mother and then at the doctor with bewilderment. What did the stories about the store-keeper and horse have to do with his sick heart? He stumbled out with his mother when she left. Oh, the air outside would have been sweet as locust blossoms if she hadn't said that he couldn't get up in the chaise.

"Now that I'm this far, I think I'll drive up and see Effie and the baby," she told them. "It isn't a good place for you to be, so you'll have to walk home."

"Walk, Mama!" Chancey stammered.

"When you're tired, you can rest," his mother said firmly. "When you get home, you can lay down. It isn't far. You can almost see it from here."

Chancey felt so wounded, he turned his head so he wouldn't see her drive away. She didn't have to go up and see Effie. No, he understood now, she just went up there so he would have to walk home. She and the doctor and Little Turtle, they were all cracked on walking. They didn't care what happened to his heart. Neither did Dezia. Oh, Libby and Huldah and Sooth would holler at him, but

they had soft hearts underneath. They would carry him a
piece if he got tired. But not Dezia. She wouldn't tease him
or jeer, and neither would she do anything for him she
wasn't supposed to. She was a little old Yankee. She'd
preach at you how good you had to be, but she never had
any mercy. If you owed her anything, you had to pay on
the dot.

"Now let's go," she told him primly. "We'll walk down
Water Street and you can look at the river. Lift your feet
and don't go so slow."

Chancey knew before he started that he wouldn't make
it farther than the nail mill. Aunt Genny used to live near
there before she moved to the boat yard. When they got
there, Dezia didn't want to stop, but Chancey sat down on
the curb of the wooden pump that stood on the street. He
wanted to lie down but Dezia wouldn't let him.

"Now don't look over at those awful Tenches!" she
told him. Before he knew it, she said it was time to start
again. He made like he didn't hear her. She tried to pull
him up to his feet, but he fought her and shrieked so dread-
fully, she let go.

"You'll be sorry," she warned. "I was just going to take
you as far as the fulling mill. You can rest there and see
the dye come out in the tail race. But if you won't come,
I'm going straight home. Are you coming? I mean it."

She did mean it, too, Chancey knew. He heard her start
away. She looked back once, and her cool eyes appraised
him. She must have seen he didn't intend coming, for she
went on this time and didn't look around. He felt a sudden
fear to see her go. She walked so fast. But he closed his
mouth tightly so he wouldn't call.

Hardly was she past the fulling mill when two boys
came out of a yard across the way. One he knew was Tur-

key Tench. He was about as big as Chancey, the other a good deal smaller. As they came close, they had that peculiar acid odor he noticed on some boys. Massey said it was because they never washed themselves all over or changed their clothing. They stood now and eyed him hard like enemies.

"What's the matter you can't walk?" Turkey jeered.

"My heart jumps."

"Where does it jump to?"

"No place. Just up and down."

"I don't see it jump."

"You can't see it, but you can hear it if you put your head on my chest. That's the way my doctor does. Right on here."

Turkey stood there skeptically. He would never do such a sissy intimate thing as lay his head on Chancey's chest. But he was willing to put his grimy hand on it.

"What makes it jump?" he asked, subdued.

"The doctor said he couldn't do anything for it."

"I want to feel it!" the little Tench cried. He felt but drew his hand away quickly leaving another black smudge on Chancey's white blouse.

"Kin Rosa feel it?" Turkey asked.

"I don't care," Chancey said.

"Rosa!" the little Tench yelled.

Suddenly Chancey felt he was their confederate and friend. They took his arms and helped his gingerly movements toward the yard. Almost at once Chancey felt stronger. This was better than going home with Dezia. The fence was of slabs and he couldn't see through till they came in the gate.

Then he felt full of wonder, for the yard was like no yard he had ever seen before. Back home everything had to be put away neatly. "A place for everything and everything in its place," his mother used to say. In this yard things were thrown anywhere. The whole yard lay choked with useless traps and belongings. Here were used kegs and barrels, a heap of trimmed stone, a hogshead with the head knocked out, nests of wet excelsior, a pile of boat lumber, a broken kettle, a row boat with a stoved-in side, some rusty iron, a bottomless cedar tub, some long oars with split and smashed blades, a sawbuck and wooden horses, a mossy drawbucket from some well, a bench with a leg split off, and a thousand things more, all worn out or worthless, jumbled helter-skelter, thrown together or strewn apart, most of them dark and damp from the weather.

Chancey stood over an old boat pole drinking it all in. It was like he had entered a different world, a new life, a place where he didn't have to take care, where nobody would make him wash his hands or pick up his traps and put them away. He felt curiously blessed and lightened.

They went on to the porch, a narrow shelf of plank with a dipping roof. The floor was tracked with dried mud and piled at one end with empty bottles, jugs, jars, earthenware, cooking pots, plant boxes and other trash.

"Rosa!" Turkey yelled.

The door to the house stood open and amid the dim disorder inside Chancey glimpsed a girl. She didn't seem any older than he or Turkey. Her face looked white and delicately perfect in this untidy and disorderly place. She came out, slow and calm, in a torn dress that showed one slender leg almost to her thigh. A grimy child clung to one hand but the girl herself looked miraculously clean and spotless as if no dirt could soil her.

"Rosa, you want to hear his heart jump?" Turkey said,

and now he boldly put his wax-filled ear to Chancey's chest, showing her how to listen.

Chancey scarcely moved as the girl came toward him. He felt in a summer trance. Not even the white chick of a sister he treasured in his mind all these years made him feel like this. Beyond the girl and around her he could see the white halo of the river. The yard was a loaded flatboat, the house the captain's cabin, and all were floating down stream. He floated with it. He could hear the river gurgle to itself. Up in the sky the great white clouds ran toward each other. So slowly they went, you wouldn't hear them when they met. But you could feel their meeting on ahead, and he could feel something of the girl running ahead of her on foot, running toward him while behind it slowly walked her other self. He stood there in a kind of daze, closing his eyes a little, waiting for her to reach and touch him.

Something in him cracked when the spell was broken.

"Chancey!" an angry voice cried. It was Dezia, and there she was walking swiftly into the yard. Now why did she have to come back and spoil it, and what made her so mad? Her eyes flashed fire.

"Let me be!" he bawled at her.

"You walked in here, you can walk home!" she said and dragged him for the street.

Hardly had they gone halfway to the gate when such a cry as Chancey never heard came after. Dezia didn't even slacken. Just as she pulled him through the gate, Chancey looked back. Something like a witch had her head out of the window. A wild mat of hair came down over her face like an animal's.

"So that's who he is!" she screamed. "Take that young

Wheeler home and keep him there and never let him come near my Rosa again!"

Chancey looked up at Dezia in terror.

"Now I hope you know better!" she told him right-eously. "That's one place you must never go to, and don't ever talk to that girl again! If Mama or Papa knew you were in there with Rosa Tench, you'd be whipped every night for a week and put to bed without your supper."

CHAPTER THIRTEEN

ROSA'S RAINBOW

Hail sweet asylum of my infancy!
CHILDREN OF THE ABBEY

IF there was anybody more hardset and stubborn than his mother, Chancey didn't know who it was. You would think she'd be shamed to have done what she did to him when it didn't work out. But never would she give in and say so.

Ever since his father had to come and fetch him home from near the fulling mill on Water Street, he was worse off than before. He had strained his sick heart trying to walk all that way home, his father said. It was true, too, because now he couldn't walk even the short pieces he used to. Oh, he'd try hard enough, take it slow and half-way hold his breath so as not to exert himself. And still he couldn't make it. Before he'd get there, his heart would flap in his chest like a chicken with its head off. It would act worse if his mother was around. He would look at her to see if she noticed what she had done to him. Just to have her standing by with her head turned away would make something come up in him so he would almost faint. How

could she be his mother and not even look at him when he
tried to walk and couldn't like her other children?

Oh, if his real mother was here, it would be different.
She would run to his side and bear him up with her soft
white arms. She would make him sit down and beg him not
to try to walk any more, for he didn't have to. As long as
she lived, she would take care of him, wait on him hand and
foot. She would wash and dress him, bring his food and
read to him. With her he would have security.

But all this woman they said was his mother would do
was turn toward him a cruel and bitter face when she
thought he wasn't looking.

"Well, what do you think of your horse doctor now?"
his father said to her one time they had to carry him back
in the house.

Not a word could she say, and yet she wouldn't give in.
He couldn't walk to the barn without stopping, and yet he
had to go to the Boatmen's Frolic. The girls daren't go. It
wasn't genteel enough. His mother couldn't go because
Fay expected a baby, and she promised to come at the first
word. Only his father had to go, for professional reasons,
he said, and now he had to take Chancey along.

"It will do him good to get out," his mother said. "He
won't hardly have to walk a step, since you're going in
boats and the grove lays right on the river."

The boy could see his father didn't want to take him.
He had to make a speech, Portius complained, and talk to
a lot of people. But Sayward was obdurate.

"Now recollect Chancey's with you," she said when they
left, and young as he was, the boy knew what that meant.
Chancey's father knew it, too.

"What refreshment I take will be strictly in the interest
of the many," he deviled her for being saddled with Chan-

cey. "The more I consume, the less there'll be to debauch others."

Fowler's Grove stood north of Americus on the far side of the river. Some days you could see its blue skyline from the cabin. From downtown its bulk stood out darkly against the hills. It was the only woods left close to Americus, they said, that hadn't been cut down. Pigeons still nested in its hinder parts where the ground was wet and soggy, and coon were trapped on its paths. You could get to it by the new bridge and a long pair of wheel tracks running through stumpy meadows and standing water. Or you could go by boat clean to the grove's edge on the river bank, and that's how Chancey and his father and most of the boatmen went today, in rowboats and poleboats and flatboats like King Sam used to have for his ferry.

It was a hot day even on the river, but from the moment they stepped off the boat, Chancey could feel the chill of the great trees. Here they grew in their native soil, standing in immense silence and shade like his mother had told him. All his young life had he heard tales of the big butts from her mouth and Aunt Genny's and from the old men and women who came to their kitchen, of the mad wolf that bit Jude MacWhirter, of the panther that tried to come down Aunt Genny's chimney and of the blood-red beast, with its hide skinned off that Resolve saw run through the trees. Oh, his mother could talk of the deep woods all day if she wanted. She hated the darkness by day and the terror by night, and by day and night the eyes of the heathen trees a watching you. At night Aunt Genny said, they made themselves into savage frightening shapes. When you tried to sleep, their long fingers tapped on your window pane. If you visited too long, they grew right up in your cabin while you were gone. And if you were fool-

[151]

ish to go out alone, they addled your wits and turned you
around so the sun rose in the West and set in the East, and
never could you find your way home again. They had
swallowed up his Aunt Sulie and never was she found
even to this day. But the worst was the Wild Thing without a name that followed you in the deep woods, and no
man knew whether it was flesh or spirit. His grandfather
Luckett had known it, and once his mother had felt it so
close that she broke out in a cold sweat and her legs tried
to run, but never did she see what kind of thing it was.

Chancey felt glad today he was not alone, that all this
end of the woods was filled with boatmen and their
families. Their colored shirts and dresses brightened the
shade, and their cheerful talk and cries warmed the chill.
He saw Aunt Genny and Uncle Will, the whole Quitman
family, the Fices and the Gannons, the Tenches and the
McCunes and many more. Young ones ran and yelled and
played. The only ones that stood still were he and Rosa
Tench.

Now why did she have to stand so alone, he wondered.
He had to hug the log where his father set him, but she had
no bad heart to hold her. And yet for a long time he saw
how she kept away from the others. Did she have no girl
friend like Massey did, he wondered. It went through his
mind that she was different from the rest, like she lived in
some other world. He sat there very still, thinking this
over, feeling the green light on his lids, the mysterious
shadows on his skin, measuring the height of the vaulted
ceiling, tasting the breath of the wild fern and the scent of
the bruised ground. When he looked for her, she was gone.

A good part of the day passed till he saw her again. For
hour after hour he had to "go out," but he didn't dare. The
other boys, he noticed, just ran behind a handy tree, anx-

ious to get back to their game. But never could he do that, stand where others could see him. Besides, with others watching, likely it wouldn't come. That's the way it was when he was little and he had to do it in the bucket while a stranger sat in the kitchen. As the day wore on, he grew desperate and more desperate still, wishing for the back house at home and peace and privacy. His father was busy, surrounded by people. He wouldn't dare to tell him what he wanted. Folks would think him a baby who didn't know he had a flyhole in his britches.

In the end he started painfully for the bull laurel where he noticed that the girls and women went. It was far but he daren't come back without what he sought. Little by little, resting on logs and roots, he made it. When he heard strange women coming, he stumbled out quickly on the other side. That's how he found himself alone in the great woods, or he thought himself alone. His eye ran down the dim aisles till it stopped, fearing to be lost, and there coming back from the depths of the forest, was Rosa.

"I saw you when you first came," she said after she got close to him.

"I saw you first," he told her, for he couldn't let a girl get ahead of him.

"I saw something else just now," she told him. "I'd show it to you, if you didn't have to go back where the others are."

"I don't have to go back," he said quickly, and took her hand like he always took his sisters' or his father's hand, and they started off together.

"Don't you want to be with your father?" she asked him.

"He's not my real father."

Her eyes widened, then flashed as if what he said had struck hidden fire.

"Why isn't he?"

"Because he isn't. My mother isn't my real mother either. My real mother's a lady with gold rings and white hands. She wears fine dresses and lives in a place far away from here. She and my real father only gave me out to raise. It's a secret but some day they'll come for me and then I'm going back."

Now what made Rosa give him such a blinding and understanding look as if he had done something wonderful for her. For a moment it seemed he could look through her eyes down a long illumined passageway in her mind. She made him tell her more, pressing him with questions. Only when he remembered that all this time they had been walking, did he stop. Why, he couldn't walk, he told himself. He got heart palpitation and flipflops. They would shake his whole body and he was liable to die. For a second he listened. He couldn't even hear his heart or feel it. It seemed like he didn't have a heart, or else it had stopped and this was what it felt like to be dead.

"What makes you so white just now?" Rosa asked him.

And now he knew he was still alive, because that old heart came back, pounding and flopping. Just for a moment. Rosa paid it no attention. She held up her finger for him to be still, and helped him down stones that looked like steps and he found himself in the strangest place. What was it like? he asked himself, looking around. Then he knew. It was like a church in the woods for gnomes. The floor was sunken and flat and covered with logs like pews, while up in front one rock stood on another like a pulpit. Green mould and moss were over everything, over floors and pews and pulpit. Even the light in this little church was green as if it came through green glass windows.

"Did you see anything just now?" Rosa whispered.

"No, but I thought I did," Chancey whispered back. He felt sure somebody or something had just left as they came. He could still feel a presence here like he could Aunt Genny's when they went in her house and she wasn't at home.

As they left, Rosa kept looking back over her shoulder. He could hear something behind them in the woods, and running ahead of them, too. Now it came and now it went, and now it talked to itself in the tops of the giant trees. Then it stayed quiet listening. Not far ahead a bush moved. But when they got there, what moved it had gone. All hung still. Rosa squeezed his hand to look. Something was there along the little run where it came out of a leafy tunnel and dripped over the wet stones and into the dark little pool beyond where the yellow sand grains went round and round as if a hand lay in there stirring them. But you couldn't see any hand, only a strange reflection in the water. Farther on a leaf trembled when no one touched it. Now it stopped and fled, but not very far. Just ahead of them it kept, so you couldn't quite ever find it or dared look at it if you did. All you could see was the curious mark it left in the wet black ground and what looked like a three-toed footprint worn deep in the round stone.

"Sh!" Rosa said when he hadn't made a sound.

How small they felt standing there or moving hand in hand through the giant woods. Up and up rose the big butts. On and on ran the trackless reaches of the forest. All the time whatever it was they felt still led or pursued them. Never would it let them see it, Rosa told him. And never would they know what it looked like, save from the light bellies of the leaves, from the shape of the snake and the way the partridge vine ran over the ground. It was heathen and didn't care for human folk, Rosa said. It came only to lead them wrong, to lose them in the swamp or quick-sands. It knew every step of the woods, all the beautiful hidden places they could never hope to find because they couldn't put their heads inside a teaberry blossom or slide up and down the long, colored spider threads from the tall trees. If only they could make themselves wild for a moment. Then, oh then, Rosa felt sure they'd see it for even now it lay under the dogwood. In a moment it would come out and show itself. The squirrel had seen it. They could tell by his chatter. But now it changed its mind and was drawing back again. All they could hear was something high in the treetops making fine sounds like tiny gold sovereigns dropped into the hanging nest of a golden robin.

Oh, Chancey never felt so close to anybody as he did today to the shy girl by his side. They understood the very thoughts of each other. Things spoke to them with the same words. What a long ways off his family and hers seemed here in the deep woods. He had to push his mind even to remember. Only Rosa was contemporary. Only she and he were real, and they were going through this wild and beautiful time together. Once in a deep shadowy place they stood and watched a tiny gold leaf come fluttering down as from another world. And once they came to an old giant of a log that had caught in the split fork of its own butt when it fell. The top layer of that hollow log had cracked off long ago and the deep bed filled up with mould. And now it looked like a monster flower box green with fern and white with strange woods flowers. Chancey wanted to pick some from the lower end where he could reach, but Rosa said he daren't. It belonged to the Wild Thing.

Once when they got tired they sat on a green log to rest

and felt the soft slow rain of the deep woods falling about them, not a wet rain but the fine drippings from the high and ancient roof of branches, leaves, needles, twigs and bark. If you listened sharp you could hear it, a dry drop on a green leaf, then a drop on a dead leaf, and now a faint drop on your shoulder. Rosa wished they could sleep here, and have it drizzle on them all night, and in the morning when they woke they would find themselves covered with a light skift of gray snow.

But they went on, sinking in leaf mould to their ankles. They tramped on flecks of pale sunlight falling through the great roof, never still but moving, dancing like ghost leaves on the dark forest floor. And once in the most deserted place of all, they heard a strange cracked voice.

"Jack!" it said, "J-a-c-k!"

"What's that?" Chancey called out terrified.

They stood holding each other and listening a while.

"It's just a tree saying 'Jack,' " Rosa said at last.

"You're sure it doesn't say Chancey?" he begged.

It relieved him it was just an old tree creaking in the wind and that it said only Jack. He would not like to hear his name called by a tree in the deep woods and never know what it wanted. As they went on, they could hear it croaking after them, "Jack! J-a-c-k-k-k-k-k!"

The only thing Chancey hated was to miss the pigeons' nesting ground. They had one in Fowler's Grove, Rosa said, if only they could find it. Her father had seen it. He claimed nesting grounds were always laid out either round or square. This one was in a circle. You would think surveyors had done it, so round it was. You couldn't find a tree with a nest in it outside the line, and if the line passed through the tree, there were nests on one side of the tree and none on the other. Oh, that was something to see,

Rosa said, especially in nesting time when everything was blue with pigeons all talking to each other like people. You could hear them a long ways off. "Ooh-coo-ooh," they said. Rosa wished she could just see a flock feeding in the beech woods. When they came toward you, her father said, they were like a long blue sea wave four or five feet high rolling along the ground. That wave was boiling with pigeons flying from in back to the front. Chancey wished he could see that blue wave boiling with pigeons. But he wouldn't like to see when you shot them. Then Rosa's father said, they always fell on their red breasts.

Chancey hated to see the woods come to an end. First white sky shone through the trees, and when they came out of the woods, there was a creek and open field beyond, all in the blinding sunlight. He felt a little shaky. But he hadn't died. His heart only flopped a little. Now wasn't it strange that over here away from his mother and sisters he could walk? It showed they weren't his real mother and sisters. And now just thinking about them, he could hear calling far away in the woods, only these were the deep disturbing calls of men.

"Rosey!" a voice like a distant hound's baying rang through the trees.

"It's you-know-who. I must go," Rosa whispered.

"Then I'll have to, too," Chancey told her.

They stood looking at each other. The spell they had found together must soon be broken, Chancey knew, and he held desperately to the last few minutes. They had been free as the birds. Now they must go back to separate prison houses and jailers.

"Don't forget me!" Rosa begged.

"I could never forget," Chancey told her.

Her eyes searched his.

"I'll give you something to remember me by," she promised. "Just wait. I'll show you."

Swiftly she led him across stepping stones in the shallow summer creek. On the other bank she found a thin whitewood slab. Smoothly she slipped off her shoes and stockings, then, keeping her back toward him her dress. For a moment she stood there in her shift. Chancey waited silent. He thought this was what she wanted to show him to remember her by, but she went into the creek, wading to the deeper part where it almost reached her knees.

"Now watch!" she called back guardedly and clapped the water with her whitewood slab. "Are you watching? Do you see it? Look and tell me! Can you see it?"

Chancey looked hard. He saw her shift, her bare shoulders and her thighs when she bent. But what was so wonderful about that?

"The rainbow!" she called back anxiously. "Can't you see it?"

Not till then did Chancey know what she meant. The spray from her whitewood slab flew high above her head, and so fast did she ply it that the fine drops hung constantly in the air. Behind them was the falling sun, before them the forest. Against the dark trees the drops took on the bright colors of the bow in the sky. But this wasn't like any bow he had seen before, and it wasn't in the sky. It hung right here in the creek around Rosa. She seemed to be standing in it. It played on her, bathed her. The drops as they came down flashed colored fire, and the reds, greens, yellows and violets dyed her scantily clad body.

Her face glistened with water and pleasure as she turned it over her shoulder.

"Did you see it? Wasn't that pretty? Do you know what it means? It means we don't have to wait for a rainbow. We can make our own. Now turn your back till I come out and dress. Then we'll go so nobody sees us."

The Boatmen's Frolic was over. Chancey's father smelled like a stale old whiskey cask as he took him on the flatboat back to town. The boy's blouse felt wet and cold with sweat, and his legs twitched and trembled. But a great peace and wonder was on his soul.

They were pushing out into the main current when shouts rang from boat to boat.

"Here they come!"

Chancey's father held him up so he could see. What looked like a long streamer of cloud was blowing up from the south. It blew very fast and when it came to Fowler's Woods, the front of that cloud began to settle, dropping to the tops of the trees in a blue wave. Only then did Chancey know they were pigeons. One of the men on a boat near the grove fired his gun, and the birds rose again. They came up like wadding fired in the air, swarmed together and circled around. Their graceful sweeps and dips made him dizzy with pleasure. All the time fresh flocks were arriving and still the column came from the south till the sky above Fowler's Woods was a great whirlpool of circling pigeons, now rising, now falling, now almost settling and then swooping up again with a sound like rumbling thunder until the boy's head swam with the spectacle and he wished he was up there with them in God's free sky.

As far down the river as he could see in the failing light, he looked back at Fowler's Grove. Oh, the woods, he whispered to himself, the terribly beautiful deep woods! How bitter he felt toward his mother for hating it and wanting to cut it down.

CHAPTER FOURTEEN

THE SUMMER

SWEETING

Oh, yellow's forsaken,
And green is forsworn.
But blue is the sweetest
Color that's worn.

OLD VERSE

S HE should have caught on sooner, Sayward told herself afterward, by the way Sooth was singing around the house all the time, and still more by the bloom on her face. Why hardly was she halfway through sixteen years old, and yet she looked like a tender white peony in full flower. But then, ever since she was a little tyke, Sooth had been a master hand for singing. And all Sayward's children were well formed and sightly, Huldah especially, though never could she match Sooth.

Sayward reckoned it just excitement coming out on Sooth. They were giving a singing play in Mechanics' Hall. An operetta, the handbill called it, "with music on the ancient Jewish cymbals and other instruments." Leah Morrison had got it up. The Thespians, they named themselves, and their show, A PLAY AT THE FAIR. Huldah and Sooth were both in it, but Sooth the most, and all day you heard her singing pieces from it. She didn't hold to her own pieces. Her voice was treble and Huldah's deep alto, but that didn't keep her from singing what Huldah had to sing, too. And she didn't stop there. No, she sang what the men had to sing, the high tenors and the low tenors, the baritones and the basses. Sometimes it sounded like she started at the beginning and sang the whole play clean through.

"Hush up, for God's sake!" Huldah would bawl at her. "I hear that most every night. Now I have to hear it all day."

Sooth's singing would shut up then. You'd think a song choked off like that would die, but it must have stayed alive bottled up inside of her. As long as she kept holding it in, you wouldn't hear anything. But the minute she forgot, the song came out of its own self and just about where she left off.

She didn't sing too much around the house for her mother. Sayward liked singing, though not all that passed for it. Once she was invited down to the Morrisons' to hear a lady singer from Cincinnati. Some must have liked it, for they clapped her over and over. But Sayward went home as soon as she decently could. She never liked screaming, not even if you had hurt yourself, and this lady hadn't. Now Sooth sang to please herself. For all she let on, nobody else heard her. It made no difference was she sweeping or hanging up clothes or taking them down or sprinkling them. Sayward held that nothing sounded so at peace with life as a woman singing to herself while she worked.

Tonight when a man called to take Sooth to practise, Sayward gave it no second thought. It would be strange if Sooth wouldn't get to know some men folks. Play practise had been going on for a long time. But that didn't mean such a man was sweet on her or that she would have him if he was. You could never tell the way it would go with a man and woman before marriage, and sometimes not afterward. There was Huldah and George Holcomb. Folks said the young iron master would surely have enough of a young girl who tried to get him by coming stark naked to his furnace house, claiming robbers left her that way. They said he'd be mighty careful after that to pick him some decent homebody to be mistress of his iron plantation. Yet all this time never had he taken a wife but had come courting Huldah instead. And still she wouldn't have him.

"Huldah, your beau's a riding up the lane!" Massey or Sooth would run in to tell her, but hardly would Huldah get giddy about it. No, let him come if he wanted to, she'd say, or let him stay away. Not too much notice would she take of him when he was there save to scorn or devil him in her heavy voice while her younger sisters sat around with bleeding eyes that she would treat a fine and handsome lover so.

Take tonight. All day Huldah knew he was coming this evening to take her to practise, that he drove four miles and crossed the river to get here, and would have to do the same going back. But do you think Huldah would get her flax work done so she could get off in time? No, all day she kept putting it off for one reason or another, for all

Sayward knew, on purpose to hold them up tonight and make him cool his heels. She was only in the last act anyway.

Now she sat on the bench in the kitchen, a carding the broken flax into rolls to spin on the big wheel. It was hot and tiring work and when George sat down alongside and tried to help, it didn't suit her. Closer he got and too close, for Huldah snapped like a bean. She took the candle and touched off the tow on the bench between them, and he had to jump from there in a hurry, for you can only work flax when it is powder dry. Up it went like gunpowder on Independence Day! Oh, how Dezia and Libby called out against her! She might have burned him and the house down besides. What's more, she burned up the tow. Sayward only smiled to herself. It was a good sign between them, she thought, and some day it would turn out all right, for never would George Holcomb give Huldah up when she was pert as she acted tonight.

It was late enough when Sooth got home. "Huldah still a practisin'?" Sayward was ready to say for greeting but Sooth stood in the door too long, letting in the cold, holding back in her own mam's house, mighty pretty in her long wrap that had been Huldah's, her white cheeks flushed. Then she moved in but she left the door open and Sayward saw somebody was a stepping in behind her. It was Captain Bernd, that eat-frog fellow who played the trumpet in the play piece.

"Mama!" Sooth asked her, and her eyes sparkled like outlights. Now what did that mean, Sayward wondered, and had it anything to do with this outlander from the coasts of Frenchland?

She turned to look at him. He had closed the door and stood by it, very stiff, his eyes polite, his boots blacked like his hair. She had to admit he cut a figure, especially for such a thick-set feller, in his dark green overcoat with a cape. She could ready see how a young girl might think it a lark to let such a one fetch her home. Especially when folks said he had been a soldier of Napoleon. He had been to Egypt and Russia with the great Bonaparte, they told. Now Portius hardly thought him old enough for that, and if he was, why wouldn't he talk on being there? It was because his emperor was beaten and disgraced, Sooth said, standing up for him. All the blood and dying, the ruin and exile, lay too heavy on his mind. Oh, that was something to move a young girl's pity to let him walk home with her on a cold November night, Sayward thought. But that was just as far as it should go.

"Is Papa home?" Sooth formed with her lips.

Sayward shook her head.

"He's not here," Sooth turned and told him with regret.

"Then I do your mother the honor," he said, nothing abashed, and you could hear the foreign saw or French locust in his tongue. He came up and gave Sayward a springy bow. Oh, you could see he had plenty of cheek and wouldn't be taken down easy. "Good evening, madame, I ask the honor of marriage with Miss Sooth?"

Libby and Dezia drew their breaths, but Sayward sat there like she was used to officers of the great Napoleon coming to seek her aid. Just the same, her mind ran fast enough. They must have been mighty thick with each other these nights at practise, she thought, for this to travel so quick. What did Sooth mean letting it go so far? Her eyes went to Sooth and there they halted.

There was out in Welsh Valley a family of brothers

named Griffin. All bachelors, they did their own cooking, washing, thread-spinning and weaving. They even sewed up their own clothes. They had a few fields of wheat and corn for bread, cows for milk and stands of bees for honey. In the winter two of the brothers burned charcoal to send to town. The other sometimes fetched in honey and a kind of apple he called the Summer Sweeting. Two or three times a year he would come along riding that two-wheeled cart of his, a blowing his long shepherd's pipe so any who wanted could come out on the road and buy.

All this year whenever Sayward heard Sooth come in the house singing, it minded her of the shepherd's pipe, and she would say to herself, "Here comes the Summer Sweeting!" But now she thought that never before to-night had she seen her so mortal fair with her pure blue eyes, her fresh white skin and light red hair. "So this eat-frog feller wants to take our Summer Sweeting!" she thought, giving him a black look. Why, never would he see thirty again, and Sooth no more than sixteen. He must have been behind the door when good looks were given out, while Sooth ever took your breath like Genny used to as a barefoot girl a running like a white-head through the woods. Why, little girls when they went by would stop stock still to see Genny like some white flower that sprouted from this black ground. But Genny had no red hair, and never had she quite come up to Sooth who hadn't been born or even thought of then.

"Mama!" Sooth reminded her.

"I heard him," her mother said mildly in her broadest woodsy accent so that he at once would see the worst of her. "I couldn't say right off. I'd have to talk it over with your pappy first."

Sooth looked at her quickly. Now what was in the back

of her mother's mind that she would say that? Why, her mother had her own opinions and would stand up for them in front of anybody. She didn't have to talk anything over with her father first. And never would she speak to one for another as she was doing now. This must be just to put him off, and to let her know that already she stood against their wedding.

Sooth was ever the one to wound easy. Her stricken glance flew to her suitor but all he did was bow as though her mother had spoken to him directly.

"I will wait till the next practise," he said. "Good evening, madame. Good evening, young ladies." He gave two more bows, stiffly, from the waist up. Then Sooth went out with him for a few minutes, closing the door behind her, and you could hear her whisper.

When she came in, Huldah and George were with her.

"Sooth's going to be married!" Libby cried before they had the door shut.

Huldah's face instantly distorted and darkened.

"Why, you young whipper snapper!" she said. "Who to?"

"Captain Bernd."

"That cheek puffer! When?"

"In December, I think — if Mama lets us."

"Why, that's next month!" Huldah declared. Her eyes had strange tongues of black venom for her young sister. "How is it you can't wait? It doesn't sound decent. People will think — "

"Huldah!" Sayward warned her sharply. "Don't say anything you shouldn't or you'll wish you hadn't."

Her oldest daughter stood there silent for a little but you could see the forbidden words working under her pretty skin.

[167]

"I thought you were cracked on a June wedding!" she jeered.

"December is a very nice month, Huldah," Sayward broke in calmly. "It's the month our Lord was born in."

Sooth had been standing there blanching. Now she threw her mother a blinding and grateful glance. It minded Sayward of the time Genny had done that. Louie had said he couldn't get a missionary to wed them here in the woods, and Sayward had said, "You might boat Ginny down the river. I don't allow she would mind." Oh, that blinding look that Genny threw her then Sayward never could forget any more than the one Sooth gave her today. It was as much to say, "I feared you were against me, Mama, but now I know that all the time you were on my side."

Huldah's black eyes didn't miss that look.

"So you think you could sneak in and get married ahead of me!" she told Sooth. "Well, you're not. I was going to keep it a surprise, but now I'll tell you. George and me are getting married next week. We made it out all along, didn't we, George? Tell her, am I telling the truth or not?" She turned on the startled young iron master who backed her up in every particular, but he looked much too pleased and thankful all of a sudden to have it go down with Sayward.

"Oh, Huldah!" Sooth stood there alive with pleasure. She ran up to her sister and kissed her. "I'm real happy for you, Huldah!" she said. She wrung George's hand. "You're getting my wonderful sister!" she told him. "And now you'll be my brother!"

Sayward could still see and hear her that evening when she made things ready for tomorrow's breakfast. Wasn't it just like Sooth to feel happier for Huldah than Huldah for herself? That was Sooth all over, blooming at night the same as by day. Early in bed in the morning, most girls looked sleepy and sulky, their skin washed out and their eyes sticky. But the minute Sooth woke up she lay there in bed like a fresh-opened daisy. Now how could Sayward trust a flower like her to this short-spoken soldier? Why, he was old and hard-wayed enough to be her pappy.

Wasn't it a pity it couldn't be Sooth and George, and the rough soldier and Huldah. Then never she need worry, for George with all his hard riding was tender and sweet as a young boy, and Huldah could handle any Great Nates who had slain men for his emperor. Why couldn't likes get married sometimes? Why always had opposites to pull each other? She reckoned it some wise plan of the Lord to keep the pretty from getting prettier and the homely homlier, the sweet sweeter and the mean meaner. But if so, the devil had spiked that way of the Lord. Little did those opposites know a standing up before the preacher promising to love each other till death did them part, little did they know what they carried inside themselves against each other. They might know the other's sweetness that pulled them together, but mostly hidden yet were their own differences that, like handspikes between two logs, would ever try to push and worry them apart.

Sayward went to the front room and undressed for bed. She felt relieved Portius hadn't come yet. There were matters pertaining to a girl child you couldn't easy talk over with a man. Especially if that girl child had been Sooth. Thank God she had outgrown it now, and could laugh at what once bothered her. But when she was a little tyke, never would she say her A B C's like her brothers and sisters. When she got to M she would start hurrying a little and say M N O Q R, slurring from O to Q so none might notice she let out the letter P, that being a coarse word she couldn't say in public. It was something like that in church when the preacher read some verse like the commandment, "Thou shalt not covet thy neighbor's wife, nor his man servant, nor his maid servant, nor his ox, nor his ass . . ." Libby's face might twitch, but Sayward used to feel Sooth's little form stiffen and tighten beside her. But the pitiful thing was the time Preacher Selin came to the house. He was a saint on earth if there ever was one. He looked like his whole face and frame were locked and his eyes saw the glory of the Lord a coming. Little Sooth sat on her young 'un's stool at his feet. When he went out after dinner, they tried to stop her, but she would tag after. Then she came a running back, all the light gone out of her small face.

"I told you he was goin' to the back house," Huldah jeered at her in her coarse voice.

"Mama!" Sooth whispered, pulling at her skirt. "Is it true, Mama? Does he have to go out just the same as we do?"

Oh, Sayward reckoned the light would go out of Sooth's face a good many times when she found out all you had to do in this life, married life in particular, and how men were. The same time, what sort of mam would she be to try and stop her? Not always could she be here to fend for her child, to try to save it from harm and hardship. Better had it find out for itself about life at the beginning than at the end. Your bones bent easier when you were young, and your flesh sooner mended. Once you were old, the marks that life gave stayed in your flesh a long time, and a right good bump could break your bones like pipe stems.

Long after Portius came home and slept by her side, Sayward prayed that God would guide her what to say about

Sooth. But make it real guidance so I can tell when it comes, she prayed, for she didn't believe in taking every stray sign and notion that came along and claiming it the hand of God. A lost person in a woods could find twigs pointing the way home in any direction it wanted to go, and even in the Bible the devil could find plenty verses to quote for his business. No, unless the Lord spoke to her strong and plain, she would fall back on her own good sense. That sense told her that the hand of the Almighty might be a little slow but it was more knowing than hers. Once she had reckoned to save Guerdon from life by tying him close to home. All that came out of it was spilled blood, and sending him away from home for good.

Oh, she would give a good deal to get this eat-frog feller alone out behind the barn and catechise him for thinking himself good enough for Sooth. And yet, who was she to do that? What woodsy had thought herself good enough for a Bay State lawyer, to make herself a wife to him and the mother of his children?

No, she daresn't complain, not even on a bitter cold night. Now she better try to get a little sleep before it was time to get up. But whoever heard of a summer sweeting ripe and picked in the winter time? Wasn't it pitiful how a mother raised a girl child, tended it loving for fifteen or sixteen years, and then before it was full-grown, some rough-handed man came along and spoiled it?

CHAPTER FIFTEEN

STANDING WATER

Here I sow hemp seed, hemp seed I sow.
Whoever wants me, come after and mow.

EARLY SETTLER CHILDREN'S GAME

Now that Chancey was at school, he didn't know if he liked it or not. Some days he'd sit at his desk blind to his book, reading the patch of window. If his heart hadn't got better, he told himself, he'd still be out there in the free air. Then if it wouldn't act up too much, he could drag around where he liked. Goods would be piled outside the stores, and the gold ball perched on the new court house roof. Hitching posts would stand to be tagged as you went by, and things in town would pull him this way and that, the boat yards, the loading docks and the Irish cemetery for those who couldn't be buried with other folks.

But the strongest call came from the canal, for the engineers were letting the water in for the first time today. As far as you could see, the big ditch ran, like a hill turned down and inside out. An army of Irishmen had scooped it out, cursing at the boys who threw stones at their clay pipes when they laid them up on the ground. Now they were gone and the ditch lay new and dry. But God help the dog or cat found in it when the water came down today. They were letting it in from the river. Oh, this would be a day to remember. Folks were coming from twenty miles to see boats floating where had been only dry earth before.

It was a high March day with the snow already gone and the ground warm in sheltered spots. Chancey had hoped they would let out school for the great event. But the master said they all had to come back after dinner. The master was a Yankee from Yale College, and the boys on their way home at noon yelled rebelliously an old round the boatmen used to jeer at the Yankee tavern keeper of the Seven Stars.

> He puts pine tops in his whiskey!
> And then he calls it gin!

Some of the boys went down to the river instead of going back to school, and Chancey tagged along. They headed for the Hollow Sycamore, for they daren't be seen along the canal. A holy feeling came over Chancey as they let him in. This was the mysterious pagan temple where men came on Sundays drinking and gambling. When the second bell rang, it sounded in here like a voice from another world, the world of the dead and imprisoned. On the academy grounds you ran like a rabbit to get in when the second bell sounded, but here it had no more power over you than a cow bell. Between the black-burned walls of this great hollow tree, you were a free man.

In fact, they were all free men now, taking turns at the corncob pipe Turkey Tench had stolen from his father. Chancey was the last to get it. He put the hard stem, still wet from the last smoker, in his mouth. Why, it wasn't hard to smoke. All you had to do was suck at the pipe. Wasn't it strange that such powerful tasting stuff could be soft as silk between your lips when you blew it out? He watched it float blue and delicate over his head and fought to keep the pipe till it rattled and went out. Something tasted bitter as gall in his mouth, but he daren't spit it out in front of the bunch, so he swallowed it.

Wasn't it a pity he couldn't do anything without getting sick, he told himself bitterly. It always used to be his heart. Now today it was his stomach. It must have been something he ate for dinner. The sunshine outside the tree was fading fast from the light of day, and all he could see of his companions were cloudy forms alarmed at the croupy sounds he made in his windpipe trying to catch his breath after puking. Waves of nausea swept over him. Oh, he had heard that this old sycamore was an evil place and that those who came here would have a bad end, but never did he dream it would come true so quick. Why, he had just got here, you might say, and this was the first time.

The boys helped him up the bank where he found himself stumbling on a littered porch while his stomach tried to turn inside out like an old umbrella in a storm. Suddenly all the boys around him except Turkey scattered like quail, and Chancey saw Rosa's mother in her wild matted hair standing inside the doorway. He didn't want to go in but Turkey pulled him.

"Can you do something for him, Mama?" he begged her. "He was smokin' grape leaves, and he's throwin' up all his toe nails."

Swaying and helpless, Chancey saw the horrible uncombed woman come toward him. She sniffed around at his face.

[174]

"Put him on a chair. He's green as a gooseberry," she said. "But he doesn't smell like grape leaves to me."

Sick as a dog, Chancey watched her go to one of the joists for tea, then the strong scent of some unknown herb filled the room. Never had the boy tasted anything so loathesome as the cup of brown liquid her claws pushed into his hands. It could be a poison for his heart, he thought as he sipped it, for she had warned him never to come near her house and Rosa again. Or it could be some witch's brew to turn him into a wolf or catamount, and then she could shoot him lawfully with the rifle that stood behind the door, and never could they put her in jail for it or even make her bury him. No, she could skin him and use his hide for a rug on this dirty floor, and the only time his father and mother and sisters would ever see him again would be when they came to watch this witch woman wipe her feet on him.

Could he have gotten out of it, he wouldn't have drank a drop, but she stood over him and he had to swallow it to the dregs. That was to make him surely die, he knew. Already he felt sicker from the vile stuff. Often had he wondered what it was people meant when they spoke of the point of death, but now his eyes found a double crack that looked like a butcher's knife on the plastered wall. Where the two lines came together for the knife's point, that, he told himself, was the point of death.

Wasn't it strange how when you were dying, things came to you clearer than ever before! Here he was half-way down to the grave, and yet he could taste the strangeness of this unfamiliar house as if it was in a cup and he had to drink it, the tick of the curious clock, the shape of these unaccustomed rafters, the litter of disarray and dirt,

[175]

the picture on the wall black with smoke and dust so that you couldn't tell if it was a cart or a camel; the cracked and broken plates and cups on the table, the coarse pewter, and shining among them, the slender shells of spoons that looked pure-spun silver, tooth marked and twisted.

But the most alien thing was Rosa's mother sitting here with him, her tangled hair falling over the soiled shoulders of her once fine dress with tassels. She was reading a book in the darkest corner as if she had owl's or cat's eyes. Right in the middle of all this dirt and disorder she sat at her ease, and in the middle of the day when women still had most of their work to do. You wouldn't reckon to look at her she could read a lick, but she'd turn the old page and suck out the meaning of the new like a bird pulling out a worm. Oh, a bird looked handsome enough on the wing, and soft as a ball of down on the treetop, but once Chancey had seen a hawk chained to its perch. Its face was fierce as a snapping turtle's, its eyes on either side of its beak a glitter and ready for the beak to strike. That's the way Rosa's mother looked at her book, like a stooped, round-shouldered hawk in an uncleaned cage, her head and neck feathers askew and disheveled; her brown back and clipped wings smutched and smirked like the filthy old shawl she had around her shoulders. Now why wouldn't she ever come out of this house, he wondered. All he knew was that boys talked of setting fire to the house some day, and then, they said, she'd have to come out. But they were too afraid of Jake Tench to try it.

Once while Chancey was sitting there, she spoke to Turkey, calling him Harold, in a mild voice. Why, never did Chancey know that Turkey had another name. To hear it said so fine astonished him. He looked to see if it could really be Turkey that his mother meant. She treated the others well enough, too, but when the door opened and Rosa came in, harsh words flew at her for staying so long. Now why did her mother feel so mean against Rosa, he wondered, for when she came in, the dark and dying world in Chancey's head lightened. The picture on the wall turned into no cart or camel but a dish of fruit with grapes and a ripe apple. The heavy close air sweetened, and when he saw it again, the knife cracks on the wall didn't come to the point of death at all but ended in a round button like Turkey's nose. His own leg that had grown numb with the sleep of death, he thought, began to waken and itch. He knew that Rosa had sat down and put her hands in her lap. Even with his head turned, he could feel her sitting still as a pin against the hostility of her mother.

Once her mother leaned forward over her book.

"What's your name, boy?" she put to him like she hadn't seen him before.

"You mean my real name?" Chancey stammered. "Or my other one? My real name's Ormsbee."

"Your real name's Wheeler," she told him sharply. "You are faithless and deceitful like your father. You think nothing of betraying hospitality and telling a lie. You can take your cap and go."

"Don't go!" Rosa made with her lips. "She doesn't mean it."

He stayed fearfully, ready to run if she came for him. After a while she sat back. The glitter went out of her eyes. She became wrapped up in her book again. What was in that book, Chancey wondered. The stained tassels of her dress would hang still for a moment and then faintly quiver or be violently shaken. He could not see her eyes. They were lowered on her book. When he could sit no longer and rose to go, she looked up, and her eyes gazed on him

with some ancient bitterness as from the pit. They gave
him the most unpleasant feeling. They would follow him
all the way home. He'd wake up tonight, and there they
would be, pitiful and accursed.

Rosa had stood up, too.

"Where do you think you're going, Miss Rosa?" her
mother asked.

"I want to see that Chancey gets home all right."

"You'll stay right here, Miss. He can get home by himself now. And he needn't honor us with his presence again.
He was welcome only in his illness."

But when Chancey got to the fulling mill, someone called
from down the side street and it was Rosa. She must have
gone out the back way and run around by the river.

"I wanted to tell you I dreamed about you last night,"
she said when she joined him.

"About me!"

"It was such a clear dream. I was wading in the water
and the water ran up hill. When I got to the woods, a fawn
came out and drank. You could see its sides go in and out.
So I knew it was afraid of me."

"Maybe it was just running fast and that's what made its
sides go in and out."

"No, it was afraid of me and it was you," Rosa told him.

"Why should I be afraid of you?" Chancey stammered.
"And how do you know it was me?"

"I could tell. You know how it is in a dream. A person
doesn't have to look like a person to be that person. Why
are you afraid of Mama? She wouldn't hurt you. We have
a picture of her painted on glass when she was young. She
has on a wonderful white dress with a fine black velvet
ribbon wound around her neck and down around her waist.
Her complexion is so fair and smooth, and she holds her

hands so you can see they're a lady's hands. They're white as milk. You wouldn't believe how beautiful she is."

In his mind Chancey could see her as Rosa described her, young and beautiful and clean so that men took off their hats when they met her on the street, and yet all the time this fresh young girl was going to be Mrs. Tench who never washed or combed and wouldn't go out of her house till she died.

"Why are you thinking of dying?" Rosa asked, watching him anxiously as they walked along. "Don't let's you and I ever think of dying."

Now how did she know that? he wondered, but all he said was, "You ought to take longer steps. Don't you know every step you take is one step less in your life."

She turned on him a sudden anguished face. Not another step would she take but sat down on the log curb.

"It's not true, Chancey?" she begged.

"I heard it's true," he said. "Maybe that's why your mother never goes any place."

"I must go back now," the girl rose and started away.

"Rosa, wait!" he asked her.

She didn't answer, only walked the faster.

"Rosa!" he called.

She didn't turn and now he knew that she wasn't going to.

"Goodby, Rosa!"

She lifted her hand as if to wave and then dropped it. She was almost running now, and Chancey stood there distressed, watching her go. Suddenly he became aware that she was taking very long steps. Even when she was only a speck, he could see her in his mind taking longer and longer steps till she was shut up in the house of that woman with the awful clouded and stagnant look in her eyes. And yet once upon a time she had been young and beautiful, Rosa said.

When Chancey reached the canal, the water was already in and the crowds had gone home. He stopped on the bridge, staring. He hadn't dreamed canal water would be slow and muddy like this. His father said they were going to let it in from the river. He thought that like the river, it would be bright and sparkling in the sun. Instead it was dirty and stagnant in its bed. Did canal water ever remember, he wondered, when yesterday it had run fresh and beautiful in the river?

CHAPTER SIXTEEN

HIS FATHER'S SIDE OF THE HOUSE

A word and a blow, and the blow first.
A FAVORITE SAYING OF JUDGE WHEELER

BOATS were ploughing the canal when Portius had it out with Sayward for a new house befitting their station.

"What's the matter with the one we've got?" she asked mildly.

"We're not in the woods any more," Portius reminded her. "We live in a growing young city. You're its largest landholder and I happen to be a leading lawyer and citizen. Don't you think we're entitled to more than a cabin to live in?"

"It's a double cabin," Sayward pointed out. He just stared at her blankly, and she went on, defending herself. "We don't need much room. Guerdon's off and Kinzie's in the navy. Resolve's married and so are Huldah and Sooth. That leaves five. By the time we'd get a house up, Libby might be married, too. That would leave only four."

"The devil plague you, Sayward! It makes no matter if they were all married. Don't you want a respectable place for yourself, if not for me? We're not savages. We've lived long enough in this confounded hole. It was useful in its time. Now it's served its purpose and should go to some canaler or millhand."

Sayward's eyes threw him a cruel whitish look. She could have reminded him what he lived in when she married him, a rough cabin of buckeye logs no bigger than a pigpen, far out in the lonesome woods where he saw no face but his own staring up at him from the run or heard a voice save his own croaking. But she would not throw that up to him. All she would do was show him that he might bamboozle a judge and jury with strong words, he could not her. Oh, she would take his every argument just and fair, but when it came to routing her from under her own roof, he might as well try to head off a gadd or talk down a whaup, as Worth used to say. Why, her father had built this cabin his own self. She had been married in it. All her children had been born between these walls, and now Portius wanted her to give it up and move to some fine new house, cold, bare and big, likely, as a church that never had the feel of living, cooking and sleeping, or of household stuff and creature comforts in it.

Her eyes mutinied and her lips got ropier, but never did she tell her true reason for not wishing to give up this cabin. It was deep down, a part of her flesh and bones, and hardly would Portius understand it, for he was of gentleman stock, used to riding and having things done for him from his youth. Now she was of common stock, a woodsy with Monsey blood in her veins, used to walking where she wanted to go and working with her own hands for what she got. Never did she believe in setting yourself up too high. Better keep your feet on the ground. Then you didn't have so far to fall, nor to get back up again. What's more, working for what you got kept your body stout and your mind sharp. But the main thing was that from down on the ground the whole world looked mortal fair above you. Bring up young ones humble and lacking in all save manners and school, and they had reason to work themselves higher. Raise them in a fine mansion house with all they wanted for the asking, and what would be the use working for anything? They'd have most everything already. Bring them up on top of the world, and they could only look down on the rest of it.

But if she had a secret she wouldn't tell, so did Portius, though she didn't know it then.

It was a warm spell in July when she found it out. In the old days seldom did they know what hot weather was in the woods, for the deep shade tempered even the dog days. Evenings in mid-summer were mighty cool and mornings fresh enough to make you shiver when you washed your face at the run. But now the run was gone, swallowed up by the canal. The woods were long since down and the sun drew the heat right out of the ground. You could look across open lots on a hot day and see it dancing in the air like fat from a griddle.

For some time lately she noticed that Portius stood a little straighter and nobler, like a pillar holding up his community. Always when sober had he carried himself with dignity, but now Genny told Sayward she met him downtown on the street only yesterday and he acted toward her like he didn't know where his own behind hung. Sayward wouldn't give into that. He couldn't have been nicer at the house. Of course he was full of sharp and shrewd sayings, of comic fiddle faddle and jawbreaking words. But ever polite if a mite puffed up. This noon he came up the new street for dinner like a ninety-foot hullhead a swinging up the canal. Sayward reckoned he must have walked off with some big case at court that had been hanging fire since spring, only she never heard of it. Neither would she ask him. He acted so munificent in his helpings to the younger ones at the table that he had no second helping left for himself, and she was at the fire frying him more when he spoke.

"Did I acquaint you, Sayward, with the death of my Aunt Unity near Boston?"

Sayward kept her face turned. Never had she even known that he had an Aunt Unity or any other kin for that matter, save the little George Roebuck had once told her. Indeed for all Portius let on, he had neither father nor mother but was born grown-up like a mushroom, nowhere in sight one minute, and the next, there it stands with the ground broke away around it under a buttonwood tree. She turned and saw him proud and pleased as Lowdermilk's hound bitch that reached her head in their oven and ate the roast.

"I feel sorry for you and your Aunt Unity," she said, sober, and added, "I'd reckon you'd be still more so, being it's your own flesh and blood, or at least by marriage."

His eye gave her that flicker of sharp respect it did at times when she caught him napping.

"I was indeed shocked and grieved at the time," he told her. "But I hadn't seen her for many years. Also, I've known of her death for some time — since February, in fact."

So he kept it back all this time, Sayward thought, turning the slice of ham she had for him in the long-handled pan. She let it rest on the coals while she got his plate from the table. The girls and Chancey sat with eyes glued on their pappy, ears big as pitchers. Neither had they known about the one who died though she was their own great Aunty. Sayward didn't mind it so much never telling her, for she was only a Luckett and a woodsy. But she shouldn't easy forgive him for not telling his children of their own blood relation. Right now Sayward saw how he held them all on tenterhooks as long as he could. Oh, he was the master hand for that, she thought, to get witness and jury under his thumb in court and then hold them spellbound, keeping back something they wished to know, bringing out some shocking or tantalizing words, then halting to let the meaning sink in before he said more, till you could hardly sit on the bench, they said, for excitement.

He buttered a piece of Sayward's baking to go with the ham.

"My sister and I happened to be the only heirs," he added, dry as dust for you didn't have to speak strong when you said anything like that.

His sister! Sayward thought. Now what might her name be? Although the girls and Chancey were done eating, none of them asked to be excused but sat there like plucked and skewered fowls ready to be basted. Were Huldah home, she would soon ask some questions in her coarse voice to get the rest of this out, but her sisters only waited.

"If you want to go back to Boston and see about it, Portius," Sayward told him, "we can get along."

"It won't be necessary, thank you, Sayward," Portius said. "My sister has put up Aunt Unity's house for sale. She has a comfortable home of her own, and there's little likelihood of us ever going to Massachusetts to live. She's also taken what pieces of furniture she wants and has shipped the rest to me."

Massey and Libby gave a little cry, but Sayward felt

[185]

grave. She was beginning to see where all this talk was
headed for.

"Out here, Papa?" Massey wanted to know. "How long
does it take?"

"Well, it was shipped from Boston by sea to New Orleans, and then up the Mississippi and Ohio."

"When did it go?"

"I'm not certain without looking it up," Portius told her.
"But I can tell you when it will get here. It arrived on the
Mary Bibb today, and I'm having it unloaded this afternoon and stored in Mr. Dyke's warehouse where I'm afraid
it will have to stay till your mother provides a lot for us to
build on."

Sayward looked at him without anger, but her face felt
dull and resigned as it had been that long time ago when
she found Louie a lying out in the woods with their Genny.
In either case, the deed was done and all she could do now
was make the best of it. Never would it be said about her
that she made her man keep his fine furniture in a warehouse because it had no room in her cabin.

She went ahead clearing the rest of the table.

"Had you any lot in mind?" she asked.

"I'm considering," Portius said, "the hundred foot lot
on the square across from General Morrison's. It should be
suitable for us."

So that's the one he wanted, Sayward thought, as she
soaped the dishes. He would put up no small house on that.
Oh, he could live with her thirty years going on forty and
never a hint of what dark secret sent him out here in the
western woods. He could read what letters came from his
folks and put them away in his lawyer's strong box, and
never a word spoken. But he could tell her mighty quick

what lot of hers he wanted, though it was the finest lot in Americus.

"A house on that would cost money," she mentioned.

"I intend to pay for its erection myself, Sayward," he promised.

"Well, I reckon your mind's made up."

"It is, thank you, Sayward," he told her. "The house shall be in both our names, if you desire."

Now what did he mean by that? she asked herself. Was it that she would have to pay half of the taxes?

After school Chancey went straight to Dyke's warehouse. They had his father's part of the canal boat unloaded already, but the girls were there chattering over the long rolls of burlap and the endless crates and boxes of every size. Chancey gazed speechless at one monster box bigger than Hector's stall in the stable. Their father said it might be Aunt Unity's piano. The girls complained that they couldn't actually see any of the furniture, but Chancey could see it all in his mind. What's more, he could see the house it came from back in the Bay State, much like the Forkville house he lay in at the time of the flood, the same red brick walls with imposing white stones under the windows. He could see Aunt Unity, too, when she was still alive, walking around her house, small, plump and sweet like the Forkville lady.

The only thing his father fetched home that night, was a high narrow box marked, "Miss U." in black paint. Inside the boards was burlap, and when they took off the burlap, there was the large painting of a grand lady in what Dezia called a heliotrope dress. It was Aunt Unity, their father told them, but she didn't look like Chancey's Forkville lady, rather like Papa. Everybody who came in

the house and saw it, said so, the same bushy hair and
fiery green eyes. She even sat on her chair like he did, noble
and firm. They hung the painting up on the front room
wall and whichever side of the room Chancey went to,
the eyes followed him.

That painting was the girls' pride. Sometimes Chancey
would sit there studying it and before he knew it, he would
be in the same room as the picture back in the Bay State.
There was something about that room he knew and which
made him feel at home. He wasn't sure if he liked it or not,
but it had the same feeling as his father, and likely the same
smell, too. He even thought he could hear Aunt Unity
talk and she talked like his father. He couldn't hear any
special words she said, but she gave sharp little cuts and
barbs like when his father said, "Your heavenly mother,
Juno," and like when he called country folks, Salt Creek-
ers, and their butter, sassafras butter. He had some things
he said over and over. If he didn't like a man, he would say,
"A pestilent fellow." On the other hand, if he looked up
to him, he might say, "Fear is a stranger to his bosom" or,
"Add to the courage of the lion, the sagacity of the fox."
"Give me a Jefferson or a Clay man," he would say, "never
a Polk, Jackson or Vanburen." Seldom did he "think,"
"reckon" or "suppose" like other folks, but was "sensible
of" or "entertained the notion" or was "profoundly penetrated by" or "had a fixed resolve." Never was he "down
in the mouth" but only "suffered my spirits to droop."

Did his great Aunt Unity talk like that, Chancey pondered, and did she tell stories like his father? For instance,
the one he told lately about Polly Becker of the White
Horse Tavern in Tateville. "Polly is the perfect tavern
keeper," he would say, "She's an especially clever cook.
She takes the bone out of every chicken so it carves easily

and beautifully at the table. She makes excellent bread in a special oven she uses for no other purpose. She's also good as a man behind the bar. But her pride and joy was the pure white steed on her tavern sign. Well, last month some of the young men rallied her about her sign. What did she mean calling her place the White Horse Tavern? they said. It ought to be called the White Mare Tavern, as anybody with half an eye could see. Let her come outside now and see for herself. That broke Polly's heart. She had to give in and call a painter to make the proper adjustment and now no one can justly criticize any more the name of the White Horse Tavern."

The ladies usually blushed and the men chuckled whenever his father told the story. Looking at Aunt Unity, Chancey wondered if she had liked to tell stories like that, dressed in her heliotrope gown and sitting in her fine parlor back in the Bay State.

CHAPTER SEVENTEEN

NOT LONG FOR THIS
WORLD

I hear a voice you cannot hear
Which says I must not stay;
I see a hand you cannot see
Which beckons me away.

T. TICKELL

Inscription in italics on
gravestone of Guerda Wheeler.

FOR a while when Portius wanted to take a dig at Sayward, he would call her Granny. But Sayward didn't
mind. Next to being a mammy would she be a grandmammy.

Her first grandchild was Resolve's and Fay's babe, named
Henry William after his grandfather Morrison. He was a
smart little fellow with a big nose from the day he was
born, and eyes that looked like they knew already what a
shilling was and how many silver levies and fips could be
cut from it. It wasn't long till he had a little sister they

called, Mary Leah. Then Sooth came along with the first
of her close-together brood. Oh, till her children got
through, Sayward was to be a granny a dozen times over.
She loved them all. Every last one was the apple of her eye.
The sun rose and set on one like the other, for she was
bound she'd be even-handed alike to children and grandchildren. But you couldn't always carry through what you
made out to do. Certain young ones had a way of crawling
unwanted in your heart like they did sometimes in your
womb. Now wasn't it strange that the least likely of all
should turn out to be her favor-rite?

The first time Sayward heard that Effie was having a
baby, she didn't know what to think. Knowing Effie, how
could she ever tell was this Guerdon's child or some other
man's, perhaps the one Guerdon had slain in bed with her?
Just the same she felt it her bounden duty to go out there,
for she owed only an extra debt to the child if Guerdon
had robbed it of its father. Besides, there was some small
chance that Effie had news from Guerdon. But Effie said
she hadn't a scrap of word from him, nor was she likely
to, and what was she to do now that she was to bear Guerdon's child, and how would she raise it without a father to
keep it in clothes and rations?

Sayward looked mighty sober. If Effie was having a baby
it must have a long time to go yet, for she gave not the
slightest sign. Also, it would be to Effie's advantage to have
the Wheelers acknowledge it as their own flesh and blood.
But the more Effie kept sniffling and claiming it Guerdon's
and the higher the stack of bibles she said she would swear
it on, the less stock Sayward took in her, though she said
nothing.

She thought from the fuss Effie made, she'd surely send
her word when the baby came. But no, not so, though

[191]

Genny fetched news that a girl child had been born to Guerdon's woman. Now why did Effie hold off letting her know? Sayward wondered. Genny said she heard the child was the image of somebody else than Guerdon, and that was likely why Effie didn't want Sayward to come out and see it. Sayward felt a strong temptation to take the easiest way and not go out at all. She had knitted a tiny jacket from her softest fleece for the baby. She could send that out with Dezia or Massey and make an end to it.

"Now this is enough holding back!" she flared at herself one day. "That poor little thing can't help who was its pap or if it was conceived in sin. I'm a going out tomorrow."

She'd have blamed herself all her life if she hadn't for when she got there and saw the babe, something went through her like the corncutter that sliced off Guerdon's finger. Had she seen that babe in Africy or the coast of Noraway, she'd have known it as her own flesh and blood. The tiny face and eyes had a stamp on them as plain as her girls' clothes hanging on their pegs in the cabin. It was a mighty pert and independent look peering out from inside that tiny skull, a certain knowing way that had been in her sister Sulie who got lost in the woods and in her own first girl child, Sulie, who was burned to her death running from the soap kettle. You'd think that would have been the last of it, but here that look had cropped up again in this bundle of flesh of the third generation. How it got here was a mystery and a wonder to Sayward. It must be that a look like hers could keep floating around in the blood-stream, first in one body, then in another, get carried around here and yon all these years, through cold and hot, sickness and famine, never getting lost in blood-letting or finger-chopping, coming all the way from old Grandmam Powelly who could say such spunky things when you'd least expect them back along the Conestoga in Pennsylvania.

The first thing flew into Sayward's mind was the fear that by some mischance Effie might call her Sulie. Guerdon must have told her the stories of what happened to his aunt and sister and Effie might think to please the Wheelers by giving the child that name. Sayward didn't believe in signs and superstitions, but just the same twice had the name turned up unlucky in her life time. Where there were two, her mother always said, there'd be three. Besides, what would be the use saddling a bad-token like that around a helpless little girl-child's neck when there were a thousand names in the world to pick from, sound and hearty names like Sarah, Betsy and Susannah, and fancy names like Rosemary, Jobyanna and Heleneor. It made her feel good when Effie said she was calling her Guerda.

Now wasn't that a nice name, Sayward told herself on the way home. Effie had surprised her. She'd have to give her credit for more sense from now on. Guerda after Guerdon, she repeated to herself. It sounded real good and clever. When she was a little bigger, they could call her Guerdy for short, like they called Guerdon pretty nearly up to the time he was married.

That name, Guerdy, fetched back a lot of water that had gone over the dam.

"Oh, Guerdon, where are you?" something inside her cried out. "Don't you know you're a pappy now! Come on home, for your babe needs you."

Every night since he run off, she had worried for him. Around Americus where most folks knew and liked him, he did tolerably well. But how would it go in a foreign place where folks wouldn't give a hait for the stranger? He might go without rations and nobody would know it. If he

got sick, who would there be to nurse him? She had felt
bad enough when Kinzie left with government men to look
after him and always tell her where he was. But who would
look after Guerdon or write and tell her where he was at,
for Guerdon himself was never one for schooling or his
letters.

"Wherever in these United American States you be,"
she called to him in her mind, "come on home, for what
you wanted has come to pass. You needn't linger in jail.
Your pappy and Resolve are good lawyers. They will get
you lawfully out. No twelve men good and true will ever
send you to the gallows."

But the days passed, and never did the stranger coming
up to the door turn out to be the babe's father, nor his face
appear among the crowd on Water Street. The only time
she saw him was in her dreams, and then he was ever a
small boy, quarreling with Resolve and Kinzie. Now why
did she never dream of him grown up? she wondered. Did
it mean he was a man deprived of life? No, it couldn't be,
for in her heart she felt him still alive, although in which
direction, whether on the prairies of Iowa, or in the back
settlements of Missouri, or east in the old states, or some
other place far from the law, the compass needle of her
heart would never point.

She was only thankful now for the small part of him he
had left behind. From almost the first, Sayward took out
for Guerda all of Massey's baby clothes. When she was one
year old, she was fetched on a visit to the Wheelers, and
after that she was at her Grandmam Wheeler's as much as
she was at home. It wasn't Guerdy any more but Gerty.
Even Portius was taken with her and liked to rally her at
the table. Ever she had a sharp pert answer waiting for him
on the end of her small tongue. When Sayward saw her

outside running, bobbing, dancing, going back and forward like her Sulie used to do, such a feeling came over her for the little form that she could hardly bear it. She wished that when Effie first complained about raising her that they had taken her off her hands, but the Clousers wouldn't think of giving her up now.

Sayward fretted somewhat the life the tot had to live in Fishtown. To offset it a little, she took her along to church whenever she could and had Dezia tell her Bible stories. Then she wished she hadn't. One Sunday Preacher Harbaugh preached fire and damnation against women who paid too much attention to frills and ruffles on their dresses when what they should wear was the humility and meekness of the Lord's commandments. The next morning Libby caught Gerty on the loft with the big shears and Libby's best dress. She was cutting off the ruffles and bows, and fought like a bobkitten to hold on to those shears.

"The Lord don't want no fancy fixens on your gown!" she kept hollering. "And I'm a going to cut them off like He said."

Oh, you didn't know whether to laugh or cry to see and hear that small tot in a white apron that came down within two inches of the hem of her red dress, with pantalettes coming down farther, with barred stockings striped around in rings and scarf hanging loose behind, telling Libby what kind of dress the Lord wanted.

Another time Sayward missed her at the house and thought of the canal. She ran down, and there the tot was on the tow path, leaning far over the water so all you could see were her chubby legs and little fat behind. She was, she said, sailing ships on the Red Sea.

"Now I don't want to find you down here alone again," Sayward told her on the way home.

"Did you fret about me, Granmam?"

"Well, I felt a mite uneasy."

"Did you reckon I'd fall in?"

"No, I didn't all-the-way reckon so. But I knew a little girl once that fell in the river, and when they pulled her out, she was a gone Josie."

"Oh, you needn't worry about me, Granmam," she bragged. "Somebody looks after me."

"Who?"

"Somebody you never saw," she said mysteriously.

"Well, I didn't see anybody around. He better stay closer so he can keep an eye on you."

"Oh, you could never see him, Granmam. It's an angel takes care of me." She said it so big that Sayward looked down stern.

"Well, I hope he's strong enough to pull you out if you fall in," was all she said.

"It's a lady angel," Gerty corrected her.

Sayward said no more about it. Was it last Sunday or Sunday before, she mused, that Preacher Harbaugh had a sermon about Elijah and how the angel of the Lord took care of him? If Elijah had an angel to look after him, she reckoned, Gerty would have one, too. But wasn't it just like Gerty to go Elijah one better? Elijah could have his man angel. She would have a lady angel.

Angel or no angel, Sayward kept a wary eye on the little tot after that. But none of them paid much attention to the strange things she said, save to laugh over them; and sometimes to cry. One evening they were having a birthday party for Libby. That afternoon Effie came in to take Gerty home. Libby said she'd bring Gerty up to Fishtown next day, but Effie wouldn't have it. The more the child cried and carried on to stay, the more stubborn Effie got.

There were no two ways about it. Grandmam Clouser was coming back from a visit and Gerty had to be home.

In the end, the child went in tears to the front room to give her Grandpappy Wheeler goodby at his desk.

"You better kiss me good, Granpappy," she said. "Because you won't never see me again."

"Are you moving away?" he asked in surprise, not knowing any of the talk in the kitchen.

"Yes, and a mighty far place from here," she let him know.

"When are you going?"

"I daresn't tell. It's a secret," she said. "But it's pretty soon, they told me."

Portius came along out to the kitchen to ask Effie where they were moving. Effie said angrily it was one of Gerty's notions, that there wasn't a particle of truth in it, and Sayward for once was inclined to agree with Effie, for she noticed that Gerty gave goodby to none of them save Portius.

That was a Thursday. Friday night a week, Libby came in and said she heard Gerty was down with a throat distemper. Early Saturday morning Sayward killed a chicken, dressed it and put it on to boil. Right after noon dinner she took a kettle of hot broth and some of the white meat out for Gerty. She took Massey along. When they got to the Clouser shack, Gerty lay in bed reading out loud to some neighbor children from the book her Grandpappy Wheeler gave her last Christmas. Oh, she could hardly tell one letter from the other, though you would hardly know it to hear her read. She knew that book by heart. But she threw it away quick once she saw who was there.

"I won't be sick long, Granmam," she promised. "The angel said I could get up Sunday and run out." But though

she tried hard, she couldn't drink any of the warm broth.
She claimed her throat wouldn't let her swallow.

"Why don't you eat it, Mam?" Effie said to her fat and
grinning mother. "It's a shame to let that good white meat
and soup spoil and go to waste." If Sayward ever begrudged
anything, it was to see that huge and sloppy old woman
take the cud of snuff from her mouth and sit there sucking,
smacking and grunting over what was meant to bring a
bit of strength and recovery to a small ailing child.

The girls and Chancey came in that afternoon to see
how Gerty was getting along. They said Portius had been
called to Tateville and wouldn't be home till some time
tomorrow. Sayward had intended to go along back with
them, but something Gerty did stopped her. Oh, the tot
was pleased as a puppy with two tails having her young
uncle and aunts come all the way up here just to see her,
and when they went she said she had presents for them.
To Libby she tried to give her Job's tears, to Dezia her
button box, to Massey her spoon wagon and to Chancey
her medicine which she said she wouldn't need any more.
Now why did that make Sayward uneasy? She told them
they could go on home. She would come later.

She didn't go after supper either. Oh, she never saw a
sick and wasted child with more signs of getting better.
She kept chattering away to her grandmam, and when
Sayward said it would be better for her throat if she kept
still, she rapped out tunes with her knuckles on the headboard and had her grandmam try to guess what they were.
And yet Sayward stayed. She told Effie and Granmam
Clouser they could lay down and get some rest if they
wanted. She would stay up with Gerty and sleep on a
chair. And that's what she did, taking a short nap now and
then.

About ten o'clock when it was time for the medicine, Sayward got the candle from the mantel. But when she fetched it close to Gerty, she stopped short. A power of sweetness, like a master secret, had come out on the child's face, and that was something Sayward hated to see worse than any rash or pox. More than once had she seen that look before, and never had she known it to be long for this world. She went straight to Effie to wake her up and send her for the doctor.

"If the new doctor can't come, get the old," she said. "Tell him I'm here and that I'll pay for it."

About eleven, there was the sound of a gig, and it was Effie with Dr. Pearsall. He came in the room, a slow Old England man, greeting Sayward with respect, paying no attention to the fat and chattering Grandmam Clouser. Sayward watched him and didn't like what she saw presently in his good eye. Some folks wouldn't have him, complaining he had been a king's man and lost that eye as a boy on the wrong side of the Revolution, but that didn't matter to Sayward if he could help Gerty. He still wore his clothes old style like Col. Sutphen and a few others. His hair, long and silvery, hung tied with a ribbon. He ordered Effie to pull a chair by the bed for him like she was a servant. But to Gerty he was kindness itself. When she couldn't swallow his powder, spilling the white foaming water on his coat sleeve and the bed clothes, he never reproached her but sat the chair by her side like a magistrate, his legs crossed, his single eye fixed on the small face, one hand on the smaller pulse, the other regularly switching his long queue. Now and then his white fingers would feel and knead the child's neck. Then they would go back to the pulse and queue again.

Sayward had no idea an hour had passed when he turned

on her in the candle light a face that told her what she must know. Suddenly the clock struck twelve, though you had to count fast to tell it. Sayward remembered with a touch of horror what Gerty had said, that on Sunday "the angel" said she could get up and run out. A curious shiver ran up her backbone. Could it be there was any truth in this wild talk of Gerty's about an angel? Other things she had given no thought to at the time swarmed in her mind, like whenever she sent the child on an errand, Gerty would ask so serious, "What will you do, Granmam, when I'm not here to help you?" And the time a canaler told her how the small tyke cried to his boy not to beat the poor mules so. The boy told her to mind her own business, but she stood right up to him and what she preached, he said, was good as a sermon. She called him a sinner but said she'd ask the Lord to forgive him when she went to Heaven.

Sayward could tell nothing from the doctor's face now, but the switching of the queue was going slower and slower. After while it stopped, and Dr. Pearsall laid down the small wrist.

"Oh, Guerdon!" Sayward called silently from the depths of her heart. "It's no use to come back now, for you have no babe asking about her pappy any more."

The sun was coming up when Sayward made her way home, but her face stayed set and cruel. A good many had she known who had to die, but never anyone who made such small fuss as Gerty did, like she was just going on a visit. Was she really out of her sick bed now, Sayward wondered, a running and playing like she claimed the angel had said? Maybe she was, but though Sayward looked hard, never had she seen her get up and run out the door or rise to heaven either. Save when her grandmammy's loving hands straightened the tiny limbs and closed the worn eyes, the scanty body never moved. Hardly did it used to take a lick of muscle for that small body to lift itself up. Yet now it lay almighty still. Just the same, if it wasn't true what Gerty told about the angel, it was the only thing that wasn't. Now how did she know that Portius would be called up to Tateville? He didn't know it his own self when Sayward left home yesterday afternoon and yet way back last week Gerty had said, "Now you better kiss me goodby, Granpappy, because you won't see me again."

CHAPTER EIGHTEEN

THE MANSION HOUSE

The last button off Gabe's coat.

OLDTIME SAYING

THE ROOF was up and the bricks laid out for the most part when Portius had enough of building himself a fine house and paying for it, too. He never said so. He had to go argue a case at an appellate court and couldn't tell how long it would drag on. At least, that's what he claimed. Then the legislature was naming a new justice for the county, he said, and Fred Godwin, the senator from Tateville, wanted him to make the legislators' acquaintance. Would Sayward look after his house-building while he was gone?

"Why don't you get Oliver Meek?" she wondered. "He's put up a good many houses."

"It would be an imposition," he said shortly.

"Well, how about Resolve? You wouldn't have to mind asking him."

"Resolve's too young and inexperienced to cope with such matters."

"He's thirty years old. You can depend on him."

"Not like I can depend on you, Sayward," he said and gave her such a good sociable smile it minded her of the night they were married. She couldn't refuse him then. Nor could she now, though by today she knew him backwards and forwards, his fine ways, his good points, and his Yankee tricks.

But she didn't know what she was in for this time till he had gone. Every day she put off going over to the house. Gowan was a master carpenter and no one had put up finer houses in Americus and Tateville. He took care of most everything, Portius said, drawing the plans, writing the bills of lumber, making contracts with masons and plasterer and overseeing their labors. None could handle a T square or triangle like he could, but his crew of journeymen carpenters did the work. His wood carver had been busy all summer on the fine Pennsylvania pine that came down the Ohio for the doorway and chimney pieces. Gowan showed him what to do. All there was to know about putting up a house, Gowan knew, Portius claimed. Gowan's word was good as his bond. Then what was the use, Sayward asked herself, of her going over?

So she waited till he came to see her, a broad man of great dignity, in a striped cotton coat, his face red against his white hair as service berries in the snow. He lifted his hat with honest respect at the door.

"I am loathe to trouble you, Mrs. Wheeler, but would you come over to the house?"

"Well, I wouldn't know what use I'd be," she told him. "But I'll come if you want me."

"It will do the journeymen good to see you take an interest," he said with great relief. "They complain they'll never get their money."

Sayward took a quick gulp and swallowed it.

"Are you saying the men are back in their wages?" she put to him.

"Not too far, Mrs. Wheeler," he said like it had to be dragged from him with horses. "Mr. Wheeler said you would make everything right when you came."

Sayward stood so quiet, never would you guess the bump she had had inside of her.

"I guess maybe I better come over and look at it right away," she told him. "You can expect me some time this morning."

So that was it, she told herself as she started up the new street. That's what she got for thinking to mind her own business and stay out of other folks' doings. All this time had she kept clear of Portius's house, for she heard enough about it from the girls and from visitors to her kitchen. Of course, she couldn't help seeing the brick walls heaving up when she went that way. She could tell it was no cabin or shanty that Portius was putting up, but she had no notion how big it really was till she came up Wheeler Street today and saw it standing in front of her on the square like Captain Loudon's brick mansion house when she was a girl along the Conestoga. Only the Loudon house stood flat on the ground while Portius had set his up high and proud. It would take many a step to reach that big front door, though now all they had was plank running up from the ground.

She hated real hard to turn in and go up that mortar-encrusted gangway. The house seemed a monster roofed shell, owning neither doors nor window lights. All stood open to wind and owls. The sight of broad vacant floors and bare high walls, the stink of wet plaster, the great lack of things still to be done and paid for before you could live in here fazed her. But she made herself tramp with Mr.

Gowan from one big empty room and floor to another. It looked like they had more room than the court house with the jail thrown in. What in the name of the white-whiskered man did Portius want with all this living space? He wouldn't, she knew, let her rent any of it out. Why, if she was a little tyke she'd have to watch out or she'd get lost in here. Oh, her eyes looked close at what the carpenter pointed out. She listened sober to all he told her, of sash and blinds, of shutters and baseboard, of door and window jambs, cornice gutters and scuttle, of back stoop and front stoop and sloping cellar door. But all the time in her mind she was reckoning how much Portius's grand house would cost her.

"I can't tell you exact," Gowan said at the end when she asked him. "But I can give you an idea."

"That'll have to do then."

"You expect to finish it, don't you, Mrs. Wheeler?" he asked and looked at her like a grandsire begging for the life of his grand littling.

"I can't rightly tell you till tomorrow," Sayward said. "But you'll have to tell me today."

Not till then did he draw from his back pocket his Master Builder's Price Book and Estimator bulging with ciphering.

Well, she got what she asked for, she told herself on the way home. That's the way it went sometimes. Run through everything you had. Let little in at the spile and all out at the bung! Make common folks point when they went by and say, "That's Lawyer Wheeler's fine house." Make tony folks a little less proud when they came calling, a climbing marble steps to a hall wide enough to drive a four horse wagon through and stairs running up and up like they went to a church belfry. Wasn't it curious, Sayward thought, how some folks had to bamboozle other folks with the clothes they wore or strike them all in a heap with the grand house they lived in!

When the rest were in bed that night, Sayward took out what bank notes she had put away between the logs behind the chinking. Under the hearth stone she took up her old kettle with a hole but heavy with gold and Spanish silver. She counted standing by Portius's desk table, summing up what she had in the bank and out with folks on interest. Oh, she had plenty to make buckle and tongue meet, and that didn't count her land leased and unleased. What went against her so hard was putting so many bells on one horse, squandering for something she didn't want in the first place and would have to live in against her will in the second. Neither did she take kindly to the Yankee way Portius had fastened it on her, running off without opening his mouth. She had no notion he had used up all his Aunt Unity's money. Likely he would get still more when her house was sold. No, he had put in what he reckoned was his half of the house. Now she could put in the other half, for wasn't she going to live in it the same as he would? That must be the way he figured.

She stayed up a while reckoning this thing out, casting up one side against the other. In the end she put back the kettle and went to bed. The mansion house was too far built to give up now, unless you didn't want to look folks in the eye any more. No use fretting all night. The more you cried, the less you had to pee, as Granny MacWhirter used to tell the young ones. If Portius wouldn't pay his honest debts, she would have to, a little slowly perhaps, one at a time like lawyers went to heaven. And if it took all she had to lay her hands on, she'd have to spit on them and take a fresh holt.

Portius came home in a fortnight, but the house took nigh onto two years to finish. The staircase alone swallowed up four months with its treads, risers, posts and handrail. Oh, Portius was back home a good while before the house was done, but never did he take over again. He had no time, now that he was a judge, he claimed, looking at her when he said it like he wanted her to see what his fine house had brought him already. He acted like he was glad enough to let her bear the brunt, now that she couldn't strike down any of the walls or rooms but would have to accept them without mutiny.

Sayward let him shirk, satisfied to do the rest to suit her. The woodwork inside and out she had painted white. It would take more dusting and scrubbing to keep clean, but Gowan told her this was the color Portius wanted. In those matters Portius had been unwise not to speak to Gowan about, she used her own good sense, choosing the plainer when Gowan assented and fetching in Fay and Resolve for their opinion when he didn't. Oh, Gowan was a great help on one hand and a thorn in her side on the other, knowing all the fine houses he did and how they had been built inside and out. "Now in the Maclay house in Pennsylvania," he would say, or "If I could show you General Gregg's house in Kentucky. . . ." Little by little she let herself be pounded or cajoled into wall paper and mortise locks, inside shutters and plenty other things she did not know much about but had to put in for Resolve, Huldah, Sooth or Gowan even though they would not live there.

The moving she put off till the very last. The truth was she hated to leave the cabin. Most of her life had she lived here. Now she would have to give it up for a place where it looked like she was putting on airs, thinking herself better than ordinary folks. The last day she kept looking about the cabin. How many times had she stood at the fire with her long-handled pan, or gone down on her knees of a morning to puff at the coals. This ladder and those steps, how often had she climbed them when one of the young ones lay abed ailing. Why, forty years of her life had she spent between these log walls. And now she had to go and leave them.

Welly Palsgrove and his one-horse wagon helped her move. Yesterday was the first Portius claimed to have been in the new house since it had doors and windows, and he couldn't get done praising how well she finished it. Today when she and two of the girls got to the square with their first wagonload, a heap of boards and crating lay in the front yard.

Massey came running out, her pigtails flying.

"You ought to see, Mama!" she cried. "Papa has all Aunt Unity's things in!"

Libby and Dezia raced ahead, but Sayward stayed behind with Welly to help him lift off and carry in. Just the same she couldn't help seeing when she got inside. A noble hat-rack, table and settee stood in the wide hall, and through the door to the room Fay always called the front parlour she had a look at stylish chairs and sofas with fine cloth seats and backs, and small shiny tables with curved legs. Rugs lay this way and that on the boards. Upstairs, when she and Welly got there with her cherry bedstead, she found beds already set up in both front bedrooms, one of yellow maple and one of some tony red wood, both with high posts. The girls were hanging up the curtains. Dower chests lay under two windows. Standing around were rush-bottom chairs and small rockers, bureaus and what Mrs. Morrison called highboys. This room she looked in had something else, like a massive redwood chest of drawers

save for the slanting top which opened to the length of a
chain, showing it a desk with red pigeon holes, the writing
part stained by blobs of black ink.

"What do you think of it?" she heard Portius ask, and
there he was behind her.

"Well, I ain't had much time to think about it yet, Portius," Sayward said. "It looks real grand though, I must
say."

"I thought I'd take this room and you could have the
one across the hall," he told her. "These are Aunt Unity's
best beds." His eyes fell on what she and Welly had fetched
up, the heavy headboard of the bed that had seemed so
fine and served them so long and faithfully in the cabin.
"Don't you want to take that up on the third floor for one
of the children?" he asked.

It came over her then and as she went on fetching in
her other things how poor and puny they looked here beside Aunt Unity's. Why, she thought she had half forgot
she was a woodsy, but this made her feel like one of those
sassafrac folks from out in the brush fetching her poor
traps in a fine mansion house. It was really her house as
much as Portius's, for hadn't she built and paid a good half
of it? And yet she found no welcome between these fine
plaster walls or among the rich Wheeler trappings. Always
had she seen a little Monsey blood in her pappy and Achsa,
but this was the first time she felt it stand out in herself.

Dog tired as she was, it went hard to fall asleep in Aunt
Unity's bed that night, lying like a corpse at a wake, she
thought, between the polished posts like mourners holding
some net over her so her flesh would not be fly-eaten. She
felt so far off the floor. Even when the gentry lay down to
sleep not knowing if they'd wake or not, they had to hold
themselves high and mighty as possible. She would hate to

THE TOWN

have the old time friends and neighbors she knew in the
woods see her pranked out at night like this. Saird has
changed, they would say. She has forgot how naked she
came into this world and in company with what worms she
has to go out.

When Sayward first woke up next morning, she had to
lie and think for a lick where she was. It came in her head
next how on both sides they had strange folks lying in bed
the same as they and so close she could throw a stone at
them. She got up mighty quick then and went down the
back stairs. It was hardly daylight, but that was all the better, for those on either side would not be out yet. She
would have given a good deal to be back in the cabin, but
she was only thankful she had a kitchen here. It helped her
to start a fire and feel her own pots and pans in her hands.
Here with the smell of mush and coffee over the fire, she
believed she could come when she got homesick and find
relief.

They reddied up the house pretty well the next few
days. Saturday about supper time it started to rain, but that,
she noticed, didn't keep Huldah and George, and Sooth
and Peter with little Sairdy from coming over. Afterwards
Genny and Will came in the back way while Resolve and
Fay came the front, without Henry and Mary Leah who
had a nursemaid to look after them. Something was up,
Sayward knew, but she reckoned it only a kind of house
warming. Not till she saw this man at the door in reddish
sideburns very wide at the bottom and in the high choking
collar and multiple buttons of a junior officer in the navy
did she guess.

"Kinzie!" she called out in that strange hollow voice
she'd heard her mother use when she was so beat out. Then
she stood like a stump while he came over. She felt her

knees tremble. Could this grown-up officer who held himself so easy and strong be the freckle-faced boy that rode east on horseback those years ago and had been all over the world since! Now how could he have got here at such a good time? It must be the girls and Portius had been keeping him posted, for he landed the first week they were in the new house. Before he reached her, his navy face broke into a freckled grin, she saw the tooth she'd know anywhere and felt the water run from her eyes as she hugged him. But only half that water, she knew, was for him. The rest flowed for his brother who wasn't here at all, and God Almighty alone knew where he was or whether still among the living.

"So this is Massey!" Kinzie said, swinging her up. He hadn't seen her since she was a little tyke or Chancey since a tot in a red plaid skirt that had come down from Libby to Sooth to Dezia and none of them could wear it out. To Massey he gave a kiss, but he only twisted Chancey's weak arm, giving a funny look at his spindly legs and the scraggly nape of his neck as if to say, is this little old feller who can't make the riffle and looks scared of his own shadder my brother?

Oh, Chancey felt himself shrink at that look. But if Kinzie didn't think much of him as a brother, Chancey didn't reckon him a brother at all. Under his navy officer clothes and ways, he was just like the rest of the Wheelers, made of some everlasting mortal stuff that never tired or flinched, never gave up or wore out. You couldn't miss that certain quality tonight now that they were all together again, talking at once, running over with vitality, each a glut for punishment, quick to go on their lip or muscle. Just to sit quiet among them drained Chancey like a sieve. He didn't mind hearing it was past his and Massey's bed time.

Up in his room on the third floor, he could still hear what his father called the Luckett Indian whoop. It was just energy and enthusiasm that came out at times like this. It spoke a great many things, surprise, anger, scorn, disbelief, congratulation, amusement or just enjoyment of life, as they whooped tonight when they saw a boyhood friend catch his first sight of Kinzie since he was back.

A new sound fetched Chancey out of bed and into the hall. Faint light came up the third floor stairs and a rich sound with it. Somebody was touching Aunt Unity's piano. The boy leaned over the bannister. He could look down the deep well of stairs to the reddish whale-oil light in the hall. He could see a green strip of carpet, the edge of the table and settee. It might be Fay showing Sooth how to play, he thought. First would come sure rich notes, then after a little, slower and less certain ones. If that was Sooth, she was catching on fast. The sure hands played again. They ran among strange keys and worked out chords that made Chancey stand stock still, his bare toes gripping a bannister post. He held his breath trying to hold his emotion. The music changed to another part, came back to the first part again. Just as it reached the most beautiful part of all, the talk, that had been going on all the time, broke out in shouts and laughter, drowning out the piano. The desecration angered the boy. His heart filled with blackness and oaths.

His toes loosed from the railing. After a moment, he went back in his room and closed the door.

When everybody had gone home, Sayward finished the girl's work in the kitchen and went to bed. Even with her door open to the hall, she felt pretty much alone. It seemed so far from Kinzie and everybody else in this big house.

In the cabin they all had lived and slept close together. But she might as well get used to it. For the rest of her life, this would likely be her lot. Portius was willing enough for her to sleep alone for style's sake now, though he had raised sand when she had done the same thing in the cabin. She set a spool under one of her windows and went to bed. Gowan had made these walls tight as the bottom of a new kettle. It seemed town folks thought the night air poisonous and wanted to keep it out. But she slept out many a night, and it never hurt her. Poison or no poison, she liked the night air, such as used to sift through the chinking of the cabin.

She thought they had been up late tonight, but it seemed like other folks were up later. Lying there she could hear the voices of a company of people coming down the square. The talk grew pleasantly nearer. Now they were going past the house and now stopping at a door beyond where some of the party lived. "Goodnight! Goodnight!" the voices called back and forward. "Pleasant dreams! We had such a nice evening!" More things were called as the rest of the party went on. A half dozen houses away a man thought of something else to shout back. It sounded like John Quitman. Oh, that was a pleasant thing for a lonesome body who lived most of her life in the woods and fields to hear. Only those who knew what it meant not to see a strange face from one season to another could appreciate how sweet was the music of human voices. She took after her mother's side and liked the feel of other folks around, although that didn't mean they had to live right up against you. Across the field or through a patch of woods would be close enough, just so you could see the smoke of their chimney and hear them call the dog, cows or young ones.

Now wasn't it a shame, she thought as she went to sleep, that little Gerty hadn't lived long enough to visit here. She'd have company then, for Gerty always loved to sleep with her grandmam. Her warm voice and running feet would take up some of the slack and coldness in this house. That's what the place needed. It wouldn't seem so empty and useless with a lively little body around, if only for a few months of the year.

CHAPTER NINETEEN

ROSA HAS TO BE
HERSELF

"You didn't e'er a thing," she said under her breath.
"Did you think you heard something a-callen?"

ELIZABETH MADDOX ROBERTS

T HE TENCH house stood along the river like a box with
two or three uneven windows, a roof of black shakes
above, and a dark slab fence around it below.

All evening in that house Rosa had the tight, stretched-
out feeling she always had before her father came. It had
started today about four o'clock when Mr. Higgins, the
man in Oliver Meek's store, put up the sign on the sidewalk.

TO RENT

By that, Rosa knew her father's boat was tied up in the
basin, though he wasn't home as yet. This kind of thing
had been going on for a long time. Whenever her father
got too far back in the rent, Mr. Higgins would put up
the sign, always the same one. Her father wouldn't see it

when he first came home. That usually happened late at night, and, besides, when he was drunk he took no notice of signs. But the next day when he went out of the house and saw it, the sign would make him mad. He'd curse terribly, pull it out by the stake and throw it down the river bank. But he would never break it or hurt it. Sooner or later he would scrape up the money to pay Mr. Meek the four dollars a month back rent he owed him. After while Mr. Higgins would come up and get the sign and take it back to the store. He knew just where on the river bank to look for it, and he never got mad like Rosa's father.

The rain reached the house tonight long before her father did. A little while after supper she had to take the big jar and pan up in the loft where the roof leaked and go up now and then to empty them in the bucket before they spilled over. She could tell downstairs by the sound whenever one was getting close to the top. The pan always got full first, and if she didn't watch out, it would run over the loft and down in the room. Oh, it wasn't a favor that she didn't have to go to bed but could sit up late tonight watching her mother read. Her mother was a wonderful reader. You never even saw her lips move. Every two weeks or so, Rosa had to go down to the back door of the Phillips' house to take one book back and get another if Mrs. Phillips had one to give her. Most times the maid had the book ready, wrapped in the Ohio Repository. The same paper went back and forward and her mother never failed to read that too, including the sermons, the advertisements and the death notices under the heading, "END OF EARTH" which always struck a kind of terror in Rosa.

Once Mrs. Phillips took her into a room in the house where the walls were covered with books.

"I've always taken an interest in your mother," she told Rosa. "I feel sorry for her in her present station."

Now Rosa sat watching her mother's eye run along the page, trying to tell from her face what she read, for her mother wouldn't let Rosa read the books for herself.

"You're much too young. Novels and plays aren't for young girls," she said sharply, but her face never changed either then or when she read, or if it did, you couldn't see it through the film of unwashed olive that had gathered on her skin ever since the girl could remember, growing a little darker green with time. But sometimes as her mother read, her eyes would dilate and gather, the light in them would heighten, and the pupils deepen so Rosa could look far back in them, and after a moment she seemed to be in there herself with the bright mysterious light of the story all around her, with things happening to the right and left, but never could Rosa quite tell what they were, for you couldn't see, just feel, them, and they had no shape save shadows.

All of a sudden she found herself sitting up in her chair. She heard them bringing her father home. It was still early, and fear like a dark flame threatened her. She knew it was her father, for she could hear his voice. No one ever brought him home before that she could remember. He came by himself, very late, as a rule. No matter how much he drank, nobody needed to help him, and yet it sounded like there were two men with him tonight. They came stumbling up on the porch and her father opened the door. Something flew into Rosa then, for he had a great rag stained with blood around his head.

The men with him would come no farther than the doorway. They were grown waterfront men and yet shied away from her mother as the boys did who ventured in the yard with Turkey.

"Jake got in a little argument, Miz Tench," Boiling William Gates broke the news cautiously. "But he's all right. It was a draw."

"It was a fight," Strap Johnson corrected.

"Tell her about Pete Easley!" Jake roared. "What happened to that Fly-Up-the-Crick!"

"Jake and Pete got in a little argument at the tavern," Boiling William started again.

"It was a knock-down, drag-out fight," Strap insisted.

"Tell her how I bit off his nose!" Jake shouted. "If my mouth'd a been bigger, I'd a bit off his head."

"He bit off a chunk of you first," Strap reminded.

"You see what I mean, Miz Tench," Boiling William said. "That's what made it a draw. Jake bit off Pete's nose and Pete bit off Jake's ear."

"Take the rag off and show her, Jake," Strap urged. "Maybe she could put some liniment on."

While they talked, Rosa's mother sat there hardly listening. All the peculiar yellow light from the novel had gone out of her eyes, as if what she looked at and listened to now wasn't real life or true. No, the real world was in the book she still held in her hand, keeping the place open, waiting to return to it as soon as this make-believe scene from a story was over. Nothing changed on her face as Jake fumbled with the bloody rag. Before he got it off, Rosa bolted, slipping between the two men at the door.

"Rosa!" her mother called.

But Rosa fled, out of the gate into darkness like a moth suddenly released from the window pane. It seemed for a minute that her feet never touched the ground. An effortless power flowed through her, lightening her legs and body, lifting her up like a bird. Never had running and the darkness tasted so sweet. The rain felt good in her face and washed it. She held open her lips to let it wash out her mouth. She let the clean night air wash through her flesh and mind. It cooled her to see nothing, nothing but shapeless shadows and the yellow lights in other houses that carried oblivion from her own. She could remember when she was a little tot how far it seemed down town, how daring she thought her father to go all that long way himself and how clever that he could find his way back.

In the dark houses people already lay sleeping. She would have the night to herself. Only the dogs in this part of town were awake, tied in their backyards, sending their alarm down the line. She walked so lightly now, hardly did she kick a pebble. Now how could the first dog to bark know that such a small body as she shouldn't be abroad? Dogs, they said, could tell if a body was good or bad. Then why couldn't they tell she was only a slip of a girl who wouldn't hurt them, not even a hair of Cottrils's fice that had bit her so she still carried the scar on her knee?

When anybody came along, she hid by the side of a house till they passed. Not that she had to. She had gone out many a time before when her mother said she couldn't. "Give me a minute, Mama, just a minute!" she'd beg and then she'd walk up and down with the moon. No matter how far she walked, the moon would walk with her, all the way and back again. She wouldn't be locked out those nights and she wouldn't be tonight. Never from one year to another did her mother bar the door, for nobody dared come in their house even in the daytime. Oh, her mother would scold her with scalding words when she got back, but they wouldn't hurt, and if they did, her walk would be worth it, getting away for a while, looking through windows into rooms where candles still burned. Daytimes you could see nothing inside, but at night her eye could go right through the glass. She could see herself living there in other folks' houses, sitting on those chairs, eating or reading at the table, lying on the couch.

Down on the Square, most of the houses still had light. Folks on the Square were the latest to bed in town, save those in the taverns. An invisible lady came out of her front door calling, "Here, pussy, pussy, pussy. Come, pussy, pussy, pussy!" Rosa moved around the Square slowly, feeling the spell of the great houses, the awe of the court house ball and the sacred presence of the church with the graves behind it. That was Judge Wheeler's new mansion house standing so high on its white marble steps. Nine regular steps it had and a little step at the top to go to the front door. Why did they have the little step, she wondered. You couldn't see it tonight. She would like to go up and try it with her feet, but somebody might come out and catch her.

That was old Judge Wheeler himself she saw through the window, with the great bulging forehead and the bush of hair on the top. He thought himself so much. Her father said he had been his lawyer, yet never would he look at her when he went by on the street, his big head down, his brows drawn over some weighty matter, the green bag in his hand.

Tonight she could see Judge Wheeler's wife with him. The house stood so high, Rosa could only see the top of her head. She was the plainest woman on the Square and the richest. She was part Indian, they said. Her hair was combed plain, parted in the middle. She was common as dirt and spoke to everybody when she passed. Twice she had spoken to her, once on the street and once when she took the flowers. But when Rosa came home and told about it, her mother said never to speak to her or any other Wheeler, and especially not with that young liar, Chancey. Better had she cross the street when she saw a deceitful Wheeler coming.

Wasn't it a strange thing about people in this world, why they were themselves and why you were the person you were? When she tried to think who it was that stood here in her flesh living and thinking, she seemed to be blown away and lost far back in her mind. She felt giddy and queer, as she did when she looked at a star and pretended herself way up there hanging on it.

She could see a light high in the house, on the third floor. Somebody must live high under the roof. The younger girls and Chancey likely. They must dress and undress and sleep up there. When they got tired of being downstairs they could run up the steps and get away from everybody and everything. Weren't they lucky to have a place to be by themselves? They could look out like birds. They could lie in bed in the morning and see green leaves wave by their window and clouds sail by. Wasn't it the saddest thing in this world that you always had to be yourself, that you couldn't be somebody else, that never, never, never could you be the person you most wanted to be?

CHAPTER TWENTY

THE BLUE STOCKING

Know him? I'd know his hide if I saw it in the tanyard.

EARLY SAYING

IT was a winter's day and bitter cold, Sayward thought, for such a poor old man to be out in the wind without a heavy coat. She was upstairs sewing by the window when she saw him. Now who could he be looking in at the house, as he went by? He had on a battered slouch roaram hat and corduroy jacket like an old hunting coat. His leggins were snowy to his knees. Just the same, he held himself mighty straight, like an old poking stick that had been used a long time, worn thin and soon to be thrown on the fire.

Hardly had he passed till he turned and tramped slowly back, looking at the house again. Why, he was turning in! She couldn't hear his rap from the stairs but she could his boots stamp off the snow on the back porch. Chancey and Massey were at their schools, Dezia at the seminary. When Sayward opened the back door, the old man stood there with a drop froze at the end of his nose, his cheeks crossed and criss-crossed with a mess of wrinkles like scrub apples still a hanging to some wild tree in the snow.

"Is this Judge Wheeler's place?" he wanted to know.

"Step in the warm," Sayward bid him kindly. At the same time she was thinking, now where did I hear that voice before and see those eyes running back in his head?

"Are you his woman?" he asked, holding back. And when she nodded. "Then you must be Saird. Don't you know me any more?"

Sayward stared at him a moment. Then she took the broom and swept the snow from his legs and boots.

"I know you but I can't name you," she complained. Something in the way he said "Saird" touched off a queer notion in her and when he came in and stood there in the kitchen with his hat on, a storm of feeling ran over her. It couldn't be. No, it couldn't possibly be. Why, all the old folks thought her father dead this long time. The last they heard, he was skinning wild bulls beyond the Mississippi, and that was thirty-five years ago. One of those wild bulls, Portius allowed, must have killed him. Hardly an Indian would, for Worth had Indian in his blood and could get along with them if anybody could. Genny thought that a Spanishman must have cut his throat for his gold. He had sent word how well off he was, but this old bushnipple in her kitchen today didn't look like he ever had a shilling to his name.

"Is it you, Pap?" Sayward asked. "I never expected to see you again!"

"You know me now!" he called out, pleased. "It took you a good while. But I don't blame you. I wouldn't a knowed you from Adam's ox. You're married to the lawyer, they tell me. I knowed him before I went but I never looked for you to get hitched to him."

"Take a chair, Pap," Sayward begged him. "I'll make you something to warm you up." She remembered how he never drank tea or coffee. Slops, woodsmen used to call them. Liquor was the only drink to stick to a man's guts, they said. Sayward made him a hot toddy, putting in lots of brown sugar, and he sat there, sucking it up from the cup from time to time with a lusty rattle.

"Achsa stayin' with you?"

"No, she's not here any more. In fact she's gone nigh as long as you have. We don't know if she's living or dead."

Some of the brightness went out of those shiny black buttons at the bottom of his eye pits.

"Well, Ginny and Louie are still around?"

"Genny is. She's married again. Will Beagle's her second man. But Louie's gone. He's the one Achsa run off with. We heard he drowned in a river up beyond the English lakes."

Worth had set down his trembling toddy cup on his knee. It took him a while to digest this.

"Well, Wyitt's all right, ain't he?" he asked.

"We hope so," Sayward said carefully. "He always was. Somebody told Jake Tench he saw him in the woods of Michigan territory, but he never sent word home himself. We thought maybe he would run into you some place out there."

Her father shook his head. He sat still a long time. Sayward thought he was thinking of her sister, Sulie; wondering had they ever had news of her. But he didn't mention her name. Likely he was afraid to, for Sulie was his favorrite.

"You know you're a grandpappy now and a great-grandpappy to boot?" she said to cheer him up. "I have nine of my own and one dead. And six grandchildren a living."

But he couldn't get up any sap over his great-grandchildren. They were too distant a relation. He didn't even take much notice of his grandchildren, once he had a look at them and they at him.

"This is Massey," Sayward said. "And this is Chancey, the youngest. This is your Grandpap Luckett. Go up and shake hands with him."

The two in their teens looked startled. This seedy and feeble old codger with shaggy white hair, ragged corduroy coat and britches worn to the rib couldn't be their famous grandfather, the great hunter and pioneer they had heard so much about, the first white man in these parts and the founder of Americus! Why, he didn't look like he could knock over a rabbit, let alone panther and bear. They went up to him reluctantly. But Worth was just as distant with them, dropping their hands like they were small fry out of the river, too scanty to bother with and had to be thrown back in. He went on talking to Sayward of where he had been and what he was doing the day he got the notion to come back and see his children before he was laid away for good.

For all the notice he gave, Chancey and Massey weren't even there, but when Dezia came in from the seminary, a full grown young lady, dressed and polite like the gentry, Worth got up to retreat.

"Sit down, Pap," Sayward urged him.

"No, I got to go," he told her.

"Go where? You're staying with us. We got plenty room."

"No, I'd be in the way."

"You wouldn't any such thing," Sayward protested. "You can have a room all by yourself. On the second floor so you don't have to climb so much stairs."

"I figured I ought to stay with Ginny," he mumbled. "She has no young ones, you say. That might work out better. I'm not used to young ones rippin' and tearin' around."

"They won't bother you."

"Oh, they're all right, I expect," Worth allowed. "But all I come for was to see you. Now I have to be going."

"Well, you're staying to supper anyways," Sayward said sternly like it was all settled. "We can talk the rest over afterward."

He threw a sidelong glance through the door to the sparkle of brass and china and claw-footed mahogany in the dining room.

"No, I got some things to do," he persisted. "Will Beagle has a boat yard, you say?"

The girls and Chancey looked relieved, but Sayward stood there half provoked. She had lost patience with her own father. She hadn't seen him for thirty-five years and now he was running off without his supper.

"Well, when are you coming back?" she asked.

"Oh, I'll be back some time to see you. I expect to stay around."

"Well, if there's no stopping you, Chancey can run along and show you where Genny lives. I hope you tell her how you put me out by not staying."

Chancey put his coat and cap back on, and Sayward went around to the front window to see them go. She hated her father going off like this, but if he wouldn't do a thing, you couldn't make him. She recollected how when her mother used to try, his eyes would get that sunken look, he'd pick up his rifle and that would be the last they'd see of him for a couple of days.

Seldom did Genny's tongue run faster than next time she came over. Wasn't Sayward struck in a heap when she saw that old man at the door? Who'd a thought their father still among the living! And the contrary old mule was still like always. He ate his supper with her and Will, but do you reckon he'd stay the night? No, he claimed he slept out all his life, and that wasn't true because he used to sleep in the cabin, didn't he? Anyway he asked Will if he didn't have a place in the boat yard he could stay in, and when Will said he had a shanty the men used, Worth had to move right out. He wouldn't even sleep a single night in one of her beds. What would people think, their father coming back like this and living out in an old boat yard shanty? They'd think he wasn't good enough for his own daughters and that she and Sayward had turned him out.

"He run off from us young ones and let us raise ourselves," Genny complained. "He stayed off thirty-five years. Now that we amount to a little something in this world, he comes back to disgrace us."

"I wouldn't say that, Genny," Sayward said mildly.

"He came back ragged and dirty, didn't he? He told who he was in front of the whole town. Why, he never used to look that bad in the woods with nobody to see him. I mind how he used to get you to shave him just to go over to Hough's trading post in Shawaneetown."

"We have to recollect he's a mighty old man," Sayward mentioned.

"He's not too old to have a woman," Genny flared. "Barney Grice told Will he knew Pap down in Memphis last fall but he didn't know he was any relation to us. Barney said Pap had a woman they called Old Profanity. They lived together on the water front. Barney doesn't know if she's along up with him here or not. But, Saird," Genny's voice rose, "I won't stand for her if she is! The minute he fetches her to the boat yard, he's got to get out."

"Well, that's his business, and I'm not a going to fret about it," Sayward soothed her. "All we can do for him now is see he gets some decent clothes."

"And then he'll never wear them," Genny said bitterly. "Anything you give him he'll hoard up like a squirrel; lock it up in the old chest Will gave him."

"Well, let's give him a chance before we jump on him. Most likely he'll do the right thing. If he won't, we'll have to rig up ways to get around him. For instance, if he won't come up to eat at my place, I'll have to send him something down to his shanty. Supper would suit me best. That's when we have our heavy meal now on account of Portius not getting home much at noon. Then I'll have one of the children free to send it down with. But I don't want you complaining it looks like you don't have enough to feed him."

That's the way it was settled. Sayward herself went down to see him whenever she could. It hurt something deep inside of her to come from her fine big house and see her father living in this poor shanty. The door was so low she had to duck her head coming in, his bed a bunk against one side. No more than two could sit in here at one time unless they sat on the bunk.

"Why won't you stay with us in the house, Pap?" she'd asked him, but he never would.

One time he told her, "Right where your place stands, I shot the deer with the blue horn. Do you mind that ole blue horn? It had a mess of points. Oh, that was a handsome spot them days. I kin see it yit with the big butts and creepers the way God Almighty made it. Why, it was so thick around 'ar, that buck never seed me. And now all slashed off and gone to rack and ruin. I kain't look at it. Only thing left is the river, and that don't look like itself with the woods killed off and not near the water coming down that used to."

She had to keep after Chancey. He hated to carry the supper basket. He and Massey hated still worse when their school mates asked, "Is your grandfather still living down at the boat yard?" But the older girls said, "Thank God the old man isn't in the house now that Aunt Cornelia is coming." Seldom if ever was it "Grandfather" or "Grandpap." No, it was, "the octogenarian" or "the ancestor" or "the old man of the Western Waters" or "Mama's old Indian fighter and painter-tracker." Portius was the one who put them up to it, especially now that his fine blue stocking sister was coming from the Bay State to visit them in Ohio.

The first time Sayward laid eyes on her, she had to admit to wonder how she and her would get along. Portius had looked for his sister by boat. That way she couldn't have got to Americus before June. But one day late in May, Sayward and Dezia were house-cleaning when they saw the stage stop in the square. Almost never would the driver go out of his way, but this time he drew up right in front of their house, and Sayward knew it must be for a good reason even before Ned Hanshaw got down from his seat and set a pile of traps on the sidewalk. Then he opened the coach door and a lady stepped down.

Could that be Portius's sister? Sayward thought. She had always reckoned Cornelia Wheeler like Mrs. Morrison, tall and sweeping, with a handsome face and gracious manner. Now this was a short plain woman more like Aunt Unity and with a face like the pope's. Her bonnet looked plain and old style enough, her hair drawn down severely on either side. Yet the stern way she held herself, the costly look of her ribbed taffeta and the respectful way Ned Hanshaw treated her told you that this was a great lady and one more to reckon with than Mrs. Morrison. Dezia fled upstairs to change her dress, but Sayward went right out as she was in her red dusting turban. You couldn't keep Portius's sister waiting in the street with her traps and everybody in the stage and square a watching.

"I'm Saird. I reckon you're Cornelia," she said and gave the white fingers in the black mit a stout shake.

"You are Portius's wife?" His sister's eyes went over her distant as Bay State Mountain, but Sayward wouldn't explain that they hadn't looked for her yet, and that's why she wasn't better dressed.

"Come right in. I'll fetch your traps," she said. "Portius will be real surprised when he comes home and finds you're here."

She spoke friendly like sisters-in-law should, but already she felt that Cornelia Wheeler looked down on her. Sayward thought she wouldn't mind too much. The only thing Portius's sister better not look down on was her children, for they had Wheeler blood a flowing in their veins the same as their Aunt Cornelia. Not so much perhaps, but enough to let them stand up and be counted, they having the Wheeler name besides.

She needn't have fretted. When Dezia came down, all dressed up, her Aunt Cornelia gave her plenty of notice.

"So this is Dezia of whom I've heard so much!" she said in her genteel Bay State voice and held her cheek to be kissed, which she hadn't to Sayward. Her keen blue Yankee eyes surveyed the girl. "Did your father ever tell you that you look like your Grandmother Wheeler, child? In

everything I may say but your hair. Your Grandmother
Wheeler used to brush her hair ten to fifteen minutes every
morning and evening. She was a very resourceful and determined woman. She was determined to have beautiful
hair, and she did."

That, Sayward found later, was her sister-in-law to a T.
She turned her sharp Yankee eyes on every young Wheeler
that came around, reminded them who they were and
started to make them over right away. No matter if they
were half Luckett and part Indian and lived way out West
here in Ohio, they had to measure up to their family back
in the Bay State. She told Massey at once that her name
was not Massey but Me'cy, that there had been a Me'cy
Hopewell who converted the Indian heathen a hundred
and fifty years ago and that no young lady of thirteen or
fourteen with Me'cy Hopewell's name and her blood in her
veins would tear into the house like a young savage or a
western tornado.

Now Chancey had to straighten his shoulders and turn
his toes out.

"You favor your great-grandfather, John Elliot," she told
him. "He had a brilliant mind. I often heard my mother
say he was one of the most fearless speakers in Massachusetts. He would have made his mark if his country hadn't
lost him at Bunker Hill."

Oh, Huldah called her Lady Washington behind her
back, and Libby dubbed her The Old Family Tree.

"Your mother tells me your husband is a young physician," she said to Libby. "I want you to bring him over. I'm
sure he would be interested to know that your father's
cousin Henry Wheeler was one of the most skilled and beloved medical practitioners in New England."

Sooth's eyes watered with pleasure when she heard that

she got her musical talent from Sarah Elliot who once sang
for President and Mrs. John Adams, which was much better than from Aunt Genny out here in Ohio. And no matter how little Resolve cared that he looked like his great
uncle, General Ezra Norris, he was glad to have a general
in his family to set up against Fay's papa. Mrs. Morrison
and the girls looked up to Aunt Cornelia, and listened im-
pressed to her stories about the Norris houses, the Elliot
brains and the Hopewell silver. Now the Wheeler silver
wasn't so much, but no family ever did so much for the
town of Quinham near Boston as the Wheelers.

Aunt Cornelia stayed for a month and, even though she
hardly raised her hands to do a tap, Sayward wouldn't have
minded having her all summer. She was better than a watch
dog on the children. If Massey or Chancey did something
outside they shouldn't, she'd tap sharply on the window
pane with her finger ring, and when they came in, they
better speak the king's English, or she'd set them straight.

"It's chest," she would say sternly. "Don't let me hear
you say chist again. And it's not banch. It's not shumac
or sassafrac, or pepmint or leevah. Now say them with me.
Bench! Sumach! Sassafras! Peppehmint! Leveh! And it's
not camphire. It's c-a-m-p-h-o-r, camphaw!"

Sayward felt beholden to her for that and for telling
them about their father's side of the house. Why, till it was
over she her own self knew more about Portius's folks than
her own. She could tell her grandchildren that hadn't been
born yet about Halbert, the queer old Wheeler coachman
who claimed that one of his horses died coming down the
Quinham hill but he held him up with the lines till he got
to the bottom; about Rover, the big black Elliot dog their
great-grandfather liked so much that he had its hide tanned
when it died and used it as a rug on the floor; and about

their great granduncle or cousin Norris who wore silver shillings for coat buttons and eleven penny bits for buttons on his waistcoat and breeches. Oh, most everything Cornelia told about Portius's folks was good. It could be lively or racy or amusing, but it ever made out the Wheelers and Elliots ladies and gentlemen of high degree.

Now why did her father have to come the very last afternoon Cornelia was here, and make the Lucketts look like fly-up-the-cricks? Why, all spring and early summer he wouldn't stir his stumps to Sayward's for a meal or visit. He claimed his joints plagued him. Even Genny herself stayed away during Cornelia's visit save when specially invited, and then she sat shut-mouthed and uneasy, not wanting to make any slips that would lower her and Sayward's side of the house in front of Portius's fine sister. One more day and Cornelia would have been gone back to her Bay State. Then didn't Worth have to come and show himself, looking like an old bushnipple.

It was pretty well along in the afternoon. Cornelia had been across the square in the court house to see her brother sit on the bench in his robes and hear her nephew plead the case of a farmer ejected from a place that had been sold. When court adjourned, Portius came straight home, it being Cornelia's last afternoon. Resolve dropped in, too. They got in a warm and lively argument, and Sayward felt it was good as court sitting there in the library a listening. In another minute, she told herself, she'd have to start supper and get Worth's basket ready. But first she'd listen to Cornelia telling Resolve right out she didn't think much of him taking the case of a man who had no honest right to stay on a place.

"That's what all the clever and smart lawyers do," she said, "take the side against an ejectment because sympathy is on their side. I should think a Wheeler would take the side of justice sometimes. This time the poor and ragged was clearly in the wrong."

Just then somebody rapped on the back door, and Massey ran to answer it. Looking up, when Massey returned to the hall Sayward could see her startled face. Sayward rose and when she got to the kitchen, there was Worth in britches like a pair of feed bags. He had on no coat, only an open buckskin vest with the hair on it and under that an old red flannel shirt. White stubble covered his chin and cheeks, yellowed with tobacco juice around the mouth.

"Do you want to come in the library, pappy?" she asked quiet and steady as she could.

"I don't care," he said, meaning he would.

Sayward might be bamfoozled a little but not beat out. She hadn't lived fifty-five years without learning that the old can be mighty shrewd and knowing sometimes, and contrary as a mule. Whatever you don't expect them to do, they are liable to turn up a doing. Just the same, your father is your father, and the more helpless and childish he is, the more he needs your help as you needed his when you were little and helpless.

Resolve's face was a picture when she brought Worth in the library with his hat on. Chancey went out one door as his grandpappy came in the other.

"I want to make you acquainted with Portius's sister," Sayward spoke, raising her voice a little so he would surely hear. "Cornelia, this is my father. Will you take a chair, pappy, and rest yourself?"

"I'll have to go directly. But I'll sit down for a lick," he agreed like he was doing Sayward a favor. His bright old eyes ran from one to another, to everybody save Portius's sister, and by that Sayward knew he was well aware that she was there, and that's why he came, to get a look at the visitor before she went back home to the Bay State.

Portius leaned back in his chair and the devil was in his eyes. You could tell he was going to enjoy this, and Sayward didn't thank him for it.

"You see before you the original pioneer of Shawanee county, Cornelia," he said in his deep court voice. "Mr. Luckett's the first settler and founder of Americus."

His sister sat there on her comfortable chair, not knowing what to make of this ancient "critter" crouching on the edge of a straight chair, his hat pushed back on his head, as a concession to etiquette. Oh, Sayward could have lifted off that hat before letting him in, but hardly would he have forgiven the indignity, and less would she have forgiven herself for trying to make him something he wasn't. What went on now behind Cornelia's stout prim face, Sayward could not tell save that she was company in her sister-in-law's house, and no matter what he looked like, she would be civil to her sister-in-law's father.

"Americus must be very grateful to you, Mr. Luckett," she pronounced.

"What fer?" Worth asked suspiciously, looking at her direct for almost the first time.

"Judge Wheeler just told us. For founding such a growing city in a new land."

"I had no idee o' that," Worth told her tartly. "Or I'd never settled here."

"You are too modest about the good you've done," Cornelia rebuked him mildly. "When you came here, there must have been nothing but a formidable wilderness. Today the country is developed and the people civilized and benefited."

"I'd say it's plumb the other way round," he said flatly.
"The country's spoilt and folks are gettin' less account
every day. If you'd a been here forty, fifty year ago,
you'd know it's gospel. God Almighty made this country
the way He wanted, and he never laid any out purtier. He
stocked it with game outa the ark and told 'em to breed.
Why, not far from this place the bucks would come so
thick to rub off their horns in the spring, it looked like the
deer park I heerd my grandpap tell about in the old country. You'd run into bear or painters most any place. Mink
and fisher fox traveled the runs. I seed squirrels thick in the
trees as pigeons. You ever hear a gray moose call, ma'am?
That's something to stir up your liver. He's a callin' to his
lady love so they kin get together and multiply like the
Good Book says. You wouldn't soon forget it. But this
town scum never heerd it and never will. They stick in one
place. They go through the whole rumpus of gettin' born
and dyin' and have no idee how the Lord Almighty meant
them to live. Moughty few ever heerd gabby birds a talkin'.
They'd sooner wear them on their hats, the purtiest birds
you ever laid eyes on. A kind of poll parrot, not very big.
I've seed the trees red and yaller and blue with them.
They'd talk to each other like humans. They'd talk to the
beaver and otter, too, and warn 'em. One time I was
watchin' a family of otter. It was up on Crazy Crick near
as I kin make out, where a fullin' mill stands now. You
kain't shoot otter in the water or they'll sink and you kain't
get 'em, but I could a shot these many a time up on them
rocks. A course it was summer and their skins wasn't much
good anyways. But them otter played together like humans. Then they'd sit on the rocks a watchin' for fish.
When they saw one, they'd tell which one had to go in for
it. You'd reckon they'd jump in doggy-fashion, but they'd

peel in that water slick as an eel. Oh, they wouldn't catch
a fish every time, specially not the young ones. But when
they did, they'd fetch it out on the rocks and leave those
bones picked clean as a human.

"That was up on Crazy Crick, and not far from them
rocks I used to keep track of a drone beaver. You know
what a drone beaver is? Well, the rest drive him out because he won't work. He'd dug hisself a hole in the bank
and lived there all alone. Just cut down enough trees to
eat. He didn't have no house and no woman. The rest
wouldn't let him. I used to feel kinda sorry for the old var-
mint and never shot him, but likely somebody else did. He
was an ole bachelor, you might say, a pore ole hermit. Me
and him got mighty friendly, though what happened to
him after I pulled out, I kain't tell you. I stayed only so
long as it was God's country."

"But there were no people!" Portius's sister from the Bay
State protested.

"Thank God Almighty, no!" Worth said fervently.
"What would we want with people? What could beef-
witted ploughmen and dainty town bodies a done in the
woods? They'd a starved to death. Oh, we wasn't plumb
alone. We had friends to visit when we got lonesome. They
was some around, scattered here and yonder. White-
skinned and red-skinned both. I don't know to this day
which was the best. I've been took in by both and give shelter and rations. Once when I had lung fever and bloody
flux, a Delyware woman nursed me kinder than my own
woman could. Another time when I was a small tyke, I
played with Injun boys. You know where the Suskyhanny
is? You crossed it when you come West. Well, right up the
West Branch where Deep Crick came in, they used to be a
Delyware town. Them was the boys I used to play with.

One time I was wrasslin' and fell off a high cliff up the crick. The water hit me purty hard and I sunk in a deep hole. I knew whar I was all the time, but I couldn't do nothin'! I couldn't move a finger. Once I laid on the bottom it seemed like I could breathe again good as anybody. If this was dyin', I tole myself, it wasn't so bad. Next thing I knew I was out on the bank over a log. Them Injun boys had got me out and were runnin' the water outa me. Best friends I ever had. They built a fire and dried my shirt and britches, and I never had dare tell their mams or paps I fell in or they'd all got jesse for near drownin' me."

Sayward looked up. She thought she heard the back door open. Genny stood there. She must have been trailing Worth.

"I was just going by," she apologized. "Father, I'm going home. Don't you want to go along?"

"Where are them good Delyware, Shawanee and Wyndotte folks now?" Worth went on, paying Genny no attention, especially that she had called him "Father." "Killed off and run off. Pushed one place, then another. Now they want to move them over the Mississippi. What fer? To give their land to men who hadn't the guts to come out in the first place. That's the kind that's mostly got it now. And what do they want with it? Why, they want to make it just like the country they left back East. Already they've put in flour mills and wool mills and saw mills and fullin' mills and all kinds of mills. Any old thing with wheels that water'll turn!" He was hollering now. "Money, that's what they're crazy about. Money! A cabin's not good enough any more. They have to have a mansion house like this. A bag of meal used to make a whole family feel good. Now it don't mean nothin'. Folks must live high these days and dress fancy — make their selves believe they're more than they are. They kain't even tramp with the legs God Almighty gave them but have to ride their selves around with hosses and fancy riggin'. At home they sit on their porch stoop or behind their window light and watch folks with nothin' more to do than their selves. Now when we come out, we didn't have no hosses. We had nobody pushin' us on a boat or drivin' us packed like chestnuts in a bur. We came on our own legs and toted our plunder on our backs."

"Father, it's time to go home," Genny said sharply.

"He's all right here, Genny," Sayward told her.

"I knew a woman done something for money once," Worth went on. "It never brought her any good either. She was one of these fine town bodies back in Pennsylvany. Her man owned three farms and a good house and stable in town. They had a smart boy, just a little feller, and his pap took him along one day in front of him on horseback out to his farm in Nippenose Valley. The Mingoes shot him and took the boy. Well, his woman got the house and stable and half the farms but she wasn't satisfied. She wanted the half that was willed to the boy. When my old Colonel got all them Injun prisoners, that woman come to Carlisle lookin' for her boy. He wasn't 'ar. She could easy tell him. He had a birthmark like a berry by the nipple of his right breast. But she wouldn't give up. She wanted the other half of those farms they were holdin' for him. So she took a boy nobody claimed. Swore that was her boy and took him home, though everybody back 'ar knew he wasn't. Well, he grew up ugly and loose. He wasn't satisfied with his share when he got old enough. He went through that and then started on her share. He ran through everything she had. He even ran through her rings and household stuff. I heerd she died on charity. The real boy they never did find. You could have told him sure by that mark near the nipple of his right breast. It looked so much like a strawberry you could almost pick it off and eat it, they said. That's how natural it looked."

"Pappy, I'm a goin'," Genny said, losing patience and forgetting herself.

"That woman was about the run of folks back East," Worth declared. "This was in Pennsylvany but it could a been in Jersey or the Bay State where you come from. They're never satisfied. When they come out here, they have to make God's country over. So they make it like the place they left. Before they come, a man's house out here was open to all that came. He took you in and gave you a bed if he had one to spare. If not, you could make a pallet on the floor. His woman gave you supper when you come and breakfast before you went, if she had any to share with you. Now show me a town body here or back in the Bay State who'll do that for you. The best folks come out here at the start, if they wasn't here already. They was all man and woman, I kin tell you. Them that come after or stayed behind were second raters. They were faint-hearted, weak-legged or money grubbing, and it's good they never come early. They couldn't have stood the gaff. They'd a starved or been scared to death. I been around, and I kin tell you. I been in the piney woods where they have runs with the purest water and yet trees die without nobody knowing why. I been out on the prairies of Ioway where horses and cattle don't need to be stabled but feed out all year on grammer and buffaler grass. I been in the mountings and in the Spanish settlements, and I'm a telling you — "

"You're talking too much, Pap!" Genny broke in angrily. "Come on home now and we'll eat."

"I'll lay a plate for him here, Genny," Sayward said. "It will save me sending his basket down."

Worth got up from his chair pretty quick then.

"No, I got to go. Well, come on, Ginny, if you're a comin'."

Dezia's face was a picture of relief and Genny's a foretaste of what she would say to him on the way home. But Portius's bold features only showed regret that the show was over. As for Sayward, she didn't see why Genny got so worked up. Cornelia would understand that old men acted mighty strange sometimes. It was their nature. Just the same, it tickled her a little how he jumped on Cornelia and her town folks. She never saw him so stuck up and proud. Why, he carried on like him and his kind were kings of creation and town folks the ragtag bobtail and small fry. Now who was the blue stocking, she wanted to know, Worth or Cornelia?

She wondered another thing. Tomorrow Cornelia's visit would be over. All this time she had been here, and not a word of the trouble that made Portius leave home and hide out in Ohio. Was it a murder? Or was it, as Sayward felt, a woman at the bottom? For thirty-five years she had hankered to know. It used to torment her what this woman was like and did Portius still have a secret wish to go back to her? When she heard that Portius's sister was coming, she told herself she would find out. Cornelia would tell her, or at least drop some broad hint. Now Cornelia was going without having breathed a word. Sayward knew one thing. Whatever had happened way back yonder, it hadn't set Portius or the Wheelers up any, and that's why Cornelia kept still.

Of course, Sayward could come right out and ask her before she went. But she hadn't seen fit to ask Portius whom she lived with all these years, why should she ask his sister she hardly knowed? Now wasn't it strange that it didn't bother her so much any more? Her children, her grandchildren and herself had got this far without knowing. Whatever it was Portius had done back there, it couldn't hurt them any more. If it still came to her unbesought in some way, let it come. But if it didn't, she reckoned she could go to her grave ignorant and unawares.

CHAPTER TWENTY-ONE

ROSA'S CLOUDBERRIES

And are we not as good as the best now, grandmother?
In everything but circumstances, my child.

ELLEN GLASGOW

ROSA was glad that her mother had three friends. The finest was Mrs. Phillips who sent the books. She was ever too busy to come herself, and you couldn't expect her to, for she was rich. Her house had a room for only books, and what would Rosa's mother have done without them?

Then there was Mrs. Clocker next door. Virtually never a day passed without Mrs. Clocker waddling solicitously to the fence and rapping on the Tench window. How did Mrs. Tench feel today? Well might she stay to her bed, for this was a cold morning. It looked like rain on her wash, maybe snow. Her lines were frozen stiff before daylight. Rosa's mother listened but said little in return, and this together with Mrs. Clocker's invariable manner toward her established in Rosa's mind the fact that her mother was of a definitely higher social position than her neighbor. Mrs. Clocker never dared to come in either, save one time when Rosa's mother lay on her bed as one dead. But when

Rosa's mother opened her eyes and saw her, Mrs. Clocker hastily beat a retreat.

The third friend was Miss Bogardus, and that was she coming up the street right now. You could tell her a long ways off. She was housekeeper for old Mr. Millard who lived on the Square. Oh, she was no common housemaid, and when she tramped up Water Street, moving sedately by the slab fence, it seemed that a faded, slightly shabby but undeniable lady was coming to call on them. How old she was Rosa couldn't guess. She seemed to be made out of some thin, sallow, yet everlasting substance. She had pale blue eyes like the finest porcelain and brought with her a whole floating cloud of the past. She had known Rosa's mother's family in Philadelphia and liked to tell about Grandmother Bartram, a real lady of the Quaker faith, and what a pity that she had to die of lung fever before she was thirty. Miss Bogardus didn't come in the house either but came closest to it, calling only in mild weather when she sat on the porch in a chair that Rosa was told to fetch out for her. Here in plain view of everybody who went by she visited with Rosa's mother who sat in the shadows just inside the door, invisible from the street but everyone knew she was there.

Looking at her now, Rosa couldn't say that she liked Miss Bogardus, but she felt pleased and honored when she came. Just to see her settled on the porch and hear her thin positive voice telling of Rosa's mother's family in Philadelphia, of great-aunts, uncles and cousins, of bonnets and gowns, of house furnishings and bric-a-brac, brought an invisible wave of respectability and peace to the girl, something so substantial she could almost lie on it and let it bear her among the scent of plush and carpets and dyes of the brick Bartram house with white scrubbed marble step in the City of Brotherly Love between the Delaware and Schuylkill Rivers.

Already Rosa had sunk to the edge of the porch out of reach of her mother's eyes. Here she waited, letting her mind and body subside to that certain relaxed, almost limp, state in which Miss Bogardus's words could levitate and transport her. But all the time while she floated and hovered, a part of her waited for the high point of the visit when for some mysterious reason Miss Bogardus and her mother invariably wanted her to leave.

At last Miss Bogardus turned her head and fixed her pale eyes on the girl.

"Rosa, don't you want to run out somewhere and play?"

Rosa didn't say anything, just sat there mildly, looking down at her hands, touching her thumb and fingers together one after the other softly.

"Rosa!" her mother ordered. "Go down and see if Mrs. Doan doesn't have something for you to do."

But Rosa kept sitting there in her trance-like repose, and inside of her the anticipation rose. Miss Bogardus was getting ready to tell her mother about the Wheelers. Oh, her mother never asked a word or mentioned the Wheeler name, but she would sit there with such silent decorum and bitter dignity that sooner or later Miss Bogardus always came around to the Wheelers, and nearly always she ran them down. There was something peculiarly vindictive in her tone. She accused, although whom she accused and why, Rosa did not quite know. Her mother listened so pitilessly and cruel. It fixed every word and scene in Rosa's mind, such as the time a summer or two ago when Miss Bogardus talked about Libby Wheeler.

"Who'd have thought that big lump would ever get married? Why most people thought she was more man than woman! Her mother could have put britches on her and few would have known the difference. Nobody ever saw her do anything but act the fool. She'd play Ducks with the boys and throw rocks with them, tussle with them on the Square. I saw her knock boys down more than once. They yelled and carried on, but do you think that woman would come out of her house or even call from the window!" (That woman, Rosa had long since learned, was Judge Wheeler's wife.) "Now, would you believe it, Miss Libby's changed! Her breasts are filled out. Almost over night! She doesn't rip and tear any more. What that young doctor from Connecticut sees in her, I don't know, but he started to court her and pretty quick they were married. Some say they had to get married, but you'd think a doctor would know how to get around that."

The last time Miss Bogardus was here, she talked about Mrs. Holcomb, the oldest Wheeler girl — "that Huldah," Miss Bogardus called her.

"Well, it's true," she told. "She and the iron master couldn't make a go of it. They're parted for good, and it's all her fault, everybody says. You know how she went out to his place years ago and tried to get him without a stitch of clothes on her shameless body! Then after they were married, she had no use for him. They lived together like fighting cocks. You'd think he'd a made her lie in the bed she made, but he let her have her way, never lifted a hand in court against her. If there'd been children, maybe it would be different, but she wouldn't bear him any. Now she's going with that England man, George Seton. The one that brought in these English sawmills. They say he'll be a lord some day if his older brother ever dies, and that's what she's after. It would make her a lady. Can you imagine that common thing a titled English lady? I thought it would disgust the iron master with the Wheelers. But I've lost my respect for him. He still comes to the house, they say, and sits and talks to that woman and asks her advice just as if she was still his mother-in-law!"

Miss Bogardus's chief spite seemed directed toward "that woman." She told with contempt how Judge Wheeler's wife couldn't read or write until her own children taught her, and even now any school child could read rings around her.

"You can tell she was never used to anything. She won't have a maid in that big house but makes the girls help. She raises things in her vacant lots as if she was still on the farm. I don't know where she gets that from, because her father isn't worth a whoop and never was. But to hear her, you'd think he was a saint. She calls him Pappy, and it's Pappy this and Pappy that. And yet she won't have him in the house. He has to stay down in that shanty in Beagle's boat yard, and she sends his supper down in a basket every day to make people believe she does something for her Pappy."

However, it was when Miss Bogardus talked about Judge Wheeler that Rosa felt the strangest, bitterest silence come over her mother.

"You remember the little Canada man that killed one of the Clarks in Tateville? He's crazy as a loon. That's why they didn't hang him. And dangerous, too. You might know, if he's a murderer. But Judge Wheeler lets him out a while every day. Calls him his messenger. Lets him run his errands. Why, he goes all over the city some days, and could kill any of us, but Judge Wheeler claims he's harmless. He lets him go in his own house and that woman feeds him at the kitchen table. I'm scared of him. If you call him Crazy Bill, he gets mad. He says, 'Johnny Meigs is crazy but I'm only simple.' Can you imagine that? It shows how crazy he is. Of course, he sleeps in the jail house at night, but he could do a lot of damage in the daytime. It's all Judge Wheeler's doings, and if you ask me, I think he's very high handed. Mr. Millard's cousin was taking up a collection for that poor woman whose husband was drowned last month. She lives down near the basin. 'I know all about her,' Judge Wheeler stopped him. 'She's a poor widow with four children and takes in washing. I won't give her a cent.' 'What do you mean?' Mr. Millard's cousin asked, so surprised. 'Why won't you help her?' 'Because she's good and virtuous,' the judge told him. 'I never help that kind of person. There's a hundred other people that will. I help only the devil's poor. When you're taking up a collection for somebody drunken and worthless that nobody else will give a hand to, come around and I'll contribute.' That's exactly what he said. I heard Mr. Millard's cousin say so myself. It's lucky for him that judges are appointed and not elected or he wouldn't get a vote except from his devil's poor. Now who would ever think that to see him walking down the street so noble and grand?"

She spoke as if Rosa's mother went abroad in the city like other people. Rosa sat on the edge of the porch missing no word. She could see Judge Wheeler in her mind, going down the street, and that's how he looked, noble and grand like Miss Bogardus said. Oh, he looked almost like God Almighty Himself in a high hat and frock coat, his lion's head sunken on his breast, his eyes looking neither to the right nor left. When he passed her, he wouldn't give her a glance. One time after he went by, a man came up and said something to her.

"You're as good as he is," he told her. "And you ought to be living in his house."

Now what had this man meant by such a saying, Rosa

often wondered, but never for a moment could she dare to ask. One or two loafers must have heard what he said because that night her father came home, his face black to all save her. He called the boys in and took down his rifle.

"I want to tell you young 'uns something," he swore. "Rosa is your sister and this is where she belongs. In this house with me and her mam. Anybody that says different, I want you to tell me. I don't care if it's man, woman or child, I'll fix him so he won't say it again. Like I'm going to fix somebody tonight who talked too much."

Rosa looked quickly at her mother but nothing showed on her tired, olive, hawklike face. Her father went on down town with his rifle, but they never heard that he shot anybody. The boys thought he might have done it in the dead of night and thrown the body in the river, but Rosa prayed that the man who spoke to her got out of town. That was the first and last time anybody said such a thing to her. Sometimes her brothers would look at her with strange eyes, but that's as far as they went. It didn't mean anything, she told herself. That man was likely just a Van Buren man mad at a Clay man like Judge Wheeler. But so long as she didn't actually know, she could always hoard the mysterious secret in her breast. Whenever she heard the Wheeler name or saw one of the many Wheelers down town, a faint unexplained excitement rose in her and the man's words came back to her ears. She kept those words in the sheltered shade of her heart. They would shrivel up if she brought them out in the light of day.

Today the magic state was on her like a spell. She could sit on the broken edge of the porch, with the empty stone jugs on one side and the sack of old rags on the other, with the trash and refuse and junk of the yard in front, and taste the scent and feeling of the Wheeler mansion house

all around her. Miss Bogardus was telling her mother today
how Judge Wheeler's fine sister was visiting him now from
the Bay State. In her mind Rosa could see her in her elegant
gray taffeta like Miss Doan's sister from Maryland wore
whom Rosa never saw either. But Mrs. Doan had told her
about her sister many times, and how she needn't lift a
hand or foot, for she had a hundred slaves to do her bid-
ding.

Sitting here today with Miss Bogardus's voice in her ear
and the pictures of Judge Wheeler's sister in her mind,
Rosa thought, wouldn't it be wonderful if Mrs. Doan's fine
sister, Ellin, came to visit Mrs. Doan while Judge Wheeler's sister was in Americus! Likely the two knew each
other back East and when they met down on Market Street
or High Street, Judge Wheeler's sister would say how glad
she was to see her friend out here in Ohio and wouldn't she
come to dinner on Sunday?

"I can come and thank you, but I can't come without
my sister," Mrs. Doan's sister would say.

"Then bring her along by all means," Judge Wheeler's
sister would tell her, for she knew that Mrs. Doan had been
the finest milliner in all of the state of Maryland before she
left.

Then of a sudden on Saturday night Mrs. Doan's sister,
Ellin, would get sick and they'd have to have the doctor.

"Jenny, I'm a sick woman and can't go to Judge Wheeler's sister's Sunday dinner tomorrow," she would tell. "It's
too late to stop it now. You'll have to go and take somebody in my place."

"Then I'll take Rosa Tench, for she runs all my errands,
and matches ribbons and threads for me at Meek's Em-
porium, and she has a good eye," Mrs. Doan would say.
She would say nothing, however, about the rum she sent

Rosa for sometimes. No, not a word would she mention about that or how she would sit and stir brown sugar in it and sip it while her face got heavier and her nose got thicker and shorter till she looked like the Houcks' pug dog sitting on a box. No, all she would do and say now with her sister, Ellin, visiting her was call a Gatchell boy across the street and send for Rosa. And Rosa would hurry down.

"Rosa, you are the truest friend I have in Americus," Mrs. Doan would say. "Will you go to the Wheelers' mansion house to Sunday dinner with me tomorrow?"

"But I have no dress, Mrs. Doan," Rosa would have to tell her.

"Then I'll make you one," Mrs. Doan would say, and she'd sew all night with her sister helping, for Ellin wouldn't be so sick that she couldn't help with the needle. And next day after everybody was home from church, she would walk down town with Mrs. Doan in her fine dress for Sunday dinner, and everybody would see her, even Miss Bogardus from the Millard windows. And Judge Wheeler's sister would look at her and say I am sorry my friend couldn't come but glad that you are the one Mrs. Doan brought. And Rosa would sit in the dining room at the mahogany table and eat from china dishes with gold and pink flowers and put a solid silver fork to her mouth. And across the table, Judge Wheeler would have to look at her and say, didn't he see her some place before? And after dinner she and Massey and Chancey could go out in the yard.

"Rosa!" a voice broke suddenly into her daydream. It sounded like her brother Turkey calling from down the street. "Rosa! Mrs. Doan wants you!"

It was a shock as if Heaven had suddenly named her. She was wide awake now but inside she felt shaking. Was it

coming true like she had dreamed? She went out of the
gate, hurrying a little, a delicious knot in her breast. Down
the street she could see the dirty little yellow Doan house
with dirtier and darker doors and window frames. A little
crowd was gathered on the vacant lot aside of the house.
She mustn't run, she told herself. If Mrs. Doan's sister was
there, she mustn't see her do anything undignified. Then
as she grew closer, the people on the lot moved so that she
could see by them, and her legs didn't try to hurry any
more.

"No!" she moaned to herself a little, but she knew it
was true. It was the same old story. Between the people
she could see Mrs. Doan's short stout body lying on the
ground. She must have got some money on a bill and was
drunk again, lying out in the vacant lot under the sun with
only her shift on.

"Get up, Mrs. Doan!" Mrs. Gatchell said, poking her.
"You're a disgrace lying out half naked in the day time.
You'll catch the distemper."

But Mrs. Doan lay quiet and peaceful, a small mountain
of flesh on the ground, never bothering, one plump hand
that could trim a hat so deftly lying open on a clump of
grass.

"Go away," she murmured. "I am in my room in bed, I
am sure. Go out now and shut the door."

"You're drunk!" Mrs. Gatchell bent down to her. She
plucked up a fistful of stones. "Are these what you got in
your house on your bed? Look and tell me, Mrs. Doan!"

But Mrs. Doan lay in fine oblivion, letting the world go
by, and that, Rosa thought, was proof that Mrs. Doan was
really of high born stock, for nothing could disconcert or
discommode her.

"Go out of my house now and close the door and leave me in peace!" she told them.

"She's drunk as a sow!" Mrs. Gatchell said to any who would hear. "She'll never listen to you, Rosa."

The name stirred life in the sluggish small mountain of flesh on the ground.

"Rosa!" it moaned. "It's about time you came. Show these rude people out and lock the door."

The girl went up to her quietly. It was curious but seldom did she feel shy or inferior with Mrs. Doan. Rather she felt like a poor but acknowledged relation. And sometimes as now like a worthy and equal relation. Even when Mrs. Doan was sober, at her best, skillfully trimming a bonnet, turning it in her hands to look at it this way and that, telling of the grandeurs of her sister's life in Maryland, she treated Rosa like a special person. With Mrs. Doan, Rosa's mother, family and house faded cleanly from her mind, and there was left only good and gentle blood in her veins. Ever Rosa felt free to act and say what she wished when she was with Mrs. Doan.

"They have a right to be here and I can't make them go, Mrs. Doan," she said in a low voice.

The bleary eyes opened and back in those round and swollen organs a distorted being regarded her like the misshapen creature that looked out at her from a pug's pop eyes.

"Are you going to tell me I'm not in my own house and bed!" she warned.

"I wouldn't say that, Mrs. Doan. But I have to tell you you're not in the right bed. If you get up now, I'll help you back to your right bed, and then all these people can't see you and bother you any more."

[253]

Grumbling and moaning and with great difficulty, Mrs. Doan worked herself up, bearing heavily on the small thirteen year old girl. She had thought all the time she wasn't in her right bed, she said. It felt too hard and lumpy. Why didn't somebody tell her? Why did she have to wait all this humiliating while for Rosa to come? She swayed on her feet like a tree with severed roots, pulling the girl this way and that. Her body stank like a whiskey barrel. Her hair had fallen completely down. No stranger, Rosa thought, would ever know her now as the finest milliner in all of Maryland. But through the puffy skin and soiled shift and disheveled hair, Rosa could still see with affection the one whose clever hands were the mistress of any bonnet and whose sister had a hundred slaves to wait on her hand and foot from morn till night and, if need be, again till morning.

"We're almost there, Mrs. Doan," she encouraged her several times. The stupefied woman let the girl lead her to the gate and into the little yellow house with the dirty yellow doors and window casings.

CHAPTER TWENTY-TWO

ANT SULIE

Blown from night and the north.

SOPHOCLES

T HE LAST month or two he lived, Worth gave Genny
plenty of trouble. Every time Sayward saw her, she
would complain.

"He won't wear those new clothes we got for him. No,
he holds like grim death to the old. He just does it for spite.
He wants to keep me mending and patching, and make it
look like we won't keep our own pappy looking decent in
front of folks. Then he won't hardly eat what I cook him
during the day. Nothing tastes good, he says. But when
Will comes home late at night, he sticks his head out of the
shanty. 'Will, fetch me something to eat!' he calls so loud
the whole neighborhood can hear. You'd think I half starved
him. If it was me, I wouldn't take him out anything, but
Will is fool enough to give him what he wants."

A month to the day that Portius's sister went back home,
Worth gave up and died. Genny cried at Sayward's neck
when she saw her. You'd reckon Worth had been a wonderful father to her.

"I made him such a nice dinner, Saird," she said, drawing back and wiping her eyes. "I asked him early this morning what was he hungry for. He answered back like usual. Oh, nothing tasted good any more. But you know the way he liked brown flour gravy. I asked if he wouldn't like some of that. Well, that would taste as good as anything, he said. So I made him some flapjacks to put the gravy over, and some boiled cabbage and some of that sausage I still have away in lard. He ate pretty good for him. After dinner, I had no idea of anything. He just sat there at the table and flushed up a little. I asked if he didn't want to lay down. He said he didn't care, so he laid down on the settee in the kitchen. I should have knowed from that. Most times he would have no other way than go back to his cabin. But you know how contrary he's been lately. Anyway he laid down on the settee and crossed his feet. And that's the last I knowed of him for a while. He did give a couple of snores and grunts, but he always did that. They sounded natural except they had a kind of rattle at the end. Mrs. Heberling was in the front room with me. She could look out through the kitchen door and said, 'I believe your pap's dying.' I looked right away and called Will to run for you and the doctor. But Pap give up before either of you got here. He died so nice and easy. Look at him. Did you ever see a nicer corpse? You wouldn't think now to look at him what a trial he's been to us all his life."

"I can see Wyitt in him for the first time," Sayward mentioned.

"I can see more of Achsa," Genny said. "Especially around the mouth."

The neighbors gone, the sisters closed the door, rolled up their sleeves and made ready to wash the silent figure and dyke him out in the new clothes he'd never consent to wear when alive. Now, how long had it been since she and Genny had done this thing for their mother? It must be close to forty years. Wasn't it strange that Worth, who never was good for very much, should have been blessed with such long life and that he should look sweeter in death than he ever had in his lifetime?

"Well, it's a blessing to go quick, and we ought to be thankful if we're ever that lucky," Sayward mentioned.

"He didn't go that quick," Genny said. "He told me something before he went. I could hardly believe it."

Sayward looked sharply at her sister. Genny went on.

"It's good I was here. He opened his eyes and saw me standing over him. Then he told me. It was about Sulie."

"Sulie!" Sayward echoed, her own Sulie coming first to mind.

"It was our Sulie he meant," Genny explained. "He found her. She's still a living — out in Indiany. I said, 'Pap, are you sure?' and he said he lived at her house a while. Her name's Harris. She has a good man and is good off, Pap said. He told me the name of the town, and Mrs. Heberling set it down. I don't know if you can read it, her hand was trembling so, and I don't know if it would do you any good if you could."

Sayward was never so beat out as by what Genny told her. So their youngest sister was still among the living! Not once all these years had she ever buried Sulie in her mind. No, she clung to the thread that some Indians had found her. But hardly had she looked to have word from her after all this time. Even Portius was stirred up. Indeed the news that Sulie Luckett was still alive after almost forty years shook the Wheeler family more than Worth's death. Why, ever since they were old enough to be talked to, the children and grandchildren had heard the story of their Ant

Sulie who got lost in the woods. The cows had come home and their Uncle Wyitt but never did she. A whole company of men had scoured the deep woods for days. All they found beside Indian signs were teeth marks on a spicewood twig, a red thread on a haw, a few small footprints in a sandy run and the bower she had made. Oh, the Wheeler children had heard plenty about that bower. Even the grandchildren could tell you what it was like, a little bitty house made from sticks, with a bark roof, a block of wood for a table and a piece from Sulie's red dress for a table cloth. Just to see it, the men could tell a small girl had done this. Away back in the trackless wilderness, far from any human this little lost tyke had made herself a play house to mind herself of her pappy's cabin and of her sisters and brother she never would see again or not for forty years anyway.

Worth was buried a Thursday. On Friday Sayward sat down and wrote a letter to Mrs. Sulie Harris, Vinita, Indiana. If she was her sister, Sulie Luckett, lost in the woods and never found save perhaps by Indians, would she write back and tell her? Their pap was dead and buried now, but his last words told about her. Would she like to know about her brother and sisters? Wyitt and Ascha had left home and were never heard from again. But Genny lived here, Will Beagle was her man. Sayward herself was lawfully married, the mother of ten children and nine of them still living as far as she knew. Her married name was Wheeler. She did not say her man was a judge; let her find that out in due course. Dezia could have written the letter in her fine backhand and saved her mother much labor, but Dezia would want to say everything grand like in the copybooks, and Sayward wanted it like she was just sitting down with Sulie and talking to her. The letter filled one side of a foolscap till it was done. But though she looked anxiously to Chancey whenever he fetched the mail after that, no answer to her letter ever came.

"If it's our Sulie, why do you reckon she don't answer?" Genny asked her.

"We let a mighty long time go by ourselves before we wrote her. We can't expect an answer right on the dot," Sayward said, but she looked mighty grave when she said it.

"Did you ever think, Saird, that Pap might a been a little out of his head before he passed on?"

"It could be," Sayward admitted. "On the other hand, Portius told me about a man up in the Firelands who was crazy for thirty years, and just before he died, his mind turned good as yours or mine. 'I wish I could see my mother,' he said, and that was the last thing he did say."

"I think it's mighty strange Pap never said anything about Sulie all that while," Genny complained.

"It wouldn't be the first time he acted like that," Sayward reminded her. "You ought to know the time we had no idea anybody was living in the woods besides us till just before Martha Covenhoven came a calling. Then Pap told us and went off hunting but he knew it all the time. No, this would be just like him as far as that's concerned."

"It still seems funny to me."

"Then you got to recollect Sulie was a little tyke the last we knew her. Now we were a good bit older and would mind her better than she could us. But I'd know her anywheres, and if I don't hear anything by the middle of summer, I'm going out."

"All the way out there!" Genny said. "Well, if you're really going, I'm a going with you. I wouldn't want anything to happen to her or me and then think I passed up a chance to see our Sulie."

They made out to go early in August. Sayward said she
would take Massey and Chancey along. She didn't like
leaving them back here alone with Dezia and Portius. It
would be something for them to see the country and their
Ant Sulie. Besides, Will, being in the boat trade, got such
low rates it was cheaper to take them along than leave
them behind.

They left Americus on a fine morning with the sun not
yet high enough to be hot and a good-sized bunch of relations and friends down to the basin to see them off. Portius and Will stood on the wharf holding up their hats, and
little Resolve kept waving till Dyke's warehouse shut them
off from view. From the Sixth Street bridge curious folks
looked down on them as they passed under. Genny wiped
her eyes as the city fell behind them. Even Chancey looked
a mite uncertain, but Sayward felt an anxious kind of hope
and peace. Oh, she hated going off where she couldn't see
all her children and grandchildren for five or six weeks.
But how long had it been since she saw her baby sister?
Hardly had there been a rainy night all this time that she
hadn't thought of her and wondered what had happened to
her that time in the woods so long ago. Could she still be
among the living, she used to ask herself, and did she still
say such grand and spunky things that minded them of
their Grandmother Powelly back along the Conestoga.

"Do you mind what she said that time we first looked
over this country?" Sayward asked.

"I mind," Genny nodded. "We were up on a hill. We
could look over a hundred miles of country it seemed like.
Woods, nothing but woods it was. I mind it good. She said
— now what was it she said, Saird?"

" 'We mought even get rich and have shoes!' " Sayward
told her. "I can still hear how cunning she said it. That

seemed like a mighty rash and bold thing to say them days. We couldn't see smoke from a single cabin."

"I wonder what she's like now!" Genny said.

Sayward had been wondering the same. Sitting here on the quiet deck of the boat, keeping an eye on Massey and Chancey that they didn't fall in, she figured that Sulie must be going on fifty years old. They'd have to remember she'd be changed, Sayward told Genny. Likely she'd be grander than either one of them, Genny agreed, with a ring on every finger but one, and three on that, for their pap said how she had a good man and was good off. She might even have a coach, for she was always one to do spunky things. Whether she had any young ones or not, pap didn't say, but if she had, they would likely give Massey and Chancey a run to keep up with them.

They came to Vinita on a Saturday, and Sayward reckoned it the prettiest country she ever saw. The canal ahead looked like it would run head on into a handsome wooded hill. But when they got there, they found the water turning against the hill till a gap opened up where it could go through, and there was the town with rows of stone and log cabins, some fine white and yellow clapboard houses and a stone mansion house with a great stone stable, while across the canal and river lay the smooth green banks and meadows of a fine gentleman's farm with the big house, farm house, barn and out buildings all painted to match, of pale green with brown narrow strips where at regular intervals strips of wood went up and down closing the cracks. It made a wonderful sight, like some place in old England, and all of them admired it together with the fat stock grazing in soft fields that hadn't a weed in them.

"That could be her place," Genny whispered. "You know what Pap said."

But when they stepped off the boat to the smooth stone
work of the basin, an old boatman standing there said Mrs.
Sulie Harris lived on the far side of town. Sayward thought
that he and the men hanging around the basin looked at her
a little strange. They were shorter spoken, too, than most
men on the trip. When she looked back, she saw them all
standing where she left them, looking after. Genny said she
guessed they made a sight tramping up the middle of the
road carrying their own traps, two women and two young
ones all the way from Ohio without a man. She said it
looked like a poor way to go visiting a sister who was
well-off. She thought perhaps they should hire a carriage.
But Sayward said it felt good to get their feet on the
ground. They had been cooped up on the boat too long,
and could tramp a mile or two without it hurting them any.

There was no house to ask at for a good ways save a log
cabin standing back from the road a little under the trees.
It looked dark from weather. The ground lay tramped
hard and bare around it. On this side stood a cleared patch
of corn.

"I declare I never saw such poor and scrubby corn,"
Genny said. "But maybe they could tell us how to go."

As they came abreast of the cabin, a pack of dogs rushed
out. Sayward picked up a stout club and they stayed their
distance barking and carrying on. A dark-faced boy about
sixteen came out hollering at them with strange words.
When he saw the four strangers in the road, he stopped.
Genny called shrilly above the hullabaloo.

"Can you tell us how to get to the Harris place?"

The boy stood stock still, never saying back a word.
After a little, he turned and went into the cabin.

"He don't know nothing. He's Injun," Genny said.

They had started on when a man still older than Sayward

came out. He was dressed in pants and shirt but was plainly an Indian. He moved stiffly, very straight, and with great deliberation. He spoke in the same language as the boy to the dogs and when one wouldn't obey him, he picked it up and threw it with such force against a tree that it ran yelping pitifully into the cabin. As he came toward them, Sayward felt the children move behind her.

"We're looking for the Harris place," she told him.

"Him live here," the Indian said. "My name Harris."

There was dead silence for a moment.

"It must be some mistake," Genny put in lordly. "We're looking for Mrs. Sulie Harris."

"Him my woman," he said.

Sayward saw Genny draw back as if he had hit her. She felt Massey and Chancey push up against her and freeze. She waited a little, gathering her thought, setting her face.

"Can we see her?" she asked friendly.

"Sure. Him in house." He made no move to take them in, only stood there with all the time and indifference in the world.

Sayward started toward the cabin.

"Saird!" Genny begged, holding fast to her arm. "This can't be our Sulie?"

"That's what I want to find out," Sayward declared. She had come this far. Nothing was going to stop her now.

"If it was Sulie, she'd be out," Genny stammered. "She'd hear us. She'd come to the door."

"She might want to fix up a little first," Sayward said.

But when she got to the door, she found no sign that anyone had tried to redd up the cabin. The door stood wide open. Inside were neither chairs, table nor stools. A younger Indian woman with three small children sat on the hard earth floor. A younger Indian man and the boy stood on the other side. At the fire with her back toward them, bent an older woman. She was cooking something in a pot. She wore a shapeless gray cabin gown, was barefoot, her feet and legs brown. Her back remained toward the door as if she were deaf, and yet something passed over Sayward when she saw her. With the dogs baring their teeth and snarling at her, Sayward stepped unbidden into the cabin.

"We're looking for Mrs. Sulie Harris," she said.

The older woman made no movement. Not till one of the younger Indians said something to her in the Delaware language did she turn around, and then aversely. Her face was brown as her feet, wrinkled, the face of an older squaw, and yet Sayward saw something in it of her own Grandmam Powelly she had seen as a girl back along the Conestoga in Pennsylvania. It shook her to her bones.

"Sulie!" she said starting toward her, but such a hard implacable look came into the woman's black Indian eyes that it stopped her. "Wasn't your name Sulie Luckett when you were a young one?" Sayward stammered.

"My name Sulie Harris," she answered, without feeling.

"But when you were a little tyke, didn't you have a family by name of Luckett? Back in Pennsylvania? Then you all went to Northwest Territory. Didn't you go out with the cows and get lost in the woods and never lay eyes on your folks again?"

"No remember."

"Try to recollect!" Sayward begged her. "Can't you mind your mam and pap? He was out here to see you not so long ago. Worth, his name was. Don't you mind your brother Wyitt and your sisters Achsa, Genny and Saird that used to live with you in that cabin? Well, if you do, I'm your sister, Saird, and out there's Genny. Don't you mind us now?"

"No. Me Indian," she said stolidly.

She was lying, Sayward told herself. Genny and the younger ones were watching from the door. Massey and Chancey turned piteous faces toward her.

"Mama, let's go," Massey whispered.

"Genny, maybe you'd sing something for her?" Sayward asked. "Something she used to know, like Fly Up. It might help her remember."

Genny looked shocked. Her face said she couldn't do that, not here in front of Indians. Yet never had she refused Sayward anything, and in the end she gave in. She started very low, not even clearing her throat. It seemed at first she was only going to hum, then the song came out as of itself, like spring water rises from the ground. So clear and strong it sounded at last that it gave Sayward a turn to hear it.

> Haycocks in the meader,
> Cherries in the dish.
> Red bird, fly up,
> Give me my wish.
>
> Chestnuts in the tree top,
> Punkin in the dish.
> Brown bird, fly up,
> Give me my wish.
>
> Ice in the river.
> Possum in the dish,
> Snow bird, fly up,
> Give me my wish.
>
> Vi'lets in the holler,
> Poke greens in the dish.
> Blue bird, fly up,
> Give me my wish.

How many times, Sayward thought, had they heard that in the old days? Till Genny was half ways through, it seemed like they were back in the woods with their mam still living, and Achsa and Wyitt still at home. It was almost like this was her pap's cabin and Sulie was a little tyke still there with them.

But when the song stopped and the spell broke, Sulie Harris's eyes looked back at her with all the stoic relentlessness of the savage as when you and he stare at each other across the uncrossable gulf.

"It's not her," Genny said very low. "Or she'd say something."

Oh, what, Sayward thought, could Genny expect Sulie Harris to say? How did she reckon her sister felt standing there in her bare feet and ragged dress, in her dirty Indian cabin with her dark Indian children and grandchildren around her? Did Genny expect Sulie to thank her white sisters for coming to see her in their soft leather shoes and fine dresses, with elegant mits on their hands and bonnets with silken ribbons on their heads, with their own clean white children along and their white husbands at home? What was that story pap used to tell of Janie Gosset who the Shawanees took from Buffalo Valley? Years later, when her folks found her, she had an Indian family, and even though her Shawanee man was dead, she wouldn't go back. She would be a disgrace to her white people, she said. Her oldtime friends and relations would look down on her and her Indian young ones. No, it was too late now. Never could she go back and never could Sulie. They had taken up the Indian life, and that's the life they had to live till they died.

Sayward couldn't look at Sulie now without her heart yearning toward her till she could hardly stand it. Gladly would she have done most anything to make it right, but what could she do? Is this what they had come all the long way from Ohio for? Is this what brave young hopes and spunkiness like Sulie's came to in the end? How far off that little tyke she used to know seemed now. Lost and alone in the woods, she had played cabin to remind her of her brother and sisters, but now that two of her sisters were here, she wouldn't give in that she knew them. One time she must have cried bitterly for them, but now she wished them far off and the biggest favor they could do her was not to claim any more that they were her sisters.

Sulie Harris stared back at her without winking. After a while, she spoke in Delaware to the young Indian who was likely her boy.

"She say," he translated to Sayward, "you and her go. But leave young ones. Wait by road. By and by come out."

Genny looked alarmed, and Chancey and Massey begged their mother not to leave them but she cut them short. They could do that much for their Ant Sulie. She saw them wince at the word. Sayward herself spoke to Sulie Harris before she went, taking the cold impassive hand in both of hers.

"I hope this won't be the last time I see you, Sulie. If you ever need anything, let me know. I'll send it to you if I can. You got my address. If you ever get that way, stop and visit me." But although Indians loved to visit, she felt that her sister Sulie never would.

As they left, Sulie Harris spoke deep in her throat to the rest of her family. The latter followed them out reluctantly, leaving her alone inside with the white young ones. Sayward reckoned she would not soon forget Chancey's frightened face at the door when she went. The Indians moved off by themselves to the other side of the cabin. The older Indian man she could see down along the river. She and Genny went to the road.

"Not a foot farther will I budge," Genny said, "till Massey and Chancey come out."

It seemed a mighty long time until they came running like deer from the cabin. Chancey looked pale and Massey was crying.

"What did she do to you?" Genny wanted to know right away.

"She didn't do anything. She just stayed in there with us. After while she took Chancey's hand and stroked it. She said how he minded her of somebody."

Sayward and Genny looked at each other.

"Wyitt!" they said together.

"She didn't say Uncle Wyitt or any name," Massey said. "She just stroked Chancey's hand and said how white it was. And then she started to cry. It looked so terrible when she cried, I had to cry, too."

"And then what?"

"She stopped and asked what I was crying for. She threw Chancey's hand down. She said white was a very bad color. She said white men were good in church but bad in the woods. They killed and cheated the Indians she said. But her man was always good and kind, she said. We should tell you he was always good and kind to her. He was a great soldier and killed lots of white men in battle. One time he scalped so many white men, his arm got tired. He was brave and not afraid to do what was right. More than once he burned white men at a fire he made himself."

Genny drew an expressive face to Sayward.

"What else did she say?"

"That's all."

"But you were in such a long time."

ANT   SULIE

"She just stood most of the time looking at us. I couldn't tell if she hated us or liked us. Then she gave us each something and said we could go." Massey opened her hand and showed a silver shilling. "She had them in a little leather bag under her dress. I saw her reach in and her skin in there was as white as mine is, Mama."

Sayward stood there, her face working. Genny put her handkerchief away.

"I'm going back and talk to her and try to do something for her," she announced.

"I wouldn't if I was you, Genny," Sayward said gravely. "You know what Pap used to say, that a white person never does the Indians any good. He always tries to make a white person out of them. Pap said he never knew a single Indian who made a good white person, though he knew plenty whites who made good Indians."

"Well, I don't believe it that strong," Genny said. "I feel terrible sorry for her if you don't. I didn't think it was really her when we were in there with her. Now I'm going back and talk to her and see what I can do. Anyway I can give her goodby when I leave and tell her I hope we'll meet in heaven."

Sayward and the children waited. Genny was white as a sheet when she returned. She wouldn't talk about it until they were some distance back to town.

"She acted queer again like she was at first," she said grimly. "She wouldn't even talk till I made her. Then she said right out she didn't know us. Said her name never was Luckett. Claimed she never seen us before. I tried to talk to her like a sister, and she told me to clear out or she'd sic the dogs on us."

Sayward said nothing. Her face felt weary and be-numbed. She should never have left Genny go back. How

[269]

she hated now turning away from her own flesh and blood
sister, leaving her behind in that poor cabin while she set
out for another state and a mansion house. She tried to tell
herself it wasn't so bad as she and Genny felt. She reminded
herself of what pap used to say that white folks liked
to think their life the only way and that any savage ought to
jump at the chance to be a white person. But, he used to
tell them, none of those white prisoners his old colonel
took from the Indians ever thanked him for giving them
back to their white folks. Most of them, he said, fought
like cats and dogs to stay with their Indian step-mammies
and pappies. Even when they got home, some ran off to
lead the Indian life again.

That was the way to look at it, Sayward told herself.
Sulie might have had a hard life, but it was better than if
she had died that time in the woods and been put under
ground. She had grown up and tasted life. She knew what
it meant to give birth to young ones, to nurse and watch
them a growing. She had a cabin, a man and family of her
own. It mightn't look like much of a life to white folks, but
you had to take life as it was and not as you wished you
had it.

Just the same, all the way to the canal and to Ohio on
the boat, something kept coming back to Sayward's mind.
Grandmam MacWhirter, long dead and buried, had said it,
the time that poor little Sulie was lost. "Sometimes it's a
good thing if you don't find a lost young 'un," she had
said. "I'd as soon see them dead and buried."

CHAPTER TWENTY-THREE

THE TREES

I am Alpha and Omega, the beginning and the end, the first and the last.

REVELATION

Now what was the matter with her, Sayward asked herself when she got back home. She hadn't felt so bad since Portius ran around with that other woman. Even then she didn't know as she was so short-tempered, sharp-spoken and mean. Nothing suited her any more. She should have thanked the Lord every night for getting her back safe and sound and having a decent home to come to. On the whole trip she hadn't seen a house she'd want to trade for hers. What was that old saying, "Travel north, south, east, west — home's best." That was a true saying.

And yet here she was, fretting, grumbling about everything around home, especially about higher taxes. Americus was getting too big for its britches, she complained. Why, the numbered streets ran high as Fourteenth already, and some were talking of them going to twenty. The town wasn't satisfied with milling, blacksmithing and wheelwrighting any more but had to brag now about its new soap works that packed pork and beef, its looking-glass works that made combs out of cows' horns, and a cotton factory with a thousand spindles and looms. There were so many different mills and works that the race couldn't turn all the wheels. The Centinel came around every day but Sunday. Nobody but an idle person had time to read it any more. Down on Water Street the Grand Central Hotel had fixed itself up like Babylon with carpets all through, and the Mechanics Society had started telling plant and shop owners what they could do and couldn't.

"Don't mind her," she heard Genny tell Dezia. "It's finding your Ant Sulie that way that done it. It's eating at her heart, and she don't know it."

Sayward never let on that she heard. It wasn't Sulie, she felt, but the pride and greed and great shakes of these town bodies that bothered her. Nothing was good enough for them any more. Twice had her own church been rebuilt during her life time and still they had to make it bigger, with a new steeple so high no workman for less than four dollars a day would risk his neck on it. The selectmen weren't satisfied any more with fire ladders in the market house and fire buckets of harness leather with the householders' names painted on them. No, they had to send for a Philadelphia fire engine and fetch it all the way around by New Orleans. This engine had a water tank you filled with buckets and a crank to pump it out. Oh, fighting Demon Fire was a good thing, and Sayward stood high on the subscription list for both ladders and engine. But even this grand new engine didn't suit them long, and now they had to have one that sucked up water from a well or cistern. They called it the Neptune, and another company was starting the Vigilance.

That wasn't half of it. Merchants were spoiling the Square, buying up houses and making them over into shops. They even tried to buy the old cemetery and put up a new bank and hardware store on the graves. Nothing could stop progress, they said, not even "Mrs. Wheeler's mother's bones." Sayward bowed up her back at that. She told what she thought to Portius who let fly a speech about disturbing the last resting place of the pioneers, and that put an end to it. But some of the business men were so mad at her, they complained bitterly about her holding on to her lots for raising truck. Land so close in was needed for business to give men a chance to work, they said.

"Why don't they say it to my face?" she complained to Portius. "Then I could give them a piece of my mind. Their houses and mills shut in all my land now. I can't see the country any more. Every way you look, you're stopped by their sawed boards or else their brick and stone."

The old order had changed, she told herself. The world she knew was going. About the only thing left around town was the ancient sugar maple half way across the square. It wasn't much of a tree any more and hadn't been for a good while. Once it had given copiously of syrup. Sayward herself had pounded spiles in the butt. Of late years it had been going down hill. The butt had a hollow place big enough for a good-sized bear to hide in. Every winter more limbs had broken off. The crown was dead, and the only green part left was its middle. But that tree had seen her pappy when first he came to this country, and the rest of them as well.

Then one night in October it stormed, and when she got up in the morning, the old tree was done. The butt had broken off at the hollow place, and what leaves it had lay yellow and mud-spattered on the ground.

"The great god, Pan, is dead!" Portius said when he got up and saw it.

Well, it was about time that it came down, Sayward told herself. Before it fell on somebody. She wouldn't want to see it maim one of those young ones always playing around it. Funny how they seemed drawn to that old tree.

Just the same she didn't sleep so good that night. When she woke up from a nap at daylight, she had the strange notion she lacked something. Now how could you miss something that you never did have? She lay there listening but couldn't hear anything. When she got up, she looked around the room. Now how could you expect to see or hear anything when you didn't know what it was you looked and listened for? The only thing missing when she went to the window was that sugar maple she used to see half way across the Square. Already it had been half cut up by Cherry Alley householders.

It couldn't be that old tree lying on the ground that bothered her, she told herself. Why, all her life she had hugged herself to see a tree come down. It meant you could see the sun and stars a little better. A mite more light and air could come in. A few more stalks of corn could grow and give meal to hungry young mouths. Why, back in the woods, she and every other settler woman hated the trees like poison. They were your mortal enemy. All your life you had to fight them, chop, split, nigger them off till nothing was left. And then their wild sprouts kept coming up to plague you. Even now long after the trees were gone, the big butts still lived on in your joints. Heavy lifting and rolling had thickened them till you sometimes felt like an old tree walking.

That afternoon from the third floor she looked out of a front window, and later out of the back. Over the whole city hardly a tree could her eyes find. She knew it had some lilac, apple and peach trees tucked away here and yonder in side and back yards, but they were puny, of no account, could hide behind outhouses. Hardly one could she see from here. The city looked all red brick and wood. Now where had she seen such a city before? Then she knew. This was the city she had dreamt about that time long ago in the wilderness, a city of red brick and white wooden church steeples and never a tree in sight. She had thought it then a wonderful sight to see, a place free of the lonesome gloom of the deep woods, and nary a big butt to have to cut down and burn up. But she didn't know how much she liked it now. It minded her a little today of one of those desert places her father told them about, of red rocks and sand and far as you could see not a single tree raising itself toward heaven.

She couldn't help thinking of some of the trees they had seen on the trip to Indiana. Not the kind she had known in the woods, standing thick as thieves with their heads together plotting against humans. No, these big butts of the countryside seemed of a different and kindlier breed, standing in open places, free to spread out on all sides, a whole woods of leaves and limbs hanging on a single trunk.

One big basswood she recollected especially. They had seen it first a long ways off across the fields. As they approached it grew taller and broader like the daddy of all the big butts, rising half way to the sky and spreading out like a monster umbrella over canal, tow path and locktender's house. It was a hot day in the sun but when the boat came under the shade, it felt cool, fresh and green like when she was a girl in the deep woods, only this wasn't something fierce but tame and beneficent to man. She noticed it again when they came back. It was a warm early September evening. All were on deck to see the sun going down and the moon coming up. They had to wait for another boat to pass through the locks, and then one of the gates had to be patched up. All the time she sat there listening to the soft wind in the big basswood. It stirred like something alive. It was immense and powerful, yet gentle as a woman holding its great arms over water and land, boats and locks, the locktender's cottage and his children.

Now why did she think all her life that trees were savage and cruel? Or were they wild in the woods when she was young, and now in the peaceful countryside did they grow tame and sweeter-natured? Or did she make up all this in her mind? Could the leopard change his spots? Maybe she was just homesick for when she was young.

All winter she looked at the naked city and square. When the ground first thawed in the early spring, she put a mattox, shovel and old axe in the chariot and had Chancey drive with her into the country. They crossed the canal on the Sixth Street bridge and drove up the hill. They had to go a long ways before they found what she was after. Once all this country had been thick woods where she and Mageel MacMahon would walk their bounds. Now there were so many houses she couldn't tell any more where her land had ended and Mageel's began. She couldn't even see Mageel's house and barn. Far out beyond where Guerdon lost his finger, they came on a patch of brush and second-growth. The farmer said he wouldn't mind her digging out a few whips. He was going to clear it for corn anyhow as soon as he was able.

She picked out three young maples, a buckeye, a basswood and a whitewood poplar. She wished she could bring home a pair of young oak trees, a white oak and a red, but hardly would they stir their stumps during the rest of her

THE TREES

lifetime. She also wished she could find an elm like the one
that used to lean by the old cabin, but she couldn't tell a
young one for sure, its leaves not yet sprouted. Every tree
she and Chancey dug out stood higher and stouter than
she did. They had to work a long time to get the roots
whole and free, and to do them up in burlap sacks with
some of their home soil for company in their new lodging
place.

They drove back to Americus with the long whips
sticking out of the back of the chariot. She had no trouble
with the farmer, but she had plenty with Chancey once she
got to town. About all he was good for was holding up
the tree while she spread the roots tenderly around and
tromped the ground down. The basswood, the whitewood
poplar and one of the maples she planted in her side yard,
the buckeye and the other maples in front of her house.
Until she finished, a small crowd of folk had gathered to
watch. Where did she get them? Did she think they would
grow in the city? Where did she get the idea — from her
home town back East? Why didn't she have the city council do it for her? Wouldn't horses and young ones break
them down? Well, she intended to have Clem Reeser
build a cribbing about these two on the square.

Small news traveled fast as big in Americus. It was too
dark for Portius to have seen much of anything when he
came home, but she could tell the minute he came in that
he knew all about it.

"I hear you've been improving the property," he mentioned.

"Well, I don't know if you'd call it that," she disallowed.

"I was always under the distinct impression that you
hated trees," he said.

Sayward went on silently with her work getting supper

on the table. Now how could she explain to him the reason
why she had done this. She didn't altogether know it herself yet, except that once a woodsy, always a woodsy. That
might explain it. She saw him watching her all through the
meal, and when they were nearly done, she came around
to it.

"I was just sitting here thinking what Mrs. Kramer told
me," she said. "This was last summer the last time she came
around with her berries. Their church out in Longswamp
Valley burned down and old Miley Hoffman wanted to
know when they were going to build it. You know old
Miley, the one that's such an infidel. They asked him, what
did he care when they built it. He said he had a good reason. When he looked over from his fields he missed seeing
the steeple. The valley didn't look right to him any more
without a church. I guess I'm like old Miley. The town
doesn't look right to me without any trees, especially not
the square."

CHAPTER TWENTY-FOUR

DOCK STREET

This house is mine,
And yet not mine.
Another comes,
And yet it is not his.

OLD ILLUMINATION

THIS year the Tenches had to move. Their house, the Clocker house on one side and the Singleton house on the other were all going to be torn down and cleaned out for a row of brick houses, they said.

Rosa stood very still when she heard the news. Never had she known their dark little box of a house to look golden as now that it had to die. Why, she had been born in that house. All her seventeen years had she lived in it. Of course six days a week she went to Mrs. Doan's, trimming hats with ribbons and bird wings, sometimes taking finished bonnets to the houses of the ladies they were made for. But all the time, the little house by the river was home in her mind, and what would she have done without it and without her mother sitting in the dim room waiting to ask her what had gone on at Mrs. Doan's today.

And now the house was going to be pulled down. Already it belonged to a strange man who cared nothing more about it than to destroy it. It gave her the same strange feeling as when her baby sister had died. It was the only sister she ever had. Rosa was just a little tyke at the time, and many a night after that she would wake up in a cold sweat over the dead baby. Nothing then would satisfy her save getting up and taking little Boicey out of the same cradle the baby had died in, making sure he was alive, and then rocking him soft, warm and living in her arms. Now evenings after work she hurried home decently as she might to spend all the time she could in the house while she still had it with its roof spreading over her and the four walls standing around her. She was small for her age and could run all the way home if she wanted to. Nobody save her mother would say aught against it.

But her father swore he was glad to get out of "Higgins's old house."

"It's too far from the waterfront," he said. He meant the new waterfront, the canal. "I have another place rented. It's bigger than this with two rooms and a goin' business in the front. Turkey kin tend it when I'm off."

The first day of April was moving day. Rosa stayed home from work to help. Her mother was of small use. Ever since the news came, her mind seemed stopped like a clock. She sat like one, too, and you could tell no time from her face. Only the pendulum tassel on her old dress moved, and that faster than Rosa remembered. Sometimes the mat of hair she never let Rosa touch kept in time with the tassel, giving little tremors as if struck by an unseen hammer. On moving day morning she went helplessly from one thing to another. She'd pick up this and couldn't make up her mind what to do with it. So she'd set it down and pick up something else. That's the way it went. Rosa and the boys had to do everything.

The wagon came right after noon to load their stuff. Her father, the driver and the boys carried out the things. The inside of the house grew bare as a nut. Rosa had never seen it look so ugly.

"We have to go now, Mama," she said.

Across the street she could see a knot of folks waiting. Oh, she knew what they waited for. They wanted to get a look at her mother. Here's where they'd get to see Mrs. Tench at last. She had never come out of her house since her first child was born, but she'd have to come out now.

"Come on, Mama," Rosa said and went out.

But her mother didn't come, and her father and the boys made like they weren't ready to go anyway, rearranging the things in the wagon. Still she didn't come.

"Go in and get her," Rosa's father told her.

"She says she'll come right away," Rosa said when she came out.

But "right away" passed and Jake went in. You could hear his loud voice outside. In the end he came out without her.

"Kin you wait a little?" he said to the driver. "We'd go and leave her to hell behind, but she kain't walk that fur."

The driver settled down on his haunches by the front wheel. His face, Rosa thought, didn't seem to have any expression. It was as if this whole business was something that happened long ago and had nothing to do with to-day. It was time out of mind, out of man's control. The minutes went by as if they pulled hard against the grain. It seemed to Rosa they'd never get away now, and here they'd forever have to stay, out of the old house but still not in the new. The loafers licked their lips watching. The horses stood sleepy and willing. Rosa listened for the tick of the clock laid some place in the wagon, but it must have stopped, like everything else.

The driver got up.

"Well, I got to go, Jake," he said and climbed up on the seat. His rough hairy hand picked up the lines. Boicey ran to the door.

"Mama, he's a goin'!" he shrilled.

Not a sound or stir came from the house. The driver clicked to the horses. They woke from their drowsing. The wheels started to turn. The axles rattled in the hubs. The wagon creaked and lumbered. Then Rosa's mother came hurrying out of the door. She had thrown her brown shawl over her head and shoulders. You could see only part of her face. She looked like a starved bird or fowl peering out of its feathers. Rosa wasn't sure she'd have known her own mother passing her on the street. She looked so different out here in the broad pitiless light of day. The wagon stopped to wait for her. Rosa ran to help her mother catch it. She and Turkey pushed her up over the wheel to the front seat where she pulled the brown shawl around her. The driver sat very still, not looking at her even when she sat up there beside him.

Rosa and her father and the boys walked, keeping abreast of the wagon. It reminded her of the baby's funeral. That's the way they had walked to the cemetery while the cart bumped along with the little coffin. But that had been winter time. Wasn't it nice this spring the way so many folks were planting trees in the city? Hardly anybody so poor that they couldn't have one or two in front of their house. In twenty years the streets of Americus would be green with dancing leaves, but where would she be then?

The wagon turned off Water Street at Sixth. Now why did the driver have to take their poor traps through the fine square? Her mother would hate it if Miss Bogardus looked out and saw her friend go by on the seat of a moving van. Rosa hoped none of the ladies who bought their hats from Mrs. Doan would see her traipsing with her father and three brothers like country jakes moving to town. That great plastered white house was where Mrs. Stowe lived who had such a lovely slope the way she sat lying back in her carriage when it went by. Next door stood the striped brick mansion house of Judge Wheeler.

Farther on the houses got poorer and smaller, one against the other, then big warehouses and little wooden houses stood together. You could smell the canal down here, with old bones from the soap works and hide scrapings from the tannery. From that brick corner Mr. Percy Yates, the Yankee, had bought all the anvils in Ohio and made a fortune, running up the price and letting his wife buy the handsomest bonnets Mrs. Doan could trim. Other rich men had places of business down here. They came only by day. In the evening they went back to their fine houses, but the people that lived here had to stay and breathe the bad smells all night when the smells got stronger and when the mills and warehouses stood dark and unfriendly on the street. Oh, it had been so open and free around their house by the river! But that life was gone to her now.

In an empty log house they passed, Turkey said that a man traveling by canal boat had been murdered. The boys wouldn't walk on the log house sidewalk but turned into the street. Next came a long stable smelling of canal mules. On beyond, the driver came to a halt in front of a faded red one-story house, hardly more than a shanty. A second shanty with a loft was attached to it in back. The front door stood fastened with a huge iron lock. Over the door letters had been painted in green on the red boards.

THE RED MULE

Rosa's father took a muddy stone from the street and hammered on the lock till the catch gave. Then he threw the lock on the floor. The boys rushed to be the first in. Rosa followed slowly. She saw that the house had two rooms like her father said. But he hadn't said everything. The front room was a rude barroom with an unpainted plank bar. An empty keg rested on one end of the plank. Behind on a shaky shelf stood a row of nearly empty bottles.

It didn't seem like a house at all, Rosa thought, never like their house. The second room was little more of a place to live than the dark hollow of the sycamore shanty. Pieces of glass and pottery, lumps of mud and plaster, drifts of rubbish all lay on the floor. The sour barroom smell hung as strong in the back room as the front. Even the walls smelled of stale mead and bitters.

Rosa wondered what her mother would say when she came in, but she only upbraided them bitterly for not bringing in her chair. When it came, she let herself down in it and sat blind to the swirling dust and dirt around her, deaf to the quarreling where to put this and that. She didn't even want to remember they had moved, Rosa thought. That's the way she kept sitting when Jake and Turkey went out for wet goods, and after dark when the sound of heavy feet and rough voices in the front shook the back room, while the scrape of mugs and glasses and the sharp scent of freshly opened beer and whiskey penetrated under the door and came through the cracks and broken panel.

"Come on and go to bed, Mama," Rosa said, "I have it all ready."

But her mother wouldn't go to bed. Not till the ugly sounds from the front room had ceased and Rosa's father came stumbling back, yawning and reeking of grog. Then Rosa's mother flew into him.

"You disgraced me!" she accused. "You brought me down right by his house like any common person in a wagon!"

Rosa, who hadn't slept a wink in the new house, pondered her words. Now whose house was it her father had brought her mother by? Was it Mr. Millard's where Miss Bogardus kept house, or the gray stone house of Mr. Percy Yates? Never had Rosa been in Mr. Millard's or Mr. Yates' houses, but once she had been in the old Wheeler cabin and once almost in the Wheeler mansion house. She wasn't ever supposed to go there. When a Wheeler bonnet was ready, Mrs. Doan took it herself. But this had been before Easter, and there were always too many bonnets for Mrs. Doan at Eastertide. She had to work half the night and drink gin to keep her awake in the day time. She was too unsteady on her feet to go to Judge Wheeler's. So she said Rosa must take the bonnet, but not until late was it finished. If the Wheelers were in bed, Rosa should put it in the usual place, back in the privy in the box for paper. Then she must close the door tightly. The first one out there would find it on Easter morning.

But there was still plenty of light in the Wheeler windows when Rosa got there. She went around the back way. Miss Dezia herself with a candle in her hand came to the door. Something flew into her face when she saw Rosa.

"I'll take it," she said, and snatched the bonnet. "Goodnight," she said and closed the door.

Rosa hardly noticed at the moment. In that short space of time that the door was open, she could see like into the golden scene of one of Mrs. Phillips' novels. It seemed her eyes could run through the whole house. Right before her lay the big wonderful kitchen with black kettles and shining copper pans, beyond that the dim dining room with the fearfully grand shape of a mahogany clawfoot sideboard. She had a glimpse into still another huge room with soft light streaming from it and deep tones of a piano, like the sound of water in a blue cavern. It was hardly more than a few moments that the door was open, not a bit longer than Miss Dezia could help, but Rosa had seen and heard everything.

She could still see and hear it tonight lying on her bed in the back room of the Red Mule. It was plain as if she stood by the open Wheeler door this minute, and Miss Dezia getting ready to slam it on her. On the way home she thought it must have been Chancey playing, for Mrs. Bernd would hardly be there so late and plain old Mrs. Wheeler in her knitted cap could never make such beautiful music. But Miss Bogardus said that Master Chancey was lazy and good for nothing and that he liked to fool at the piano so he wouldn't have to do an honest day's work.

CHAPTER TWENTY–FIVE

THE OFF–OX

All of a piece of what they said before.

EARLY SAYING

CHANCEY didn't want to go to the Independence Day celebration in the first place, but he had no idea anything would happen to him there.

He only knew he'd feel like a lost sheep at the big gathering. He always did. Most everybody else enjoyed it with an energy and zest that weakened him just to see it. They wouldn't have missed it for the world. They arrived early and a wild light came into their eyes the minute they got there. They revelled in meeting old friends, in playing old games, in eating old-fashioned rations and talking and praising old-fashioned customs in which, try as he might, Chancey could see nothing except a harder way to live and do things. What made people like that? Why did they want to leave the brighter present for the dark and painful past?

Take today. The high light of the celebration was a cabin raising. There was utterly no use for it as far as Chancey could see. It was just to show the younger generation and especially city folks how they used to put up a house in the old days in the woods. They had to go to a

great deal of trouble for the event. Logs had to be bought
far up the country, boated down the canal and hauled to
the scene by ox team. No timber was left standing around
Americus any more. The settlers and sawmill people had
cut it all down. There wasn't even a grove left to hold the
celebration in, only patches of scrub overgrown with
brush. So the last few years after decorating the graves, the
people went to Brown's pasture where the fairs and cir-
cuses came.

The worst of it was that Chancey had to take part in the
raising. There must have been a thousand other sons of the
pioneers who would have jumped at the chance. The trouble was, they didn't have Judge Wheeler for a father. All
Chancey wanted was to be left alone, and yet he had to get
right out in front of the crowd and help carry logs to the
end men.

The committee was a little simple-minded, Chancey
thought. Indeed he felt sure all pioneers were more or less
simple, almost like children. More than once he had noticed
it in his mother. She could be hard as hickory denying him
some small thing he wanted to do, but let somebody tell
her a noble story of old times and water would be liable to
run from her eye. Like the story she told of the boy in
Dark County who had no boots. In the winter time he'd
warm two boards by the fire, run out in the snow and stand
on them in his bare feet while he chopped firewood.

Any grown-up moved by that story was a little pathetic,
Chancey told himself, but then all pioneers were a little
that way. Take these Revolutionary and Indian war veterans brought in carriages and who now sat in a place of
honor to review the cabin raising. It was hard to believe
that these ancient and tottery old codgers had ever fought
the British or Indians in the primeval forest. Why, they

didn't look as if they could find their way in the woods, let alone outsmart war-whooping savages. Doddering, palsied or half-blind, they sat on the platform like they hardly knew what was going on. When the veterans of 1812 fired a salute, Major Phillips, who was deaf as a post, got up and squeaked:

"I kain't hear your volley, men, but your powder smells good."

That was the kind of partner Chancey had the luck to draw for the raising, a little dried-up fellow named Mac-Nulty, with bandy legs. He looked a hundred years old beside the boy. Youth and age, Chancey's father, called them. He was master of ceremonies.

"The first ox team will now stand at their yokes!" he called out, and Chancey and five other men took their places where three handspikes had been laid on the ground and a log rolled on them.

Chancey was at the last handspike. He reached down to take hold but he could hardly get his fingers under the iron, and when he tried to pull it up, it felt like his end had been spiked to the ground. He glanced over at Mr. MacNulty, but that little shriveled old man had his end up already, and no matter how Chancey heaved, Mr. MacNulty's side stayed so much higher that the log kept sliding against the boy's fingers.

"Let me give you a little more handspike, boy," the old man croaked.

"No, sir, I got all I can carry now!" Chancey shouted, to make his partner hear.

The older settlers had a good laugh over that.

"He's got all the handspike he can carry now," they said.

"Your off-ox is a calf, Judge!" a Tateville democrat bellowed.

Chancey felt his face burn. Oh, he lifted his share from then on. He vowed he'd raise his end if it tore him apart inside. If that little old dried-up runt with one foot in the grave could do it, he could, he kept telling himself. He did it, too. Now wouldn't you think folks would give him credit for that and forget what he said? But, no, they wouldn't let him rest. That little old devil, MacNulty, was the worst. His nose and chin came mighty close together, but they'd spread apart with glee every time they went back for another log.

"Some more handspike, Chancey?" he'd twit him.

As soon as his stint was over, Chancey tried to melt away in the crowd. But wherever he went, folks recognized him and grinned. His father wouldn't look in his direction, and he daren't meet his mother's eye. Libby, when she saw him, told him out in front of everybody that maybe now he'd take the powders that Harry had given him, but the worst was the silent pity from Sooth's brown eyes. He felt relieved that Kinzie was away in the navy and Huldah in Cincinnati, soon to go to England to stay.

The only one of the family Chancey wished for was Guerdon. Good old Guerdon would have stood up for him. He'd have knocked down the man who called his younger brother a calf. But Guerdon was so long swallowed up by the world that at times he seemed to Chancey like somebody he had once read about in a book.

From across the field he heard the quavering voices of the old soldiers singing Sinclaire's Defeat.

'Twas November the fourth in a year that is done,
We had a sore engagement near to Fort Jefferson.
Sinclaire was our commander, which may remembered be,
For there we left nine hundred men in Western Territory.

All afternoon Chancey had to listen to the pioneer singing and story telling. Their theme was ever of hardship and tragedy, of drowning and starving, of mourning, and sudden death. Now how could these old people be so pleased and comforted by such dark and terrible tales? They engulfed Chancey in gloom. He found coming up in him today all the small creeping terror that used to plague him in church when as a child beside his mother, he listened to the long, shouted sermons on dying and being cast into hell. He could always see hell plain as if he was there, the deep red pits, the brimstone flames and waist deep in them the poor naked people he had known in life, now repentant but too late. Their clothes were burned off but their bodies could never be consumed for that would be unjust to the mercy of God. In hell they must stay not this year and next but forever, crying for mercy, getting not even a drop of water to wet the ends of their tongues. How they could stand it, Chancey didn't know, for he himself would almost expire in rebellion and sympathy. And yet when he looked up at his mother, there she would sit calm as could be. Only great firmness and peace flowed from her, and she could join in a strong quiet voice when they sang:

> Thee we adore, eternal name,
> And humbly own to thee,
> How feeble is our mortal frame,
> What dying worms are we!
> Our wasting lives grow shorter still.
> Ourselves we cannot save.
> Whate'er we do, whate'er we will,
> We're traveling to the grave.

How could she? the little boy would say to himself. And how could all the others, for when he looked around, there the congregation sat undisturbed, singing with a great fervor that had no resemblance to dying worms at all. Even Massey when she was twelve years old, sewed that awful motto on her sampler and never dropped a stitch. It hung in the hall today.

> There is an hour when I must die,
> I do not know how soon.
> How many children young as I
> Are called to meet their doom?

It never bothered Massey. Not for a lick. And still didn't. There she was now in a bunch of young ladies, all seventeen or eighteen, in their good dresses, and yet playing Father and Son like simple-minded children. You played it in pairs, racing to a mark and back. Each had a switch. On the way over the son tried to birch the father and on the way back it was the father's turn if he could reach the son. The girls held up their dresses and ran, switching each other unmercifully and pealing with laughter. Only their silly heartlessness, Chancey told himself, could make them cheerful in the face of all the gloom. And yet the sounds of their high spirits drew him hungrily closer, too unsuspectingly close, for when Hester Patterson saw him, she put her thumbs to her ears with her hands out like two flaring horns.

"Moooo!" she cried. "Moooo!"

Chancey withdrew with what dignity he could muster while their screaming and howling came after. You'd think his own sister would stick up for him, but he could hear her laughter with the rest. He dreaded meeting the family at breakfast. He hadn't much faith in his mother's philosophy, but one of her expressions came to him. "You'll have to live it down," she used to say. That's what he'd have to do now.

Living it down was a harder job than Chancey looked for. Till it was over, he thought the cure worse than the disease. For three weeks he couldn't walk across the square without the back of his scalp twitching, fearing the call, "Moooo!" after him. But when July was out, he breathed deeper. The month of his disgrace had been lived through. Perhaps August would be better.

His father seemed a little better, too. Since the night of the celebration he had been ill of the gravel, with pleurisy on the side to plague him. The doctors said he had had too much cheer on Independence Day but Chancey felt a burdening sense of guilt, although he couldn't tell why. Whenever someone called at the house to ask about him, Chancey felt himself unaccountably flinch. Callers came from over the county, clients, voters, lawyers, court attendants, canal men and friends. Some of them stayed for a meal or the night. But outside, Chancey gave no sign, moving like a sleepwalker through all that went on at the house till Little Turtle came, cutting through his shell to the shrinking and indefensible self within.

It was morning when Chancey walked in the kitchen and found the Indian chief there, journeyed all the way from another state, older now, dressed in white man's clothes. He had become heavy, his rugged face layered in brown fat. But he carried himself with great dignity, and there was still something in his black eyes that struck fear to those remnants of childhood surviving in Chancey's breast.

"Hanh, Chancey, big boy now," Little Turtle smacked his lips as he shook hands. "Good um not dead. Better that way. Come back for um now. Bring squaw. Help take um back to Indian."

Chancey knew he was only joking, and yet a great abhorrence came over him. He could barely bring himself to
touch the hand of Little Turtle's squaw. Her hair was
greasy, her skin a mass of wrinkles, her expression such that
her face seemed a blur, a broad mass of flesh like a buttock, almost devoid of features. She eyed the preparations
for dinner greedily, and Chancey's mother gave her a
melon to eat before the meal would be ready, setting the
pail of kitchen slop beside her so she could throw away the
seeds. The squaw cut the melon with a knife and drank all
the insides including the seeds, cut off a large piece of
melon, stuck it on the point of the knife, then shook it
around in the slop and ate it. Little Turtle laughed broadly
to cover his pride. The others smiled but Chancey couldn't.
Just the way she had done it filled him with uneasy loathing.

Chancey's father sent word he'd be down for dinner and
stay until the doctor came. He looked like a member of
some weak and bloodless race beside the coppery face of
the Indian, but was glad to see his old friend. Little Turtle's face glowed like some oaken knot in the fire. Oh, you
could see he was pleased seeing his friend, the white judge
again, and especially sitting up to his dining table. To him
this was a ceremonial room with its white cloth, blue china,
great sideboard and mirror hanging there. He carried himself like a Roman senator. Everything had to be just so.
With great dignity he tried to instruct his squaw in the use
of fork and spoons but it was no use.

"Can't do so," he defended her. "Squaw good. Never
cross like white squaw. White man court too long. Maybe
get good wife. Maybe get bad. Bad scold all time. All same
white man must keep um. Well, how do Indian? Indian see
good squaw. Him go right up. Put two finger like this,

hanh? Make two look like one. Squaw know what him mean. Take um home. No danger him be cross. Squaw know what him do if be cross. Throw um away and get other one. So live happy. Go to heaven."

In the parlor after dinner, Little Turtle showed his squaw what a piano was.

"Make music!" he explained. "Go toot toot." He turned to Portius. "Him like music. Him father like music. Him fight General Wayne. Say General Wayne make music. Have big dinner horn. General Wayne dinner horn go toot, toot here. Go toot, toot yonder. Gun crack. Indian whoop. Dinner horn go toot toot. Much music."

The Indian woman's face never changed and Chancey didn't think she looked like she cared a hoot for music, but Little Turtle went on to praise her.

"Him Christian," he said. "All same like you. Go church. All sister, brother. One sister get up talk. Talk all night. By and by him get tired. Choke sister down. That stop um. Make talk, pray. Sister start sing hymn. Sing loud. Drown um out. Nobody hear. Have choke sister another time. Then can talk, pray. Sing. You want hear um sing?"

"I think that would be very nice," Chancey's mother said from the doorway.

Little Turtle turned to his squaw and urged her in Delaware, encouraging her by singing himself as you do to start a child. Chancey didn't recognize a word, but he could make out the air of the doxology.

> Kain nom moo tooqk owk woz.
> Kain nom moo waim uh keeng ah yaigh.
> Kain nom moo wuh Koung kagh tay laick.
> Kain nom way gweez mint wauk w'jih joqk.

The squaw wouldn't join. She only grunted in Delaware.

"Him want hear you make music," Little Turtle said.

"Tell her I'm extremely sorry I don't play," Portius said courteously.

"Wife play?"

"No, the only one at home now who plays is Chancey."

"Him! Well, glad can do something. You tell um play."

All eyes were on Chancey. He wished now he had sneaked out after dinner. He never enjoyed playing for anyone, let alone for a heathen Indian and his squaw who wouldn't know a black key from a white one.

"I don't know what to play," he protested.

"Play the Lady of Loti Polka," Massey suggested.

Chancey shook his head. If he did play, never would it be anything gay and fast, or the Indians might want more. No, if he had to play, it would be something they'd never want to hear again. He'd make it so dismal and sad they'd be relieved beyond measure to have it done. He went up to the piano and sat for a little. Then he began the harrowing strains of "On Nebo's Lonely Mount" or "Moses' Funeral March."

Before long he was conscious of extraordinary interest behind him. He couldn't look around, but in one of Aunt Unity's mirrors he glimpsed the Indians manifesting unusual excitement. Even the old squaw had become alive and was swaying back and forth on her chair while Little Turtle had got up on his feet and was doing a kind of dance. The boy couldn't see him continuously, only when he came in range of the glass at which times he perceived wild and terrifying arms flung over him.

When he got to the end of the piece, Chancey felt considerably relieved.

"More, make more!" Little Turtle shouted.

But nothing could have induced Chancey to play again. "I don't know any more," he lied.

The Indian was disappointed. Almost at once his animation dropped from him and he became his old resolved self. Grim dignity wrapped him like a blanket, and he sat down. But you could see he felt cheated by Chancey.

"If can't make so, can't make so," he grunted. "Minds me like story. Indian scout take out white men. Tell how to go. Come on tracks in mud. White men say buffalo track. Scout say maybe no. Maybe Mingue take sticks, make track. Fool white man. Maybe Mingue wait, ambush, scalp. White man be careful. Go slow. Look every bush. White men do so. By and by find dung of buffalo. Indian scout laugh. Now all right, he say. Mingue can't make so. Only buffalo can make so. Minds me like Chancey here. Only music man make so. Chancey can't make so."

While Chancey's father was laughing, Dr. Howie came. The boy tried to sneak off, but the doctor caught him.

"Wait a minute, Chancey," he said. "I want you to recover my other bag from the carriage."

The boy went reluctantly for the bulging bag and its evilly clanking contents.

"Now don't go away," the doctor instructed him, "I suspect I am going to need you."

Ever since Libby had married young Doctor Harry, Sayward and the children had called him faithfully when ailing. Libby thought her father should have him, too, but Portius said he had had Dr. Howie ever since Dr. Pearsall died, that he liked the man and his wit and felt it an injustice to discriminate against him simply because he was no churchman or son-in-law. Not that he had any prejudices against Harry Conyngham, he went on, who was an estimable and rising young physician. Libby told her

mother that her father just wanted his complaints kept secret from the rest of the family, but Chancey thought he
understood why his father liked the ironical Dr. Howie.
They were two of a kind.

The doctor stood here now, a tall delicate-appearing man
who nearly always looked nearer death than his patients.
He moved delicately, too, like one on his way to heaven,
but when he opened his mouth, you knew he had no intention of going there, nor was he delicate. He liked to say
that he would prescribe pills to the goddess Diana and ad-
minister physic to the vestal virgins, but the only patient
he'd practise phlebotomy on would be a brass monkey. It
was too messy. However, today at the sight of Chief Little
Turtle and his squaw, some perverse humor seemed to pos-
sess him. It appeared to please him to have savage Indians
for an audience and the judge's grand parlor for a lancing
room. Not for a moment did he suggest removal to the
kitchen. He helped the judge off with his coat, then rolled
up the patient's white shirt sleeves with his own white
tapered fingers.

Now, pleased with himself and the attention, he handed
Chancey a wicked looking gallipot from the bag and held
up half a dozen fierce and bloodthirsty lances to select
from. Chancey had an uncomfortable feeling at the pit of
his stomach.

"Hold the vessel here," the doctor said dryly, "and don't
look so terrified. It's not you I'm going to lance, but your
father, and I daren't let him bleed to death or the bench
might forfeit my license."

Chancey bore up, screwing his nerves to the needed
pitch, holding the gallipot at the required place. He saw the
unhealthy white flesh of his father, with black hairs curling
like worms, the cruel curve of the rusty lance, then his

father's warm red life's blood gushing out like from a steer's throat at the butcher's. A violent wave of sickness went over him, and the next thing he knew, he was lying on the sofa with Massey applying cold cloths to his head. Strings of unrecognizable words came from the doctor's mouth while Chancey's mother worked with a rag on his blood-stained pantaloons and Dezia on her knees wiped up the floor where the gallipot still lay.

Chancey wanted to scramble up, but his father sternly bade him lie. He had never seen his father so grave and pale. The boy lay there with his eyes closed, every muscle conscious of itself and aquiver. Once he lifted a lid and saw Little Turtle regarding him with contemptuous eyes. Presently the Indian spoke sardonically to his friend.

"Long time past Little Turtle say give um Chancey. Indian make um over. Make um do what don't like. Make um walk in snow. Make um sleep on ground. Make um man or be with Great Spirit. Not now, you say. By and by. Now by and by come. What have you? Look like man. Eat like man. Walk like man. But act like baby. Got pigeon heart. Indian can't make um over now. Better be with Great Spirit."

Chancey's father said nothing. The boy still lay rigid like a prisoner at the scaffold. He heard the doctor go, then his mother help his father upstairs. Soon as his parents' feet sounded in the upper hall, the boy sprang up and fled. As he snatched his cap from the rack, he could hear Little Turtle's hoarse laugh after him.

The air outside, when he reached it, was sweet as wild honey. It seemed at that moment that if he drank enough of it, all his troubles would be ended, wiped out of existence. But that, he found, was only his fancy, for as fast as he outraced his dishonor, it caught up to him in painful hu-

miliation. He fled the square and headed for the waterfront
where fewer would know him. The canal smelled good as
he approached it, the scent of stale water and tarry ropes
and frying eels, of wood and paint drying in the sun, of
mules and down-to-earth manure. The very sight of the
district soothed him, the shacks and warehouses, the humble little shops, the muddy street and all the boats tied up in
the basin. The canal had a kind of bay dug out from it for
a boat yard. They called it the Level. It was another world
than the square. Boat carpenters sawed, hammered, pounded
with calking mallets. The hot foreign scent of tar was
stronger here. On the decks of condemned boats, men sat
fishing; a huge darky fried his fish over a fire of oaken
chips, using a shovel for a frying pan. Running wild on
the condemned boats, a gang of naked boys played Whoop,
jumping from boat to boat, hiding between, climbing down
into empty holds and cabins, and diving out of open windows into the yellow water.

Chancey sat for a while with his feet down over the side
of an abandoned boat, rocking faintly in the small waves
stirred up by the boys. Then he lay down on the deck. The
rocking, the sound of small lapping against the boat soothed
him only for a while. He started to tramp aimlessly again,
crossing the lower bridge and back over the next, threading
the narrow streets and alleys, his eyes devouring glimpses
of strange life through open doors and windows. What he
searched for he never knew till he passed an open door on
Dock Street. Above it was painted THE RED MULE, and
inside he saw Turkey Tench behind the bar.

Then he thought he knew. The bitter scent of whiskey
and gin flowed like a slow river of air from the door. He
had always hated the smell, and the stuff worse, even when
diluted with water for himself and others as children. He

remembered once they had made him drink rum and milk in the Ferry House, and the awful mess he had made over his father on the way home. The clear persistent pattern of it shook him. Then he was only a child. Now he was grown, and yet today he had fainted dead away, defiling himself, his father, the doctor and the carpet.

"How are you, Turk?"

"Why, how are you, Mr. Chancey?"

"Will you stake me to a drink? I'll pay you next time I come down."

"Why, sure. You have all the credit you want." Turkey's look of surprise had not abated and his small black eyes continued to scan Chancey's face. "What will you have?"

"Brandy." Chancey heard himself say it like his father. He would drink it if it burned out his throat like a soot fire did a chimney — if he had to drink a second glass to hold the first one down.

Turkey poured him half a tumblerful, and Chancey stared at the thick glass, trying not to smell it. When he lifted it up, it tasted of fire and musty old cellar barrels. He saw Turkey watching him and the almost imperceptible ebb of the liquor from the glass. After while a girl's voice sounded in the back room, and Turkey opened the door between.

"Rosa!" he called briefly. "Somebody in here you know."

He left the door open and went back to the bar. When Chancey turned his head again, she was in the doorway, looking extraordinarily slight and sensitive in this uncouth place. So this was where she lived, he told himself, here in this waterfront barroom shack.

"Rosa! Who is it?" her mother's sharp voice called from the unseen room.

She didn't answer.

"Rosa! Come back here. I want to talk to you!" the mother demanded.

The girl moved with quiet surety into the tavern to stand with Chancey at the end of the bar.

"Don't mind her," she begged in that gentle way he remembered.

But Chancey couldn't help minding or feeling for Rosa. She was like he, wronged by the stars, caught in the blind machinations of birth and life. For himself he could do little as yet, but for her he would do a great deal. It made him feel stronger. He could swallow this liquor now. Once he had it down, his mind and tongue began working on all the bitter injustice that had been done him, but before he could bring out half of it, he was stopped by the quick uncommon shadow on her face. When he looked around, he saw through the open door a group of ladies approaching in the street. In their fine gowns, bonnets and manners they looked out of place on the waterfront. They picked their way across Dock Street and formed themselves directly in front of the Red Mule, where they stood meekly enough with open hymn books in their hands as in church. One of them struck a note. Then their voices rose oddly high, pure and mild in this rough place.

O, for a heart to praise my God,
A heart from sin set free!
A heart that ever feels Thy blood
So freely spent for me.

"Don't mind them," Chancey said. It was his turn now to apologize, for these were intruders from his own part of town. His father frowned on the Temperance Crusaders, but Sooth belonged, joining the group on certain days, helping to besiege some tavern, singing the most reproachful hymns they knew to melt men's hearts. They went summer and winter, knelt in snow or driving rain to pray aloud for the men inside. Chancey had often seen them on Water Street. More than once he had stopped amused to listen. But it was less amusing to be caught inside, especially if your own sister happened to be among the besiegers. When the hymn was over, a voice that sounded like Fay's sister, Leah, started to pray for the salvation of the poor souls and sots within. Inside among those sots themselves, all was interest, respect and a little perplexity. This was something that had to be handled with care like walking on eggs or smoking around black powder.

The prayer done, another sacred song was begun. It sounded nearer.

"I believe they're coming in," Rosa said.

Chancey looked around for escape.

"You can use the back way," she told him and showed him how to go. He had a passing glimpse of the same sort of dim room as in the other Tench house along the river and the same Mrs. Tench uncombed and unaged, staring at him like an outraged owl.

"Rosa! Who is that?" she demanded but Rosa did not reply.

"Wait, I'll go with you," she whispered at the back door. She threw on a wrap and guided him through several alleys. They came out on the waterfront again and they stood on a deserted dock, taking up their talk where they had left off until dusk descended. "I don't want to go home yet," she told him. "Will you walk with me to Butterman's Lock?"

Was it he himself and what he had heard or was it Rosa's mother and what she said, or why did he have this feeling all evening that he and Rosa were surmounting the world in being together? The canal basin tonight seemed like their inland sea with a faint mist already rising and making the rows of moored boats on the other side seem very far away.

Silent barges lay nearer. A loaded boat was pulling out, the mules moving like shadows along the tow path, the dark hump of a boy on one of their backs. Rosa and Chancey slowed their pace to keep even with the boat. When it entered the long stretch to Butterman's Lock, the captain's horn called to the locktender over the aisle of dark water. The wild note hung in the air, lingered, trailed off and came again like the dying strain of the vanished spirit of the wilderness.

"Can you float on it, too?" Rosa asked him. "Especially in the night time like this? Most every night I lie in bed and close my eyes and go on it wherever I want to. And the longer they draw it out, the farther I can go."

It wasn't the boat horn but themselves, that did it, Chancey told her, their rebellion and liberty that lifted them up. That's what made life tonight richer and wiser than he remembered it. Seldom had he been so aware of the warm musky scent of the water, the half moon in it and all around him the velvet night, including Rosa. Something appeared to flow from her slight body to his. She seemed like someone he had known a long time, longer than his mother or Aunt Genny, closer than Sooth or even Massey. No one else knew like she did the words he was about to speak of the troubles and problems that lay on his mind. Sometimes he could tell in advance what she was about to say, but not always. Frequently her fancy rose like the strange killdeer to circle and cry its wild note over water and cloud. Then often he had to go back to childhood to follow, to know what she meant, to a time when he was very young and could stand in a floating leaf and steer it across a mud-puddle sea. For a moment then his feet felt extraordinarily tiny, like the feet of the little old boatman Rosa told him about, who could dance a jig on a dinner plate and never once get off or break it.

It was much later when they came back down Dock Street. They had passed the cabin of the Wizard of the Dell, Rosa said. A little farther on, her young arm stopped him. Ahead in the darkness stood a house of one and a half stories with a squat ugly roof. Save for one lonely window, the house was dark. In that window a woman stood mysteriously swinging a lantern. Boldly, almost blasphemously, she would bisect the window from top to sill and from corner to corner. Afterward she would make occult signs and symbols across her head, across her feet, and then around in circles that grew gradually larger or smaller.

"They say she's a witch," Rosa whispered. "Something evil is surely going to happen now."

Chancey had never seen anything like it before. He watched with a kind of horrible fascination while the woman performed her secret rites. She seemed to be writing on the night. All she did was of a pattern, had to be done exactly right, and when she finished one series, she would remain utterly still and grim on her feet and rest. Then suddenly, almost vengefully, the lantern would start again. Chancey and Rosa stood a long time watching while the streaks of light were drawn across the darkness in mysterious design and while around them the shadows rose and fell with obscure implications.

CHAPTER TWENTY-SIX

THE FLOWERING OF
THE WILDERNESS

Come day, go day, God send Sunday. ⁓

OLDTIME SAYING

SAYWARD was beat out about Chancey.

She hoped she didn't show it too much, but hardly did she know any more what to do with her youngest. Most everything else she had ever got up against, she found she could lick if she stuck to it long enough. But this little old feller from her own womb baffled her. Wasn't it singular? You could wrassle down famine and solitude, the wilderness and the big butts, but the Lord knew just where and how to lay His hand on you to fetch you to your knees.

From the year he was born, Chancey had been a cross laid on her. She didn't mind it so much for her own self. She felt thankful enough for all the good luck her other young ones had. If this littlest one had to be puny, she'd nurse and feed him best she could. She'd give him from her own self what he needed. She'd make a man out of him yet. But all the time, she knew now, the cards were stacked against her, and against every other mother like her. Oh, a mother can do most anything she wants for her young ones while they're little. But she better recollect they grow up mighty soon. And then they do as they please. Next December Chancey would be eighteen years old and had his own mind this long time. It was a good mind, too, from his father's side. His stubbornness likely came from both sides. But where, she pondered, did all his strange notions and ways come from?

Ever since he was little, he had made up stories and claimed they were true — like riding on a cow that time and that she and Portius weren't his real mother and father. No, according to Chancey, they were just some hirelings, his real folks had left him with till they'd come for him. Genny said that was the most ungrateful thing from a young one she ever heard, but Sayward reckoned it wasn't bad as all that. Some young ones just took curious notions like they did ailments such as St. Vitus dance. Given time, they'd outgrow them. But Chancey never did grow out of his. She thought it was the St. Vitus dance that made him go around by himself. This was a good while ago. He didn't want other folks looking at him when he jerked and twitched, and she didn't blame him. But when that was over, he shied from folks just the same, and then for a while he made an awful fuss about going to church, claiming that people in church whispered about him.

"You're fourteen years old and too big for such bosh!" she told him vigorously. "Folks have more important things to talk about than you."

It didn't do much good, and in the end she blamed herself that she hadn't raised him right. If she'd worked him

harder, he'd have been stout enough to keep up his end of
the log that time at the raising. If she'd kept on doing her
own butchering like she used to and made him help, he
wouldn't have swooned at the sight of blood and had the
names Off-ox and Butcher Boy, called after him. Where
she made the mistake was letting a little sickness coddle
him. Had she brought him up rough and tumble like his
brothers and sisters, he'd known how to call back worse
names than he got, and then the others would be glad to
leave him alone. Of course it would have been still better
to knock down and drag out a few. Then he'd had some
real peace. But never would Chancey stand a hitch with
anybody. He wouldn't turn on his tormentors, the only
ones he ever answered were some harmless old men that
teased him down by the bridge, and then he said the wrong
thing. It went all over town.

"You can make fun of me now!" Chancey called back.
"But remember my name. If you live long enough, I'll make
you ashamed that you ever made fun of Chancey Wheeler!"

That was a summer or two ago. This spring he tried
every excuse to get out of working in the lot and garden.
When she held him to it, he cried out it was a disgrace.
She was thunderstruck though she tried not to show it.

"Why is honest work a disgrace?" she wanted to know.

"It's all right for those who have to," he told her. "But
you're the richest woman in Americus and I'm your son
and yet we have to go out and work like hired men in the
field."

It came to her mind to say, I thought you said you weren't
my son, Chancey, but never would she cast that up to him.

"Work's the best thing we can do, Chancey," she said.

"Robert Owen didn't think so and he was one of the
greatest thinkers of our age. He said if you make a man

[308]

happy, you make him virtuous. That's his whole system — making people happy."

"We want to make you happy, too, Chancey," she said mildly.

"That's what you say. But what you mean is you want me to work and be happy. You're so used to working all your life, Mama, you can't live without working. You wouldn't know what to do with yourself. Thank God I've never been spoiled like that."

"Spoiled?" Sayward swallowed.

"Yes, you won't even have a hired girl in this big house. You insist on doing all the work yourself. Don't you understand, Mama, there are more important things than work in this world?"

"What for instance?"

"Well, Robert Owen said that one of the main occupations of working people should be play. He practised it, too. He arranged in his factories that the laborers could dance, relax, talk and sing and amuse themselves all they wanted. He was the real pioneer, Mama, not you and the settlers. Now phalanxes are taking up his revolutionary ideas. Every member of a phalanx is going to be equal. Nobody can order another around. Everybody can choose his own work and do as little of it as he wants to. That's in the constitution."

"If everybody can pick the easy work, who'll do the hard and ugly work?" Sayward asked meekly.

"Of course there'll have to be a little repulsive labor at first," Chancey admitted. "But progress will do away with all toil and labor in time. Meanwhile those who do that work will get a little more credit against their rent and meals. They'll also get a share of the profits. Everybody else will share alike. There'll be no rich people and no poor

people, just brothers and sisters. And everybody will have
security and happiness."

"Everybody but your mother," Portius put in. "I can't
conceive of her being happy there."

"Not if I had to work to make up for all those lazy shirk-
ers who wanted to dance and play and have a good time
all the time!" Sayward agreed bitterly. "I'd sooner go out
on the desert with savages and rattlesnakes for my brothers
and sisters and live my own life and get paid for my own
labor. Such schemes never worked in this world and never
will, but the're always cracked people getting born who
try to get something for nothing."

"See, I told you!" Chancey said to his father.

"Now just a minute, Sayward," Portius rumbled in his
easy powerful way that made you feel small for getting hot
under the collar. "I don't support everything the boy stands
for, but he has a point. It was essential for you and me to
toil and sweat when first we came to the wilderness. We
had to cut down the tremendous forest and break in the
new land in order to live. If the young folks had to do that
today, I believe they could — "

"And a good thing it would be for them, too," she inter-
jected.

"But the point is they don't have to do it today. And
you don't have to any more either. We are well off and so
are our children. Things have changed."

"I don't see our grandchildren coming in the world with
didies on now that things have changed and folks are so
well off like you say," she retorted. "There always was
work and there always will be. Some folks just never want
to do any. Even those who had to slave and sweat the most
to get their heads above water now say they don't want
their young ones to have to go through what they had to.

They'd never reckon to train a young horse by letting him stand in the stable or pasture. They know mighty well the minute they'd put him in a plow or on the road, he'd sweat his self to pieces. He'd be too soft. But that's the way they coddle their own flesh and blood. Well, what they don't learn their young ones about work and hardship, life will learn them later on."

"That's a cruel and outmoded thing to say," Portius declared. "People are more enlightened now in the nineteenth century."

"Robert Owen says, Papa," Chancey put in, "relieve the people of want, and you relieve them of evil and unhappiness."

"Bosh and nonsense, Chancey!" his mother flared. "Making a body happy by taking away what made him unhappy will never keep him happy long. The more you give him, the more he'll want and the weaker he'll get for not having to scratch for his self. The happiest folks I ever knew were those who raised their own potatoes, corn and garden stuff the first spring out here. They'd been half starved but they found out they could get the best of their own troubles. They wouldn't have traded that first sack of meal from their own corn for half of Kentuck. That kind made good neighbors, too, and mighty handy to have around in time of trouble. If making your young ones work off their own troubles is old-fashioned, and out of date, then the good Lord is out of date because that's the way He lets us sink or swim with our troubles."

"I'm not acquainted with the ways of the Almighty," Portius said with irony. "But the Indians practised the philosophy you mention, and you know how far they got with it."

That's the way it went, on and on. She would fire one

barrel, and Chancey or Portius the next. In the end she saw
it was no use. Talking never got you anywhere. You can't
make somebody believe what he doesn't want to. Besides,
she didn't like falling out with her own boy. If he couldn't
make the best of her as she was, she could of him as he was.

"You said folks had to do a little work at first, Chancey,"
she said humbly. "If you don't want to work out in the lot,
what do you want to do?"

"Work in my room upstairs," he told her.

She had to admit she was bamfoozled.

"What do you aim to do up there?"

"Write letters to the newspapers. Exchange views with
leaders like Robert Owen."

Sayward turned away. So that was his idea of work! It
was bad enough for her own son to take stock in all these
crack-brained schemes for lazy folks to shirk work and have
a good time doing what they wanted to do. Now he was
going to shut himself up like a hermit, the way his pappy
did years ago before she broke him of it.

A month passed and all this time Chancey hadn't worked
in the lot. Sayward did his share herself. Whenever she
went by in the upstairs hall, she saw him sitting at his little
table by the window. He had made it his writing desk.
Most times when she made his bed or changed it or while
she cleaned up his room trying to make no more dust with
her rag and broom than she had to, he sat there looking out
of the window. Only once in a while did she hear his quill
scratch. What he was setting down on the white paper, she
had no idea, save that it must be something serious the way
his lower lip pushed out and his blue eyes were on fire.

"Is this what you like to do, Chancey?" she asked one
day timidly, and he nodded like his thought was far away
on something grand and more important.

What would come out of such strange makeshift for work, Sayward didn't know. But one day Genny came and asked had she read last week's Centinel. It had a poem in it she said that Sayward ought to know about, if she didn't, for some said the person, Ripheus, who signed it, was no other than Chancey, and he and Portius might have reasons of their own not to show it to her.

When Genny was gone, Sayward hunted till she found the paper and spelled that poem through. Could it be Chancey who did this, she pondered. Oh, from his school work she knew he could write. Many a rhyme of his had Massey or Dezia read to her. He stammered sometimes when he talked, but not on paper. Portius said he would some day put his father to shame with the pen. But never had that devilish quality of his father so come out in Chancey like it did in this poem. She felt queer all over when she read it, for this sounded like some of her own talk against progress turned back against her.

THE FROGS' PETITION

To those who rule Americus
Our meek petition we address:
Return unto the status quo
Of forty, fifty years ago!

Reverend sirs, today be known
Our race has grievance with your own.
Hard have we suffered by your rude
Assaults upon our solitude.
By thoughtless youth we've pelted been
Till bones were broken, also skin.
Not satisfied with this, you've schemed
A human course we never dreamed.

THE TOWN

You drained the water from our land
And left us perish or be damned.
Your only reason for our fate
Is progress, to be up-to-date.
Now beg we that this thing you do,
Our great just cause take into view.
Return unto the status quo
Of forty, fifty years ago.

Remember that our nightly song
Your children's sleep would much prolong.
From early in the evening hours.
You all have heard when copious showers
From Heaven descend upon our dwelling,
It makes our throats with joy be swelling.
Do then, kind sirs, take pity on us.
Let water once more be upon us.
Shut up this ditch, then we will pay
Our best respects and humbly pray
That you who are so very clever
May live in peace with us forever,
Close by our sweetly stagnant stream,
The insect's hum, the panther's scream,
Back in the golden status quo
Of forty, fifty years ago.

                                        Ripheus.

The strange feeling the poem gave her discomfited Sayward long after she laid it down. Everybody who read it must know she was the one it meant. The city had wanted to drain land that would drain her Beaver Gats and she had got up a petition against it. When she wanted her land drained, she said, she would drain it herself. And now Chancey had gone and poked fun at his own mother, siding her with the frogs. But she had to give in that it was a master poem and clever. Portius could not have rhymed it better. She hadn't reckoned Chancey could be so sly. Oh, if it was he who did it, she felt proud of him. She'd tell Portius and the others they needn't have held it back from her. The only part that made her feel bad was that somebody else had to tell her about it. With careful shears she cut out the poem and laid it in her Bible. It was, she told herself, the first rhyme any Luckett ever had printed in the paper.

But she had a curious notion it was not the last. Only yesterday the girls told her they heard that Chancey was trying to get a position on the Centinel. They didn't altogether approve. They said working in General Morrison's bank would suit him better because it didn't open till ten o'clock in the morning and closed shortly after noon. But Sayward rather hoped it was true. Barnaby Lane from Rhode Island had started the Centinel. He had printed it first in Tallow Alley on a hand-press he fetched up the river. Sometimes in the early days when stock was scarce, it would come around on pink or yellow paper. The girls and even Resolve used to call it the Palladium of Human Liberty because that was the motto printed under the name.

"Well, I see the Palladium of Human Liberty's come," Libby would say, fetching it in. But Sayward stood up for it then and now. She said Barnaby Lane had gone into business without running out and borrowing money like the bank did, only the bank called it capital. What's more, Lane put in an honest day's work. She had passed his place one time at night and saw him setting type by the light of a tallow candle. Now who ever saw one of these bankers in their offices after dark, she asked.

This afternoon an envelope from the Centinel came to

the house for Chancey. A boy fetched it. She laid it at
Chancey's place for supper, hoping he would say something. When he sat down at the table, he opened and read
it, but not a word to anybody what was in it. That evening
when she had to run up on the third floor, his room was
empty.

"He's gone," Massey told her. "I saw him right after supper going toward the canal."

It had been one of those days, Chancey told himself,
when hardly could he stand it any longer at home. Even
in his room on the third floor he could feel the strong vibra-
tions of his family below him, the robust exertions and
pleasures of their lives. It was in the banging of pots and
pans, the certain sound of doors and dishes, in the vigorous
pitch of their talk, for company and other members of the
family were always dropping in.

They were so sufficient to themselves, he thought. That
was it. Nothing stopped them. Any one of his people could
go it alone, ask for no quarter, do without your help. There
was Huldah across the sea in England now. All the wild
things she had done that she shouldn't, and yet she thought
it fitting that she should be mistress of a castle and have
people call her Lady Huldah since George Seton's father,
the lord, had died. Hardly could Kinzie wait till his ship
docked in England so he could put on his finest uniform
and visit her. The Wheelers were like that, ready for anything, afraid of nothing. His mother called it snap; his father, the dash of the pioneers.

If only there had been another in the family puny, lazy
and cowardly like he! Just the thought of having such a
brother or sister, perhaps one even worse than he was, lifted
him up, made him feel better. But his mother wouldn't ad-

mit he was puny or cowardly or anything else that wasn't good. He was strong as anybody else, she claimed. He could see through her stand. She would hound him till he was hearty as his Uncle Wyitt, ambitious like Resolve, smart as his father and musical as Sooth. But nobody could make that much out of him, Chancey told himself, for none understood him save Rosa.

Tonight at supper when he read the penciled note from Mr. Lane, it came to him what he would do. Now as he left the house, he felt at once like a different person. When he came down Sixth Street and saw the Basin ahead shining in the late afternoon light, his body turned ten pounds lighter. The soft heavy smell of the canal relaxed him. The broad letters of a boat's name, like M A R Y   E L L E N or B E T S Y   A N N, painted around the stern, gave him feelings he never had at home, as when sometimes through the murky water of the river he had seen a great fish swim and was gone. Scarcely anybody down here knew him or expected anything of him. He could do as he pleased. He was just Chancey, and if he was a Wheeler, that was as good a name as the next. They didn't hold it against him that he was of the gentry, so long as he put on no airs. The Wizard of the Dell told Rosa he liked him because he was common as anybody.

But let him turn back toward home right now, and he would feel his family take hold of him like he was a horse suddenly hitched to a mill's machinery. At once he would be fast again, pulling the heavy interlocking wheels and cogs of the Wheelers, the brick mansion house on the square, the court house where his father reigned like the priest in his robe and Resolve like a prince of the realm. Just to think of his brother standing up so cool and composed in front of a crowded courtroom made him feel all

[317]

funny, for it was not Resolve but himself standing up there in his mind, and he wasn't cool and collected at all. Had he told them tonight at the table about the note from Mr. Lane, he knew in advance how it would go. "A position on the Centinel!" Dezia, who was home for supper, would say. "How much does it pay?" His father would nod sagely. "Lane is not too brilliant. But he has sound views. Are you going to take it?" And that cruel look of strong secret feeling he knew so well would come out on his mother's face.

Never would Rosa unsettle and debase him so. He waited to tell her tonight till they walked up to Butterman's Lock. It had started to get dark when he gave her the letter, but it was still light enough to read the large penciled handwriting. Seldom had she given him such a blinding look as when she handed it back to him, and not a word should he take the position or how much would he get.

"I knew from my dream last night that something wonderful was going to happen to you," she told him. "We were on some high place with castles all around. They brought you a royal diary out of a stone tower. It said that once you had come secretly to see the queen. They pointed up at a circle of stars in the sky and called it the Crown or Corona. Two or three bright shining stars were moving in the circle. The people called out it was a good sign. You were pleased. I remember you wore a cream-colored robe with strips of soft brown fur around your neck and shoulders. You looked like a king or a high judge of the land."

He kept perfectly quiet, waiting for her to go on. She always said things that made him feel so wonderful, gave him such confidence in himself. Never were they the same thing, always new, ever a surprise. He thought she would say more now, but she didn't. He wondered if there was something else in the dream that she didn't want to tell him.

"Next Saturday's the end of the month, and when I get paid, I'm going to buy you a present," he told her.

"That would be wonderful, Chancey!"

"Either a brown or a green parasol, I haven't made up my mind yet which."

Her eyes were brilliant.

"Brown, if you can, Chancey. A golden colory brown!"

Now he was almost sure that there had been nothing bad in the dream. Her eyes were clear as amber. All the mysterious dark flecks and shadows had vanished. He felt their world rising around them, his and Rosa's private world, but mostly was it Rosa's, textured by her dress and face and voice and by the things she said. All evening he would live and move in it, and so hard was that world to die that even after he left her for the night, its half-painful sweetness would follow him home.

Of the three worlds which Chancey knew, it was the one most to be desired, never to be given up, always to be held to. His first world, of the Square and his family, was the heaviest. The second world, the one he used to retreat to in order to get away from the first, was the lightest, of fragile weight and fabric so that when he returned from its dreams and shadows he could scarcely remember what it was really like, although he knew and understood perfectly while he was there. These two worlds lay far apart and never would they meet. But his and Rosa's world moved at will into one or the other, could be at the same time apart from and parcel of either, and all the while be both real and insubstantial, remembered and forgotten. The talk of the first world was hard and clear, that of the second world in few words at all. But the talk of his and Rosa's world was sometimes spoken, sometimes thought, and ever held meanings more subtle and significant than either, like the poems he

wrote for the Centinel which were meant to go far beyond
the inky newspaper office, to be carried over city and countryside, to be read, remembered and forgotten days from
now in houses and under trees and on decks of boats following the canal as far as Cincinnati.

Chancey dropped no hint to his mother about the Centinel when he got home. Not often had he risen so early as
he did on Monday morning, nor had bed ever tasted so
sweet. If he was surprised to see his mother already down
in the kitchen, he didn't show it, and neither did she to see
him, although he had to admit hers might be the bigger
surprise. Presently he found himself among other silent
men tramping the misty streets of Americus toward work.

He had thought to sit most of the day at an office table
writing as he did at home. But there was no low table in
the Centinel office. Desks stood four feet high. In the shop
he found type cases as high or higher, stone tables and
presses. He learned he had to run errands, collect mercan-
tile announcements, deliver proofs and printing jobs, help
turn presses. When he hadn't anything more to do, he
could stand at a desk and write copy for the paper. Hardly
could he crawl home those first nights. So this was what
men went through who toiled for a living, he told himself.
As long as he lived, he felt that the six a.m. bells would give
him a sick feeling at his stomach. A fierce gratitude came
up in him for Robert Owen and all those revolutionary
thinkers who would lighten labor, the curse of the world
since Adam, and root out its evil. They knew what it did
to human souls.

He didn't believe he'd have lasted through the week save
for the image of Rosa in his mind, a bright Rosa in the
gloom, a fresh Rosa when he was sweated and wearied, and
in the heat, a cool Rosa like one of those statues they prayed

to in the Irish church. Thank God today was Saturday. Now he could lick his wounds for the week and spend his wages. He noticed with mixed feelings that the apprentices received no pay. The printers were handed envelopes heavy with money, but to Chancey, Mr. Lane gave no more than a slip of paper.

"What's this for?" the boy stammered.

"That's an order for your wages. Cash is scarce, but if you take it to Harley Fry, I think he'll pay you the two dollars he owes me. He's owed it for eighteen months."

Chancey took the order and left for uptown at once. If he hurried he could collect his wages and still get home in time for supper that his mother never failed to keep warm for him. Harley Fry was a cabinet maker. The long double front room stood crowded with bedsteads and footboards, bureaus, wash stands and coffins. The house smelled of paint, varnish and supper.

"I can pay you," the old man said. "But not in ready money. You can see for yourself all the goods I have on hand. But I'll give you an order on Albert Logan. He owes me a good deal more than that. Maybe you can get two dollars out of him. I can't."

Chancey felt the life go from him like air from a blown bladder. He left Harley Fry's slowly, ashamed to go home so late now without his wages. It took a long time and desperation to get up courage to knock on the Logan door. He knew before it opened that he would not get his money. Had he been Resolve or his father standing there with power and presence, it might have been different, he felt. But these men would only shoo a boy from one to another. He found Albert Logan a big man and stone mason. Like a hammer knocking off pieces of rock with each word, he gave his opinion of Harley Fry and other well-to-do men who pushed him for money and still worse, those who owed him and wouldn't pay. He hadn't a dollar, he claimed, but if Chancey sat down and wrote him out an order on Minor Jones, the jobber, he'd sign it.

Chancey never did get his supper that night. Minor Jones wasn't at home when he got there and the boy had to wait a long time. When he did come, he said he had been down town for Saturday night and had spent what cash he had in his pocket. The banks were closed. It was late. He would have to give him an order on Tom Brill, the grocer. If Chancey hurried, he could still get his money from him. The boy left as soon as he was able, but it was ten o'clock and Brill was putting the heavy wooden shutters on his store windows when the boy got there. The grocer stood reading the order, his dour lips moving.

"It's too late to send me to anybody else tonight!" Chancey begged to forestall him.

"Well," the storekeeper said shrewdly, "sign it 'Received in full' and I'll pay you. But you'll have to take it out in trade. Now be smart about it. I'm closing."

Chancey wanted to cry out that the grocer surely must have the money in his till. It was Saturday night and he had done business all day. But the words wouldn't come. Desperately he looked around the store. If only it had been a general store, there would have been umbrellas among the blankets, piece goods, queensware and such. But here were only things to eat, not a parasol or bolt of goods in the house. In the end, goaded by the grocer, he let himself be loaded down with flour, loaf sugar, stick candy and milk lunch crackers. He had to pay a penny for each paper sack. Then hoping that Rosa would take the things for her mother and understand, he stumbled out into the darkness for the waterfront.

CHAPTER TWENTY-SEVEN

WINTER IN

Sweet Phosphor, bring the day.

ROBERT HERRICK

WHAT had come over her, Rosa whispered to herself, that she didn't like winter any more? Why, it had always been her favorite season! Of course, so was summer when it came, and so were fall and spring. But only winter had coasters and skaters, the black and white she passionately loved and the crispness of being that her secret self fed on. Only in winter could she ride the north wind, survive the frost and prove that she was immortal.

Then how was it that already in December she hungered for spring, for green and warmth, for the sun? Every evening, the six o'clock darkness and long winter night came bitter and cruel. They had never seemed so before. Was it some deep disorder or foreboding — what her mother called "a messenger"? Or could it be Chancey, that he didn't come around to her mother's little house behind the Red Mule any more?

In January, at a safe distance, Rosa stood in the snowy square one evening and looked across at the great Wheeler house. How high it looked and wide! You might think it needn't be very deep to hold the needs of the Wheelers, and yet as she moved on and more of the house came into view, it astonished her again how far back the side walls and windows reached. It was a brick world in itself. Chancey's folks must have more space than they knew what to do with. If some of the family were in one room, the rest could go to another. And if company came to that room, they could move on to another and still another room, all downstairs, not counting the hall nor the rooms upstairs.

What was it about the Wheeler house gave her this strange feeling, she wondered, half burning hot, half icy cold. It came to her on the street, when she sighted one of the Wheelers or heard the name spoken. Was it her bond with Chancey? Or could it be what some folks whispered to her, that she wasn't a Tench and ought to be with the Wheelers? Hardly could that be true, she thought, for, save Chancey, none of them would look at her when she passed, only he and that old woman, his mother, with her face brown as an Indian's, her hair combed tight as could be, and she not a Wheeler anyway save by name.

Well, except for Chancey, neither did she, Rosa, give a hait about any of the Wheelers, but she couldn't say that about her own family. If she wasn't a Tench, why did she look forward all day just to see them again in the evening, although she had left them only that morning? And when one of her brothers lay sick in his bed or was in trouble for doing what he shouldn't, why did pity flood her like a hemorrhage, proving he was truly of her own flesh and blood? She even felt loving toward Turkey's wife, Lulu, who came to live with them and she could hardly wait for the day when Lulu's baby came to make her Aunt Rosa and bring more life to their little house, for how could it crowd them as some folks said, a tiny helpless thing no bigger than a minute?

But where was Chancey? Before Christmas, the canal had frozen up, the boatmen had gone home, if they had any, and there was skating all along the waterfront, especially in the basin. Then for a day or two the weight lifted on Rosa, for she felt sure Chancey would come. She came home early on purpose Saturday afternoon. The lively scene lay in front of her, the bright reds and greens of the skaters, the children on sleds, the long chains of boys and girls, the graceful ladies with skirts almost sweeping the canal, the stout men and old men light on their feet as dancing masters. But nowhere among them could her eye make out Chancey though she watched till the misty hills looked furry in the sunset light that was blue with the woodsmoke from a thousand chimneys. The first time it snowed, the men and boys swept it off with a will. It snowed again heavily the third day and this time they shoveled only a wide path to skate up and down and another from bank to bank. The third time it snowed, only the children came to clear a ring or two, and that for a long while was the end of the skating.

So far, since winter had set in, there hadn't been a day of thaw. The first snow still lay on the ground under all the rest. Was it to be this way all winter, she asked herself, no break in this long bitter stretch until spring? The first snow had been pleasant enough when it fell, casting such a friendly feeling upon everybody out on errands or shoveling paths. It made even the grumpy cheerful, and uptown among the big houses all seemed so cordial and gay. On the night of the second fall, Rosa stood a while out in the back yard, drinking it in; the pale light, the utter stillness and the snow lying thick over houses and out buildings, bushes and fences. This is what she used to do as a little girl when they lived along the river, stand out somewhere alone in the evening and feel the magic of the new world she found herself in. It was like nothing else she knew. The soft fragrant smell of the snow was in her nostrils. Sometimes she could feel a fine rain of flakes from the roofs in her face. The snow on the roof edges rose like bread, and she thought of the rabbit sitting in his warm nest. Winter is the best time of the year, she told herself, if you are snug and happy. She could hear the fine bells of cutters uptown and the bobsleds' deep bells down Dock Street. Oh, winter was far and away the finest season, she thought, but why when everything lay so white and pure in the world, should such dark shadows lay on her mind?

The cold set in after Christmas like a strong man settling himself in bed. Night after night Rosa could hear the house crack like a fowling piece with the frost. A big thermometer hung nailed with a hundred other signs to Meeks' store front. Mornings on her way to the millinery shop, Rosa saw that the mercury was swallowed up, vanished. The red crept out a little until she came home in the evening. Sometimes it rose high enough to foretell snow again, but by another morning or two the glassy upright line would stand pale and bleak once more. Roof icicles stabbed toward the ground, and over the shoveled piles of snow you could see little more than the driver and the nodding heads of his horses.

But where was Chancey? Had his heart's blood frozen in his veins like the red stuff in Meeks' thermometer? She kept remembering all the good times they had had last summer, especially the night at Dixes' wake. Chancey hadn't wanted to go at first, and once there, he looked like he would bolt, for the Dixes had no cool room to put the corpse in but had to keep her in the kitchen-sleeping room with the company. All the time somebody had to stand there sopping baking soda water on one cloth over the corpse's face and on another cloth over the folded hands so the smell of Death would not rise too strong.

Rosa thought nothing of doing her turn, but Chancey stood from her as far as he could, looking like the whitewash on the wall.

Then after the barroom closed, Turkey came.

"I been working all night and I'm hungry!" he bawled and went to the cupboard. "What! Didn't she bake anything before she died? Well, she'll pay for it, I'm a tellin' you."

He went across the room and tickled the bare feet of the corpse's older sisters lying on the bed. They thought it was flies and kept twitching and shooing. The whole company had to choke to keep back from laughing, and that was only the start. When Rosa and Chancey got outside, they had to hold each other. She wasn't over it by the time she got home. Her mother asked her what could be funny at a wake, and she hadn't dared tell on account of Turkey.

Oh, Chancey and she had a good time that night, but where was Chancey now? Her mother claimed she knew. She wouldn't say right out who told her, but let it be known she had talked it over with Miss Bogardus. According to her, Chancey never gave a hait for Rosa, and it was good he didn't, her mother hinted darkly, because he couldn't give her the rights and rewards of a decent girl. All the time he came down here to see her, he had somebody else picked out for himself, a young lady who would fit in with the Wheelers and Morrisons and their fine houses on the square. No, there was nothing honest in Chancey Wheeler's coming to see her, and if she knew what was good for her and him, too, she'd thank him for staying away from her and clear him out of her mind.

All the times her mother said this, and when she didn't, she sat there wrapped up in herself by the stove, living her life in her chair. Hardly had she changed, Rosa thought, since she first remembered her, although these last years she let Rosa comb some of the wild tangles out of her hair. Rosa's father's coal black mane had streaked long ago, and now it looked like iron strings dipped in lime. But her mother's brown head hadn't a gray thread woven in it. The only way you could tell she was older was by her glasses. All these years she had sat in her dark kitchen reading like an owl in a hollow tree. At last she claimed she could hardly tell any more who came in at the door. Rosa fetched pair after pair of glasses home to try until she found one to suit. They suited her in more ways than one, Rosa thought, for now no matter what was said, her mother could sit behind those spectacles in her own world and all you could make out from her eyes were the hard lights glinting on her glasses.

When her mother spoke of Chancey and his fine young lady, Rosa kept still. Not even to herself would she admit it. She went on just as if her mother hadn't spoken. She would give it no room in her mind, no shred of existence. Then it couldn't hurt her, for so far as she was concerned, it wasn't true and couldn't be, like the story of the child that never knew about Death and never would believe it, and even on her death bed, Death couldn't harm her, for it had no power over her. But if Rosa wouldn't mention it, a mysterious voice in her mind would. Many times it plainly said, "Who is this fine young lady?" She would be sitting sewing a ribbon or combing her hair and suddenly in the

silence this voice would ask, "What is she like that Chancey likes her better than you?" Never did the voice sound
like her own or any voice she knew. Now whose voice
could it be, she pondered, saying, "you" and not "me" in
her own mind?

When it wasn't another voice breaking in, it was her
mother's.

"I hear he took this young lady to Tateville Saturday
night," she would say. "You can be glad you didn't go."

That would throw Rosa's thought to the sleighing par-
ties. They had started in January. First seven sleds had come
to Americus from Tateville crowded with young folks
shouting and singing. They carried a white flag with a
green face and a thumb held to its nose. The young ladies
of Tateville, it was said, had sewed it up, but what young
ladies, Rosa's mother asked, would sew up a thing like that?
She said it must be a made-up story, but Dennis said he
saw the flag with his own eyes at the Washington House
where the Tateville people ate their supper. A good many
others saw it, too, and said they couldn't let Tateville get
away with that. The next Saturday night sixteen four-horse
sled loads went to Tateville from Americus crying out
they wanted that flag. They got it, too, and lost it the next
Saturday night when Tateville came back with twenty-
three sleds. From then on every time Americus went to
Tateville or Tateville came to Americus, it took more sleds
and folks to get the flag.

Now this was the last of February and everybody said
that any day the snow would go. And yet it held on. Tateville had come to Americus last week with nearly eighty
sleds, and all Americus prayed the snow would last another
Saturday night. The biggest sleighing crowd in the history
of Ohio would journey to Tateville then. The whole coun-

try around Americus, on both sides of the river, was scoured
for the promise of teams and sleds. Nearly a dozen sleds
were going from the waterfront alone, and Rosa told Idilla
and Vic that she would ride along.

And then she wished she hadn't. It was all right, she saw
clearly, just to lay eyes on Chancey again, but not if this
other person was with him. Once her eyes glimpsed them
together, never afterward could her mind deny her mother's
story. Perhaps their sleds would stop side by side, or they
would all have supper at the same table. The sight of him
and her together would be like a knife. She wished now
she hadn't said she would go, but it was too late. She
couldn't bear to go and see him, and yet now that she had
gone this far, she couldn't bear to stay away.

There were ninety-six sleds that went to Tateville from
Americus that night, counting the two-seaters and cutters.
Not that many lined up on Sixth Street in Americus to
start, but at every side road halfway to Tateville sleds
with shouting and singing young people waited to join the
procession. From the top of the Long Swamp hill Rosa
could see against the snow an endless dark train of teams
ahead and a longer one winding behind them. And instead
of thawing, it was still snowing. Now and then flurries
would come licking their faces with melting flakes, bringing the mighty chorus of a thousand voices ahead. Then
when the wind stood still, she could hear the concord of
another thousand voices behind her. It was a curious and
wonderful thing to hear, the great song waxing and wan-
ing and turning upon itself with distance and the wind. The
same words and bar would come a second and third time
with such power that blood was fetched to her head. After
the snowy swirls, the early moon came out, racing through
the clouds, making the countryside bright as day. Oh,

never, Rosa thought, had she seen and felt such deadly loveliness before.

Half of Tateville lined the streets to welcome them when they got there. Only the first section of sleds could get near the square. Rosa and her friends had to get down a long way out. Where his sled would be later on, the driver did not know. Nobody cared. It was good to use your legs after so long a ride. Tonight Tateville belonged to Americus, with Americus folks tramping the sidewalks and streets, calling and laughing in a monster open-air party from one end of town to the other. But Rosa's laugh didn't carry very far. She was unwilling here to look at folks directly. She moved along taking care to see over heads and past faces. It would be too hard a blow for her eyes to come on them suddenly together. She had no fear to miss him. If Chancey were somewhere in the crowd, his face would make itself known to her, or his proud head or stiff spindly shoulders. The smallest part of him would jump to her eye from the crowd like the name, Wheeler, always jumped from a crowded column in the Centinel. What she would do then, she didn't know.

She and Idilla and Vic were standing outside the Rising Sun when she felt a hand on her arm. She knew without turning whose hand it was. She could tell by the violent feeling that went over her. She had been waiting with the others to get their supper. For a long time they had stood in the crowded line, moving by inches toward the dining room. They were almost at the door. Another minute or two they might have been in the warm. But now Rosa's arm wasn't hers any more but belonged to the hand that had touched it, and where it drew her, she went also.

Shame rose before she went very far. Was she so weak that all this winter he could stay away from her at home without a word sent or written, and then when he chanced to see her in a strange city, he need only touch her arm and she would follow like a blind woman the hand that guided her! She would go with him only a little way, she told herself, just far enough to be out of hearing of Americus folks. Idilla and Vic could think she deserted them. Right now they had likely turned to watch the white scarf on her head ride through the crowd like a duck on the river. But if they waited a little, they would hardly know she had gone, for in a minute or two she would be back. She had said no word when she went, and it would be the same on her return.

"Now I'm going back!" she would tell Chancey suddenly in a way so he knew that nothing would stop her. At the first stretch of empty sidewalk she would say it, or in the middle of this long dark block. Surely at the next lamp post she would do it, where she could see his face when she told him.

But he was the one who turned first.

"You shouldn't have come," he blamed her. "I promised I wouldn't see you again."

"Promised!" she blazed at him. "Why should you promise if you don't want to?"

"My father made me."

Rosa let that turn around slowly in her mind.

"How did he make you?"

"He said it wasn't right for us to go together."

"Why?" she asked though she thought she knew.

"Because it's evil — who you are and who I am."

Now she wasn't sure that she knew at all. That strange, half-hot, half-icy cold feeling of the Wheelers went over her, mysteriously strangling her and at the same time freezing the soft inner marrow of her bones.

"Who am I?" she asked him so low that scarcely could she hear herself.

"You can ask your mother," was all he said.

"Why must I ask her? She wouldn't tell me anything."

"She told my father. That's why he talked to me. She wrote him a letter. She said it was wicked and immoral, our being together and he had to keep us from ever seeing each other again."

"My mother!" Rosa whispered. Hardly could she believe it. Her mother, sitting in her chair in the brown dress Rosa herself had made for her, with the book Rosa fetched for her in her lap, with the glasses Rosa bought for her on her nose, and all the time it had been she who had kept them apart.

"We'll come back when we won't have to wait for supper," he promised, but Rosa scarcely heard him.

"Is it true that it's evil for us to go together?" she whispered.

"It's against the law — and the church."

"Then we can't ever see each other again?"

At his answer Rosa's foot slipped in the snow and she would have stumbled had he not held her. The strangeness of the street at night was a dark cloud around her and he was the wind carrying her here and yonder. Her body might have been a snowflake blown this way and that, yet always coming back in the end to the shape of her body. Already the square was far away, Idilla and Vic small and distant in her mind. Could it be just a few minutes ago that she had stood there talking to them at the Rising Sun? So much had happened since Chancey had touched her. Where they were going now she didn't know. These dim streets seemed all alike to her. Only the last one they came to she thought she knew. She had heard of Tateville's Front

Street, and here was the river. In summer it must be grand
with the great houses getting the breeze, but now all was
locked in a wintry and snowy death.

A few blocks more and the street changed. One-sided
above, it was two-sided below, with dark and deserted
workshops crowding each other. She and Chancey could
be alone here. They could find solitude among the silent
warehouses and mills, the factories and brew houses. They
could say anything they wanted and none except themselves would hear. Yet hardly a word passed between them.
Always afterward would she mingle this night, she thought,
with the warm soft smell of dyes, the cold hard scent of
iron and the sweetness of malt and hops, with the mysterious stillness of the darkened buildings and visible between
them on one side the bleak white expanse of river.

It was late when they got back to the square, yet he
would have it no other way than that she have her supper
with him in the elegant Mansion House. The dining room,
almost bare of both food and diners now, received them.
When they came out, the square lay almost empty of teams
and sleds. From far through the city and the country beyond, they could hear the stream of song and sleighbells
drifting back to them.

"They're gone!" Rosa said, meaning Idilla and Vic.

"Not everybody," Chancey said. "I'll get you home." He
took her hand and dragged her over to a long low bobsled
with four black horses. "We missed our party, George,"
he called to the driver. "Can we go back with you?"

Like a Wheeler, he didn't wait for a yes or no, but lifted
her over the low board to an open space among the dark
forms. Rosa slipped quickly down in the thick straw under
the covers. Already it felt warm down there, but around
her she thought she felt a slight chill. Though she couldn't

see their faces, they could have seen hers coming out of the Mansion House. She was aware now that there were no coarse quilts here as in the sled she had come in, only soft blankets. The scent of fine fabric and leather told her this was no common sled. She wished now she had held back. Sooner would she have walked all the way home with Chancey, if need be, than this.

Once out in the country, the couples turned to themselves, became blind and deaf to the others around them. Rosa crept farther down under the blankets. The sled mounted the hills, slid through the high white banks, sped over snowy fields. They passed farm houses and barns standing extraordinarily still in the winter night. The road went so close, they could smell mows and horses and the soft milky scent of cows. Once through a wintry woods, Rosa fancied she smelled spring. Most of the time she lay back, making all she could of the night and of Chancey so close beside her, tasting it over and over, making it last. Such a feeling she never had before as when she lay there looking up at the sky. The sled slipped so effortlessly over the earth, it seemed to drop away and leave her riding, drifting among the great flying clouds and the sudden blue stars that flashed out between.

Once when the low western moon came out she raised her head to see the snowy countryside crusted with lighted silver. Presently the magic was darkened. Cattycornered across the sled she was aware of the cool eyes of Chancey's sister, Mercy, fixed upon her as if upon something wicked and unclean. All the rest of the ride Rosa tried to rid that evil from herself, but it lay too deep. It seemed like some dark stain in her blood, and she couldn't tear it out or scour her white flesh clean.

CHAPTER TWENTY-EIGHT

SUMMER OUT

Where the deer and the roe bounding lightly together
Sport the long afternoon on the braes of Balquether.

SUNG IN EARLY AMERICA

W HAT Chancey's sister told her father about them, Rosa
never knew, nor wished to know. But it must have
been something bad for Barney Shand to come to see her
mother. He was the sheriff of Shawanee County and Judge
Wheeler's right hand man. In the parlor of his house, they
said, he kept the rope of every man he had hanged and the
last dishes the doomed man had eaten from. Barney Shand
came to the waterfront on the softest day, the first mild
day of March, a day full of the mercy of God and of the
elements and of everything else save man. With winter and
the snow gone, with spring in the air and the kindly sunlight lying on the sidewalks, he called at the little house
behind the Red Mule, a stout man with small eyes and
flabby jowls, and was alone with her mother a long time.

Rosa felt herself steel when she went in the house afterward.

"I know all about your going with that young Wheeler

to Tateville," her mother informed her bitterly. "So does Judge Wheeler. Now he forbids you two seeing each other under the penalty of the law."

Inside Rosa shook a little, though she would give small heed outside. So there was no limit, she told herself, to the cruelty that wicked old men and women practised on innocent young people who never harmed anybody. It hadn't been enough for them that somewhere inside of her the dark eggs of some obscure taint had been laid to spoil and set her apart from the rest. Now they had to brand her flesh, tell her what she must do and mustn't, and where she must never walk or pay the penalty.

All the rest of the day a strong disquiet possessed her like that of the moths caught last summer behind the window pane. Hardly could she keep still or wait to clear early supper from the table, and when she slipped off and out into the free air, she felt like the moths must have felt when she raised the sash and let them soar.

She went straight in the face of the setting sun to the Sixth Street bridge that spanned the canal, and when she got there, Chancey was waiting as they had planned. He had his back turned, looking the other way, making as though he didn't expect her. But just the anxious desperate way he stood she knew that they had bullied him as they had her.

"Don't tell me anything!" she begged him.

Scarcely speaking, they walked out Sixth Street and took a back road into the hills. The deeper they went, the more the feel of evil and shame fell from her. Never, she thought, had the country been so beautiful as tonight after the sheriff's call. One day or another each March she had noticed that a fine indeterminate haze hung in the air, but she couldn't recall that it had ever been so delicate before or when it had given her such a grateful shelter. It was softer than smoke and dryer than fog. Indeed as the dusk deepened, it was like some mysterious and exquisite mist distilled by the gods to hide the secret and stealthy union of earth and heaven. She and Chancey walked through it tonight as if only half awake and yet with all the wisdom of dreamers.

That was it, she told herself, it was like a dream. Through the luminous vapor the land, fields, trees and fence rows appeared as in a dream. The cries of late birds and of men and women across the fields had the same unearthly insubstantial quality. The ugly unreality of the day had dissolved. This was reality. Earthly time stood still. Even the rigs and wagons on the road moved in a curious, almost sleepy fashion while boys and girls standing in the lanes or outlined against the glowing red of brush fires seemed motionless, wholly under the spell.

Coming back to the waterfront was like waking up in the morning to her lot, to the coarse wornout bed clothing and hearing the early tipplers grumble and cough in the saloon. Only the enchantment of this evening and their triumph over the law supported her. If Judge Wheeler and Barney Shand hadn't been able to stop their happiness tonight, who would keep her and Chancey apart? The law would only draw them closer. As she neared her house she could feel her mind rising, resolving, sharpening, devising to protect themselves against her mother and those wicked old men. She would be cunning as the fox and watchful as the savage. Never would she and Chancey submit to such as they.

And that's the way it worked out the rest of March when the soft baby fur of the pussy willows opened to them by the tow path, and in April when the yellow daffodils bloomed in the locktender's garden and the white blood root in the woods where on Sundays they wandered. After May, they met on the other side of the level, in the boat yard, where they sometimes glimpsed others beside themselves meet like shadows and disappear into one of the long line of boats moored for repairs. More than once as she and Chancey sat rocking on the deck or in a sheltered cabin from the rain, she caught sight of a pair of eyes from an adjoining cabin staring at them. But she knew that she and Chancey were safe. Such as they would never tell.

Often on a condemned boat, watching rings in the murky water where a catfish had come up to gasp, or hearing the endless wash of waves against the hull, Rosa could not help but think of those who had drowned here. There was the Man with the Hook. Though his arm had been lost at the elbow, his hook, they said, was just as good at work or fighting. But when he got drunk and slipped in the water, the hook was no good at all, and he never came up. Then there was Florry Hughet, who fell in too, the wife of a boatman, and Polly Baker tried to reach her with a pole. Ever afterward Thirsty Hughet used to say, "Polly Baker, you drowned my Florry with your pole." But the worst was the Early girl who threw herself in the canal none knew where, and when they found her and fished her out, her body was covered with eels.

Oh, whenever she thought of the Early girl, Rosa would give a secret shudder. Not an eel had she eaten since that day. She would rather have put the waterfront behind them on their holidays, but Chancey liked the basin. He used to say that ever since he had gone down the river on the old bridge, water and boats were in his blood. Rosa didn't mind stopping with him to watch the Privateer as they called the Flour Inspector. A little man with a long hollow augur like the letter, U, with a screw bit on one end, he would run it down through a barrel head and draw it out full of flour, then hold it over his bucket to sift it through his fingers. If free from specks, he branded the barrel, SUPER-FINE, otherwise FINE. From every boat he took home a bucket of flour.

The trouble was that Chancey would stop and spend their precious hours talking to anybody they met. He liked to visit Bigger, the black who lived on his boat with a white woman and six mulatto children, and Teeny, the biggest boatman on the canal, who on a summer's day would float in the water asleep or reading the paper, his head resting on a block of wood; and Paddy Doran, born in Ireland, who always told the same tale, how his mother was a maid of the sea and had swam up the River Shannon and shed her scales by a hay rick, and after bearing him, she had put on her scales one night and left his father, swimming out to sea again, and never had she been heard from since, so they mustn't take offense if he had been drinking.

Oh, Chancey was a strange one, interested in all these things. It was to gather material for his writing, he used to claim and that's what made him curious. But what made him stubborn and willful he didn't say, or why he leaned on her like a cane. She had to stop with him and listen to all he talked to, though she'd heard the story many times before. When summer and camp meeting came around, she had to go along and stand in the shadows with him and listen to the praying and preaching that Chancey ever claimed he didn't believe in.

The first time Rosa heard how God told Abraham to kill his own son and sacrifice him on the fire; when she heard that God ordered Joshua to destroy the people of Jericho and of Ai and Makkedehad and Lachish and Libnah and

Hebron and many other cities so that not a single man, woman or child nor even a calf or lamb had dare to remain alive; and that all who disobeyed would go to hell and burn in pits of fire forever, Rosa put her fingers to her ears and wanted to cry out, "Liars! Stop!" The savage preaching, the gloomy singing, the violent praying, the threats and imprecations dismayed her. One preacher would fall from exhaustion and another and still another took his place till a dozen had manned the pulpit. Under their unceasing fire, the people would stir and moan, cry out wordless things, throw up their arms, leap and wrestle with each other. Often a mighty jerk would go among the women like the plague, their heads snapping and their hair coming down to lash and crack like bull whips in hypnotic unison. Then Rosa would close her eyes from the terrifying spectacle and not look save now and then at Chancey. There he'd stand pale and irresolute, consumed and tortured by what he saw and heard, yet drawn and held to it like he couldn't help himself.

But the good of summer far outstripped the bad. What atoned for the blot of camp-meeting was God's country and the Welsh Valley. They'd walk up the tow path past Butterman's Lock and cross the aqueduct over Welsh Creek. Here they'd leave the canal for a little road that ran through a break in the hills. It was just a small narrow valley, thinly settled and full of the wild beauty of God. The road wound along the creek. At every step you had the curve of the road and the white of the water through the leaves. In the lanes you could stand on log bridges and look up the stream and down. Such particular beauty she had never seen, the long reaches of water with the trees meeting overhead, the wet mossy stones and logs below, and the clear water tumbling through.

Oh, she loved every minute in Welsh Valley. She liked the natives they made friends with, and the best were the Griffins, all brothers, all bachelors and never a woman over their log doorsill till she had come, they said, to bless their house. The oldest brother would show her his corn and hogs. The middle brother showed her how he wove his homespun and mixed his salt rising bread. And the youngest brother would play for her on his shepherd's pipe, walking up and down and only stopping to tell her where he had first heard the air in the old country.

She gave a little cry of pain that day in August to think that summer was almost over. Why, in June it had seemed that it would last forever. She had put out of her mind that there could ever be an end. Each week, she fancied, was a little warmer than the last, July hotter than June, and August than July. Then suddenly she saw the first buckwheat shocked in its dark green forester shade in the field, and a hurt gripped her heart. Why, only the corn-cutting in late September was later than buckwheat harvest. Now she held to what was left of summer with all her might, trying to hold it back, praying it to slow down and linger, that it would not pass. But in her heart she knew that winter was just ahead, that soon all the flowers, open windows, green leaves, birds and grasses would be gone. And where in the cold and snow could she and Chancey see each other then?

Even if it hadn't been for the shocked buckwheat, there would have been the Sign to tell her. It had been their last day at the Griffins, such a wonderful day with the air clear as Welsh Creek water, the sun like a bright shining stove and all the grasshoppers still calling in the fields. They had stayed till late, and evening was clear with stars when they reached the aqueduct. Here they waited for a down boat to take them to town and the Basin.

They were sitting on the locktender's bench outside his cottage when it began.

"Did you see it?" asked Chancey who saw everything.

"I see you," Rosa said softly. "What else must I see?"

"It was something in the water," he told her.

She watched, and there it was in the brimming lock like he said, a streak like phosphorus this way and that. It brought to her mind the tale a riverman had told her father, that far around the curve of the earth under the Southern Cross every creature left its trail of light in the warm sea water. You need only dip your hand and see the mysterious light glow and sparkle. Watching now in the full lock, Rosa could almost feel herself on some far-away isle watching the train of some strange swimmer in the tropical ocean.

"Rosa, did you see it?" Chancey cried.

She looked up and found that what she saw was not in the water but in the sky. Over the face of the heavens, stars were falling, not directly down as a stone would plunge but across like cannonballs fired from heavenly breast works. They left in their wake long trains of white fire that died slowly in the black velvet night. Most of them seemed far away, but now and then a huge bolt of blue or greenish light would flash dangerously toward them or another streak so low across the face of the earth that it seemed they must hear the hiss of its passage and the violent report when it landed. The lock keeper, aroused by their excited voices, came out to see and called his wife who looked for a brief moment and then ran back to hide her head under the bed covers. All the time the spectacle was growing stronger, grander and more terrifying. In the end the heavens appeared to be raining fire and that surely they, the lock house and canal must presently be hit.

In the midst of all this celestial display, a distant earthy

horn sounded for the lock, and a down boat loomed up
calmly in the eerie light. The boy on the mules looked
panic-stricken, but the tall old boatman at the helm said he
had seen snow and hail that bothered him a sight worse
than falling stars. He hadn't heard a single splash or come
on any "b'iling" water. Furthermore he wished one would
come a little closer. He'd like to catch it in a wash basin,
cool it off in the "drink" and tie his rope around it for an
anchor.

Chancey seemed to shrink from boarding a boat whose
master dared the stars to strike him, but Rosa felt a sense of
strength and safety in his presence. All the way down the
long ride to the Basin, she pondered what could this sign
mean to her and Chancey? That it tokened something, she
felt certain, for if she and Chancey hadn't gone to Welsh
Valley this day, if the Griffins hadn't asked them to stay
for supper, if it hadn't been the summer's last weekend so
that they agreed, and if it hadn't turned out that for the
longest time no boat came so that they had to wait out here
on the locktender's bench, they would never have seen the
sign. She would have been asleep in her bed and Chancey
in his. But the sign spoke to both of them together, and
that it was a true sign, she knew, for stars ever spoke the
purest truth. The sailor on the trackless oceans sailed by
them and never did they lie. Nor were they lying now. But
what they said in their fearful message, neither she nor
Chancey could make out.

When she got home, the lamp still burned and her mother
sat in her chair, her old brown shawl around her shoulders.
Her eyes you couldn't see behind the clouded glasses, but
her face looked sharp and the mouth bitter and thin.

"Where have you been on a night like this?"

"Out in the country."

"Till this time in the morning?"

"I just got in."

"Who with?"

"I didn't say I was with anybody, Mama."

"What were you doing?" insinuating, incriminating.

"I was walking."

"All alone at this hour?"

"I didn't say I was alone, Mama."

"Don't tell me you went against the law with that young hellion?"

"I don't know who you mean, Mama."

"You know exactly who I mean — that degenerate Wheeler?"

"He isn't degenerate."

"So that's who it was, was it?"

"I can't tell you, Mama."

"You needn't tell me, I know."

"All right, then you know, Mama."

"Don't all-right me, Miss Rosa! If you don't want to tell your own mother, I can't make you. But don't tell her, either, when the law brings your sin out in court. Don't say I didn't warn you. Never did I dream I would have a daughter like this!"

Her mother went about making herself ready for bed then, and soon her peculiar breathing rose to the loft, but Rosa in her bed could not sleep. Too much hung over her this night, her mother's talk, the warning of the stars, the close of summer as if she had come to the end of a golden rope. But what Chancey told her before he left was the worst. It might be better if they didn't see each other for a while, he had said. The coming week he would be busy. The week after that was the Americus fair, and never dare they be seen together in front of so many people. Rosa wasn't sure that she heard him right at first. Then something like a wheel stopped inside of her, and all night his words lay like a dark unknown specter by her side. Was it going to be like last fall and winter, she kept asking herself. Was it truly the end of summer then, and was this the start of his forsaking her and perhaps of their final parting?

When a week went by and not a sight of his thin unforgettable face, Rosa turned at last to her other self for aid. Always before had this other self helped her. Who or what it was, she didn't altogether know, save it might be her conscience or the self she might have been had her hopes had their way, for its qualities were nearly all those she had not. No matter how upset she could be, her other self was always cool and unalarmed, as much as to say to her, very well, it's all right, go and do it then if you must, the world won't come to an end. Sometimes when in great emotion or pain, Rosa thought her other self calloused and aloof. If it had to suffer fever or shame as she did, she thought, if needles could pierce its fingers or its back ache, then it would soon learn to have more pity and feeling. Just the same it was a comfort and a friend, like an older, sometimes difficult but infinitely wiser sister whose counsel was ever open to her.

But tonight when Rosa turned to it for help, no other self was there. Never had this happened up to now. Why, she couldn't recall the time when it had not been ready with an answer. It shared her every thought and feeling. Indeed she always fancied it part of herself and that when she died, it would have to die with her. How then could it have vanished while she was still alive? In faint panic she turned, calling within herself and then, still in her mind, to the spaces about her. No answer came, no feel or intimation of that familiar and dependable presence, no characteristic words of advice or rebuke rising in her mind. It was as if she had called into a great void, empty of life, one that had never known her existence.

If only she could talk five minutes with Chancey! What a bitter thing that never could she see him or share his company up town like other young folks, but must meet him by stealth down here at the waterfront behind boats and people's backs. She would not endure, she told herself, such a life of disgrace and debasement any longer. Often had Chancey talked to her of leaving Americus. They could go to Cincinnati or Indiana, he said, and start anew. No one would know them there or care. They could live their own lives without interference or dishonor. But always when he begged, she had held back from such cruel leave-taking of her family, never to see her mother or brothers again, not even to let them know she was still alive. Now she had waked up with a shock. God give her another chance, and she would in a moment leave them all behind. Hardly could she wait till she and Chancey went away and started their new life together.

Such a week she hoped never to live through again as this last. Monday and Tuesday of the new week were interminable. Wednesday she grew hopeless, and Thursday desperate. Friday she told herself she could hold back no longer. By noon the waterfront looked almost deserted. Every one else had gone to see the balloon ascension, the great bag and its fearless rider mount the sky. Under the silent accusing gaze of her mother, she washed and dressed in the brown dress that Chancey like best. Then she took the precious gold piece from her keepsake box and slipped out into Dock Street.

If she were blind, she thought, she could find her way today. The great voice of the fair drew her, like the voice of the sea she had never heard but always hoped to. Could this be Brown's field where the peaceful white cows had grazed all summer, this city of booths and stands, of tents and enclosures, of the calls of show folk and medicine men, the blare of horns and beat of drums all playing furiously! The rich booths stood laden with goods and trinkets. She could smell the frying fish and warm pop corn of the stands, the pickles and mustard. Men dipped from tubs of lemonade and from huge black kettles of coffee. Outside the tents, posters and barking men pictured the marvelous sights within. But today she had no taste for the giant giraffe, or the snowy bear, or the hairy woman from Abyssinia or the dreadful Turk who swallowed fire. For small silver she could have heard David's Pedal Harp played by one of his descendants or the Campanologians, the Swiss Bell Ringers, in rusty coats, red boots and blue pantaloons, their caps with white plumes and a bell in either hand. She could have seen rope dancers, sapient and performing brutes, the wax figures of Cain and Abel and of Delilah cutting the hair of Samson.

But all that mattered today was Chancey. From every part of the fair she could see the monstrous bag of the balloon floating, bobbing over the tops of booths and tents, straining with the breeze on its slender rope mooring. All day it had carried people fifty or a hundred yards into the sky. For two dollars each a pair of passengers could ride and see the world as a bird saw it. Then the balloonist's crew would pull them down. Four times she came back to the balloon without finding Chancey. The fifth time there he was, climbing into the basket.

"Oh, Chancey!" she cried aloud before she thought. "Take me with you!"

By the look on his face she knew she had made a mistake

[348]

in front of all the people. The balloonist looked at her coldly, guessing something was wrong. "The aeronaut par excellence" Chancey in the Centinel had called him, and he looked it, dressed in black jersey trunks and slippers.

"You can go up later, Miss," he said.

"But I must go with him!" she testified, trying to reach the basket.

"It would cost you two dollars, Miss!" he said sternly, barring her way, hoping to put her off, but her hand in her purse quickly found the gold piece.

Even when she stood in the basket, Chancey kept his face turned away as if he had never known her. "Oh, Chancey, couldn't you give me one small sign that you saw me before!" she wanted to say to him but never would she till they were free from the crowd. Now wouldn't you think that this aerial car would feel foreign to her, but her shoes seemed to find firm and familiar footing among the sacks of sand and among the extra ballast of blackened iron that lay in broken scattered pieces on the floor of the basket, broken stove plates, pieces of chimney rods and the rusty heads of two eelspears. The crew was letting out the rope now, and the bag surged upward like some live celestial thing eager to return to its world. She could feel her and Chancey rising, the heavy ground falling away beneath them, and in herself a growing and effortless lightness of being. So this was how it felt, she whispered to herself, to leave Americus? Never if she could help it, would she ever return again.

How long they let her and Chancey up in God's free air, she didn't know, but the time must have been very short. She could hardly believe it was over when she felt them starting to pull the basket down. Why, scarcely had she time to say the first word to him. He still stood silent, stiff and obdurate. She could see the upturned faces of the crowd waiting cruelly below. Must she now go back and face them, return to the heavy air of Americus, to the smell of frying fish, to the crowded little house behind the Red Mule saloon and her mother's mouldy chair! It looked like such a slender little rope that pulled them down. Where it pressed the rim of the basket, the hard-woven willow and many winds had frayed it. Not much would it take for the strands that were left to give way. Only a touch, and she and Chancey could go where he had so long wished, not to return again.

Never had she known her hand to do such a swiftly reckless and irresponsible thing before. Chancey's back was still turned, but she thought she felt him give a start at the lightened jerk of the basket. Then he must have looked at her when it was too late, with the rusty bit of eelspear head safely out of sight in her bosom and the parted rope falling unseen below. The quick bag had leaped like an uprushing pheasant. It took a moment for the cry of the crowd to reach them. Then it came like a storm on the already distant earth. What the look must be on Chancey's face, she could only faintly guess. She was alone with him now, and such a sensation came up in her as she had not known since riding the sled last winter and coursing in fancy among the clouds. Her hands held tightly to the basket rim, but inside of her something had let go and was flying free. Was this how birds felt, she wondered. Heavy and awkward on the ground, with what ease they spread their wings and returned to the sky.

Over their heads the buoyant bag rode magnificently, the basket swinging in stately rhythm below. They were racing toward a high golden cloud. Below and beyond on the eastern horizon, a fleet of small white cloud boats sailed in a turquoise sea. Looking down, she could see the earth still falling away from them. Already they had left the fairgrounds behind them, the cross lines of Americus and the green square where Chancey lived. Around such were tied the wide and narrow ribbons of river and canal, white with sky, and the round blob of basin and level. That smudge of gray near it must hold Dock Street and her mother's ugly little house although she could not see it. Never, she told herself, would she see it again. Let God blow them eastward now, over fields and towns, over streams and woods, ever eastward over the wide Ohio and on to the mountains and Philadelphia where her mother's people had lived in respect and decency so long.

But she hadn't reckoned on Chancey. When first she turned to smile courage to him, his face was yellow with fear and he crouched back in the basket where he need not see how high and far they had gone. But now he was on his legs, grim and atremble. One hand gripped the basket rim. The other hunted for something overhead in the nipple of the bag. Suddenly she saw he had hold of a red cord and it flashed through her mind that this must be something the balloonist had told him about for his piece in the Centinel.

"No, Chancey! Don't!" she screamed, but her cry was lost in the wind and sky.

She saw him pull the cord so hard that it tore out in his hands. Almost at once the great bag above them reeled like a stricken thing. Life seemed to bleed from it and from her as well. The effortless lightness of her body fled from her. She felt her old weight return and with Chancey's bear down on basket and bag, forcing them to the ground. The golden cloud no longer seemed akin to her, and she knew now she would never reach the horizon to sail with all those small white boatlike clouds floating in a turquoise sea. She looked down. The strong sweep from earth was irretrievably lost. The earth's face came up to meet them, a broad heavy face marked with the shapeless features of fields and brush patches. Looking back she could see on the last rim of earth before the sky, a faint dot that was the city. Hardly had they even got away from Americus. Someone with sharp eyes or a telescope at the fairgrounds must have seen them falling from the heavens like a dark burned-out star.

The bag caught in a fence row of trees between two patches of swamp land. They had to climb down as best they could, watched by a farm boy and his dog. Rosa was still at the farm house that night when the first team from Americus reached them. In the second were the balloonist and Sheriff Shand. Rosa thought she knew at last what it meant to come to the end of things. She would have to go back to Americus now.

She felt herself an old woman next morning walking into her mother's kitchen. Could it be that ever she had lived here? It seemed like some small, crowded and airless cave.

"So you thought you'd run off?" her mother greeted her grimly.

"The rope was nearly worn through," Rosa faltered.

"Yes, but the rest was cut, they say. Did you or that young hellion cut it?" And at Rosa's silence, "Where's the knife?"

"I don't know any knife, Mama."

"You don't need to tell me anything. I know. I told you what would happen to you if you didn't watch out. Do you know what they're saying about you now?"

"I don't and I don't want to, Mama."

"It's all over town," her mother informed her. "You know that dead baby they found on Pine Street Wednesday morning. It was wrapped in a dirty Centinel. Well, they say that was yours and young Wheeler's baby!"

Rosa stood very still. Her head felt numb. It seemed that she must move her brain with her hand to think. A little later she caught a glimpse of herself in the glass. Her face looked shapeless, lifeless, like the stricken bag of the fallen balloon.

CHAPTER TWENTY-NINE

ALL HER BORN
YEARS

God buy me for a penny!

OLD SAYING

CHANCEY didn't believe it when they told him. Of course, he knew that news traveled fast in Americus. More than once when his mother served him breakfast, she had told him something that had happened since he had gone to bed the night before. But this Saturday morning she said nothing, only gazed at him with her tight mouth and the cruel look in her eyes that he had seen so often. He knew what it meant, or thought he did, her bitterness over what had happened in front of everybody at the fair-grounds yesterday, that he and Rosa had brought out into the open the ugly thing about his father that had been buried so long. What his mother didn't know, nor would he tell her, was how little he had to do with it. The whole thing had just happened to him. He had gone alone and unsuspecting into the basket. It was really Rosa who was responsible and to blame.

All the way to the Centinel office he went over the in-
cident in his mind, checking it step by step, and it only
proved his contention, even though he could never come
out and say so. Mr. Lane looked up at him searchingly
when he came in. A tall spare man, his hair hung down behind his ears, and a stained black stock crossed around
his stand-up collar. His thin face was mostly bone, the forehead seamed with parallel lines, his mouth wide and his eyes
sunken pits, like the eyes of a man who had died and which
still followed you about from his portrait hung on the
court house wall.

He seemed to be writing unusually savagely this morning, Chancey thought, his fingers holding a very thick
pencil, the whole arm moving from elbow to fingers, making sharp dots and dashes. When done, he held the long
foolscap sheet up to read, but he turned and spoke to
Chancey instead.

"You want me to write the news column today?"

"Why, no, sir," Chancey felt surprised.

The deep eyes did not spare him.

"You've heard the news?"

"I don't know what news you mean, sir."

The fierceness on the editor's face dissolved, leaving his
head like a kind of skull.

"Well, I'm sorry to be the one to tell you. Your little
friend, the Tench girl, died last night. She took her own
life. They found the body this morning."

That was when for the moment Chancey couldn't believe
it. Rosa dead, and by her own hand! It couldn't possibly
be and yet inside of him he felt all his blame against her
collapse suddenly like a house of cards. Mr. Lane's face
was inscrutable. For a time he held it stiff and grave, as if
this was a moment of importance, of dignity to the dead, or

perhaps he couldn't find the exact words he wanted to say. He went on finally.

"We can say nothing of that in the paper, of course. Merely state that the deceased met her death at her mother's home early this morning, exact time unknown. Everybody knows about it anyway. I understand the whole town is shocked by the details."

Chancey stood there rigid and confused. What were these shocking details, part of him cried out to know, but the rest of him closed its ears and would hear nothing. He felt Mr. Lane's eyes search him but whether with pity or scorn, he had no means of telling. It would have been better, he knew afterward, to have had the whole story then instead of filling his mind with horror and uncertainty of the unknown. He tried to prepare himself by fearing the worst, but it turned out to be so much worse than he had dreamed. He couldn't escape it anyway. Everywhere he went that day he heard snatches of the cruel talk and exclamations.

"You'd reckon she'd throw herself in the canal, wouldn't you, sooner than make such a mess!"

"It was an old eelspear head she done it with. They said it was honed sharp as a razor."

"That was something to see, for fair, the blood dripping down through the loft boards. It turned my stomach. I couldn't eat a bite of dinner."

"She done it after she went to bed and was that quiet, nobody in the house heard a blessed thing."

"If it wasn't true what they said about her, what did she ever do it for? Folks don't make way with themselves without a reason."

"That old witch! Do you reckon she'll go out of the house now to the funeral?"

"Didn't you think it queer, the blood dripping down on her own mother? You suppose she done it on purpose like that? Anyway, it gave me the creeps when I started to think about it."

"Dr. Keller said she was all cut up. He didn't see how a body could cut their own self that way. He said it looked exactly like she thought she had something wrong inside of her and was trying to cut it out. But he couldn't find a thing the matter with her."

All the time Chancey went about his work, while he set down the facts that Miss Martha Fuller and Mr. Mayhugh Jones were united in holy matrimony in the First Methodist Church, or while he wrote an advertisement for Mr. Wells, the storekeeper, "Don't mind loud cries of others but call and you shall see more new goods and cheaper still, grandurells and fashionable bonnet trimmings at the Enterprise on Water Street," the ugly words about Rosa were the ones he kept writing over and over in his mind. Now he felt sickened by his own treatment of her at the farm house. Could that have been only evening before last? Something inside of him struggled and fought to reach across that short space of time, trying to get back to Rosa still alive when he could make everything all right. Even then, he remembered, that through his sullenness, Rosa had stayed her own gentle self. It must have dashed her hopes to the ground to have to go back to Americus, to her mother and their shabby house on Dock Street, and yet she had been the one who had tried to cheer him. He remembered now the strange thing she had told him that evening, but then Rosa was always telling him strange things.

He was not to worry too much, she said, about her not getting away from Americus. Now that she had seen him again, she would be all right. And she could always get away to her secret places. He knew what those words meant. One of her "secret places" was the canal. More than once as they walked the tow path or stood on the bridge, especially on a clear day, she had pointed to the world of reflection in the water.

"At first it looks upside down," she had said. "But if you look at it long enough, it changes around and our world up here is the one that's upside down. See the sky down there! It's just like the sky up here, but isn't it lighter and softer and a more beautiful blue? And the trees and grass! Everything's so peaceful and free down there. When I go down in it, I feel I'm getting back to a wonderful place I know."

"It's just your imagination," he had told her. "You can never really go down there."

"Oh, yes, I can," she had said.

"Not with your body."

"With my body," she had insisted. "I can move my arms like I'm swimming and float right over those trees."

"It's impossible," he had told her sharply. "If your body went down there, you'd get wet and drown."

That had stopped her for a moment, and her face went grave.

"If I don't go down with this body," she had said slowly, "then I must go down with some other body that's just as good as this one."

It had made him angry at the time but now it only gave him pity, like the pity you feel for a child, while recurrent tingles ran along his spine. He cursed his own stupidity. If he hadn't been sullen and blind the other evening, he might have known of what dark things she was thinking.

Tonight as he tramped the dark streets everything that Rosa ever said or did came up in his mind, things she would never say or do again. He could see her lying slight and still in that little dark house, dressed in her green or brown silk, while rough hands sopped her white face and her small folded hands with baking-soda water. That night he scarcely closed his eyes, and in the morning nothing could have kept him from her burial. Oh, never would he dared to go to it directly. By a devious route he went to the waterfront and stood around the corner from the Wizard-of-the-Dell's cabin. There he waited till he saw the six young women in white dresses come out of the front door of the saloon. They were bearing the unpainted diamond-shaped coffin to the Basin delivery wagon. Cold and sweating, Chancey watched the stream of mourners follow. Everybody, he thought, was there, everybody but her real father and her Wheeler half brothers and sisters. In life they had ignored her and in death deserted her. Of all that side of the family, only himself attended, and that by stealth, sneaking cowardly as he had in her life time.

What rats these Wheelers were, he told himself, as moving by different streets he followed the funeral down along the canal, across to the river and the little old cemetery they called the Devil's Acre. Here a jockey had been buried, a gambler, some bad women, a few Negroes, several men and women who had been hung or who had hung or drowned themselves or had otherwise placed themselves beyond the pale. Among them Rosa had to lie. Had it been out in the country he might have forgiven it, but here the shabby fringes of the city had grown around it, shutting it in. Coarse uncut river grass covered it, hiding the sunken graves and the few board markers, most of them flat and rotting on the ground. Chancey thought he had never seen such a pitiful sight as that group of mourners and white pallbearers standing for a few minutes in grieved attention

before leaving Rosa to her desolation. From time to time
the words of the preacher, some of whose beliefs had only
horrified Rosa, drifted across in the cold wind. Later Chancey could see yellow clay flung into the air. Not until all
had gone, preacher, singers, pallbearers, mourners, the tag
end and curious, Ed Malcolm's delivery wagon and finally
the gravediggers themselves, their shovels on their shoulders,
did Chancey go over and stand close by that bleeding
mound of earth. Only then he realized that he hadn't even
brought flowers. At the thought of her lying down there
in the wet ground, with the desolate scene above and the
bleakness of winter coming on, such a feeling went over
him that he didn't believe he could endure it.

It must pass, he told himself, for time heals all things, but
day after day it never did. When he woke in the night, it
was there. What he would have done without his work at
the Centinel, he never knew. He seldom read in print what
he wrote or remembered it afterward. But it was something
to hold on to and lose himself in. He was aware of Mr.
Lane's eye on him when he answered strangely and of the
silent watchers at home when he came stumbling in. But
none of them spoke to him about what lay like lead in his
breast, none but his mother and he shut his ears to her as if
he hadn't heard and climbed the stairs to his room.

One of them must have spoken to someone else, for Dr.
Shotwell, the family minister, sent Chancey word that he
wanted to see him. Half unwillingly, half in faint secret
hope, he went across the square.

There had been a church standing on the corner ever
since he could remember. When he was a little fellow, it
had been frame, and before that, something else. Now it was
of brick, the biggest church in the city and with the greatest congregation, a huge structure with wide steps running

up to a portico, with three front doors topped by carved fan lights and four huge white fluted pillars. There were two rows of white windows all around, one upstairs and one down, and the white steeple went up so far that God help the people around there if it ever blew down. From its belfry on a clear day you could see Tateville, and once when the wind was right, it was claimed they heard the bell out there, although many doubted. Anyhow, it was a long way from the first little log church that had stood there not much bigger than a cabin, his mother said.

The maid took him in, and Dr. Shotwell met him at the door of his study, a tall dour looking preacher with iron gray hair curling up defiantly on the top of his head. His low collar showed the strong sinews of his neck. The black tie had been furled with carelessness and melancholy. His face was gentle and forgiving, and yet the heavy eyebrows told that on principles he was uncompromising.

He talked to Chancey a long time about his poems and newspaper writing, then he took him down and outside where he produced a heavy key and unlocked the church door.

"Come in, my lad," he said with a fierce tenderness. "I want you to bare your head in your own church. It's been a long time since you were here and that's a reproach to your Maker. Your family is responsible for this church in the first place. Your mother gave the land. Your grandmother lies, the first silent inhabitant of the churchyard. Your brother heads the council, a fine man and our next governor, everybody says. Your sisters and their families attend. It would make us all very happy if you could see the light and come, too. We have missed you, but whether you realize it or not, my lad, you have missed us too, and the peace and blessedness of giving up sin and the world."

He said a great deal more than that. Chancey listened hungrily, wretchedly, bracing himself against any possible mention of Rosa's name and yet all the while secretly thirsting for some word of charity for her that would lighten the leaden weight in his breast. But nothing rose to the good doctor's lips save piety and justice and the uncompromising word of God. When Chancey left, all that persisted in his mind was the bitter thought that his sister, Sulie, could rest in peace in the sacred ground of Dr. Shotwell's churchyard, but her half-sister Rosa must lie like an outcast in desolate and unhallowed ground.

Chancey never went back to his mother's church, but sometimes he would slip into yellow-painted St. Martin's on Willow Street. Not that Father Murtrie of St. Martin's ever sent for Chancey, even to have a sermon printed in the paper. Tense and still the boy would sit there in the strange-smelling dimness hoping to find a moment of peace. St. Martin's was not so large as his mother's church, but no one had to unlock the door for him to enter. Nor on a weekday was it empty and deserted. The yellow flames of candles billowed in the dimness and the red of the sanctuary lamp glowed like a coal in the cold. Seldom did he sit long that others did not come to kneel at pews or altar or to make their round of the stations. The boy liked especially when he saw the white habit of St. Dominic nuns in the dark church and thought he could feel then how those white-clad forms must have looked coming through the dark forest to early Catholic settlers like the MacMahons, who, his mother said, had cried for joy at the sight.

When Father Murtrie saw Chancey, he stopped and spoke to him. He liked to tell about Father Guntz who had founded the mission. "I think your father and mother knew him," he would say, though seldom would he go so

far as concede that the early priest had been nursed by the
boy's mother once during a bad spell of woods fever. It
was just that he didn't like to admit the saintly priest's debt
to some one not of the faith, Chancey thought. Ever he
gave Chancey the feeling of strength and secret martyrdom,
of vast authority behind him and of the church's closely
guarded treasure of security and peace. If only, the boy
thought, he could break into the papal fortress and take
some of that peace for his own without giving his soul in
exchange! Any word of cheer or reassurance for Rosa
from Father Murtrie's lips would have carried the weight
of centuries with Chancey. The boy's gaze hung wretchedly
on the lips of the priest and on the signs of his office, hoping that he might recognize in his eyes the nature of his
illness and cure it. Just a sentence of forgiveness for Rosa
would do it. He must have known about her, Chancey
thought, and his silence could only mean that the matter
of lost souls was inexorably fixed and discussion futile forever.

His own mother and father were the last Chancey would
have thought to go to for sympathy. Even should he die,
all he would expect his mother to say was "The Lord
giveth and the Lord taketh away. Blessed be the name of
the Lord." But one Sunday when Sooth and Libby and
their families had been invited home to dinner, an untoward
thing happened. They were sitting around the table talking of Dr. Shotwell's sermon. It must have been a powerful
one, for Sooth kept referring to it uneasily until Chancey's
mother took a firm hand.

"Now that's enough about hell," she said. "I never was
there, I don't look to go there, and so long as we lead a
decent life, none of us need to."

"Not even Papa!" Sooth faltered.

A grave silence ran around the table.

"I think you have a better father than you have any idea of, Sooth," her mother said calm as could be and with a still calmer look at Chancey's father.

You could see that Dezia wasn't satisfied.

"Well, I know one that's not so far from us that's burning in hell right now!" she came out with, which was as far as she dared say.

As her meaning fell over Chancey he pushed back his chair and hastily left the table. After perhaps a half hour there was a knock on his door.

"Papa wants to see you," Massey called.

Chancey waited as long as he dared. He smelled his father's cigar before he got there. His father had drawn on his long coat with the black satin collar and now stood in the hall waiting for him.

"Put on your hat and come along, Chancey," he ordered. "I want to talk to you a little."

Of late years this was the last thing Chancey wanted. There was no surer way to feel himself shrink to little or nothing than to walk out on the street beside his imposing father. The boy ever tried to avoid speaking to certain persons in this part of town, but his father greeted fearlessly everyone they passed. Sometimes his word was brief, sometimes cordial, sometimes severe, sometimes genial, but always with dignity and power.

Today he turned in at the silent courthouse and Chancey followed. The empty stairs and stale halls rang with their footsteps. Upstairs his father unlocked the door to his office. What was coming, Chancey wondered. His father did not take off his hat but seated himself in his immense red leather chair.

"I want to have a little talk with you, my boy." He

shook the ashes from his cigar to the bare floor as if to set an example to the boy not to take things too seriously. He went on not unkindly. "I've been watching you for some time, Chancey. You are too much like Sooth. You let things depress and upset you. Take for instance, the remark Dezia made at the table. Mark you this, my boy, there is nobody burning in hell right now. That is, nobody who has departed this life. The living may suffer, but the dead are free. Despite what your mother's church tells her, she and I and you and all whom we know in Americus today will some day be only unthinking and unfeeling clods whirling on this dead planet. There was no heretofore to worry about, and there is no hereafter."

He looked at the boy with beneficence, but instead of a feeling of relief, one of tragedy and horror sickened Chancey. His father went on.

"I want to give you a measure of counsel. Don't give credence to everything you hear. There are a thousand conflicting religious beliefs. Reason should tell you that they can't all be true. If you are wise, you won't let yourself be deceived by any man-made theories of God. Formulate your own philosophy as you find it. Make that your religion. If your logic is sound, no one can hurt you, and you will never attempt the dangerous and impossible. I mean trying to right the mistakes of the dead. Justice must be shown during life. It cannot be administered to those who are gone. That's why I brought you in here today. I want you to have a glimpse of my religion."

Chancey stared. His father sat there noble and untouched. If he felt any shade of remorse or regret for the tragedy he had fathered and remained indifferent to all his life, he admirably concealed it. Rising, he led the boy through his private entrance to the court. The large white assembly room lay silent and peaceful. Golden October sunlight streamed through the long ecclesiastic-like windows and over the empty benches that might have been pews.

"This is my church," his father said with feeling. "And these are my altar and pulpit." His hand indicated the platform and the raised white bar with the tall solemn bench, like pulpit chairs, behind it. "Here we dispense no superstitious punishment and reward for the dead, but practical justice to the living. Over there is our Amen corner, the honest seats of the jurors drawn from the people. This is our witness box and we admit no visions but the straightforward testimony of competent men and women. The prisoner's dock I call our judgment seat. Here the penitent or unrepentant sinner must have his innocence or guilt proved in the presence of living witnesses and a congregation drawn from the entire county. It's very much of a religious service to me. Like my friends, the Catholics, I like to come to my church sometimes when no service is being held. I sit here in the peace and quiet and meditate on the justice meted out in this and similar institutions all over the world dedicated not to some unknown god but to man."

He stopped. It was plain from his voice that he was greatly moved. But Chancey felt no tingle of contagion. Only a bleakness and numbness came over him as if he had been shown a vast world of desert and rock in which no spark or hope of life might flourish or be born. Was there no balm in Gilead then, the boy cried to himself, no rhyme or reason in living, no solace for the cheated and deprived dead!

Not until winter did Chancey dare to go back to Welsh Valley. Had it been summer or early fall, he felt, he could never have endured the warm sunshine, the trees still in leaf, the fields in their growth that he and Rosa had seen together. But now the warmth had vanished, the sun thinned, even the corn gone from the fields, the grass dead, the once green leaves withered and fallen. He took a satisfaction seeing it so, to pass under trees bare and frozen, to tramp on the lifeless leaves and grasses. If Rosa was dead, then it was right that so much of what she loved was dead too.

But the Griffins he found more alive than ever, their house laid about snugly with cornshocks. At his step they came to the door like bright-eyed woodchucks to the mouth of their burrow. But their cries of welcome at the sight of him soon turned to gravity as they took him to the warm kitchen. He had feared to explain why Rosa was not along but even here in Welsh Valley they knew all about it and, like true country folk, did not try to hide or gloss over the way she had died.

"Wasn't it a pity?"

"Who would have reckoned that was the last time we'd see her."

"You never know who'll be next."

"Why couldn't it have been one of us old ones? Why did it have to be her?"

"What got into her? We always said we never knowed anybody happier than she was."

"She wouldn't have had to done it, would she?"

"No, because if it had anything wrong with her, she could have come out and lived with us."

"Yes, we'd have took care of her — and everything that came along."

At their honest declaration of friendship and bounty, something which for weeks had been frozen in Chancey melted like icicles in the sun.

"There was nothing wrong," he told them with feeling.

"We didn't think there was," the middle one said quickly. "Not with her kind. But she could have stayed here just the same."

"Yes, we have plenty of room."

"It might as well have been her as Old Johnny. You know, he always comes with us for the winter. But he had lots of other friends he could go to."

As they spoke, Old Johnny himself came out into the kitchen. Chancey looked at him with interest. So this was the man his mother used to talk so warmly about! Why he was just a simple old man, thin as a rail and dressed in bulging ragged clothes. His patched linsey shirt open at the neck showed a coarse coffee sack he must have slipped over his head for an undershirt. His waist and seat bulged as if with two or three pairs of pantaloons, one on top of the other. He shook off his shoes in the kitchen and padded around the floor in his bare feet.

"This here's our friend we told you about," the oldest Griffin said. "You know, his true love's dead. She done away with herself."

Old Johnny turned quickly at that and his eyes had a strange brightness in his witless face.

"She's not dead!" he cried in his peculiar voice. "We're the ones who sleep. She's awake now to glory unknown and in a body unchanged. She's in the new life. 'Today thou shalt be with me in paradise.' The son of David and the Lamb and Prince of Peace didn't say, on resurrection morn. No, today she lives in Beulah Land. Hallelujah! Give glory to the Lamb! Oh, that man would praise the Lord for his wonderful goodness to the children of men!"

Chancey was too astonished to say anything. Old Johnny went on with fanatic zest.

"We were never born, my lad, and we never die. Before

Abraham, I was. The sun sinks, but it shines on another land. Love never dies. If she loved you then, she loves you now. Emanuel saw the true vision. He laid eyes on those who had died and they were not in their graves, praise the Lord. Emanuel saw the blind see, the lame run, and the miserable happy. 'And I will restore unto thee the year that the locust hath eaten.' 'Oh, death, where is thy victory! Oh, grave where is thy sting!' Graves are empty, my lad. The dead are not there. Their joy is the happiness of the Lord. If they loved the good and beautiful here, they love it there. Call nobody damned, for the one the world calls damned may be the one the Lord loveth best. 'Judge not that ye be not judged.' We're all pilgrims on our way to heaven and there our true selves will be known. Praise the Lord."

His unshaven face and dirty gray mane, his simple look and the wild gleam in his eye unsettled Chancey. The smell from his unwashed body repelled him. He tried to move away but the grotesquely clothed figure saw his advantage and pressed closer so that his breath and spittle nearly overwhelmed the boy. In the end Chancey left before he had intended, declining all invitations to stay.

"Take along some pearls of truth!" Old Johnny cried. His bare feet padded upstairs and when he returned he carried a book in his hands. Chancey thought he meant to give it to him but he only tore off some pages as if to start a fire and pressed them into his hands. "Read and be free. Hallelujah! Praise the Lord!" When the boy got outside he found the pages weren't from the Bible at all but from *Heaven and Hell* by Emanuel Swedenborg.

So that was Johnny Appleseed and his holy book, Chancey thought with distaste. And yet as he went down the lane and crossed the bridge to the road, he thought he felt a little better. At least now he could endure looking on the loveliness of Rosa's beloved Welsh Creek, which he couldn't when he came up. Certain sayings of the strange old man kept coming back to him, especially what he said about Rosa not being dead but living, that if she loved the good and beautiful here, she loved it there; and that the one the world called damned might be the one the Lord loved best.

Why, he wondered, did the philosophy of life that most eased and satisfied him have to come from a ragged, unwashed old beggar? Why was it, if such things were true, they couldn't have been spoken by Dr. Shotwell or Father Murtrie or by his father or some other scholar of dignity and respect? Then he might have been able to receive and accept them. As it was, who could believe a fanatic voice crying in the wilderness, a lowly, unlearned wanderer who lived on the charity of the humble and the poor? By the time he reached the canal, a growing skepticism of the whole business had come over him, a sense of anger against his father and mother, against preachers and priests, philosophers and pioneers and all the rest who saw any good in the unjust and meaningless torment of life.

CHAPTER THIRTY

SAYWARD FEELS THE EARTH TURN

I propose to alter that old phrase, a speaking aristocracy in the face of a silent democracy. I am democratic and I am certainly not silent.

CHANCEY WHEELER

I T struck Sayward all of a heap the day Chancey told her he was leaving home. Oh, she couldn't help noticing the bitter looks he had been giving them the last few months, but she hadn't looked for this.

"Can I ask, Chancey, where you're going?" she said humbly and saw him set his lip.

"I'm of age now and intend to board with a family on Seventh Street," he told her.

"You mean you're staying right here in Americus!" was what came up in her mouth to cry out, but all she said was, "You got a home here, Chancey. You don't need to pay board. We hoped you'd stay with us a long time yet."

His thin face only hardened.

"I've let you support me too long now. It's time I broke away and stood on my own feet and felt free to say the things I ought to say."

"You can say anything you want to now, Chancey."

"Not against you and Papa and what you stand for. Not when I sleep in your house and eat from your table."

"What don't you like about us that we stand for?" his mother asked him.

He threw her a look and met hers full on. She thought for a minute he was going to light into her for fair.

"Old time people would never understand," was all he would tell her.

When Dezia came home and heard about it, she said Chancey was just plain spoiled and ungrateful, but Massey said it must be the new society Chancey had joined.

"You know that woman from Connecticut and Charley Hollenbeck are in it. They call it, I think, the American Peace Society. It's all over the country. They're cracked on peace and don't believe in doing anything that might make friction. They say all this talk about freeing the slaves is criminal because it makes bad feeling between the North and the South. They claim Papa is a war maker because he's such a strong abolitionist. And you're the same, Mama, because you helped all those darkeys get away, especially the time you stood off the sheriff from Kentucky and gave my pink dress to that black wench in the cellar."

Portius saw it a little differently.

"These societies are nothing to get agitated over," he said magnanimously. "I've watched Chancey for a long time. And, I might say, some of the other young people, too. I see all this chiefly as a revolt of the young against the old. It has always been and, I suppose, always will be.

The young — not all of them, but the weaker members — are easily bruised by the hardship of the world. They can't endure it and think it shouldn't be. Not having the experience of the old, they imagine they can form a society and do away with it. Perhaps," he added gravely, "they can. We should let Chancey go and see what he and his kind can do. Perhaps they can move this dark old earth a little nearer to the sun. Certainly if they could wipe hardship from the face of the earth, they would be the greatest saviors of mankind."

At his last sentence, Sayward felt her face grow bleak. She didn't trail along with Portius on that. Take away all the hardship from the world, and man wouldn't amount to much, she opined. He'd just lay back and grow fat and feeble as a pug on a lap. Not that she wanted to start an argument with Portius. They had wrassled the subject too often before. She didn't want to see a war start in this country either. But sometimes you had to stand up for your rights or lose them, and you couldn't stand up sitting down. It went hard enough for her to sit down and let that Peace Society drive Chancey from home, make him give up that nice room of his on the corner and three meals a day she took pleasure cooking for him.

But she said nothing though it gave her a bad turn. The others, save Guerdon, she hadn't minded going. They had taken care of themselves in the past and there was no reason to fret they couldn't do as much in the future. But Chancey was her baby. She'd had to nurse and pray him into growing up. Now that he was grown, he had got it into his head to leave, and no thanks to her or Portius. Well, she didn't know as she looked for any. But neither had she looked for it to be like this when he went. But who would have reckoned any likeness between Chancey and Wyitt!

Why, Chancey took to books and learning like a duck to water, while her brother, Wyitt, could hardly write his own name. And yet when they got to be their own men, nobody could hold either one. Could Wyitt wait till he got off by himself? No! Could he be satisfied eating her rations and sleeping where she knew he was safe and sound? Not him. And now her youngest and puniest, the last she could ever give birth to, was a following him.

Chancey went on a winter's day when the snow lay deep in the street and the cold blew down from the English Lakes so that she had to worry all night did he have enough covers where he was at to keep him warm. Most every day she looked out the window on the chance she might see his thin face and shoulders coming back across the square. He might have forgot one of his traps, she thought, or got hungry for a taste of her pigeon pie or what he had called Blubblub ever since he was a little feller, a couple pieces of toast swimming around in a dish of hot milk and butter. Or he might have wanted to see again the house where he was raised, to climb the stairs one more time to his old room that she kept just like he left it. Portius mentioned seeing him in the court house, and the others dropped word of running into him here and yonder. But although often during the day she would catch herself stopping to listen, it was a long time till she heard his familiar step at the door. She thought surely he'd drop in sometimes for dinner or supper. Twice she had Dezia stop at the Centinel and bid him home for Sunday dinner when the family would be there. The first time he sent word back that he couldn't make it on account of something else. The next time Dezia said he wasn't there any more. He'd had trouble with Mr. Lane over something he'd written. So he quit last Saturday and went to Cincinnati where they said he was going to

be editor of the New Palladium and the youngest editor in
Ohio.

"It's that peace society woman," Dezia said. "She bought
the paper and made Chancey editor. She's ten years older
than him if she's a day. Leave it to him always to be taken
in by some woman."

It was just talk, about this woman, Sayward told herself.
Perhaps Dezia made it up. She and Chancey never got along
together anyhow, not even when they were little. But if
it was true, at least Chancey was an editor. Now don't go
feeling so proud over him, she told herself. She had Portius
send money for the paper and there it was, The New Palladium, two long sheets, printed both sides, and Chancey's
name down as editor. She'd have known it even if his name
wasn't there. The minute she started reading, she could
hear Chancey's voice speaking the words in her mind. Friday evenings when she laid down the paper, she could
hardly believe that he hadn't been sitting here talking to
her and had now just gone up to his room, so strong and
clear the impression of him remained.

Oh, there were some things in the paper that gave her a
turn until she got used to them. Especially the editorials
which she spelled clean through. She used to ponder over
the paper's motto printed with a raring horse on either end.
"Liberty, Equality and Peace," it said, but Sayward found
a lot more in the paper about equality and peace than about
liberty. Most everybody who had made something out of
himself around this part of the country got digs from the
New Palladium. Could it be, Sayward pondered, that
Chancey was trying to pull such folks down to make himself feel a little better?

Resolve's face sobered when he saw the paper in his
mother's hands.

"I'm surprised you read that scurrilous sheet, Mam," he said. "I understand Chancey writes all the letters to the editor himself. There's one against me and my candidacy most every issue. There was also a very bitter one against you. It didn't give your name but called you the Petticoat Plutocrat."

"I read that one," Sayward admitted calmly. "Just what is a plutocrat, Resolve?"

"It's a very rich person who makes everybody dance to his money and influence. Chancey's against you. In fact, he's against everybody and everything."

"He's not against the railroad coming in," she defended.

"No, nor anything else that will save him from the exertion of walking or doing any kind of honest toil," Resolve retorted.

Sayward looked mildly grave. Now that wasn't very partial to facts. You'd still have to walk or drive your horse or ox to the railroad. You could tell Resolve was the lawyer for the canal company. Canal folks claimed the railroad a crack-brained swindle. They said all the land it bought was waste and extravagance, that the low places it filled in and the hills it cut through would stand useless as Indian mounds after the bubble burst. It would be a monument to folly and anybody who put his money in it deserved to lose it. Sayward hoped for Chancey's sake it wouldn't work out that way. It would be a shame not to win out after the way he had stuck up for it. Most every time his paper came, it bragged up the railroad. In her mind she thought of it as Chancey's railroad, and, despite what Resolve said, she put a little secret money into it to help it along.

Nothing would have kept her from the celebration that day the railroad's locomotive came. The paper said it had run under its own steam as far west as there were rails to travel on. Then mechanics had taken it apart and shipped the pieces down the Ohio and up the canal. When Sayward got downtown they had already fetched the pieces from the boat to the Fourth Street crossing where they had about put them together. The crowd was so thick she couldn't get nearer than Dr. Keller's drug store and he took her upstairs where his family and friends were watching from the windows.

She had to admit Resolve nearer right than Chancey when first she laid eyes on the thing setting down there on the rails. Black and besotted, with a vicious iron point in front to cut you to pieces and a fierce stack belching smoke and fire, it looked like it came from where canal folks claimed, the pits of hell. On the side in sulphurous letters was the monster's name, SHAWANEE. A gang of boys carried pails of water from the nearest pumps to fill the greedy belly of the boiler, while men fed stacks of cord wood to the furnace. The first time they blew the whistle, folks started to run in the street. Seeing the steam and hearing the shriek, they reckoned the boiler had exploded. At last slowly with more hoots and screechings and a great hissing and grunting, the engine began to move. Dogs dropped their tails between their legs and ran off howling, while men in front of the engine cleared ditches and fences at a single bound. Old men and women leaned on their staffs and gazed as if doomsday was at hand. Only the young seemed unafraid, running alongside the engine with leaps and capers.

The Shawanee moved as far as Buttonwood Street and came back drawing an open car behind it. Sayward made out Portius, Resolve and Dr. Shotwell among the notables on the car. But where was Chancey? Why wasn't he standing on the first train of his railroad? Dr. Shotwell prayed the Lord to bless this new instrument of man. Resolve was introduced as "our next governor" and spoke a few words. But it was Portius who gave the oration. Standing there on the strange movable platform, he appeared to pay no attention to it or the strange iron contraption in front. Instead he started telling quiet as could be how he had found the woods hereabouts when first he came. You could have heard a pin drop. He went from the woods to the axe and plough, from the cabin to the court house and mill, from the Indian trace to the ox and canal. Not till then did he come to the railroad; but he hadn't need to before, because all the while he spoke the iron dragon stood there in front of everybody's eyes breathing out smoke and steam.

Oh, Portius was getting up in years like she was, but he could still spellbind you. Sayward reckoned she wouldn't easy forget the last few words he spoke.

"When I look back on the unbroken forest that stood here when first I came — when sight of and communion with another human being was a rare privilege and blessing — when our only light was the fire, the tallow dip and lard lamp — when the time made on horseback was considered exceedingly fast — and when I stop now and look around me at the growth of civilization, at our countryside flowing with milk and honey, at our cities humming with humanity and the spinning jenny, and now at the steam locomotive able to transport people and goods for a hundred miles in less than half a day — when I think of all these stupendous and undreamed of changes, all within the span of one short life, speech fails me and my power of astonishment is almost exhausted."

That night after supper, sitting alone in her kitchen which she had let dark on purpose, Sayward thought of Jary lying mouldered away yonder in the old churchyard

and what she would say could she come back and see what
Sayward had this day, the fine buildings on the streets, the
boats a swarming like fish in the canal, and the shiny new
steel road they called the railroad. "By Jeems' cousin!" she
could hear her mother say. But what Jary would be taken
with first, Sayward thought, would be her grandchildren
she had never seen.

"Lawsy me!" she could hear her mother say. "I kain't
git over our Kinzie a ship captain a knowin' the seven seas.
But never did I reckon one of my seed would go back on
the United American States for Old England! Now how
is it, Libby, a doctor's wife, is blessed with nary chick nor
child, while Sooth has so many she don't know what to
do with 'em? And Dezia is much too smart, a teachin'
school all day and readin' books half the night. She better
watch out her head don't bust. And that Massey! How kin
she stay so lively? At her age, with one in the cradle and
another on the way, women in my time used to settle down.
Then that little old feller, Chancey, writin' pieces for the
paper all the way from Cincinnati!" But what her mother
would come back to again in the end would be the tall,
three-and-four-story buildings standing right here where
the woods used to be, and now the unbelievable wonders
of the railroad! "By Hokey day. I'm plumb beat out," she
could hear her mother sigh.

After while Sayward rose and walked out in the yard.
The sky hung covered with fine clouds like small pieces
of cotton batting. Down here on the garden walk all was
still, but up there those clouds ran to the east like sheep
over the moon. If you stopped and looked at them a minute,
it seemed it was the moon that ran and the clouds that
stood still. Now what was that funny feeling it gave you?
All her life she had heard it was not the sun and moon but

the earth that moved, turning like a fat old turkey carcass on the spit. Tonight she could well believe it. Looking at that old moon a rushing to the westward she could feel for the first time in her life the old earth rolling to the eastward, turning under her, pushing against her feet and carrying her along.

Yes, she knew it now, if she never had before, that the world really moved.

CHAPTER THIRTY-ONE

PAST AND PRESENT

A-ah, law! That was a time gone.

LAMB IN HIS BOSOM

I F it hadn't been for Mrs. Wray, Chancey felt he would never have gone near Resolve's reception. He had no intention to let Resolve think that now he was governor, his youngest brother was running after him and would support him in office. The impressive invitation from the governor's mansion only aroused his criticism. He told Mrs. Wray that the money for the reception could be better spent giving bread to the poor and education to the unenlightened.

But he noticed that Mrs. Wray's fingers kept tight hold of the card. She was an intelligent woman with a long, narrow aristocratic head. An upright collar like a cleric's stood above the dark collar of her dress. Her highly bred face almost never seemed to get its quota of blood and life. Yet now a faint warmth and color softened it.

"After all, he's your brother, and I think you should go," she said. "There will be very important people there. I only wish we had their names on our subscription list.

Your presence won't hurt the cause — or the paper either. Perhaps you would be considerate and let me come along. After all, the governor is your brother, and I could do a little missionary work."

Chancey wished then he had never shown the invitation. He was caught now and would have no other way than go and suffer the torments of the damned, which he did. All the way from Cincinnati to the capital he dreaded the evening at the governor's mansion and once there among all the blazing candles and whale oil lights, he felt distressed and oppressed. Why, he asked himself, did he always feel like this among the ruling class, especially among strong, successful, self-made people? It was their great power and self-assurance, he told himself, their blind devotion to themselves, to their families and their particular rounds of duties. Hardly ever could they be instructed or enlightened in their own duties and affairs. The more rugged their struggle with life had been, the more they clung to what they knew and believed. They were sure as eggs is eggs of all their old beliefs and resisted like flint any ideas that were new.

"Most potent, grave and reverend signiors, my noble and approved good masters!" he repeated to himself bitterly, quoting a once-favorite quotation of his father's. Well, tonight he would try to plough some of these stick-in-the-muds loose from their earthy roots, sow what seed he could on their rocky soil and let time struggle to bring in a crop of reform.

It grew late before he had the chance. Once Mrs. Wray was welcomed to the big house, she forsook him for an evening of gayety and social chatter. That was a woman for you, he told himself. Well, he would neither forget nor be bribed. He would give an account of his presence that these infallibles would long remember. Meanwhile austerely he resisted all advances. Most everyone treated him too cordially to please him. It was for his mother's or his father's sake, he knew, because he was a Wheeler. No one showed fear or consternation as he approached, not even those he had pilloried in the New Palladium. His father greeted him as always. If his stalwart mother felt emotion, she showed none when she hugged him. Not until now that he had been away from her so long did he realize what a creature of past ages she was, a relic of the deep woods, with her heavy skirts, her stout waist, firm mouth and her severely parted gray hair. Little wonder, he thought, that as a child she never seemed like his parent. And yet on her part she took him around tonight, introducing him as her youngest son and editor of the New Palladium. The way she said it, as if it were the Cincinnati Gazette or Boston Advertiser, made Chancey wince.

All evening the forces of restlessness and rebellion in him gathered. When he blundered into a large back room upstairs, he knew instinctively that this was his Battle of Armageddon. There were only men in that room, swimming in the strong fumes of whiskey and tobacco. His old aversion to both rose to sicken and trouble him, but he dare not back out now. His eyes took in some of the most important men in the state: a lordly white-headed supreme court justice; a fierce general with a cane whose only command now was as marshal preserving order at funerals; a famous abolitionist preacher whose red nose said, Drink, and whose tight mouth said, Be Damned; and a thick silent man whose name Chancey recognized as that of the most influential business lord and financial power in the state. There were present also, besides men he did not know: Chancey's father; Fay's father; a senator from Washington; several congressmen; a pair of leading lawyers one of whom had thrown a chopping axe across the court house roof; the governor and a tousled ex-governor. Of them all, the senator was the one with whom Chancey felt most congenial, because of his courageous saying, "If I were a Mexican as I am an American, I would welcome the American troops to Mexico with bloody hands and to hospitable graves." School boys in Ohio liked to recite that, dyeing their faces and hands with pokeberry juice.

"Come in, Chancey, and join the crowd," his father said, not too enthusiastically. "No, Tom, you'll have to drink that yourself. I'm afraid that Chancey doesn't indulge."

The boy was sensitive that the words belittled him. In the awkward lull that followed, he made his way to a scarlet-covered stool in the corner. He felt he had interrupted something, a discussion evidently of extreme importance, probably matters of state, perhaps a national policy. Nothing less could be talked about when such leading and influential men got together. He sat down meekly on his stool, and after a moment or two the parted atmosphere joined and flowed over him again.

"Go on, judge," Resolve prompted.

"Well, as I was saying, Governor," the justice resumed, "their father left those boys in the woods all winter, and a mighty severe winter it was, too. They lived alone in an open cabin till spring and, mind you, they were only nine and eleven years old. All they had to eat were the rabbits they caught in hollow logs and what was left of a deer after the wolves got through with it. Once in a while they tramped fifteen or twenty miles down the Indian trace to Hiram Sadler's place for a little cornmeal. They had no gun, only an axe between them, and yet when their father fetched their mother back in the spring, they had made a considerable clearing."

"Oh, that was common, common," the gray-headed congressman rumbled. "I was brought up in the Firelands. One summer everybody in Claysport was down with both ague-and-fever and bilious fever. Everybody but a boy named Charley Snyder. He had only the ague-and-fever. He was considered quite lucky. Every day he tramped five miles through the woods for a peck of cornmeal. He mashed it first at Judge Hamil's where he got it, in the judge's hand-mill. Then he waited till his second attack of ague came on. After that he fetched the meal to Claysport and we all had rations for another day."

Chancey listened with growing astonishment. Was it possible that these distinguished and influential men had closeted themselves together for nothing more important than that fallacy of the good old days and how much better they were off then.

One of the lawyers stirred.

"I've told you this before," he rumbled, "but it may not hurt to tell it again. When I was a boy, my father read to us evenings by the light of pine knots. I had to gather them. Later on when he found that hickory bark made better light, I had the chore of gathering that, too. I can still see him sitting there in the cabin with the fire blazing and a book in his hands. I'd be hatchelling and carding wool. My mother would be spinning. He'd make us take turns reading sometimes while we chored, but we would all rather work ourselves and hear him. When our books ran out, he bought a share in the library. Nobody had any money. They had to buy things with the skins of game. They called it the Coonskin Library, and I'm sure some of you heard of it. I can name you today every book they had in that library, in my time. We read them all, history, geography, theology, law. In fact, that's where I learned the rudiments of my Blackstone."

"Is that where you learned your law in the Thomas-Acton case, John?" the old justice twitted him.

"No, judge," the other came back at him. "If anything ailed my law in the Thomas-Acton case, it was all the law books and luxury I've seen since. What gave our generation enterprise and a keen mind was the deprivation we had in the woods, the hard work we enjoyed and the freedom from deadly refinement and ease."

"I can go one better, John," the preacher said. "In fact I will say without fear of contradiction that I am the only one in this room who ever wore a nettle shirt. Some of you must know the old nettle patch. It always grew in the richest ground. Everybody avoided it like the plague. My mother rotted, broke, scutched and spun it like flax. If you ever walked barefoot you know how nettles sting. But you should have worn one all winter next to your skin. The holy men of ancient times had their hair shirts to carry them as they thought, to heaven. Well, I would prescribe nettle shirts to the ease-and-pleasure-loving youth of to-day."

Chancey could hold himself back no longer.

"That would be unjust!" he cried. "Nobody, not even you, reverend, wore that nettle shirt because it was good for you. You wore it because you were poor and had no wool or flax. But today we are rich and have sheep and woolen mills. To inflict nettle shirts today on the young would be tyranny in its worst form."

"Saving the soul of our youth would be excuse enough, young man!" the old abolitionist answered fiercely.

"I would try to understand youth before you try to save it!" Chancey replied, trembling. "Especially when you commit it to a life of hardship. And to the scourge of civil war on the excuse of freeing slaves!" He did not stop there but launched into an eloquent defense of youth and peace. The words came fast. He wished Mrs. Wray could be there to take notes so he might use them in an editorial. And yet of all the telling things he said, he could remember only the last few sentences. "You gentlemen speak of the past. But the past is dead and gone. Soon you old men who belong to it will be gone, too. Only youth will be left. The old can never understand youth nor the problems of youth. Only youth itself can. Youth is the native of its own times and carries with it the key to its own salvation."

Nobody answered when he finished this time. There was a long, grave silence. Then the senator spoke.

"It wasn't only the shirts that were strong in those days, doctor," he said. "It was the pants, too. My mother made me a pair out of the hide of a buck my father shot on the way to Sunday meeting. Whether that made it any better, I don't know, but I couldn't wear those pants out. No brush or thorns could make a dent in them. After they got wet once or twice, you couldn't cut them with a knife. When I'd get through ploughing, I'd hold on to the bar and let Buck and Berry drag me down to the barn, hoping to rip those pants to pieces but nothing fazed them. Well, sir, one time I was ploughing in our swamp field. My father talked about draining it but never got around to it. There was a locust stump in that field he never could get out, either. The sprouts came up all around every year like locust does and that day the thorns gave old Buck a bite. I don't know if Berry felt it too, but he was willing. The minute Buck lit out, Berry did, too. I held on to the plough handles. My pants caught on the stump and when we got to the lower end of the field I found we had pulled out the stump, dragged it behind us and dug the prettiest drainage ditch you ever saw clean across that swamp."

When he first started telling it, Chancey thought the senator must be on his side, but he wondered at the laugh that came at the end. He could overlook, he thought, the man who had made the speech against the Mexican war, but he never would forgive the general for his story.

"Your oxen, senator, remind me of the sheep that said baa to old Forley. Old Forley came over from the old country, he claimed, to escape service in the army. Unless he died lately, he's still living in the Appleton Valley just outside of Center City. He once knocked a neighbor's calf dead with his fist. When the neighbor took him to court, he claimed the calf kicked him first. When he had a little too much to drink, the boys in Center City used to follow him home calling, 'Mooo! It kicked me first.' He had a favorite sheep and one time when he came home drunk, he gave the sheep what he gave the calf. 'It was baaing at me like them boys,' he told his wife."

Chancey could feel no point to the story, and yet he felt the cold chills go over him as the general gave it. He thought the excessive laughter from the men at this time cruel as their prescription for youth. As the anecdotes went on, one catching fire from another, he could feel that the old-timers were belittling him, putting him in his place, killing his argument with hilarity and savagery. He looked around. Savagery was the word. He saw that unmistakable flame he had noticed before in pioneer eyes, that wild mark of violence and passion that seemed to go hand in hand with their strong comradeship and mutual understanding. Bitterness for their souls possessed him. Here were gathered together some of the master minds of the state, leaders of government, and they degraded themselves in cruel horse-play and blind delusions of the past.

When he could, he rose and slipped out. He had the feeling he was neither noticed nor missed. But what was that shout of laughter and extra pitch of exuberance that seemed to follow him down the hall?

CHAPTER THIRTY-TWO

A SLIPPED COLLAR

Be still and know that I am God.

TEXT FOR JUDGE WHEELER'S FUNERAL SERMON
IN WHICH THE CHURCH HAS THE LAST WORD

SAYWARD sat in Portius's bedroom upstairs waiting for the funeral to start. Sooth with her big family to get ready had just come in the room, but Libby with only a man to fetch, hadn't showed up yet.

"Now don't be hard on her, Mama," Massey said. "It's all right to be a little late."

But not for your father's funeral, Sayward thought, although she said nothing. She just sat tightly in her strong basque and the voluminous folds of her black silk. If Libby and Harry were late, they were late. But when it came to the last thing they could do for Portius, she would rather they were on time.

The air seemed close in here. The bed stood piled with family wraps. Chairs from neighboring houses crowded the floor. Sayward had a little trouble catching her breath, but none of the others said anything, so she kept still. Out of the window she could see the overflow of folks in the front yard. She wished Portius could know the big turnout for his funeral. Resolve had wanted it in church. So did Dezia and the others, and Dr. Shotwell had supported them, but Sayward had stood firm. Portius never went to church when he could help himself, and she wouldn't play such a trick on him as take him there now when he couldn't. She would make him out no hypocrite or turncoat at the last minute. Whatever faults he had, they were not those. Some of the rogues and knaves out there in the cold of the yard looked like they would rather stay out anyway. It was nice of them to pay their last respects to Judge Wheeler, and they were welcome to come in the warm if they wanted, but a few of them might not feel at home sitting down with pious, God-fearing folks. Portius had lent a hand to so many scalawags in his time, jailbirds, drunkards and bad women. Hardly ever would he give to a good cause.

"That's a fine and noble charity," he used to say. "I wouldn't give it a penny. I give only to the devil's kin, the sinners nobody else will help. Even the door of Heaven is closed against them."

A good many of those he helped or their friends had come to the funeral. Now here were Libby and Harry saying something about a patient who made them late. And there was Dr. Shotwell's voice from downstairs, coming right on behind like a pedlar's pack. It was plain that this was what he had been waiting for. His voice rang out brisk as an auctioneer's through the house. The family, mourners and the rest might be stricken with grief and fright before the specter of death, but he wasn't. Death was everyday to him. Disposing of it was his trade. His words came matter of fact like this was an old story to him to be put through without waste of time on corners and edges. All the sweat and fire would be saved for the

funeral sermon to crown the saint and punish the sinner
and put the fear of God and of hell in all who heard him.

Sayward had to get hold of herself once or twice. It
wasn't easy to sit calm and hear yourself parted forever
from the man you lived with for going on forty-five years
and the father of your children. Nor would she have just
bad said about him at his funeral when he lay helpless and
silent in his box and couldn't rise up to defend himself.
That's why she had taken Dr. Shotwell into Portius's library
last night, closed the door and come right out with where
she stood. What Portius believed, she said, was his and the
Lord's business, and what end he came to. The Lord would
judge and the Lord would know what to judge from. Oh,
Portius had made some mistakes in his time. He was no
saint. But she had lived with him long enough to know a
lot of decent things about him, and if the bad would be
played up more than the good, she would have no funeral
sermon said over him at all. To herself she added that nobody looked more peaceful than Portius a lying there in
his box. If he had gone to a bad place, he certainly gave no
sign of it.

She had to admit Dr. Shotwell did an honest job. He
didn't whitewash but he said the bad first, and gave it no
more talking about than it deserved. Then he started on
the good. Sooth was the first to sob. The other girls followed. When the choir sang "The River Between," Sayward saw even Resolve and Chancey wipe their eyes. Sayward tried to, too. It didn't look right, she felt, sitting there
like a dry stone in the run. Those crowded in the upstairs
hall could look right in and reckon she still held against
Portius what he had done to her thirty years ago. But she
couldn't help it. If she couldn't cry, she couldn't. Tears
had never come to her easy. Not even when her mother

went, coughing up her heart's blood, or when little Sulie spoke the last time with her blackened lips, looking up at her with no lashes on her eyes, begging her not to scold her that she had burned herself. Even when the news came about Guerdon, at last, how he had paid back the life he took, giving his own for his country, enduring wounds to die of fever and be buried in some heathen place with a Mexican name two thousand miles from his Ohio home, she couldn't give way and melt the cruel knot twisted inside of her. If she hadn't then, how could she cry for Portius now? He had been luckier than most, going quick, one hour on the bench and the next being carried home a corpse. She hoped it might be that way with her when her time came, still in harness and all over in a hurry, but whatever way it came, she would have to take it.

The funeral service seemed mighty long. It comforted her a little to count it in her mind the service for Guerdon, too, who didn't have much of any. Later she stood at the grave, leaning forward like a tree on the river bank with some of its roots washed out. When she turned away, she told herself, that much was behind her now. She would have to leave the dead with the Lord and think about the living. There was Chancey getting into the carriage behind her, looking like he needed clothes and rations. He had fallen off since she saw him last. For months she had heard rumors that his lady, Mrs. Wray, had flitted to some other flower patch and left him with the paper. Business was shaky. The stores wouldn't advertise any more in what they called a copperhead paper. Creditors were pushing him. Now what could Chancey do when he had no paper to sound out his views in?

Sayward just felt thankful that she could feed him today at the funeral dinner. This would be the first time he sat down to a meal in his mammy's house since he pulled up stakes and left. Wasn't it a pity that it took the death of your father to fetch you home to your mother's table! Even so, it was uncommon that he stayed long enough to eat. Sayward reckoned she knew what he waited for. It was to hear how much his father left him.

The girls tried to drag her away, but she had to see that folks at the second and third tables got enough to eat. Resolve called her twice before she would come to the library. The rest of the family was already inside. Sure enough, there was Chancey, sitting like he didn't care, but none of them had bigger ears. Already his face looked filled out since he had a square meal inside of him. If only she had him home for a while, she could plump him up and put roses in his cheeks. She would ask him today, wouldn't he stay and keep her company, but she had no notion he would agree. He would say he had to go back to Cincinnati. That was the way it went! And here she would be all alone in a big house with no one to cook for but an old woman who hardly got hungry any more save for a crust of bread and a cup of tea.

Now wasn't it a shame that Portius didn't leave Chancey an inheritance so he could keep on with his paper! Sooth could have used something, too, with her big family. Even in his will, Portius had to be himself and leave his children their youth, their wit and their sense of humor, as he called it. He always had to have his little joke. It was true he had given his children their wit and some of their being able to laugh, but he hadn't had much to do with their youth. Some of them weren't even young any more. There was Resolve, high in his forties. Portius might have left Resolve his law books, but then he would have had to match that gift to the others. It was better, he must have reckoned, to bestow on his widow what he had to by law anyway. The rest could go to his fund for rogues and sinners.

Oh, his heirs looked at each other with hard eyes when Resolve laid down the will. Massey and Libby spit out what they thought. But Chancey acted like when as a small boy he would get hurt easy and hide in the loft. One minute he was here, and the next Sayward couldn't find him.

"Chancey! Did you see Chancey? I want to talk to him!" she called going about the house, but Chancey had left neither hat nor word behind him.

One by one, friends and family followed. Resolve had an important meeting. Sooth and Massey had to get their young ones to bed. Libby said she ought to be at home now for the evening patients. The members of bar and bench had long since paid their respects and taken leave. The Morrisons, the Sutphens, the Quitmans and the rest had drifted off. A few stayed on, George Holcomb and Will Beagle among them. George wanted to hear about Huldah, and likely Will hated to go back to his lonely house, after a funeral fetched up in his mind about Genny. Sayward was glad to have him stay. Will was one of the oldest friends she had left, the only brother-in-law she owned, save for Sulie's Indian man. It was a pity Genny couldn't have given Will some young ones in her time. They would be a comfort to him now in his old age.

Every time the door shut, the house felt a little lonelier. In the end, it looked mighty empty with just her and Dezia. She was thankful Dezia didn't have to go back to her teaching at the ladies' seminary till Sunday. Now Dezia, you better go to bed, she said. She would come soon her own self, she promised, but in her heart she felt grateful for the few things that neighbors and friends had left undone, small things that only the woman of the house could attend to, redding up here and straightening out there and putting back yonder. When she did climb the stairs, it wasn't to sleep. God knows she had been up enough the last few days to drop off the minute her head hit the bolster. And yet her eyes didn't want to shut tonight or her body let go to such a point where she wouldn't know where she was at.

The big house stood mighty still around her. Once upon a time on nights like this it was filled with sleeping, restless, snoring young life, charging up energy to be spent violently on the morrow. One by one they had cleared out, taking something out of the house with them. And now you could tell that Portius was gone too. That certain living power of his presence was missing from the rooms, that feel and flavor she had had of him from the day Will Beagle had told her how he had caught the Bay State solitary tramping up and down outside his cabin made of buckeye logs, reciting Latin and Greek or some other dead language.

She could see Portius now as he was then, a bushnipple and no mistake, standing up to marry her in his ruffled linen shirt pied with doeskin patches and his homemade buckskin britches shrunk and dried and clapping like clapboards when he walked. And she could see him as he was these last years, the eminent Judge Wheeler, in his long coat and broadcloth britches, starting for court on a weekday. Now on the Sabbath he would go out in the oldest suit he had, with his stick across the back of his shoulders. He did it on purpose, she always thought, setting out at that hour with his walking stick and old clothes so he would pass Christian folk dressed in their Sunday best on their way to church. He liked to devil them as he did her when he came to the kitchen for cake stuff.

"Any gingerbread, my love and my dove?" he would

say, and yet all the time she knew what he was after. He had no sweet tooth for her baking. No, he only wanted the gingerbread to set out for the mice so they would spare his law books.

Oh, sometimes he had been hard to put up with, and yet that was the very part of him she would have parted with last. His feeling for rogues, she always thought, came from his being part of one himself. He liked to take sly digs at folks, and none was so honest or sacred as to be spared. He would poke wily fun at Resolve's mother-in-law's table by telling how he had that day seen the Morrison goat — it belonged to another and poorer set of Morrisons — so thin it followed the handbill man around and licked the flour paste off the put-up handbills. And when somebody's brandy tasted weak, he would say it reminded him of Ferry House whiskey. "I never knew King Sam to buy but one barrel of it," he told. "Every time he drew a gallon, he replaced it with a gallon of water." Even poor and simple country folk were not immune from Portius's jokes. He liked to tell of the farmer who bought a wagon from the Tateville Wagon Works and then hung around waiting for the discount they promised him. "Why, I gave it to you!" the manager said. "Oh, no you didn't," the farmer said craftily. "I've been sitting here looking for it all this while and I ain't seen a thing."

He had no shame, and nothing fazed him. Hardly would she forget the time long ago she had got him to camp meeting and the preacher for something to say called out in his sermon, "Where is that winebibber and agnostic who sits in high places!" "Here I am, sir," Portius said cheerfully, standing up. It had shamed her so no end and scared the preacher nearly out of his boots. The story went all over the county, but people had respected Portius more than ever. "Honest Judge Wheeler," they called him. "He'd send himself to prison if he done any wrong."

Favorite words and sayings of Portius came back to Sayward's mind tonight. Never would he say "Christmas" but "at the time called Christmas." He would make common things sound noble like when he called some good-for-nothing, "that scurrilous and epithetical piece of rascality" or when he'd refer to Sayward's family's humble tramp west as, "Their long and arduous exodus from the Eastern states." A dead man was "a man deprived of his life"; a gentleman, "a man of parts." If a guest praised the food on Sayward's table, Portius would invariably agree and add slyly, "As Fred Pynchon used to say, 'Yes, it's good, what there is of it, and there's enough of it such as there is.'" When Chancey was still at home and would lie abed late in the morning, Portius used to call in stentorian tones up the back stairs, "Chancey! Don't you know that the great majority of people die in their beds!" You could never get the best of him. Even when he made a mistake and you proved it, his eye would twinkle and all he would admit was that old Wheeler household saying that Mathias Cottle first said, "I was just a thinking, and if I hadn't been a thinking, I wouldn't have thunk that way."

He liked especially to tell stories against aristocrats and the gentry like the one of the driver who said to the lord, "Are you the man to take the carriage? If you are, I'm the gentleman to take you." But most of his stories were about the law. One they told about him so often that Sayward knew it by heart. At one time it was Resolve he was supposed to be talking to, another time some other young lawyer. "What do I do if the law is on my side and justice against me?" the apprentice lawyer was supposed to ask. "Advocate the majesty of the law," they said Portius answered. "Well, suppose justice is on my side and the law against me?" "Advocate justice though the heavens fall," they said Portius thundered. "But what do I do if the law and justice are both against me?" "Oh, then saw the air and talk of glorious liberty for all men," Portius told him.

That story had gone far and wide among lawyers. She heard them telling it at the funeral table again today along with the one about the tattered Bible Portius had for years in his court. Thousands of witnesses and several judges had been sworn on it. Then one day somebody opened it and found it was a copy of Arabian Nights.

Well, she better try closing her mind for a while, Sayward told herself. She could lie here till New Year's Day if she wanted to recollect all the things Portius said and did. It must be getting toward morning. Not that it mattered any. A woman needed small sleep and less passtime when she got old. The clock and calendar passed fast enough for you then.

CHAPTER THIRTY-THREE

THE WITNESS TREE

Come from? Why, I didn't come from any place. I been here all the time.

OLD SETTLER

SAYWARD was in her kitchen, supper eaten, what she had of it, the few dishes washed and put away. She had made it herself around five o'clock as usual. Now she sat here, not doing anything, just thinking. It was singular how she had it in her head tonight about Hugh McFall's locust post. Portius used to tell of the time he was in Hugh's field and Hugh laid his hand on a fresh-cut-and-peeled post he had just put in. Portius said Hugh felt and patted that stick of wood like it was a colt.

"I just wish I could last as long as this post," he told Portius.

Hugh must have been failing then or had second sight, for he was dead in the year. Twenty years afterward Portius said he went in the field a purpose and found that post sound as the day Hugh had put it in. And now Portius himself was dead and buried eight years. She declared it didn't seem that long. Now what made her think this way? Oh, yes, it was Hugh McFall and his locust post. But what made her think of that in the first place?

Why, it was most dark already! She had seen a slew of winters in her time, and it still surprised her how early night came of a fall afternoon. She pulled herself up and made her way to the front of the house. Now what did she come in for? It must have been something or she wouldn't be standing here with a candle, lighted at the kitchen stove, a burning in her hand. Oh, yes, how could she forget what she did every day at this time for nigh onto thirty years? The big hall lamp she lit blinded her for a minute. Now she had to watch out she didn't let it burn too high and smoke like she did last week.

Going back to the kitchen she dropped the candle. Well, it didn't matter so long as she hadn't set fire to anything. She didn't need the light. It felt good to pass from a lighted to an unlighted room and feel the darkness wash over and soothe her. She had always liked that, from the time Portius built a second room to their cabin. Even since they had the big house, she liked to sit and rest a minute in the dim kitchen when her evening's work was done, taking notice of the pleasant glow and sounds of life coming from some other rooms up yonder in the front of the house.

She went to the high narrow closet with the little doors behind the kitchen fireplace. There was no light save what came down the long hall, but she didn't need any. Her fingers could find what she wanted. When she was little, the touch of a clay pipe used to go through her like eating a persimmon. Now it felt like an old friend. Her unsteady hand cut plug in her palm and her thumb pushed it in the bowl. When she had lighted it with a spill from the stove, she sat back in the rocker. Oh, this, she knew these last years was why her father smoked. The small fire in the bowl warmed you, body and soul. The smoke drifted up like chimney smoke. A pipe in truth was a piece of household comfort you could carry with you far into the lonesome tracks of the deep woods.

If only she could take off her shoes and stockings now and have her feet free against the floor by the stove. The girls reckoned it unladylike, but she even liked the scent of sweat and tan bark leather from her shoes. Some could crack their toe knuckles but she never could. Folks who wore their shoes all the time like she had to these years missed the good feel of grass and leaves, the bare toes a working in earth or sand. But she better not do it now, not till she went to bed.

Wasn't that the front door and somebody in the front hall? Sayward put the pipe back to its cup on the shelf behind the little door and went front. Yes, there was Libby a few steps up the stairs.

"I was just going by," she said, as if her mother didn't know she came by here every day on purpose, "What do you have it so dark for? I'll light the sitting room lamp for you."

"A body gets tired being in the light all the time," her mother told her. "Won't you take off your things?"

Libby waited till she had done her work with a spill from the mantel lighted from the hall lamp chimney. Then her eyes critically examined her mother as she took off her cape and promptly slipped it back on again.

"It's cold in here. I don't see how you stand it with only that knit thing around your shoulders. You ought to be in a warm house. How do you feel tonight?" Her mother didn't answer and Libby lifted her nose to sniff. "It smells exactly like somebody was smoking in here." And when

Sayward still kept mildly silent. "Why don't you ever want to tell how you feel, Mama?"

"You just asked me last night or night before," her mother complained. "I don't think about it till you ask me."

"We're concerned about you, Mama."

"You needn't fret so much. I can get along real good."

"We're thankful you can. But what if something would happen and you all alone in this house?"

"Then I reckon it would happen," Sayward said, resigned.

"I don't see how you can be so cold-blooded. Think what people would say about us? And think how we feel! We never know night or day."

"It's better sometimes if you don't know," Sayward said shortly.

"That's foolish, Mama. If Harry knew in time, he could do something for you. He's your doctor. He knows more about you than anybody else. More than you do yourself. And he says you're not fit to be alone."

"I don't know what he says that for," Sayward said stoutly.

"He doesn't mean only your leg. He means the way you are lately."

"What way?"

"Well, just the way people get when they get old. They ought to have somebody with them. They can't be trusted."

"You mean I'm getting queer?" Sayward put to her.

"Well, not queerer than anybody else your age. People must expect it when they get up in years. They're forgetful. Take yourself. You don't remember things any more."

"I can remember as good as you, Miss Libby," her mother said sharply.

"Yes, right now, but not all the time. Especially when

you're alone. You eat things you shouldn't. You won't take your medicine. You keep runaways in the house, no matter how big and black and dangerous they are. You cook their meals and give them money. They could knock you on the head so easy. Then you won't listen to your children. You won't come to live with any of us. You say we should come and live with you, but if anything happened, we'd have to move again because the square's all business now and getting worse every day. Even if we did come, we'd have to do everything like you said. We'd be living in your house and you'd be the master. It wouldn't work, especially with the man of the family. Besides, you said yourself you'd rather be alone. If you'd only have a regular maid in the house, so there'd be somebody here with you all the time, it would be different. Why, there isn't a house in Americus half this size that doesn't have one maid or two. But all you'll have is just Matty to clean a couple of times a week. And she's pretty near as old and feeble as you are."

"The house don't get upset with just one person in it," Sayward protested.

"It gets upset enough. Folks come in here all the time. If it isn't somebody to pay rent or interest, it's somebody trying to borrow or get you to donate. Or it's somebody who stayed with you once, and there were thousands of those. Or they knew Papa or Resolve when he was governor. If it's meal time, you cook their dinner or supper, and if it isn't, you give them cakes and whiskey. Or it's somebody who knew you when you were a girl."

"Folks that knew me when I was a girl are all gone, Libby," Sayward said.

"Well, you shouldn't have to lift a finger," Libby de-

[404]

clared. "Not with your bad leg and all your other ailments.
You must remember you're an old lady, Mama."

"But I'm not dead yet, Libby," Sayward said mildly,
"and I like to have something to do my own self."

"Well, I should think there'd be other things for you to
do than go out and pet those trees of yours in the side
yard. Now don't get mad at me, Mama. You asked a while
ago if you were getting queer, and that's one queer thing
you do. Your neighbors over the Water Company say you
go around to every one and pat it with your hand and look
up at it and talk to it. Yes, they do. They claim you do it
twice a day. They can't hear what you say, but after little
Sooth stayed with you the last time she said you give those
trees good night and good morning. We told her not to
dare breathe a word to anybody. We can't imagine how
you would do such a thing. You used to tell us how you
hated trees. Just what do you do it for, Mama?"

Sayward's face set and she didn't answer. How could she
explain that to Libby? She couldn't even explain it to herself. At her silence, Libby's face set too. Studying it, her
mother could well believe that this was the child whom
folks said favored her the most. Sayward could see some of
her stubbornness and resolve in her now.

"Mama, there's no need deceiving you. We don't like to
tell you some things, but you won't listen to us. Harry's
told us for a long time to expect anything. It's not only
your leg although that's bad enough. The veins are clotted
and abscessed, and if it isn't watched and dressed, it might
turn into gangrene any day. But what he's worried most
about is a stroke. One time he came in and you couldn't
talk to him right, he says. You've worked too hard ever
since you were a little tyke. It's telling on you now and

[405]

something has to be done about it. We'd have gone ahead
before but we didn't want to disturb you too much before
your picture's painted."

Behind Libby in one of the long looking glasses that had
come down from the Wheelers, Sayward could see herself.
So that, she thought, was the face her family and the Pioneer Society wanted painted so they could show genera-
tions still to come how the first settler of Shawanee County
looked. Libby was right when she said that she was getting
up in years. The skin of her face had pulled together and
worn away like old cloth when the nap is gone and you
can see only the warp. Crisscross ridges ran across her
cheeks like on old trees and Indians. Her neck had shrunken
mostly to up and down tendons. Now what made the top
of her head slant away more than it used to? Her nose
stood out plain enough but her mouth pinched and drew
down like she had seen on old folks in their coffins, bitter
at that bitterest of all things, death. She reckoned it was
partly that her teeth were gone. Her hair had turned gray
long ago; then white, and now to another color. It had that
dirty "yaller" look she had seen on old women in her time.
When she was younger she thought those old women just
had dirty hair, but now she knew better. She couldn't wash
it out. Even soap she made her ownself wouldn't take off
the tarnish. Once she had been light complected but now
her skin looked dark brown. It was the Indian in her, she
told herself. Only her blue eyes belied it. They looked out
at her straight and "cam" like always.

"Do you hear me, Mama?" she heard Libby's voice say
sharply.

"Yes, I hear you," Sayward said, looking back to her
again.

"What I want to say is that this isn't something sudden.

We've been facing it a long time. Ever since last winter we've done nothing but talk about it. We wrote to Huldah and Kinzie. We talked to Dezia when she was home. We came to the conclusion we couldn't let you in the house another winter alone. Not in your condition with all the fires to keep up that you wouldn't be able to. We decided there was only one thing to do and that was bring you to my house where you could have care."

"You mean winter next year?" Sayward asked.

"No, I mean this year. In a week or two."

Sayward sat silent, with a kind of shocked grief.

"Your father and I built this house," she said at last. "I've lived here for over thirty year, and I wouldn't have it torn down for a store or something. Not while I'm alive."

"We talked that over, too. It's handy to the court house, Resolve said he could use it for his law offices. Not the whole house, but he could rent the rest out. They wouldn't have to change a thing, and the furniture could be stored on the third floor."

"The other children mightn't like Resolve having the house," Sayward mentioned cautiously.

"We took that up with Huldah and Kinzie. They said it was all right."

"Did you take it up with Chancey?"

"We thought what's the use talking to him. He's against everything and everybody, especially Resolve. But we did then, and he said so, too. It surprised us after all he's printed against Resolve. We don't understand who pays the money to keep up that terrible paper of his. It doesn't make any money. It isn't you, is it, Mama?"

Sayward sat there a moment with a cruel face.

"I haven't seen Chancey but once since his father's funeral, and then I didn't have a chance to speak to him."

"Well, I didn't think you'd do a thing like that, give him more than you gave us, but I told the others the first chance I had I'd come right out and ask you."

Sayward's mouth set like it used to years ago.

"I've always tried to be even-handed, Libby," she reminded sharply. "But if one gets a lick more than another while I'm alive, the others will find it taken care of in the will."

"We know you want to be impartial, Mama," Libby said humbly. "Just the same, it's mighty funny. But I didn't come here to talk about Chancey. We wanted you to know about this so you could be ready and we wouldn't have any trouble with you when the time came."

She said a great deal more than that, explaining to her mother just how they had everything worked out so it would be best for her. When finally she got up to go, Sayward wet her lips.

"Did Chancey say right out you should move me, Libby?"

"Why, yes, Mama. We asked him and he said he hadn't a thing against it." Libby started for the hall. "Now don't you dare get up! I can let myself out."

For a wonder Sayward obeyed. She heard the door close and Libby's step outside.

"Even you, Chancey!" then she said aloud.

For a while she kept sitting there in a kind of stolid brooding. In her time she had looked forward to a good many things that came to pass, but never had she looked forward to outlasting her time. Where were those now she knew as a girl in the woods: Genny and Achsa, Will and Mary Harbison, George Roebuck, the Covenhovens, the MacWhirters and the Tulls, Jake Tench, the McFalls and the Browns, the Morrisons and the Sutphens, even Will Beagle? They

were gone, all gone. More than once as a girl she hadn't
seen a strange face in the woods from one month to the
other, and yet all the time she had her pappy and her
brother and sisters. But when your brother and sisters and
then your man drop off one by one; when the friends and
neighbors you grew up with are dead and buried; when
all the folks you knew who lived and felt like you did, are
gone, lock, stock and barrel never to return; and you're the
the last of your generation, then you can drink a draft of
loneliness you never drank before.

She reckoned she knew now how one of those old butts
in the deep woods felt when all its fellows were cut down
and it was left standing lone and gaunt against the sky, with
only whips and brush and those not worth the axe pushing
up around it. The second growth trees you saw today were
mighty poor and spindly specimens beside the giants she
had known when first she came to this country. Those
wild shaggy mossy oldtime butts would be out of place in
Americus today as would the shaggy oldtime folks she had
known. Yes, and she was out of place her own self, living
her old life like she did in her day, taking care of herself at
her age and doing her own work, giving no thought if she
lived or died. That's one reason why her children wanted
to move her. Younger folks couldn't stand seeing her do it.
It was too hard on their "narve strings."

What gave folks "narve strings" today and made them
soft so they couldn't stand what folks could when she was
young? Oh, she was no learned judge like Portius, just an
old woodsy woman who hadn't learned to read and write
till her own young ones taught her. Her eyes were not so
good any more and her mind would lately forget. But she
had her own notions. It had taken a wild and rough land to
raise the big butts she saw when first she came here, and

she reckoned it took a rough and hard life to breed the kind
of folks she knew as a young woman. If you made it easy
for folks, it seemed like their hardihood had to pay for it.
Didn't she know? Which one of her young ones was it she
had raised the softest, done the most for, coaxed and prayed
along, saved from bad things one time after the other?
Wasn't it the same one that now could take life and his
country the least and wanted to change God's world over
from top to bottom? It was the same with sick folks, Sayward noticed. Once they had been taken care of too long,
they got to feeling the world ought to be changed and softened, centered toward themselves.

But what in God's name did soft and weak folks want to
make the whole world over like they were for? In her time
in the woods, everybody she knew was egged on to be his
own special self. He could live and think like he wanted to
and no two humans you met up with were alike. Each had
his own particular beliefs and his reasons for owning to
them. Folks were a joy to talk to then, for all were different.
Even the simple-minded were so original in their notions
they either made you laugh or gave you pause. But folks in
Americus today seemed mighty tiresome and getting more
so. If you saw one, you saw most. If you heard one talk, it's
likely you heard the rest. They were cracked on living like
everybody else, according to the fashion, and if you were
so queer and outlandish as to go your own way and do
what you liked, it bothered their "narve strings" so they
were liable to lock you up in one of their newfangled
asylums or take you home where they could hold you down
to their way of doing, like Libby wanted to.

What was the world coming to and what hearty pleasures folks today missed out of life! One bag of meal her
pap said, used to make a whole family rejoice. Now folks

came ungrateful from the store, grumbling they had to carry such a heavy market basket. Was that the way this great new country of hers was going to go? The easier they made life, the weaker and sicker the race had to get? Once a majority of the men got weak and soft, what weak, harmful ways would they vote the country into then? Well, her pap's generation could get down on their knees and thank the Almighty they lived and died when they did. How would they ever have come and settled this wild country if they said to each other, "Ain't you afeard?" How would her pappy have fetched them the long way out here on foot if he'd kept asking all the time, "Are ye all right! How do ye feel? Do ye reckon ye kin make it?" No, those old time folks she knew were scared of nothing, or if they were, they didn't say so. They knew they ran bad risks moving into Indian country, but they had to die some time. They might as well live as they pleased and let others bury them when the time came. Now Libby's generation, it seemed, lived mostly to study and fret about ailing and dying.

The knocker on the front door sounded. Who could that be? Likely some other fearful soul to ask was she all right and wasn't she afeard to stay in the house by herself at her age not knowing what might happen? She turned down the light. She didn't know as she wanted to listen to any more tales tonight of how some other bodies living all alone got sick or fell and there they lay till strangers came in and found them. Rat a tat! Yes, it was some timid soul. Already he or she was getting discouraged, for that knock was not so hearty as the first time.

What a difference it was when Alec came last year, or was it the year before! Anyway, she was sitting in the kitchen that time when the knocker sounded. She had had a run of callers all day. She had her pipe in her mouth and her shoes off taking her ease, and she thought she wouldn't go to the door. Then she heard that big brass knocker with the Wheeler name on it cast aside and a fist pound on the door. Didn't it sound good again to hear plain knuckles rap on the wood? And when she didn't answer that, a stick beat on the door. That wasn't a town body, Sayward told herself. No! Such would have fretted she might be upstairs or sick. It would be a terrible hardship to rouse an ailing woman in her eighties and run her downstairs to the door her own self. But this rowdy body, whoever it was out there now, didn't care if she was up in years or not. He reckoned she could come to the door. By hokey day, she told herself, she would put on her shoes and see who this was that didn't think she ought to lay abed and have somebody wait on her.

She opened the front door and there standing looking up at her was a smiling young girl she ought to know and a little old man with snow white hair, red cheeks and a cane. She reckoned she never saw him before. Now wait a minute! There was something familiar about those little bear eyes and the small mouth and face swollen around the cheeks. Then suddenly she knew who he looked like. It was old Judah who died of a mad wolf bite way back when Resolve was only a whip of a boy.

"Alec MacWhirter! What on earth! I thought you were dead and buried long ago up in Wisconsin or wherever you went to. Come in both of you. And to think I almost didn't go to the door!"

"Oh, we'd a gone around to the back if you didn't come to the front," he told her. "And if you didn't come to the back, we'd a come in and hollered. And if the door was locked, we'd a gone to your neighbors to help rout you out. You wouldn't a got rid of us that easy."

What a treat that had been for her to visit with Alec
MacWhirter, one of the few of her own kind left. You
might say of her own family. Why, the MacWhirters and
the Covenhovens had been the closest to the Lucketts there
was, the oldest settlers around here save themselves. All evening she and Alec talked of the old days. Hardly was Portius decently asked about and buried till they were at it.
She asked if he remembered the time his brother Dave's
bare feet got cold and he stepped in his granny's kettle of
hominy to get them nice and warm. And Alec asked her
if she recollected when Achsa took her pap's saw up on the
leaning elm and sawed off the branch she was setting on.
Sayward minded him of the time Jep walked for miles in
his sleep, scaring the wits out of some folks who reckoned
him a spirit in his bed gown. And Alec told of the first he
ever tasted coffee. It was in a cup, he said, set in a bigger
and flatter cup and tasted like neither milk, nor mush, nor
hominy. The tears ran down his face, he claimed, while he
drank it. Oh, one thing that night led to another. She would
tell one story, like the time Tod Wylder got mad at his
wife for giving his red mittens to the Indians. Then he
would come back with another, like the time Will Beagle
drank her pokeberry juice.

"I kin still mind it plain as day," Alec told her. "We
were all boys together. Your brother Wyitt told Will the
pokeberry juice was wine and Will drank it. Then Jake
Tench told him it was dye, and a course, it was. But Jake
said it was pure poison. He said Will would be stiff as a
frozen skunk in two hours by the clock. The only thing
that could save him was hog fat. Now Will believed him,
for everybody knew that hog fat was why a rattlesnake was
no good against a hog. Well, sir, I don't know where you
were at, Saird, but Jake fed him your hog fat. Wyitt

showed him where you kep' it. Now Will hated fat, especially hog fat and most of all when it was soft and slippery. He could hardly get one piece down. And then he hollered he couldn't look at a second piece. But Jake gave him no rest. He said, do you want to die and be buried in all this sloppy weather? Till it was over Will was sick as a dog puking in the grass. But do you reckon Jake would let him be? No, he had to get one more piece down to live. Every time it was just one more piece."

Sayward could still see Alec sitting there a telling it with his small mouth and swollen around the red cheeks. His little bear eyes would look at her fierce, then his face would crease and his throat give out such a yell of laughter that his great-niece would jump. No, they didn't do things by half in the old days. That little grandniece of his must have reckoned they were both wild and crazy as whaups. Only when it grew late and Alec got up to leave, did they let themselves get serious. He stood there holding her hand and neither knew if they'd ever see each other again, and then you could see it for the first time in his eyes.

"Folks loved each other then, Saird," he said sober. "It ain't like now. Pride and style have took the place of religion. You may go where you will, you'll have a hard time finding folks like when we were young."

"Not around here anyways," Sayward agreed. "A good many ask me lately about those days. How was it on the frontier, they say. To hear them talk, you'd reckon our life was terrible, something flesh and blood couldn't put up with. They say, but didn't you have a hard time, and I reckon we did, but gladly would I live it all over again, Alec, if I ever got the chance. If I was young and there was such a place, that's where I'd go to."

Yes, that had been such a nice visit from Alec. He had

sat right over there on that hickory chair, laughing fit to kill. Hardly a year ago it had been, or was it two? And now he was gone like the rest, those red cheeks of his in the grave. Sayward heard some whistling boy go by out in the square. When he passed, the stillness settled over the house again like the tomb. It seemed like she had lived a long time, longer than anybody that ever lived, and all those days back in her youth were like the time of Greece and Rome that her young ones used to write school papers about. She could recollect how dead those days from Resolve's history books used to seem, like they'd never really been. Well, that's the way her and Alec MacWhirter's early days must seem to young folks today.

She picked up her lamp to go to the library. She had promised young Monroe Cottle to set down her accounts every day before she forgot them. Now what was she standing here in the hall for, and what was she a listening to? For a while she didn't know. Then she heard it again and it took her back to the deep woods. Why, it sounded like the wind in the great white oak at the MacWhirters. Judah had left it stand over their log house, and when you went there you could hear the air draw through. She could still see that monster tree in her mind as it looked when she and Portius would go to call. The MacWhirters' house was two stories but it looked like a child's play house under that white oak. Some folks claimed it would draw lightning. But it never did. Old General Washington, Cora used to call it.

Well, it was too far over to the MacWhirters. What she heard must be from the sugar maples standing by Portius's log academy. Where was Portius tonight and why wasn't he home yet? She went to the kitchen and took her old shawl from the back of the settee. Out in the faint moonlight she stood a little confused and uncertain. Why, what were all these buildings a looming up yonder! She had looked for black woods a raising against the sky. But the only trees she could make out were these few in her side yard. She went up to them squinting and peering. Why they weren't wild trees or first growth at all! They'd be no more than step-children to those big butts she was looking for.

Then her eyes made out her own stable, and she felt shamed. Why, that stable wasn't here or hardly anything else when the academy stood. No, she recollected now, the academy wasn't up here at all. It was down near the cabin where they used to live. This was her and Portius's mansion house she was at, and these trees out here were the ones she had planted her own self so it wouldn't look so naked and bare. Portius was dead now, and all those old time trees, she remembered, had been cut down and burnt up long ago, the big white oak at the MacWhirters, the twin walnuts of the Covenhovens and the sugar maples by the academy. All that was left around here today was poor and spindly second-growth.

Now what was she so hard on these young trees of hers for? She hadn't meant to be. Her mind had just slipped a little. It wasn't their fault they weren't any bigger, that they were town trees instead of wild butts. They couldn't help being mild and tame any more than humans could today. Wasn't it Chancey or Portius who said once that present day folks could cut down the woods and break in new land, if they had to, but they didn't have to. That was the trouble. When natural hardships petered out, the government ought to set up some hand-made hardships for the younger generation to practise on. No, she couldn't blame these young trees of hers. They did uncommon well since they were planted. Sometimes at night, especially when there was no moon, she thought they changed into wild trees. Then they looked mighty tall. They stood like Indian chiefs, letting the dark come over them, like this was still their land and they were the masters of it, like they hadn't lost heart. Oh, she had to admire their spunk and feel for them, three young forest trees against a whole city. Sometimes she wished she could give them back their land, for it was she who had taken it from them. But all she could do now was save them from their enemies. Whoever had his eyes on this lot when she died, expected first to cut down these trees and build. He'd have a jolt when her will was read that the lot could only be leased. The trees would have to stand unharmed. Resolve hadn't liked to set that down. He acted like she sided with these trees against her own children, for how could they get the full value of the lot if the buyer couldn't chop down the trees?

All this time Sayward puttered around, patting and talking to her basswood, maple and whitewood poplar. They needn't worry, she told them. She'd look after them. Nobody with an axe or saw would come in to fetch them low. She had done enough of that her own self in her time. Oh, she hadn't dare be too sorry for what chopping she'd done. It had to be, she reckoned. No, it was something else of late made her feel that way toward the trees, although she couldn't say what it was.

Now she better go in before Libby came along or Harry drove by in his new buggy and caught her out in the night air. Besides, she had to get a mite of sleep. That painter fellow would be here with his brushes in the morning.

She woke up before daylight like usual and went down to cook her breakfast. She thought she better eat a mite extra this morning to try to fill out her loose skin. She wouldn't like to show up on that painting looking poor as a shad. After breakfast she fetched in her broom and dust rag. If any of her parlor was going to get in the picture, it had better be clean. Libby came about nine and made a fuss that her mother wasn't dressed. She took her upstairs and brushed her hair, putting it up to suit herself. Then she ran down to answer the knocker.

The painter fellow was there when Sayward got down. He was a nice-enough man with a brown goatee and a velvet corduroy coat to match. He bowed over her hand like an eat-frog feller, but before he straightened up Sayward could see that his eyes were taking in her and the room. He told her just where to sit, with Portius's bust in back of her on one side and the painting of Portius's grandfather on the other. Sayward said she didn't know as she liked that, having her likeness painted under one of the gentry like he was somebody from her side of the house when he wasn't. But the painter and Libby saw no harm in it.

Once the artist went to his easel, Sayward felt rueful sitting there. She had never looked for them to do such a monster picture of her. Why, there was enough canvas there for a barn door. He'd have to draw her big as a cow. The painter's hand moved fast as his eyes. Whether he was drawing her natural or not, she couldn't tell, for the picture was turned away. Several times he had her move her chair or hold her head just so. It was going to be a "tejus" job, Sayward saw, a good deal worse than a tintype. But she stayed meek as she could and did all they told her to, at least until they brought in the cushion.

It was the painter who started it, although Libby was just as bad. He told Libby something and she fetched the red velvet pillow from the blue brocaded stool. The painter said it was the very daddle. He laid it on the floor in front

of Sayward's chair and had her lift one foot on it, so her
shoe showed outside her skirt.

"Now what's that for?" she wanted to know.

"It's for composition, Mrs. Wheeler," the painter said.

"It's the fashion, Mama," Libby told her. "It makes you
look ladylike and genteel."

Libby should have known better than say that. Up to
this time Sayward had done everything they told her though
it meant feeling foolish and acting like a body in her second
childhood. But now they had gone too far. This she would
never submit to, sit here for her picture with her shoe resting in plain sight on a red velvet cushion, as if the floor
wasn't good enough for her feet or anybody else's.

Before she knew it she had raised up and kicked that
pillow out of the way, not caring if it knocked down the
easel or not.

"Now I've had enough of this," she said, heaving a little.
"If you want to draw me like I am, you can. If not, I'm
going upstairs and take these Sabbath things off." That's
all she said, but she could see her daughter and the painter
fellow look at each other.

Well, she told herself when the painting went on, she
didn't know as she had ever done that before, kick anything, let alone her own pillow. It must have been that business about the house yesterday flying out of her at the
same time as the pillow. Now that she had time to think on
it, she didn't know as she would give in about the house
either. No, they could wait for her to get out till they carried her out like they did Portius. They shouldn't have to
wait too long.

CHAPTER THIRTY-FOUR

THE WOODCUTTER

The tree casts its shade upon all, even upon the woodcutter.

OLD PROVERB

CHANCEY stood it as long as he could, but when they started auctioning off his faithful old Washington press, he turned his back and went to the window. That press had been his ally and friend. It had printed his burning words of liberty and equality, of progress and peace, and sent them across the country for all to read. Now the press was lost to him, the New Palladium was lost, and the work for peace was lost, too. Outside the window he could see a regiment of Union troops, eager for glory and mad for death, marching down the street on their way to answer their backwoods president's war call.

Why couldn't his unknown patron, he thought bitterly, have supported the cause a little longer? All he knew of that nameless subscriber was that he demanded a statement each month of the money Chancey took in and spent. If his admirer had only waited a little while! Any day now Chancey looked for his mother's death, and then there would be money to keep the paper going for years to come.

That is, of course, if she gave him his rightful share of the estate. But would she ever do that? Sometimes he doubted it. He knew her and her practical kind too well. Likely he would have to use it for something a dead woman in her will approved.

The most ironical of all was that now he had no further justification to stay away any more. He would have to go home and see her before she died. Libby had written him. Sooth and Massey had written him. Resolve had stopped in at the New Palladium office and abused him for staying away, as if he could drop his paper's fight for life and run whenever they whistled. Only last week Dezia had telegraphed him. But evidently his mother was living as yet, for no word had come of her death. How he hated death and dying! That's why he fought so bitterly against war. It was the horror of suffering, of wanton crippling, of gangrene and early extinction. Never would he forget the degradation of Rosa's youth in the grave.

He stored with friends his few personal things. His precious file of the New Palladium, he put in their attic.

"I'll be back soon and start all over again," he promised them. "Meantime I may write an answer to Uncle Tom's Cabin."

At the Americus railway station nobody seemed to know him in his brown beard, for which he felt grateful. How huge his native city had grown! Wandering these busy streets among all the uncounted new buildings, he could hardly believe that here as a small boy he had been carried across the fields. As he approached the square, he felt the old telltale nearness of his mother's house come over him, that timid, helpless and angry feeling in the face of his family's boundless strength and confidence, its great animal courage and decision.

The square had changed. All was business now, stores, offices, churches, a new court house and this morning, a cattle market, with steers and calves bawling and the government buying horses for war and death. But his mother's house showed no change, as he knew it would not so long as she lived. There it stood, tall and deep, its faded red brick, its white lintels and steps, flaunting the uselessness of its old-fashioned side yard in the face of all the crowded progress.

A maid he didn't know answered his mother's door. Then at the sound of his voice Libby came down the stairs.

"It's about time," she said as she cooly kissed him.

"I came when I could," he told her with dignity, and after a moment, "How is everything?" carefully avoiding any reference to his mother, but Libby knew.

"Mother's just the same. There's no change. Harry says he never saw such an iron constitution."

Thoughtfully he hung up his hat and moved toward the library.

"Then there's no hurry. I'll go up and talk to her after while."

"I'm afraid you won't talk to her after while or any other time," Libby told him in the library. "You're too late, Chancey."

"I thought you said — "

"She doesn't know anybody, not even Harry or Manda."

Chancey felt appalled, but it was swiftly followed by something like relief.

"Then there's no need for me to go up at all, if she won't know me," he said, taking a free breath.

"She might not know you, but you'll know her!" Libby told him sharply. "You want to see your own mother, don't you? You feel a little grief for her dying, surely?"

"Certainly I do," he said warmly. "No, not exactly grief, perhaps. She wouldn't want my grief. She's had a long life, longer than you and I will likely ever see. She's also had a great deal more than she ever expected. She's never had much trouble. For instance, she's never been sold out by the sheriff like I just was. No, she wouldn't want me to grieve, and if I did it would be over somebody who died young and unhappy and had nothing but misery and degradation," he added bitterly.

"Who's that?" Libby asked.

"Your sister and mine."

"Well, I must say you didn't act toward her like a sister."

There they were, at it again, he told himself. Before he was here three minutes. And after all these years! He felt the blood drain from his face, the old passion to be free of house and these creatures of his own flesh who bullied and angered him. But he must remember he was no small boy now. He must move temperately to the hall and take his hat from the ugly old walnut octopus of a wall rack.

Libby stood angry and formidable between him and the front door.

"Oh no, you don't, Chancey. Not this time. You're the only one that's footloose. The rest of us have our families except Dezia and she has two weeks more of teaching. Huldah is on the ocean now. Can't you wait for once in your life anyway until they come? Don't you want to do a little something for your mother you haven't seen for five or six years? Or is it longer?"

Chancey felt echoes of the old childish sense of terror.

"What could I do?" he stammered.

"You don't need to do anything but live here in your own home. Hatty will get your meals and Manda will look after Mama. The rest of us come every day and stay with her and help out as long as we can. But there ought to be a member of the family in the house with Mama all the time. Harry says you can never tell. She might go suddenly. She might get back her mind and speech for a minute beforehand. She might call for us. Then there'd be one of her children that could be at her bedside when she went."

Chancey felt the old sense of suffocation in his chest. Why he hadn't had that since he was a boy. It showed how this house acted on him. He wanted to get away. Everything in him cried to escape while there was still time. But he was a grown man with a beard, an editor of some years. He couldn't run away like a child. He would stay then, he said with dignity, until Dezia came. To himself he added that he had nowhere else to stay or money to pay for lodgings until his mother died and he came into his own.

He didn't mind it so much as he feared, especially while other members of the family were there. He liked best when the grandchildren came. Then he could even stand in the doorway of his mother's sick room untroubled by the silent shape in the bed, so long as they were about. It was at night when he minded it the most, or when he had been out for a breath of fresh air and came back. To enter the old house at such times was like returning to the tomb, the musty smell of ancient carpets and hangings, the stillness and shadows on the stair. There was an air of decay and dissolution, of death and dying. He had begun to see now that the real corpse wouldn't be his mother. No, it would be the whole fabulous legend of pioneer days on which he had been bred and raised. Then the legend had seemed heroic and very real, but today it had been moved into its proper perspective, and you could see that it had been only a dream, the self-made illusion of a rude and primitive race back there in the twilight of the forest.

Somehow it seemed fitting now that before she died, his mother's lips had been closed. He and his younger generation must interpret her and her kind from this on, reconstruct her from their better knowledge. Surely he knew and understood her generation more clearly than that generation understood itself, the strong fare they lived on, their incredible epic tales like the nettle shirt and the buckskin pants, Guerdon chopping off his finger and the two Welsh children living through a wilderness winter alone.

And so he listened with a polite but faintly mocking air to all those who came to ask how Mrs. Wheeler was and stayed to tell him some memory they treasured of her, some trifling thing that had happened perhaps far in the past and that they had magnified into nobility and importance. Now that they knew he was there, the maid wouldn't satisfy them. "Could I see Mr. Chancey?" they'd ask. Or, if he went to the door himself, "Aren't you Mr. Chancey?" and they'd go into a long story about his mother, making a great deal of some minor connection with this rich old woman dying in her landmark of a house. Sometimes even tears would come into their eyes.

One woman with an old black cap and gray curls sticking out in front told how his mother had fed her father and mother when first they came through. "That was before you were born," she said. And a stout bareheaded woman from the country told how her mother had come to town one day when it was still Moonshine Church and had been sheltered in the Wheeler house. "Your father was away and she slept with your mother that night. I often heard my mother tell how Mrs. Wheeler shared her bed with her. That was when you still lived down in the cabin." The callers weren't all women. A very black Negro with the whitest fleece told him of the time "Miz Wheeler" stood off the Kentucky sheriff and his posse, wouldn't let them lay foot on the steps of her house where he lay trembling in the cellar. And a man with a green baize bag who said he came only to ask how Mrs. Wheeler was today, insisted on coming in and sitting down and telling a long story how when he was a young lawyer on his first big case, he had complained to Chancey's mother that Judge Wheeler was prejudiced and had ruled against him on every exception. "Maybe he believes in your side and is just doing that so he can decide for you later on. Then they can't say he favored you," Chancey's mother said sagely, he claimed, and so it turned out.

Even the girls together with Manda and Harry contributed to the myth. Manda said she asked if she wasn't scared of the Rebellion, and Mrs. Wheeler said, why should she be, she was a war baby herself, born during the Revolution. But she didn't like Harry coming to see her every day with his doctor's bag. "You can't help me any more. What do you come so often for?" she complained. "I have to give Libby a daily bulletin," he defended himself. "People want to know how you are." "In my day, there was no such thing as a daily bulletin," she told him bitterly. "You either got well or died right off and that was an end to it." Even then, before she lost the power of speech, she had picked the text for her funeral sermon. It was from Luke, "Now let thy servant depart in peace," and that text had gone all over the city.

But it was a doughty little old lady named Miss Jenkins who annoyed Chancey the most. She sat a whole evening lecturing him like he was a small boy, telling him how his father was "brilliant but flighty and even queer" and if it hadn't been for his mother marrying and saving him, he'd "a gone crazy and been plumb ruined" when he was a "solitary" out in the woods. "What's more," she said, "your father was queer more or less all his life, and if it hadn't been for your mother to keep him on an even keel, he'd a never been a judge or amounted to anything."

She fixed her pale blue eyes on him.

"Aren't you the baby of the family, the one that writes? You ought to write a piece about your mother. You'll never find a truer body in this world to write about. I could tell you a lot and so could some others. If you wasn't lazy, you could get up enough for a book like the one they printed about General Harrison. He wasn't one-two-three with your mother. I'm sure a good many would want to read it. Especially here in Shawanee county."

Chancey kept a cool silence. Miss Jenkins would be surprised, he thought, should he write a piece about his mother and interpret some of the things about her he knew. Those who praised her hospitality to the skies would be astounded to read that hospitality was a savage virtue, like Tallyrand said, and his mother was hospitable simply because all those years in the woods she suffered a need and thirst for human companionship that wouldn't be satisfied long after the need was filled. The Negro slave she saved from the sheriff would be startled and confused to hear that it wasn't "Miz Wheeler's" kindness of heart that had protected him from his owner so much as an inbred intolerance for others who believed in something she did not, such as slavery. All their lives the pioneers had to fight Indians, wild game, the trees hardship, starvation, and it was this habitual contentiousness and resulting cruelty that had made his mother accustomed to and even eager for the horrors of war. Didn't he know? Hadn't she refused to let her own sick son be taken to school in a carriage but compelled him to walk every day to and fro. And the lawyer who believed her a sage

would be confounded to learn how little she really knew of
life and the world outside, how she couldn't even read or
write until her own children taught her, and then her lips
would move and hiss painfully and, while writing, her
tongue twist and writhe in her mouth.

He himself was surprised, when he started to think about
it, how many stories and anecdotes about his mother there
were, and how revealing their interpretation. There was
one she liked to tell of the time Resolve was governor and
a French dignitary came to see him. "He's out on the farm,"
they told him, and then, "He's out in the field." The Frenchman went out and saw a man helping to cradle wheat. "But
I want to see the governor of the state, not a working man,"
he said. "That's the governor," he was told. The French
dignitary couldn't believe it, that the head of a great American state would work like a common man. When he found
it was true, he couldn't get over it, and apparently neither
could Resolve's mother. Sooth said she told the story at
every opportunity, and Chancey thought that both Sooth
and her mother would be shocked to know that it wasn't
the story and moral that made his mother repeat it so much
as the impulse to remind her visitors and self that her son
was governor, which made herself more in their eyes and
her own.

It was one thing for Chancey to think this out and another to tell it to Resolve. He thought he told it amusingly,
but his brother turned on him in anger.

"And the reason she kept your paper going all these years
was so she could tell people she was the mother of an editor, I take it!"

"I don't know what you mean." Chancey was taken
aback. "She never paid me anything but her subscription."

"So you charged her even for that!"

"I didn't charge her anything. She paid up her subscription years in advance, and that's the only money I ever saw from her."

"She fooled us, too," Resolve said grimly. "If you don't believe it, ask Monroe Cottle when he comes. She wouldn't trust me. She was afraid I'd tell the girls. So she gave the money to Monroe and Monroe sent it to a Cincinnati lawyer named Hartzel who gave it to you. She's also fixed it that once she dies, you can go on printing what you like as long as you live."

Chancey stood there thunderstruck. He couldn't, he wouldn't, believe such a thing – that his cherished patron, his philanthropic and ardent reader, who had supported not only his paper but his own courage and spirit, was nobody save his own mother. His pride and world of achievement came crashing down around his ears. But, no, it couldn't be. Why should she spend her money making it possible for him to say and print what he wanted, things she didn't believe in, even attacks upon herself and her kind? Certainly he would never have done such a thing for anyone, and wasn't he far more progressive, enlightened and humane than she?

Despite himself he found his steps drawn toward his mother's room. The sick smell, the solemn and gloomy air, the plain and ancient furnishings repelled him as formerly, the dark wall paper, the gray and red stripes of humble rag carpet on the floor, the rough table and bench that had been in the cabin. Here she had kept all these years the crude box for fixens that his Uncle Will had made for her out of rough hickory bark. It looked uncouth as the picture of her homely and beloved backwoods president standing on top of it. She had the picture faced toward her so she could see the ungainly face from the bed. This was the same cherry bed that she and his father had once slept in. Finer beds had come from his Grandfather Wheeler's in Massachusetts, beds with tall polished posts and handsome canopies, but his mother always said she could never sleep well under frippery and vanity such as that.

On the small pine table near the bed, he glimpsed his mother's large-type Bible. Often as a child in the evening he had seen her laboriously spelling her way through it. Today the book looked worn and singularly fat and flabby. It bothered him a little when he opened it and found it stuffed with familiar clippings. Her own hand must have cut them from the New Palladium, all poems, articles and editorials he had written. Even that savage piece attacking her and her generation she had saved. He winced now as he picked it up and read a few tattered lines. Could it be true then that she was the one who had kept the New Palladium going! He couldn't deny it any more, for in his heart he knew that it was just since his mother had been paralyzed that the mysterious money through Lawyer Hartzel had stopped coming.

A strange, uneasy feeling ran over him. If he had been wrong about his mother in this, might he by any chance have been wrong in other things about her also? Could it be even faintly possible that the children of pioneers like himself, born under more benign conditions than their parents, hated them because they themselves were weaker, resented it when their parents expected them to be strong, and so invented all kinds of intricate reasoning to prove that their parents were tyrannical and cruel, their beliefs false and obsolete, and their accomplishments trifling? Never had his mother said that. But once long ago he had heard her mention, not in as many words, that the people were too weak to follow God today, that in the Bible, God made strong demands on them for perfection, so the younger generation watered God down, made Him impotent and got up all kinds of reasons why they didn't have to follow Him but could go along their own way.

Hardship and work, that's what his mother always harped on. Once when at home he had refused to work on the lot, she had said, "You're going to live longer than I do, Chancey. Watch for all kinds of new-fangled notions to take away folks' troubles without their having to work. That's what folks today want and that's what will ruin them more than anything else." Could there be something after all in this hardship-and-work business, he pondered. He had thought hardship and work the symptoms of a pioneer era, things of the past. He believed that his generation had outlived and outlawed them, was creating a new life of comfort, ease and peace. And yet war, the cruelest hardship of all, war between brothers, was on them today like a madness. Did it mean that the need for strength and toughness was to be always with them; that the farther they advanced, the more brilliant and intelligent they became, the more terrible would be the hardship that descended upon them, and the more crying the need of hardihood to be saved?

He had always felt a little scorn for those who came to ask his mother's opinion, especially grown men and women. Even his father used to do it. But now there were just one or two questions he wished he could put to her, not that he would accept her answers as infallible or sage, no matter how matriarchal and wise she looked lying there.

"Mama!" he spoke to her aloud.

She paid him no attention. He had half expected it and yet at the experience an incredulous stunned emotion crept over him. Why, he was her favorite, her pet, they all claimed. Massey had written him once that if he only came home, it would make his mother well just to see him. Now here he was by her bed and she took no more notice of him than a chair.

"Her mind's on another world," Manda said piously.

Standing there, Chancey observed that his mother's eyes continued to hang on some point off to the right beyond the foot of her bed. He followed their gaze. All he could make out was the narrow bar of light from the window where it had been opened perhaps a foot and the shade lowered save for the same distance.

"It's the trees," Manda told him. "We moved her bed when she first took sick. She wanted to see the trees."

Again that strange feeling ran over Chancey. Why, she had always claimed how as a girl and young woman she had hated the trees. He remembered a dozen stories of her abhorrence and bitter enmity for what she called "the big butts." And yet now all she lived for was the sight and sound of those green leaves moving outside her window. Was there something deeper and more mysterious in his mother's philosophy than he and his generation who knew so much had suspected; something not simple but complex; something which held not only that hardship built happiness but which somehow implied that hate built love; and evil, goodness?

He bent closer to her. Something in him flinched at her face shriveled as a mummy's, at the ancient brown skin marked with great purplish liver blotches. Were those blotches like her faults, he wondered, part of his mother's strength, like roughness and hardness are part of an oak, and if you take them out, you destroy the strength also?

"Mama!" he called louder.

There was no quiver of the eyelids. His mother only lay there, silent and oblivious as in the majesty of death. He knew now that she would never answer him again, that from this time on he would have to ponder his own questions and travel his way alone.

A NOTE ON THE

Type

IN WHICH THIS BOOK IS SET

THIS book was set on the Linotype in Janson, a recutting made direct from the type cast from matrices (now in possession of the Stempel foundry, Frankfurt am Main) made by Anton Janson some time between 1660 and 1687.

Of Janson's origin nothing is known. He may have been a relative of Justus Janson, a printer of Danish birth who practiced in Leipzig from 1614 to 1635. Some time between 1657 and 1668 Anton Janson, a punch-cutter and type-founder, bought from the Leipzig printer Johann Erich Hahn the type-foundry which had formerly been a part of the printing house of M. Friedrich Lankisch. Janson's types were first shown in a specimen sheet issued at Leipzig about 1675. Janson's successor, and perhaps his son-in-law, Johann Karl Edling, issued a specimen sheet of Janson types in 1689. His heirs sold the Janson matrices in Holland to Wolffgang Dietrich Erhardt.

The book was based on designs by W. A. Dwiggins; printed and bound by Haddon Craftsmen, Inc., Scranton, Pennsylvania.

In this superb novel—the longest Mr. Richter has written—Sayward, eldest daughter of Worth and Jary Luckett, completes her mission and lives to see the transition of her family and her friends, American pioneers, from the ways of wilderness to the ways of civilization. Here is the tumultuous story of the Lucketts, an American family born in the wilderness, grown to face the changing ways of America during the turmoil that was the first half of the nineteenth century.

The Trees began the story of Worth and Jary, a wild and woodsfaring family who lived a roaming life, pushing ever westward as the frontier advanced and as new settlements threatened their isolation. How young Sayward and her family, facing the realization that the forests had become fields and settlements, took up the arduous task of tilling the Ohio soil was the story continued in *The Fields*. But *The Town* is a much bigger book in every way than its predecessors; it is in fact a major literary event and with them comprises a great American epic.

BY CONRAD RICHTER

Early Americana (SHORT STORIES) (1936)

The Sea of Grass (1937)

Tacey Cromwell (1942)

The Free Man (1943)

Always Young and Fair (1947)

The Trees (1940) WHICH IS CONTINUED IN

The Fields (1946) AND

The Town (1950)

The Light in the Forest (1953)

The Mountain on the Desert (1955)

The Lady (1957)

The Waters of Kronos (1960)

A Simple Honorable Man (1962)

The Grandfathers (1964)

A Country of Strangers (1966)

The Awakening Land (1966)

WHICH CONTAINS The Trees, The Fields, AND The Town

The Aristocrat (1968)

THESE ARE BORZOI BOOKS, PUBLISHED BY

Alfred A. Knopf

1980